FOOD, DRINK, AND THE FEMALE SLEUTH

CONTENTS

PREFACE

Among the things in common between the Sisters Wells is a longstanding preference for women detective novels as escape reading. A couple of years ago, after guffawing together over Sue Grafton's latest Kinsey in her minimalist kitchen, the psychologist asked the editor, what goes into a novel anyway? You mean, what are the components? I guess. Well, okay, there's first and foremost the primary character. Then there are secondary characters, their development. Main plot. Settings. They can be general, like New York City, or specific, like a fastfood Mexican restaurant in a run-down part of L.A. How time is dealt with is important, also suspense. Why?

I have a book idea. Wouldn't mystery readers get a kick out of seeing all their favorite food scenes gathered together? And see how authors used things like the fridge full of nothing or trips to McDonald's to help define their heroines. As a matter of fact, I think women writers use food scenes more than men do, so the book could stick to women writers with women sleuths. It could just do writers of mainstream detective series and just American writers. So, I'm describing a book of excerpts that highlight the authors' use of food scenes to flesh out the main character and secondary characters. And how food is used to move the plot along, set settings, add suspense. Whatcha think? Let's do it together, she replied, What fun. And I know for a fact it hasn't been done. So it's Unique with a capital U!

So *Food, Drink, and the Female Sleuth* was born on a couple of Adirondack chairs on the Olympic Peninsula in 1998. It was supposed to be finished in the spring of 2000, but the process of permissions began then, totally consuming the editor, and the psychologist went off to London reading, reading, and adding on by the process of "briefly describing" rather than fully excerpting. Which process required no permission.

We started putting the book together way back in 1998. We'd stick post-its on relevant paperback pages, and at the book's end look them all over and select the winning scene. We did this independently; one did half the authors, one did the other half. Our first evolving chapters had to do with partners, kids, helpful relatives and friends, junk food, coffee, alcohol, unhelpful relatives and friends. So where an excerpt was most needed did come into choice.

As we progressed, new chapters got added, and finally we were selecting "the best excerpt," regardless of where it filled in. And every six months we'd revise the book outline, redistributing our largest among an expansion of chapter titles. We started with our own libraries that were dominated by Marcia Muller, Susan Dunlap, and Sue Grafton, the West Coasters hugely responsible for the stereotypical PI image—young, gutsy, independent, and fastfood-addicted. Also Linda Barnes, Patricia Cornwell, Jo Dereske, Sara Paretsky, Julie Smith, Laura Lippman, and Dana Stabenow.

We got into the permissions process out of respect for the authors. Basically, simply, we wanted them to see and be happy with our choices and get their approval. But it turned out to be anything but simple. (See Acknowledgements and note in References that certain titles were not excerpted, but instead briefly described which is indicated by "desc" rather than page numbers.) So while the editor spent hundreds of hours faxing and phoning, the psychologist fumed that, inasmuch as we had followed fair use all the way, the publishing world was not playing fair with us. After all, the excerpts were well under 300 words (acceptable to our previous publishers), they were not a major part of the work from which drawn or a major part of our book. Our book's content was review and commentary, and contained a good bit of us. The excerpts in no way could harm the authors monetarily or any other way; indeed, they'd get added publicity and exposure, guaranteeing more not less sales. And finally, once we had covered our expenses, half our royalties were to go to Hedgebrook Farm on Whidbey Island, a retreat dedicated to women writers.

It could be this book was unconsciously motivated as well. The psychologist's first book after retirement was about women police officers, and the book following it involved interviews with women police officers. The editor's first job after retirement was/is that of senior volunteer police officer. And, incidentally, the reason the editor knew for a fact the idea was unique is that her collection of nonfiction books dealing with crime is rivaled only by her collection of cookbooks. Ah. Other audiences. People who like to cook. People who like to eat.

CHAPTER I
THE PRO'S AN AMATEUR AS A COOK

A prime example of a fastfood junky who not only doesn't cook but doesn't shop for food is Linda Barnes's PI Carlotta Carlyle. In *The Snake Tattoo* Carlotta answers the door midway through a dinner of leftover takeout pepperoni pizza with a can of anchovies dumped on top. Fortunately it's only her best cop friend Mooney come to call. How'd Carlotta get this way? In her case it has something to do with growing up in a kosher home. The statute of limitation on kosher has not yet run its course with Carlotta, so ham-and-cheese sandwiches and pepperoni pizza are doubly delicious forbidden fruit.

There are individual differences. To quote PI Kinsey Millhone, "As far as I'm concerned, the only reason for cooking is to keep your hands busy while you think about something else." (From Sue Grafton's *"I" is for Innocent*.) On the other hand, "Private Resolver" Emma Rhodes tells a prospective client that maybe he'd been reading too many lady-shamus books if he expects her to subsist on Big Macs and pizza like Carlotta and Kinsey.

We're going to start the book out with scenes from the lives of the stereotypical professional female sleuth. But first, two brilliant examples of the ways women writers play around with food.

Even though Susan Dunlap lets Berkeley Detective Jill Smith consume little else besides donuts and pizza, Dunlap is a master of figurative food-speak. (From Susan Dunlap's *Time Expired*. PB. NY: Dell Publishing. 1994.)

This was one of those days when the fog never clears. Looking into the canyon, I could see where the common allusion to soup had arisen. The canyon looked like a huge tureen, and the fog in it, one of those chowders that had been thick and warm and wonderful the night before. Too good to have merely one bowl. Sufficiently heavy to weigh on you all night, viscous enough to have rolled as you did and when you lay on your side to pull your overstretched stomach down toward the bed. In the morning when you opened the fridge door looking for ice water to pour over the Alka-Seltzer, you would see that tureen holding a dirty beige congealed mass with wrinkled edges of mushroom and wizened celery slices. Or in the case of Cerrito Canyon, live oak branches.

Sergeant Kathleen Mallory of the NYPD is wrapping up multiple, interwoven cases. One involves a thirteen-year-old junkie prostitute whose pimp is a cop. Mallory has told her she's taking her someplace safe in the country and shows her three bags of white powder, letting her believe these are part of the deal. But Mallory did not confide in her old friend, medical examiner Dr. Edward Slope, just how she was going to get the girl to cooperate. We're at the hospital. (From Carol O'Connell's *The Man Who Lied to Women*. PB. London: Hutchinson, Arrow Books Limited, Random House UK Limited. 1996.)

Mallory kept silent until she and the girl were in the lobby which might have passed for the ground floor of a fashionable hotel. When the girl saw the first white-coated attendant, she tried to bolt...."You said you wouldn't turn me in! You promised, you promised!"

She was crying now, the garish make-up washing down her face like yesterday's Halloween mask....

Dr. Edward Slope was glaring at Mallory. "I told you to prepare her for this. You never listen to me—or anyone else."...

"Kathy, sometimes I think you're growing into a real human being, and then you exasperate me this way. You got her this far, that's good. But after the detox—what then? You can't just dump off a little girl like she was a sack of potatoes."

"Doris does all the cooking in your house—that's her job, right?"

"What?"

Mallory's hands went to her hips. Her words had a cautioning edge. "If you'd ever tried to prepare a meal, you'd know what an art form it really is, making every dish come out at the same time." Her voice was on the rise now, and angry. "Well, I'm cooking. I've got six dishes going at six different speeds, and they all have to be done at exactly the same time or the whole thing falls apart on me." One long fingernail jabbed at his chest. "You go do your own damn job! Get off my back!"

And the cook with a gun walked through the lobby and out the front door.

Susan Dunlap's book covers proclaim that she is the leading proponent of tough, gutsy, no fluff female sleuths. Her cop (Jill Smith) and amateur (Vejay Haskell) both have bare cupboards, fridges, and utensil drawers, and eat mostly in cafés. It is Dunlap's medical examiner, however, who takes disinterest in food preparation to new heights. Kiernan is over forty and wealthy enough to own a duplex on the beach in La Jolla and to employ a genuine houseboy, Brad Tchernak, who is a gourmet cook. Ezra is Kiernan's wolfhound. (From Susan Dunlap's *High Fall*. PB. NY: Dell Publishing. 1995.)

..."What's cooking?"

"The garlic polenta rolls with no-longer-secret herbs and spices. Hot from the oven." He waved a hand at the baking pan....

..."How'd you ever get the recipe? I certainly couldn't."

"Wasn't easy. I drove up to the [movie] set this morning and bearded the cook. My working MO is charm," he said, grinning. "Okay, so it doesn't work as well on guys. But with Correra, the cook, it was zip...."

He scooped a polenta roll from the pan and held it out to her, watching as eagerly as the now-alert wolfhound.

She took a bit, chewing slowly, savoring....

"A miracle." Tchernak inhaled, deeply, smiling so broadly, he had to stop and reposition his face before he could eat.

She held out a taste to Ezra. Normally she loved being in Tchernak's kitchen with its chaos of greensauce and golden batter-coated bowls, its Eiffel Tower of used and abandoned pots, wooden spoons, stainless spoons, spoons that were round, oval, shallow, deep, full of holes or edged with lips, and knives and saws the like of which she hadn't seen since she'd left the coroner's office. She loved the smells she couldn't possibly have named. It pleased her to watch Tchernak moving from counter to stove in one long stride, humming the Beethoven he insisted was essential to the culinary art. Every time she walked in on him cooking, it comforted her at a level too deep to touch that someone was cooking just for her.

How does cooking become an aversion? Here Kiernan is on the brink of confiding to a co-investigator that hers is linked to a food fight involving Jell-O that preceded the death of her beloved sister. (From Susan Dunlap's *Pious Deception*. PB. NY: Dell Publishing. 1990.)

..."You know, Kerry, if we were near my place, I could make my famous Wiggins Breakfast Tacos."

"You cook?" she asked....

"Kerry, you're looking at a damned fine cook here. Might be every bit as good as you."

Kiernan laughed. "If you can open a can you're that good. I don't have a houseman for nothing."

Wiggins slowed down at a sign announcing OLD ADOBE SHOPPING CENTER. "Kerry, with the amount you chow down—"

"I didn't say I don't like to eat. My housekeeper played offensive line. He used to spend his days with guys who weighed over three hundred pounds and ate twelve egg omelets filled with half a hog. I went out to dinner with them—if you ever want to see a restaurateur in heaven...I sat between a center and a left tackle and was still eating when both of them shoved back from the trough...."

"And you don't cook?"

She sighed. "You cooks are such snobs. You just can't accept that there are those of us who don't cook, and don't care."

"But Kerry, how do you—"

"See? You really can't accept it." She laughed halfheartedly. "You're not going to let up on this, are you?"

"Probably should, but I'm a nosey old fellow....That's what you like about me."

"Okay, Stu. But I warn you, it deals with my sister's death and my adolescent reaction." Already she could hear the catch in her voice. "Ben's Burgers doesn't exactly sound like breakfast," she said. She knew she was stalling.

"They've got a breakfast burger with guacamole, egg, and better sausage than you deserve, on a roll your football friends would consider a meal."

Another Californian, Kinsey Millhone, gets the prize for the smallest kitchen in the world. In *"I" is for Innocent* she first mulls over a case while eating a dinner of Cheerios and skim milk at the kitchen sink, staring out the window. Here she continues to mull over an equally exciting lunch, probably at the sink and window again. (From Sue Grafton's *"I"*. HB. NY: Henry Holt and Company. 1992.)

...There was precious little in the refrigerator and I was forced to open a can of asparagus soup, which I think I bought originally to put over something else. I've been told novice cooks are chronically engaged in this hoary ruse. Cream of celery soup over pork chops, baked at 350 for an hour. Cream of mushroom soup over meat loaf, same time, same temp. Cream of chicken soup over a chicken breast with half a cup of rice thrown in. The variations are endless and the best part is you have company once, you never see them again. Aside from the aforementioned, I can scramble eggs and make a fair tuna salad....I eat a lot of sandwiches, peanut-butter-and-pickle and cheese-and-pickle being two. I also favor hot sliced hard-boiled egg sandwiches on whole wheat bread with lots of salt and Best Foods mayonnaise....

What was bugging me at this point was this question of Morley's death....What if Morley was getting too close to the truth and had been eliminated as a consequence? I was torn between the notion of murder as too farfetched and the worry that someone was actually getting away with it....

I finished my soup, washed the bowl, and left it in the dish rack with my solitary spoon. If I kept up this cycle of cereal and soup, I could eat for a week without dirtying another dish.

San Diego deputy district attorney Judith Thornton has to feed a bedridden mother, the mother's live-in aide, and Judith's young daughter. So she's a sleuth with a big refrigerator and no time to keep it filled. Eleven at night is just asking for trouble. (From Patricia Benke's *Cruel Justice*. PB. NY: Avon Books. 1999.)

...There was no milk in the refrigerator and there was no bread. Or butter....

...She reached into her pants pocket for the grocery list she'd been compiling over the last few days. It wasn't there. She looked in her purse. It wasn't there either....How could she forget it?

Judith moved quickly through the store, trying to remember what was on the list, finally pushing the cart into the vegetable and fruit section.

The peaches looked ripe. The strawberries, they were a risky proposition....Across the bin, a woman in her seventies was watching her. Their eyes met for a moment and the woman shook her head. Judith nodded and put the strawberries back....

"Paper or plastic, ma'am?"...

"Plastic's fine."

Somewhere in the middle of her response Judith remembered something. It was her driver's license. She wasn't sure she had it with her....And now she was certain it lay on her desk at work. She needed it to cash her check here. One glance into her wallet confirmed her fears....

..."I forgot my driver's license."

When there appeared no look of sympathy on the checker's face, Judith offered, "I'm a deputy district attorney, you can find me if there's any problem...and there really won't be."

A twinge of guilt made her face flush red. She'd violated one of her own cardinal rules: She never used her position to curry favor anywhere....The store closed at midnight and that was now fifteen minutes away. She'd never make it back from the office in time.

Why is Willie Whelan, professional fence, being followed? Not a likely case for PI Sharon McCone, but she figures maybe she'll learn something, and, besides, fences have rights. Distraction is welcome in the person of Don Del Boccio, star disk jockey, who moves in with Sharon during a visit to San Francisco. The following two food scenes, one from the beginning of the book and one from the end, tie up their developing relationship. (From Marcia Muller's *Leave a Message for Willie*. PB. NY: Warner Books, Mysterious Press. 1990.)

...I lifted the lid and smelled tomatoes, onions, garlic, oregano, and other less definable spices. It had to be one of the wonderful Italian sauces that were Don's specialty....

"We're barbecuing tonight?"

"I thought we would."

"So what's that in the pot on the stove?"

"Barbecue sauce."

"*Italian* barbecue sauce?"

"Sure. You don't expect a Del Boccio to look like a Texan, do you?..."

Don got up and went to the barbecue....Don had dark Italian good looks that had attracted me immediately when we'd met last fall while I was on a case in his hometown of Port San Marco....he loved Brahms and Tchaikovsky...he adored salami and cheese and rich red wine....

The last scene of the book takes us back to Sharon's kitchen. Willie keeps her company while she fixes spaghetti sauce and they wait for Don.

I lifted the lid of the pot...and then sniffed its contents. Something was not right here. "Oregano," I said, "maybe it needs more oregano."

"I'd be careful; that's powerful stuff." Willie sat at my kitchen table, drinking beer and—by all intents—supervising.

"Garlic, then?"

He just looked at me.

"Well, I don't know. I wanted to make a nice dinner for Don when he comes back and announces he's got the job at the radio station. But I can't make this sauce smell right!"

They discuss who did what to whom by way of wrapping up the case. Don arrives with champagne to celebrate his new job.

"So, what's for dinner?"...

"Um, it was going to be lasagna…but I'm not too sure about the marinara sauce."…

Don sniffed at the sauce, drew back…

…"Babe, would you do us the honor of accompanying us to dinner tonight? There's a wonderful little Italian restaurant that just opened over on Union.…"

Back to Boston PI Carlotta Carlyle. She and a new lover, Keith, both a neighbor and a psychiatrist, have got the important stuff out of the way and are now satisfying their other basic need. Roz is Carlotta's upstairs tenant. (From Linda Barnes's *Hardware*. PB. NY: Dell Publishing. 1996.)

I kept glancing over my shoulder while we foraged for breakfast, wondering why in hell we'd wound up in my bed rather than moving two houses down to the relative privacy of the doctor's digs.…

Roz does the weekly shopping and cleaning in exchange for greatly reduced rent. I doubt she could do a lousier job at either task, but she might try.

I opened another cupboard. Can after can of fruit cocktail. Why? Who eats this candy-colored stuff? I make a shopping list, I honestly do, but Roz, using Stop & Shop coupons as her bible, buys whatever's on sale.

What would I say if she waltzed in and discovered us *in flagrante* munching stale toast and jam, smiling across the table, holding hands, basking in the shiny afterglow?…

…I liked the fact that he hadn't criticized the meager fare, hadn't sat like a stone and watched me fetch and carry. I could put dishes on the table, find the butter in the fridge, make coffee.…

I gulped coffee. I needed caffeine to clear my head.…

I chased Keith out as soon as I could, sidestepping his efforts to set up a date for the evening.…

I hate the word *relationship*. I'd enjoyed the night. Enough. I'm not a clinging vine. I didn't even ask if he'd call.

Part of me whispered, secretly smug, "Because you know he will."

It shouldn't surprise fans of Janet Evanovich to learn her favorite "drug of choice" (her words) is Cheese Doodles. They destroyed her last laptop with all that grease and orange stuff. Now she keeps a cannister of air beside her computer to blow the crud away. Evanovich has done for numbers what Grafton did for the alphabet. Enter her sleuth, bounty hunter Stephanie Plum, in *One for the Money*. On page 12, we're permitted a glimpse of her refrigerator where a hungry Stephanie finds a depleted mayo jar, a bottle of beer, blue bread, liquid lettuce, and hamster nuggets, the latter for her hamster Rex. She wonders if nine in the morning is too early for beer. Hey, it's four in the afternoon in Moscow, so...

When the story opens, Stephanie's just lost her job as a lingerie sales rep. She's a broken woman, selling her few pieces of furniture to pay for things even more basic—food. It's easy then to bend to the will of her mother who wants her home every Sunday for dinner. The setting is Trenton, New Jersey, a neighborhood Stephanie calls "the burg," where food is all. (From Janet Evanovich's *One for the Money*. PB. NY: HarperCollins Publishing, HarperPaperbacks. 1995.)

...The moon revolves around the earth, the earth revolves around the sun and the burg revolves around pot roast. For as long as I can remember, my parents' lives have been controlled by five-pound pieces of rolled rump....

"You should wear a dress," my mother said to me, bringing green beans and creamed pearl onions to the table. "Thirty years old and you're still dressing in those teeny-bopper outfits. How will you ever catch a nice man like that?"

"I don't want a man. I had one, and I didn't like it."...

"I hear Loretta Buzick's boy is separated from his wife," my mother said....

..."I'm not going out with Ronald Buzick," I told her....

"So what's wrong with Ronald Buzick?"

Ronald Buzick was a butcher....I found it hard to think in romantic terms about a man who spent his days stuffing giblets up chicken butts.

Here Evanovich uses food scenes to flesh out the fastfood junky side of Stephanie's character and introduce us to her two partners: Ranger, an experienced bounty hunter, and Lula, hooker-turned-file clerk for Vinnie, their boss. Each partner tries to influence Stephanie's culinary habits in opposite directions. Ranger wants her fit. One morning he breaks into her apartment. (From Janet Evanovich's *Three to Get Deadly*. HB. NY: Scribner. 1997.)

"Ranger?"

"I made you some tea. It's on your nightstand."...

"I hate tea," I said, sniffing at the noxious brew. I took a sip. YUK! "What is this?"

"Ginseng."

"It's weird. It tastes awful."

"Good for your circulation," Ranger said. "Helps oxygenate."

Lula has the greater influence. Here they are on the lookout for a candy store owner called Mo who missed his court date. They drive by his store.

"I'm starving to death," Lula said. "I need a burger. I need fries." I could see the glow of a fast-food drive-through shining red and yellow through the misting rain....

"I want a triple-decker burger," Lula yelled at the box. "I want bacon and cheese and special sauce. I want a large fries, and I want lots of them little ketchup packets. And I want a large chocolate milkshake." She turned to me. "You want something?"

"I'll have the same."

Back to Evanovich at her laptop, air cannister at hand. Could she ever give up the Cheese Doodles? She claims not, that all that "salt and cheese and crunch make all my creative synapses come together."

Here's an end of the chapter pop quiz about a PI as defined by food. She won't eat liver, sweet potatoes or okra, but everything else is fair game including mountain oysters. She has a serious love affair with Twinkies. Ditto chocolate pie. She likes her coffee decaf, her margaritas *sin sal.* For breakfast she likes flour tortillas wrapped around eggs scrambled with cream cheese and salsa. Potato and salsa sandwiches or *carne seca* burritos for lunch. Dinner might be a couple of frozen tamales zapped in the microwave with a glass of merlot. Tamales with pitted olives are one of her homemade specialties. She meets up with folks at Dunkin' Donuts and the Rainbow café where chicken-fried steak with gravy is a breakfast special. She has a problem with mustard which mesmerizes her until some gets smeared on her clothes. Her truck, Priscilla, always carries a box of Cheez-Its. Cocoa's her comfort food. Old-fashioned feed stores are an anxiety reducer, while anxiety manifests itself as a "pasty lump" in her tummy. All this in just the first two books of a brilliant new series.

CHAPTER 2
A DOZEN WAYS TO FEED YOUR LOVER

"Max liked sushi. Annie adored fried pies. Peach, not cherry. Max admired nouvelle cuisine. Annie was passionate about Texas chili. Max detested pretzels. Annie loathed quiche....It was great fun, but it couldn't last." (From Carolyn Hart's *Death on Demand.*)

The stereotypic PI or cop is single or divorced one or more times. She doesn't want to commit herself to a long-term, stable relationship. It's part of preferring to live alone, of being answerable to no one, of being such a tough cookie she doesn't need a man around to take care of her. Instead, she has a lover. They may not live together but they eat together, a lot.

Because professional sleuths don't have an ordinary home life, these are not ordinary scenes. For starters, because pros don't have nine to five jobs, meals can occur at all hours. But the big question remains, where *do* they find some of these extraordinary guys?

Marcia Muller's Sharon McCone is a PI for the All Souls Legal Cooperative in San Francisco. She fits the mold—unconventional vis-a-vis career, independent of mind. She is absorbed by her work and if she eats well, somebody else has done the cooking. She keeps an emergency Hershey bar in her handbag and drives to McDonald's when she wants sit-down. Her major food groups are chocolate, white wine, and caffeine. Here McCone is holed up in a small motel in La Jolla, where she feels safe from pursuers. Food holds no appeal, but she knows she has to eat. (From Marcia Muller's *Wolf in the Shadows*. PB. NY: Warner Books, Mysterious Press. 1994.)

Finally I went to the kitchenette, found a fork, and wolfed down my salad, barely tasting it. Made a sandwich and poured another glass of wine. Wolfed that down and went back for seconds. And decided to call it a day and see if there was anything worth watching on TV. Maybe tomorrow things would seem clearer....

That was a good day for Sharon. On a bad one she forgets to eat altogether. She leaves La Jolla and travels south to Baja California, trying to locate lover Hy Ripinski, an investigator who's been kidnapped. She's on a beach alone, helpless, when she remembers...food.

The darkness deepened. Fires danced down in the riverbed; I smelled fish and tortillas frying, heard men and women laughing. I twisted around and saw that the villas on the hill were now ablaze with light; music and cocktail-time chatter drifted down, as did smoke from mesquite barbecues. My stomach growled forlornly....

She finds Hy, wounded, and wants to know what happened, but...

"What say we eat first?"
I had to admit that the smell of the food was making me ravenous. We sat cross-legged facing each other and burrowed into the basket. The tortillas were wrapped around a fiery fish-and-vegetable mixture and fried. The melon dripped sweet juice. In contrast, the wine was raw and very, very dry. We ate with our fingers, wiping them on our jeans; we drank from a shared paper cup. When we'd eaten all the food, Hy poured another cupful of wine and we leaned against his carryall—shoulder to

shoulder, arm to arm, thigh to thigh, toes touching occasionally—and told our respective stories.

This is the first, but not the last time that you will encounter one kind of hunger being swapped for another. NYPD Lieutenant Marian Larch is working round the clock with an attempted kidnapping linked to two murders. But she's finally had a good night's sleep. The "he" in this scene is her lover, Curt Holland. (From Barbara Paul's *Full Frontal Murder*. HB. NY: Scribner. 1997.)

She turned the showerhead setting to its most needlelike spray. Marian felt a lot better this morning; that deep, undisturbed sleep had done her good....

On the dining table lay a Carnegie Hall program with yesterday's date. Kiri Te Kanawa. So that's where he'd gone last night.

Marian started the coffee. But the concert wouldn't have lasted until 1 a.m.; he'd gone someplace else afterward. She wouldn't ask.

He came in while she was spreading cream cheese on a toasted bagel...."Caffeine," he muttered.

Marian poured him a cup. They sat at the table and she waited until he started to look more awake. "So, how was Kiri?"

"Magnificent, as always." He reached over and took the other half of her bagel. When that was eaten, he said, "After the concert, I picked up a couple of chorus girls and we did the town."

She got up to toast another bagel. "Did you have fun?"

"Oh, yes. A ton of fun. We snorted a couple of lines and went to an illegal gambling den on West Forty-fifth."

"Hmm! Living dangerously."

"And when we ran out of money, we sold our bodies. I had more customers than the girls did."

"I'll bet you did."

"Then Sigourney Weaver came along and asked me to marry her."...

"I went back to the office and did some work," he muttered. When she laughed, he said, "Well, this has turned into a working weekend, hasn't it? You'll probably have to go in again today."

"Probably." She looked at him with a gleam in her eye. "But not just yet."

This comes from the eagle-grabs-the-poodle mystery in which PI Kate Shugak speaks French—acquired to fulfill the foreign language requirement for a B.A. About her years at the University of Alaska in Fairbanks, Kate doesn't say much. Now back in Fairbanks with her lover, Jack Morgan, over a riverside picnic, she explains the terror she felt as a freshman who had never used a phone before, or watched TV, or driven down a paved road, or met people all on her own. From Dana Stabenow's *Play with Fire*. PB. NY: Berkley Publishing Group, Berkley Prime Crime. 1996.)

She took the rubber band that held the butcher paper around her deli special and used it to fasten her hair up off her neck....

Jack unwrapped his meatball sandwich, opened the bag of Olympic Deep Ridge Dippers, placed bags of green grapes, red grapes and Rainier cherries at strategic intervals, set the package of Pepperidge Farm Soft Baked Chocolate Walnut cookies within reach, and sat back to survey the scene through critical eyes. For the moment Kate feared they were going to have to return to the store, and then he raised one finger upright in inspiration and went to the truck, returning with a six-pack of Heineken, for him, and one can of Diet 7-Up, for her. He settled on the bench across the picnic table with a long, satisfied sigh and set to, reminding Kate of nothing so much as a vacuum cleaner in overdrive, but she knew better than to get between him and food....

"You haven't been here in a while?..."

..."No. This is the first time I've been back to Fairbanks since I graduated."

"Why?..."

..."The food was weird, no moose, no caribou, no seal, no fish, just a brown lettuce salad bar and mystery meat in gloppy sauces and too much grease. It took all semester for my stomach to settle down."..."Once I got brave enough to go to meals. I dropped twenty pounds that semester; Emaa called me a skeleton at Christmas and wanted to force-feed me fried bread morning, noon and night."

You can write to Dana Stabenow at *dana@stabenow.com* or visit her web site at *http://www.stabenow.com*.

In one of the earliest scenes in *Blood Money*, West L.A. homicide detective Jessica Drake is fixing dinner in her home with ex-husband Gary. He wants back. She's ambivalent. They do a kind of dance getting the broiled trout and dilled new potatoes on, all the while discussing her latest case, a death from heart attack that looks like murder. (From Rochelle Krich's *Blood Money*. HB. NY: Avon Books. 1999.)

"Ten-to-one he's a Holocaust survivor," Jessie said, slicing mushrooms on a wood cutting board. "That's why the numbers—it's his concentration camp ID."

"You're probably right," Gary said. "So why are you so upset?"

..."I'm not upset. It's just a comment."

"Okay." His dark blue eyes said otherwise. Reaching across the narrow room to the opposite counter, he opened a white drawer and frowned. "Where's the garlic press?"

She set her knife on the board and handed him a press from another, nearby drawer. "I rearranged some things," she said. *After you left.*

"Hey, it's your kitchen."

She was glad he'd invited himself over for dinner, but she felt strange, too. Though they'd been dating for almost three months, it was the first time since he'd moved out two years ago that they were preparing a meal together in the house they'd fallen in love with and fixed up together. And made love in.

She studied him as he minced two garlic cloves and added them to the wine vinegar and olive oil....

She'd been up front with Gary about wanting to keep their renewed relationship nonintimate. She didn't want to confuse sex, and a longing for companionship, with love....Though Gary wasn't pressuring her about the sex, he'd been dropping not-so-subtle hints about remarrying.

She wasn't ready for that. Most days she thought she was in love with him....But she'd been in love with him before and there were issues they still had to resolve....

The broiled trout and dilled new potatoes were ready....

Gary came to the table with the salad, a corkscrew, and a bottle of red wine that he'd brought....Uncorking the bottle, he poured wine into the Orrefors goblets...."I remember these," he said....

Maybe this was a bad idea....When he lifted his goblet, she knew he was going to make a toast, and felt her stomach tighten.

"To good friends and happy days, Jess," he said....

You can read more about Rochelle Krich by visiting her web site at *http://www.rochellekrich.com.*

On-the-road bookseller Honey Huckleberry suspects there's something neurotic about her lifestyle, but it's safe. After all, when your wardrobe is organized by tags that say "Spring—Second Week," how can life possibly trip you up? One thing's for sure, she knows too many people by the name of Steven: There's the accountant, the car repair guy, and her best friend, who's out of the country. So when a fourth Steven calls and poses a riddle only the friend Steven would understand, and then threatens her life, she knows all her self-imposed routines will not protect her.

She may have to operate on a more visceral level, but she's learning how from a customer named Harry, British bookseller who's located on Padre

Island. Author Margaret Moseley, incidentally, says, "In my travels, I've always used food for directions, such as 'Turn right at the Black Eyed Pea and left at the Pizza Hut.'" (From MM's *The Fourth Steven*. PB. NY: Berkley Publishing Group, Berkley Prime Crime. 1998.)

It was my third visit to the island, and the second time Harry had asked me [to] have dinner with him. We'd started late, just barely had settled onto Scampi's bayside deck before the sun dipped beyond the liquid horizon, causing such an arrogant display that we spontaneously applauded its descent. Hungry and thirsty, we sat on the deck, peeling shrimp and downing scotches. I fussed at him for not knowing more about his merchandise, forgetting to be the daughter my mother raised and generally getting very drunk....

I thought this trip was no different, except for my secret about Steven. We enjoyed our walks, stopping to read the delicate script the sea oats endlessly scratched out on the sand....We ate all our favorite foods at our favorite places: big kahunas at Blackbeard's, breakfast at Ro-Van's and nachos mariachis at Palmetto's.

I would have liked being with Harry even if we weren't...you know. He knew things that were interesting, like the Lord Mayors of London only serve one-year terms or why ships have round windows or that you could stand behind the falls at Niagara Falls....

I had fun with Harry. I had never had fun before—just plain fun....

I finished in Brownsville—I sell mostly Spanish translations there—and then headed for Alice, my last stop for the day, feeling the resisting pull of Harry....All the way, the car and the wind kept whispering to me. "Harry, Steven, Harry, Steven."

Relationships don't stand still. They either move forward or backwards. Sometimes it's the intimacy of a great meal that forces the issue. Callahan Garrity's an ex-cop turned PI, and owner of a house cleaning business in Atlanta that pays the bills. She shares her small bungalow with her mother

Edna, an arrangement that suits them both. Callahan's lover Mac works in Atlanta too, but his home is a lakeside cabin 40 miles out of town that he shares with his black Lab Rufus. Tonight, she's tired and Atlanta is hot, hot, hot. She grabs a cold beer, calls Mac, and heads out for rural North Fulton County. (From Kathy Hogan Trocheck's *To Live & Die in Dixie*. PB. NY: HarperCollins Publishing, HarperPaperbacks. 1994.)

Local old-timers bitch and moan about creeping suburbanization, but most, like me, welcome the opportunity to shell out $4.99 a pound for a bacon-wrapped filet mignon, $3 for a loaf of fresh-baked French bread, and $11.99 for a decent bottle of wine. It beats the hell out of a can of Vienna sausage and a Yoo-Hoo....

Mac was on the back deck, dropping two foil-wrapped bundles on the glowing coals. I dropped my sack of groceries on the wooden picnic table and gave him a quick, grateful kiss....

..."Crack open that wine and feed me a little something and you'll have a happy woman on your hands."

Rufus loped onto the deck and licked my bare toes....

Mac emerged from the house with two water glasses of wine and two bowls of tossed salad cradled in his arms....

The wine was nice, the salad was cold, and the French bread was warm and crusty and dripping with real butter. We ate the steaks and potatoes slowly and I piled extra sour cream on my potato to console myself for having endured such a long, difficult day. I hadn't realized just how hungry I was until I pushed the last crust of bread around to mop up the last bit of steak juice.

"God, that was good," I said meaningfully....

"Then I'm glad you called," he said simply. "Any time."

"Okay."

"No, I mean it," Mac said, suddenly serious. "I've been thinking about this off and on lately. What would you think about us living together?"

Homicide detective Jill Smith and her lover Seth Howard are having their most serious communication problem to date. At eleven p.m. when Jill leaves the station she realizes all she's had to eat was a stale donut. Howard's no dope. He knows nothin' says lovin' like something from Dunkin' Donuts. (From Susan Dunlap's *Death and Taxes*. PB. NY: Dell Publishing. 1993.)

I sat in my Volkswagen waiting while the engine warmed and realized that…the thing I wanted most was to hash over the case, to stretch it like pizza dough, sticking a finger in one option…and pulling that as far as it would go before the dough split and I had to discard…a suspect. Howard was great at that. He'd been known to stretch the pizza dough of a case so far that it ended up as a breadstick. But Howard, if he was home, was going to be in no mood to talk.…

I took a shower and climbed into bed.…

"Your case," he murmured. "What happened?"

It wasn't a giant step into admission of error. It was a toe inching forward, testing the waters of truce.…

…"The case has dead-ended," I said, my voice tight.

He started to roll over toward me but stopped. Clearly, he knew what he'd committed himself to tomorrow and that a truce is no more than a truce. "Nothing has to be a dead end. What have you got?"…

Howard turned away, grappling on the floor beside the bed. The light was still off—we weren't ready to face each other—and I could hear a paper bag rustling. He sat back up and held the bag in front of me. Another time we would have sparred about the dangers of my sticking my hand in. But we weren't ready to face that either.

I reached in. "Ah, chocolate old-fashioneds. You knew I'd be starved."

"Safe guess."

At times like this, there's something to be said for sublimating one appetite by sating another.

"Let's move on to motive, Jill.…"

Annie Laurance's Death on Demand bookstore is located on an island off the coast of South Carolina. The island abounds with writers who flock to her store to buy books and gossip. Annie helps it along with her Sunday evening socials, although this Sunday the lights go out and the speaker is killed by a poisoned dart.

Enter Max Darling, an old beau from New York whose vast wealth embarrasses Annie. He doesn't work at anything. She doesn't approve. Still, might they have enough in common for a permanent relationship? (From Carolyn Hart's *Death on Demand.* PB. NY: Bantam Books. 1989.)

They took the container of Kentucky Fried Chicken to the beach. Max looked suspiciously at each piece as Annie emptied the barrel onto a paper plate.

"Perhaps we aren't compatible," he mourned, setting up camp chairs from the Porsche's trunk. Trickling sand through her fingers, Annie thought of Mary Roberts Rinehart and a trip she had made in 1925 into the desert near Cairo. At night her party rested in tents decorated with scenes from tombs. Oriental rugs covered the sand in their dining and bedroom tents. Dinner included soup, appetizer, roast with vegetables, salad with quail and dessert. Then fruit, Turkish coffee and candy. Gourmet picnicking. Max would have fit right in.

"I love Quarterpounders, too."

He winced.

Annie bit into the lushly crusted half-thigh, half-breast while Max turned an oddly shaped piece around uncertainly.

"Was this chicken double-jointed?"

"It provides variety—and surprise," Annie retorted, mouth full.

With an air of incalculable bravery, Max began to eat.

By meal's end they had admitted to irreconcilable culinary tastes....

Then they walked, hand in hand, up the beach, stopping to look at sandpipers' tracks, turning over a shell-encrusted piece of driftwood and skirting the tendrils of a Portuguese man-of-war.

We are midway through PI Catherine Sayler's investigation of the murder charge against her PI lover, Peter Harman. He's been framed and it's up to Catherine, her partner, Jesse, and Peter's assistant, Eileen, to uncover the real murderer. (From Linda Grant's *Random Access Murder*. PB. NY: Avon Books. 1988.)

We ate on the pier. There were places with better food in town, but Peter wanted to look out over the water. He stared at the sea as he'd been doing when I arrived at the Shoals. Finally he said, "It's very healing, isn't it?"...

He was silent for a moment, then the waitress arrived with our orders. Peter's plate was covered with something that looked like large spiders and rubber bands dipped in batter and deep-fried.

"Calamari," he said. "Want some?"

"No," I said firmly....

I gave him a brief summary of the information we'd collected...."I thought you might want to hang out at Spades a bit," I suggested.

He nodded. "Just my thing," he said. "You sure you won't try this? It's delicious." He extended one of the spiders toward me, with a twinkle in his eye that told me he knew very well that I did not want anything to do with his dinner.

I shook my head. "I try not to eat eight-legged creatures," I said.

Our banter hid the subject I'd been avoiding, my role in the investigation. Peter had been very clear about his desire that I not be involved. I didn't expect that he'd changed his mind. Now that he was out of jail, he'd want to run things....

"Where do we go from here?" I asked.

"You mean with the investigation? What you're already doing seems right....More wine?"

I was too busy being amazed to answer....

I raised my glass. "To working together, then."

He touched my glass and grinned lecherously. "Very closely," he added.

New York mob attorney Matt Riordan whispers to attorney Cass Jameson outside of the courtroom, "Call me." They used to be lovers, but this very sexy guy is dangerous and in big trouble with the feds. Whatever he wants, it won't be good news. Can she resist? (From Carolyn Wheat's *Mean Streak*. PB. NY: Berkley Publishing Group, Berkley Prime Crime. 1997.)

One of my very favorite things about Matt Riordan was his voice. It was as rich and dark as fine Belgian chocolate....

"Matt?"...

..."Cass," he replied, filling the single syllable with a flood of warmth, as though hearing from me was a wonderful surprise.

..."I got your message," I said....

"Would you be free for dinner?"

"Tonight?"

"It could be tonight," he said...."Shall we say an hour from now, at Tre Scalini?"

An hour. An hour to shower, do my hair, change into a silk blouse...

"Make it two hours," I said....

I was twenty minutes late....

Date behavior. I was exhibiting definite date behavior, something I hadn't done with regard to Riordan in a long time.

He was sitting at a quiet table in the corner....

"One thing about eating with you," I said, sliding into the seat next to his, "you always know where to get the best clam sauce."

He laughed. It was an old joke between us but he laughed anyway. "I guess when your clients are named Scaniello and Cretella, you tend to eat Italian."

"Good Italian," I amended. I opened the menu....My eyes bypassed the real food and went straight to the section headed *Dolci*. "Does this place still have *tiramisu* to die for?"

He smiled....

It wasn't until we had steaming plates of *linguine alla vongole* and an enormous *insalata verde* in front of us that he revealed the purpose of this meeting. I choked on a clam....

"You want me to *what?*"

"You heard me. I want you to represent me...."

"Riordan, you don't need me. You need Alan Dershowitz. Maybe F. Lee."

"No, I don't," he cut in...."I need you. I need you because you're smart and tough. You don't run away from a fight and you don't think prosecutors walk on water."

For a wild moment, my heart filled with pride. The pride a daughter feels when Daddy praises her....

Indemnity Only, an early V.I. Warshawski book about insurance fraud, offers up two choice excerpts: In the first, V.I. is explaining over dinner to one of her men friends why her job as a PI and marriage just won't mix. It's quintessential V.I., but it also serves to explain why so many of the professional female sleuths go it alone. In the second, she's sitting down to dinner with another guy but this time suffering from a swollen lower lip, damaged jaw, and incipient black eye. Enough to drive most people to their beds, and it eventually does, V.I. style. (From Sara Paretsky's *Indemnity Only*. HB. NY: Delacorte Press. 1991.)

I drank some more wine and poked at my salmon.

I pushed my plate away. I'd only eaten half the fish, but I didn't have much of an appetite. "The trouble is, I guess I'm a bit gun-shy now. There really are times when I wish I did have a couple of children and was doing the middle-class family thing...."

..."...I'm a good detective, and I've got an established name now. And it's not a job that's easy to combine with marriage. It's only intermittently demanding, but when I'm hot after something, I don't want to be distracted by the thought of someone at home stewing because he doesn't know what to do about dinner...."

         *   *   *

...Ralph ordered oysters and quail, but I opted for Senegalese soup and spinach salad. I was too exhausted to want a lot of food....

...The waiter brought the first course. The soup was excellent—light, creamy, with a hint of curry. I started feeling better and ate some bread and butter, too. When Ralph's quail arrived, I ordered another bowl of soup and some coffee....

Ralph was finishing off his quail and ordering coffee and dessert. I asked for a large dish of ice cream....

..."...I'm fading...Maybe I could wake up enough to dance...."

"You look like you'd fall asleep on a disco floor right now, Vic...."

"If you keep the blood circulating, it keeps the joints from stiffening so much."

"Well, maybe we could do both—sleep and exercise, I mean."...

I suddenly thought that...I'd like the comfort of someone in bed with me. "Sure," I said, smiling back.

Thirty-year-old NYPD sergeant April Woo still lives at home, except when she lives with detective colleague Mike Sanchez on the twenty-second floor of his Queens apartment. According to her mother, April is not only an old maid, but has a most unsuitable suitor. April's answer to her mother's belching fire is to call her "Skinny Dragon" behind her back.

Mike has broken his homicide case and wants to celebrate, but he can't reach April on his pager. Inspired, he buys two cell phones on the way home. April has her own plans to improve communication. (From Leslie Glass's *Stealing Time*. PB. NY: Penguin Putnam Incorporated, Signet. 1999.)

…She arrived with two shopping bags at quarter past nine….

She let her arms slide down his sides and around his back….Still kissing him, she raised her knee up the inside of first one leg and then the other like a spy on assignment, looking for a weapon….

"…You have a license for this?" she asked, giving him a friendly squeeze.

"What's going on?"

"I'm making dinner," she said….

April started unpacking her shopping bags. "Well, you had a better day than I did…." She took two jars of nasty-looking stuff with Chinese labels out of the bag; then came garlic, ginger, scallions, and something that looked like green beans but were way too long….

"I needed a break," she said.

"Hmmm…This cooking and break thing is new with you. What am I supposed to do…?"

…She finished unpacking the bags, finally taking out a whole roast duck…."Want to fool around?" she asked….

An hour later April was still drunk with love. Gone was the gun at her waist; gone was her heavy shoulder bag with all its necessary supplies like her second gun, notebooks, beeper, Mace, flashlight, rubber gloves, tissues, breath freshener, plastic bags, wallet, and keys; gone were her sweater, jacket, tights, and boots. Without all the paraphernalia of life as she knew it, weighing down her every breath, both her soul and body felt light….

...*"Me amas tu?"*...

Did she love him? What kind of question was that? How many people did she cook for?...

...Just as she was heading out the door, he gave her the cell phone....She thought it was so unbearably romantic she actually cried in the car on the way home.

Readers can become as attached to lovers and other secondary characters as they can be to sleuths. When you've finished with Dana Stabenow's *Hunter's Moon*, you might want to get ahold of Dana at the addresses we gave above.

Chapter 3
Bribing with Food

Female sleuths, when not on the edge of poverty, typically don't make all that much money. Little wonder they pay for information with pizza rather than a C-note. But even women who could afford it prefer to deal in food. Take Kiernan O'Shaughnessy, in San Francisco to investigate the death of Carlos Delaney, deckhand, and the sinking of Robin Matucci's boat. Kiernan's prowling in the wind and fog of Fisherman's Wharf at five a.m. asking questions. "Tchernak's breakfasts" refers to the blueberry corn muffins and killer-chili pepper scrambled eggs her houseman-cook dishes up. (From Susan Dunlap's *Rogue Wave*. PB. NY: Dell Publishing. 1992.)

Kiernan smiled. This was a man ready to deal. "Did you know Robin Matucci?"

"*Early Bird?* The one who went under? Sure."

"Tell me about her over breakfast."

"And a ride back to my room?"

"Done. Come on."

The fancy restaurants may have been still closed, but a tourist mecca was not without its advantages—plenty of motels with 24-hour restaurants or coffee shops. The nearest was two blocks away....

…Zack looked like a sack of garbage left behind by the last shift. His frayed wool cap and salt-stained windbreaker seemed ridiculously out of place behind the lime-green tablecloth and pink napkins.

"I've traveled enough to know the safest bet for breakfast in places like this," Kiernan told him, glancing at the menu. "Eggs scrambled medium—it's hard to screw that up, but get lots of ketchup in case they do; wheat toast and plenty of jelly. Lots of coffee, regardless of what it tastes like."

"Bacon?"

"Right, bacon or ham." She smiled. "Never order sausage if you haven't counted the strays."

"How about a beer?"

…"The offer was breakfast."

"I have beer with breakfast."

"Don't wheedle…."

The food arrived. Zack glared down at it. Ignoring him, Kiernan mixed the bacon in with the eggs, lathered the jelly on the toast and dug in. After Tchernak's breakfasts all others huddled together in mediocrity, but that didn't keep her from downing them. When she looked up, halfway through, Zack had finished the bacon and toast. His face looked less gray, and the fearful squint of his eyes had relaxed.

Kiernan put down her fork. "Tell me about Carlos Delaney. Was he as dumb as Robin liked?"

As head of Port Frederick's civic foundation, Jenny Cain is practiced at getting people to do what they don't want to do. What she wants today is information about her mother's mysterious past from her mother's former priest, now retired. She calls him first on the phone but he tells her he doesn't want to be bothered, after all she's not a member of his parish. (From Nancy Pickard's *I.O.U.* PB. NY: Simon & Schuster, Pocket Books. 1992.)

"I want to ask you some things about my mother," I told him, not at all abashed by his bad temper…."I'm gathering memories of her. And I have a gift for you."

"Things! I don't need any more *things*."

"It's food, Father Gower, cookies."

There had been a pause, full of suspicion. "What kind of cookies?"

"Chocolate chip, like my mother used to make."

"I don't believe it," he said, but he sounded as if he wanted to believe it. "I hear you're a working woman. Everybody knows working women don't cook, which is the reason their husbands run around and their children take drugs."

I laughed, and sweetened the bribe: "Two dozen."

"You're sure it's her recipe?"

"Out of her very own recipe box."

"All right. Ten o'clock in the morning. Put the cookies in a paper sack, and be sure you give them to me and not to anybody else, do you understand?"

"No," I said, "but I'll do that."

"Not to anybody else!"

At my phone, I raised my left hand. "I swear it."

He grunted, and hung up.

V.I. Warshawski uses food and drink to extract information from clients and suspects alike. It's even better if they are chauvinists and insist on grabbing the bill. In *Deadlock*, she begins an investigation into the waterfront death of her cousin Boom Boom by having drinks with the chief engineer on the *Lucella Wieser*, a ship connected to Boom Boom's death. (From Sara Paretsky's *Deadlock*. PB. NY: Ballantine Books. 1986.)

The waiter brought our drinks, white wine for me and vodka and tonic for Sheridan….

Sheridan drank some vodka. "I have to admit I knew who you were when you were standing on the wharf….People gossip a lot in a place like this...Your cousin was coming over to talk to John Bemis, the *Lucella*'s captain, that afternoon. He claimed to know something about an act of vandalism that kept us from loading for a week...."

So now she knows what Boom Boom was doing on the wharf the day of his death. V.I. and Sheridan are spotted by Niels Grafalk, owner of Grafalk Steamship, who asks them to join him for lunch. Grafalk has also suffered some losses to his fleet.

The waiter came to take our order. I asked for a whole artichoke stuffed with shrimp. Grafalk chose grilled lake trout, as did Phillips. Sheridan ordered a steak. "When you spend nine months of your life on the water, beef has a solid earthy appeal."...

I suddenly wondered what Grafalk was doing eating a leisurely lunch when he had several hundred thousand dollars' worth of damage sitting outside.

Martin Bledsoe joins them, owner of the Pole Star Line, which includes the *Lucella*. Soon after, Bledsoe and V.I. dine out.

...Over champagne cocktails we became "Martin" and "Vic"....I told him a bit about my childhood on Chicago's South Side and some of Boom Boom's and my adventures. He countered with stories of life on Cleveland's waterfront....

She later meets with Grafalk at his estate on the shores of Lake Michigan. She tells him about an attempt on her life. Grafalk drinks martinis, V.I., sherry, as they discuss suspects.

...He was turning something over in his mind. "How much do you know about Martin Bledsoe?..."

"…No one gave me a whiff about his background that sounded as troublesome as you're seeming to imply."

"It is buried deep. I've never told anyone about it, even when Martin left me…."

Chocolate got a bad rap for years. Now they say it prolongs life, like a glass of red wine before dinner. Works for us. And for sleuths. When you eat on the go, you need an instant fix, something small, cheap, robust, that enraptures on first bite, and pumps your system full of life-affirming stuff—sugar for high energy and theobromine for the waning libido.

It can also be addictive. Sleuths understand this, and will use it to get what they want. What Carlotta Carlyle, PI, wants today is a car to do a stakeout. She goes for it where she always goes, to her old employer, the G&W Cab Company. A cab has the advantage of a radio from which Gloria can relay messages from Carlotta to the cops. But most of the time, a dispatcher's job is boring and a dispatcher needs escape. (From Linda Barnes's *Snapshot*. PB. NY: Dell Publishing. 1994.)

Gloria, massive dispatcher and half owner of the Green & White Cab Company, was sitting in her wheelchair behind her battered metal desk, phone to ear, listening, talking, and eating at the same time, a trick perfected only by Gloria and certain politicians on the campaign trail….

I glanced at the top of her desk in shock. On a typical visit, I expect to find, within arm's reach, a sampling of America's best, say a box of Bugles, a six-pack of Hershey Bars, a one-pound bag of M&Ms, an openmouthed jar of marshmallow fluff, and a can of Planter's peanuts.

There was nothing but a single sack of Orville Redenbacher microwave popcorn, empty and forlorn.

"Dieting?" I asked, my voice layered with disbelief.

"My dumb-ass brothers," she said angrily….

"You want food?" I asked….

"Hell, long as they make pizza to go, I ain't gonna starve. And I got stashes they ain't found yet. They let me have this popcorn stuff, but where's the butter?"

"I need a cab," I said. "You got something barely functional?"

"Let me guess. You want a cut-rate lease."

"Ask me, all your junkers ought to be cut-rate."

"You just gonna charm it right outa me."

"Give me a deal and I'll bring you a package of Hostess Cream-filled Cupcakes."

"Make it four packages." She patted one plump dark cheek and let a laugh rumble up from deep inside her. "Chocolate's good for my complexion."

"You drive a hard bargain."

"And you get to drive an old Ford. Keys on the pegboard. How long you gonna keep it out?"

"You'll know when I get back."

"Six packages. And some Twinkies."

For more about Linda Barnes, go to her web site: *http://www.lindabarnes.com.*

New York, New York. Chinese-American PI Lydia Chin finds herself the bribee when she agrees to meet with anti-unionist restaurant owner H. B. Yang, a powerful Chinatown political figure. She's already been warned not to investigate the disappearance of four missing Chinese restaurant workers, but Yang's offer proves to be irresistible. As she tells her partner later, "Our new client fed me the foods of my childhood. That's not fair, is it?" (From S. J. Rozan's *A Bitter Feast*. PB. NY: St. Martin's Paperbacks. 1999.)

…"Please," he said, "help yourself," and he pointed to the covered blue-and-white dishes. I lifted the tops to find in one preserved plums, and in the other the little sesame-covered balls of fried dough my father used to make for us on his rare days off. Their warm, rich scent suddenly brought back to me our cramped kitchen and my father's voice. "See how they smile when you cook them?" he'd say as the balls split in the hot oil. And my mother would reply, "It's a lucky thing the dough is smiling, because all the children in this house are quarrelsome."...

I reached for a Smiling Face from H. B. Yang's dish, wondering whether it would live up to my memories....The seeds were crunchy, the dough was soft and sweet. What was missing was the sense that came with the taste, of being surrounded by people who, confining, annoying, and dismissive as they were, nevertheless wanted the best for you....

"My staff is...quite good," he went on. "But most are peasants...when they come to me. I train them. I look after them...."

"...I need you, Chin Ling Wan-ju, to follow something through for me."

I reached for a preserved plum to hide my confusion. I'd thought I was going to be told to follow my nose out the door and leave Dragon Garden and its union problems alone....

...As I bit into the salty-tart plum, H. B. Yang continued. "I've lost something," he said. "In fact, someone. Four men, employees of mine. I would like you to find them for me."

NYC actress Josh O'Roarke has just attended the laying out of actor-director Rich Rafelson. Suspected of his murder is Josh's good buddy, Texan P. J. Cullen. The police have released P. J. for the time being and Josh wants his ideas as to whom else had a motive. (From Jane Dentinger's *Who Dropped Peter Pan?* PB. NY: Penguin Books. 1996.)

"Let's see, I'll have corned beef hash with a poached egg on top and home fries on the side. And a large Coke Cola," Cullen said to the peroxide blonde waitress in the Lord Camelot coffee house. She scribbled his order and turned to Jocelyn, who was looking a little bilious.

"What would you like?"

"Coffee and an English muffin."

"That's it?"

O'Roarke looked over at P. J. and asked, "You gonna pour ketchup all over the stuff?"

"Natch."

"Yeah, that'll be all for me," she told the waitress, adding, "Trust me, it's the safe choice."

After spending a decent amount of time at McDermott's [funeral parlor], she had hauled P. J. off for further pumping....Knowing that Cullen needed to consume at least his own body weight each day, and that food worked on him the way shopping worked on Cher, she had acquiesced.

Carefully averting her eyes, she waited as he dug into the dog-food doppelgänger on his plate. Then she heard the hum; P. J. always hummed, mostly show tunes, as he achieved culinary nirvana. When he had finished the first ten bars of "Have an Eggroll, Mr. Goldstone," she broke in on his bliss....

...He tried to distract her by dumping more ketchup on the hash. She snatched the bottle away from him.

"Stop potchkying, Tex. You know what I mean. Who else was Rafelson screwing with—literally or figuratively?"

"Aw, man!"Cullen crumpled his paper napkin ...."I *hate* this kind of gossip."

This was like Liz Taylor saying she hated weddings, but Josh didn't point out the irony; she merely said, "Close your eyes and picture a state penitentiary. Now picture yourself *in* one."

It should be noted that one of Jocelyn O'Roarke's salient features is her unspoken motto, While there's food, there's hope. (From Jane Dentinger's *Death Mask*.)

Leigh Ann Warren, Washington, D.C., cop on disability leave, needs to get rid of two well-meaning minders who have been trailing her at the behest of her ex-lover. Said ex-lover has left town for destination unknown at the same time Leigh comes home to a very dead body at her kitchen table. But there's no way she can get into investigating with six-foot-three Tank and four-ten Tina on her case. How to get rid of the pair? (From Chassie West's *Killing Kin*. PB. NY: HarperCollins Publishing, Avon Books. 2000.)

…"Smells like somebody's cookin' last month's garbage."
Tank tried to shush her. "That ain't food, Tina, that's—"
"How 'bout we talk about it later?" I cut him off.
"We're on our way to get something to eat. You coming, Tina?"
"You buyin?" she asked me…."Then what y'all waitin' for? I'm starving."…

…Tina might be my ace in the hole. I was certain she wasn't happy about the role he'd assumed….With her along to nudge him in the right direction, there was every possibility that by the time I paid the check, I'd be seeing the last of Tank and Tina. This meal might be worth whatever it cost me….

Over a buffet dinner at a local restaurant, I presented what seemed to me to be perfectly logical reasons why I had no need for a baby-sitter….

"…There's no reason for you to hang around, Tank. You'd be bored silly…."

Tina managed an affectionate smile between mouthfuls of the second plate she'd loaded with so much food it resembled Mount Kilimanjaro. "Nothing my Tankie hates worse than being bored."

"…Think I'll get another slice of that coconut cream pie." He headed for the dessert table, and I breathed a sigh of relief….

Tank demolished another piece of pie, and Tina worked her way through a chunk of cheesecake the size of a cement block before declaring that she thought she'd had enough to last until she got home….

…there was no doubt who jumped through whose hoops. Tank had it bad.

Karma introduces readers to Susan Dunlap's longest series based on Jill Smith, beat officer on Berkeley's Telegraph Hill. In keeping with the gutsy image of Dunlap's women sleuths, this is *the* food scene in *Karma*. Heather—a questionable source at best—says she has information about a murderer and she'll pass it on to Jill if Jill will let Heather leave town with her lover, Chattanooga. So Jill takes her to a fastfood joint. (From Susan Dunlap's *Karma*. PB. NY: Dell Publishing. 1991.)

Heather turned, stalked to the patrol car and treated me to an icy silence all the way to the restaurant. It wasn't till after we were seated and she had ordered herself a cheeseburger deluxe, their special salad and a Coke that she said, "Okay."

"So who's the killer?" I asked in a half whisper.

"Vernon Felcher, the real-estate man."

"Felcher!"

"Felcher. Yeah."

I leaned forward. "How do you know it was Felcher?"

"I don't *know*. I didn't say that I knew for sure. I just figured it out because everything points that way."

"What things?"

The waitress arrived with Heather's meal and my cup of coffee. Seeing the food, I wished I'd ordered something to eat, too....

"Yeah, Leah told me. I remember because I was surprised he'd have the gall to come, particularly on that night when there was so big a crowd they'd had to turn people away." She looked more confident now. Biting into the cheeseburger, she watched my reaction. My mouth was watering—one reaction....

"Anything else?" I asked as Heather started in on her salad.

"What more do you need!"

"Then that's it?"

"Yeah. Isn't that enough? Can't I go? Chattanooga will be leaving."

"I can't let you go until we have an arrest. It could be soon, or maybe not. Get Chattanooga's schedule and meet him along the way. If it's true love," I said with a straight face, "it will survive."

"Shit!"

Ignoring my suggestions to hurry, Heather dallied over her salad, ordered a slice of banana cream pie and, finally, announced that she would get home alone.

During a late evening shoot in L.A.'s MacArthur Park, independent film producer Maggie MacGowan is hustled by a teenager girl ("You can call me Pisces"). Pisces introduces her to Sly, a nine-year-old "foul-mouthed, evil-smelling little wretch" who "looked old…more like a small animal. Something feral." Pisces turns up dead in the park the next night, her throat slashed. Sly is placed in a juvenile detention facility. Maggie wants to question him about what he saw, but first the little animal must be fed. Wendy Hornsby can be reached at *whornsby@lbcc.cc.ca.us*. (From Wendy Hornsby's *Midnight Baby*. PB. NY: Penguin Group, Signet. 1994.)

I passed him the bag of burgers. "Thought you might be hungry."

He fished out a drippy cheese burger and, staring blankly at a point in front of him, wolfed it down in four huge bites.

"Sorry the food got cold," I said.

"Doesn't matter." There were two more burgers, a jumbo order of fries, and a chocolate shake still inside the bag. He rolled the top of the bag closed and set it on the floor between his feet.

…"Can you talk about her, Sly?"

He said nothing, but a single tear finally rolled down his cheek. I moved closer to him and put my arm behind him, not touching him. When he didn't shy away, I let my hand rest on his shoulder.

"Did you see it happen?"

He nodded.

"Tell me about it."

"Why should I?"

"Because I want to nail his balls to a tree. Don't you?"

Sly's chin quivered, but he held on to his composure. He also pulled himself out of his stupor to speak to me. "She picked up this guy."

"What did he look like?"

"Just a guy...."

"Would you know him if you saw him again?"

"Yeah...."

"You know, Sly, you can tell me anything and all that will happen to you is you'll get a pat on the back and maybe some more burgers. Whatever went down, it's not your fault. You're a kid....Do you understand that?"

He thought about it. Then he turned in his seat to face me.

"No shit?"

Could a healthy choice bribe possibly work? Brenda Midnight, NYC milliner, has turned amateur sleuth when her best friend, Carla, dress designer, is found murdered. How she got to be a vegetarian is revealed when she invites a man to dinner for, incidentally, one purpose and one purpose only—*information*. (From Barbara Jaye Wilson's *Death Brims Over*. PB. NY: Avon Books. 1997.)

Food was a problem. I don't eat meat. The whole time my mother was pregnant with me, she worked as a secretary at the stockyards amid the stench and sounds of death. Somehow it sank into my formative brain and I never could stand the taste of the stuff. My parents tried everything....They stuck small chunks on the end of a fork and flew it into my mouth, airplane style. Nothing worked. As soon as I had a choice, I spurned it totally. This, combined with the fact that I'm a lousy cook, made it a real challenge to come up with a meal somebody else could actually eat.

However, with fresh ingredients, I could throw together a salad that would knock almost anyone's socks off. Lucky for me, the mecca of fresh, locally grown green stuff, the Union Square farmer's market, was still going strong....

I have a strict personal code of visual and gustatory aesthetics that dictates which vegetables can be served together. It has nothing whatsoever to do with nutritional science; the complicated rules are based solely on appearance and texture....Let's just say I would no more combine asparagus and broccoli than wear a wide-rimmed straw hat after sunset....

I stopped at several vendors, eventually filling my canvas bag with the makings of a wonderful salad—all carefully color and texture coordinated....

On the way home I stopped at the pasta shop on Greenwich Avenue for a meatless entrée. The owner recommended his wild mushroom ravioli. "It's the most satisfying," he claimed....I got the sauce too.

Pam Nilsen, who works in a collectively-run Seattle print shop, is trying to find a young prostitute whose life is in danger. She's in Portland where a lawyer friend Janis invites a prostitute, Dawn, for tea and cake to fill in amateur sleuth Pam on the oldest profession. Dawn thoroughly enjoys this break from work since it also allows her a sweet escape into food. (From Barbara Wilson's *Sisters of the Road*. PB. Seattle: Seal Press. 1986.)

...Dawn settled herself on the couch with a sigh of satisfaction and crossed her plump legs. "Cut me a big slice, forget the diet."...

"You're organized like the Pentagon," Dawn laughed [addressing Janis], lolling comfortably back on the couch with a huge slice of carrot cake. "Only you're the generals and the staff all rolled into one. So, Pam," she said, without a pause, "I hear you're looking into prostitution in Portland?"...

"I'm actually looking for a girl who's a prostitute...."

"Well, I tell you," Dawn said, cutting herself another piece of carrot cake....

…"It's easy work and I've got my regular customers, had some of them for years."…

Dawn chuckled…."Men aren't going to change, honey. And it's men who're on top, like it or not. All we can do is stick together and try to get fair treatment." She stirred her cup and sipped….

"But what about kids in prostitution?" I asked. "The girl I'm looking for is only fifteen. She didn't make the choice as an adult, she was pushed into it."

"If there were strong hookers' unions we could do something about that," said Dawn firmly, succumbing to another slice….

"You think about this, Pam," said Dawn, polishing off the last of the carrot cake. "If you want to find this girl you've got to decide where you stand. Because she's not going to listen to you if she thinks you're judging her….But now I'm late. I'm visiting old Mr. Taylor at his hotel. He comes in from Hermiston once a month to have a nice time." She stroked Janis' wispy brown hair. "Janis, I didn't *mean* to eat all your carrot cake. It was just too *good*."

In San Francisco, Julie Smith's Rebecca Schwartz gets us up close and personal with a visit to *Tadich's* restaurant—of which we also have fond memories—then on to shrimp and mushroom dumplings at a nameless café, sandwiches at the Embarcadero Plaza, parties at the Bravo Caffe. But the scene that sticks from *Other People's Skeletons* (Ivy Books, 1993) is bringing breakfast to the classiest madame in town, one Elena Mooney, whom Rebecca had met when she was the lawyer for HUENA, the hookers' union. It's lunchtime but Elena is still waking up and her blood sugar's down, so Rebecca brings hefty portions of bagels, cream cheese, and lox. Elena admits to losing half her words until she's breakfasted, but in no time she's able and ready to talk. Unfortunately, the hooker Rebecca is asking about has moved to Alaska. However, a cordless phone call elicits the news that the murder victim was weird, weird, weird.

Bribery's not a very nice thing to do. Getting out your wallet and saying "There's a twenty in it if you'll tell me what you remember" may be efficient, but it's insulting, patronizing, crass, and cold. On the other hand, leisurely breakfasts where bribees get to select bacon, ham, or sausage, lunches like corned beef hash with home fries, tea-time cakes and cookies—mean you're treating a fellow human being as a real person. Someone you're willing to spend time with. Somebody who'll let you nurture and comfort them. Something female sleuths are pretty good at.

CHAPTER 4
HANGING OUT

"…The menu for the deputies that day was lasagna, grilled ham-and-cheese sandwiches, french fries, and corn. Not quite enough fat and carbs for my taste, but it was coming close." (From Sue Grafton's *"J" is for Judgment*.)

Cops and PIs are renowned for their hangouts—bars, restaurants, and fastfood joints where they are known and welcomed. They can let their hair down with owners, cooks, and wait persons who know what to bring them when they step in the door. They can shoptalk, swear, badmouth superiors, reveal indiscretions, gossip, vent, and moan. No one cares.

A typical hangout is NYC's Empire Diner where assistant D.A. Alexandra Cooper regularly reviews notes with detectives Mike Chapman and Mercer Wallace. In addition to the plot moving along over their breakfasts, what each chooses from the menu tells us who they are. Alex is a bowl of Raisin Bran, Mercer is a plain bagel, while Mike is a mushroom-and-cheese omelette, home fries with ketchup, side orders of crisp bacon and sausage, lots of toast and coffee. Mike says it's all Alex's fault, she being so tough to work with, he needs to fortify himself several times a day. See for yourself in Linda Fairstein's 1999 *Cold Hit*.

Hangouts are also good places for PIs and amateurs to connect with cops. Here forty-something PI Lauren Laurano gets together with good friend, NYPD Lieutenant Peter Cecchi. (From Sandra Scoppettone's *My Sweet Untraceable You*. PB. London: Little, Brown and Company (UK), Virago Press. 1996.)

I am having breakfast in the air-conditioned Waverly Place Luncheonette with my friend Lieutenant Peter Cecchi....

We eat here a lot because it's a cop hangout, cheap by New York standards, and the service is fast. The decor is the same as in any other luncheonette—a square room with booths, small tables, a counter and stools....

..."We got a stiff on Eighth Avenue and Twelfth in a Dumpster."

I wipe my mouth and stand up to go with him.

"I don't know," he says.

"Yes you do."

"Okay, Lauren, but stay out of the way."

*   *   *

I go into the Waverly Place Luncheonette with hopes that I might locate Cecchi. Also, I know I'll find a phone book. Probably the only public one left in New York City.

In one sweep I take in the room. No Cecchi.

Ruby zips past me, a tray of breakfasts balanced on one hand. When she comes by again I stop her.

"Hi, Ruby. Seen Cecchi?"

"Not today." White shoes spirit her away with the silence only an older New York waitress can manage.

*   *   *

...It's 2:00 a.m. Ruby's not on duty at this hour. Instead, there's a surly waiter and a sullen counterman. I long for Ruby.

I've brought Cecchi up-to-date....

I take a sip of my five hundredth cup of coffee. Cold. I wave to the waiter for fresh. Scowling at me, he pours the dark liquid that's beginning to look like beach tar. I try to see things from his POV....

"Cecchi, do you think the waiter thinks we're lovers?"

"No."

"Why not?" I tell him my scenario.

"First, he doesn't give a rat's ass, and second, he doesn't give a rat's ass."

Sandra Scoppettone can be reached at *sandrasc@optonline.net*.

When Baltimore PI Tess Monaghan wants to meet with her cop friend Martin Tull, she's not surprised when he suggests the Daily Grind, a coffee house right across the street from the recreation pier at Fells Point, which is a stand-in for police headquarters in the production of the TV hit *Homicide: Life on the Streets*. There's always the chance you're going to see somebody famous while you're sippin'. But Tess insists she pay for Tull's latte and chocolate biscotti. (From Laura Lippman's *Butchers Hill*. PB. NY: Avon Books. 1998.)

Tess smiled. Leave it to Baltimore, usually so finicky about its national image, to embrace a television program that spotlighted its murder rate....

"But it's why we always meet here, isn't it? Because you like to sneak peeks at the actors."

"I like coffee, and I don't like bars," Tull said. "You live in Fells Point. Where else are we going to meet?"

"Another coffeehouse?"

A blonde at the next table was trying to catch Tull's eye with no luck....

Tess didn't have any romantic yearnings toward him. She would remain under her self-imposed dating ban until she figured out why her judgment in these matters had been so historically wretched....

"Do you have a drinking problem?" she asked suddenly.

"Now that would be a cliché, wouldn't it?" replied Tull. "The alcoholic cop."

"A cliché is merely a truth that's become banal through repetition."

"What if I told you I think *you* drink too much, so I make you meet me here, where you can't abuse anything but caffeine?"

Tess considered this. Such personal observations fascinated her, even unflattering ones. Did she drink too much?...She followed H. L. Mencken's tips for responsible alcohol consumption: Never drink before sundown and never drink three days in a row. Well, she more or less followed those rules....

"I'd say you were trying to change the subject on me," she said. "Besides, talk about clichés. Everyone thinks I do everything to excess. I can go cold turkey on anything, any time. Just try me."

"Like men. Which means I can't try you." He was teasing her. Tull would have run for the exit if he thought she had a romantic interest in him.

Massachusetts native Jenny Cain has been coaxed to New York City to sub for a murdered friend...who headed up a foundation much like the one Jenny used to run. Almost everyone had a grudge against her friend, including foundation supporters. Here, Jenny taxies to Brooklyn to an unusual crime-related hangout—a halfway house for ex-convicts—one of the foundation's projects. (From Nancy Pickard's *But I Wouldn't Want to Die There*. PB. NY: Simon & Schuster, Pocket Books, a Pocket Star Book. 1994.)

Robin Stewart was all genial smiles when he greeted me at the front door....

"I'll apologize before I even say hello, Jenny. Mother's changed her mind again, she's not coming down to dinner after all...."

I stopped him as he began to pull out a chair for me. Apparently, I was to sit at the table in regal solitude while I waited for everyone else to appear.

"Robin, you don't have to do this, maybe I should leave—"

"No!...I've seen enough of men to last me a lifetime. No, stay, please."...

He disappeared through swinging doors into the kitchen and soon the table began to fill up with food brought in by several different men, and within minutes after that, there were nine men and me gathered around the big table, digging into huge platters of spaghetti and long loaves of hot garlic bread. Robin took a seat at the head of table, like Dad, and I was ensconced at the opposite end, like Mom....He quickly introduced me to Fred the counterfeiter, Robinson the sex offender, Paulie the arsonist, Eddie the enforcer, Manny the armed robber, and three murderers: Jackson, Quillin, and Allen Cheskey....

It was unnerving but weirdly entertaining—if you could manage not to think about details like innocent victims—because they regaled me with stories of their crimes and incarcerations as if they were characters in a crime caper novel....To hear them tell it, they were all smarter than everybody else, just unluckier....

Robinson the sex offender stared at me all through dinner without saying a word. Whenever I noticed him, however, I wanted to utter five words: Get me out of here.

PJ Gray is a divorced forties-something head of the Computerized Homicide Investigations Project (CHIP) with the St. Louis Police Department. Assigned to her (as a naive civilian) is fifties-something Detective Leo Schultz. Both have just been chewed out royally by their boss. Millie's is where they go to share. (From Shirley Kennett's *Chameleon*. PB. NY: Kensington Publishing Corporation, Pinnacle. 1999.)

…The plates and coffee mugs were heavy and white and didn't say Taiwan on the back, and there was always a Daily Special.

He rapped his knuckles a couple of times on the counter. "Service!"

The proprietress, a formidable woman who could fry eggs on a grill with one hand and refill coffee cups with the other, approached the two of them. She pointedly ignored Schultz, but reached out and patted PJ's hand.

"Nice to see you, dearie. We've got a wonderful three-cheese soup today. You sure you want to sit next to this guy? I always got to wipe the stool with disinfectant after he leaves." She beamed at PJ.

"The floor, too," the two women said in unison. It was a familiar ritual.

"I'll have the soup and a side salad. Lemon slices, if you have them."

"Of course I do. This is a high-class joint."…

"So how did it go with [bossman] Wall?" PJ asked.

Schultz shook his head. "It's a wonder I can sit down on what's left of my ass…."

*   *   *

…PJ's cheese soup didn't smell half bad. PJ snatched a French fry from Schultz's plate as Millie set it down in front of him.

"Watch it, dearie—"

"Ouch."

"—those are hot," Millie said. "Love to stay and talk, but the place is hoppin' like a frog on the Interstate."

Schultz grabbed the hot sauce and liberally doused his fries before PJ could take any more….He plucked the little flag on a toothpick out of the bun of his hamburger. It was Millie's trademark….If he'd collected them since he first started coming to the diner, he'd have enough to decorate Arlington National Cemetery on Veteran's Day by now.

PI V.I. Warshawski meets Murray Ryerson, a newspaper reporter for the *Chicago Herald Star*, for drinks to discuss why she thinks her apartment was broken into and why her friend Lotty Hershel's clinic was recently attacked. Their hangout is the Golden Glow, a bar that V.I. introduced to Murray five years ago. (From Sara Paretsky's *Bitter Medicine*. PB. NY: Ballantine Books. 1988.)

The Golden Glow is the closest place I have to a club. It's a bar in the south Loop for serious drinkers. Sal Barthele, who owns it, stocks twenty brands of beer and almost as many of whiskey, but she doesn't do happy hour, little quiches, or anything else exotic. After holding out for two years she reluctantly brought in a supply of Perrier; if someone asks for it they get waited on by the barmaid, not by her.

Sal was sitting behind the horseshoe mahogany bar when I came in, reading *The Wall Street Journal*. She takes her investments seriously, which is why she spends so much time in the bar when she could retire to the country....No one behaves in an unseemly fashion at the Golden Glow when Sal is there. I went over and chatted with her until Murray arrived....

We took our drinks—two bottles of beer for him, a glass of water and a double whiskey for me—over to one of the little tables lining the walls....

I drank the water before taking any Black Label, then felt a welcome warmth spread through my arms and fingers....

"Okay, Ms. Warshawski. I want the truth, the whole truth, and nothing but—not such little crumbs as you may choose to hand out."

I shook my head. "I don't have it. I don't know it. Something mighty weird is going on and I'm just beginning to get the hang of part of it. If I tell you, it is definitely off the record...."

On Sara Paretsky's web page, Murray Ryerson interviews V.I. and tells her that some readers are troubled by her drinking. V.I. is puzzled. "I'm not a heavy drinker. I never drink and drive. I can't figure out if people are shocked that a woman drinks neat whisky, or just that she drinks. But you remember old Philip Marlowe? He always had a pint of rye in his glove compartment. He drank when he was concussed, he drank when he was depressed. He drank. I don't know how he ever functioned well enough to figure out what was going on around him. But different strokes for different folks," she tells him. Check out Paretsky's website and see what else V.I. has to say about food and drink: *http://www.saraparetsky.com*.

Any cop will do when you need hard information. Callahan Garrity knows where they hang. She was an Atlanta cop once, a job she abandoned to become a PI. She's about to let her PI license expire to concentrate on House Mouse, her new cleaning service. Just too busy to do both jobs. Tonight though, she's doing a favor for an old friend, tracking down a nanny who's run off with her employer's jewelry and business papers. (From Kathy Hogan Trocheck's *Every Crooked Nanny*. PB. NY: HarperCollins Publishing, HarperPaperbacks. 1993.)

It looked like a fairly slow night at the Yacht Club....

I scanned the room until I saw what I needed to see: a cop. Tonight it was a guy named Charles "Bucky" Deaver. Bucky is about my age and he is a big boy....

He was concentrating on a monster hamburger and didn't see me walk up until I slipped behind him and gave him a little goose.

He didn't even look up. "Callahan Garrity, you hot-blooded vixen. You never could keep your hands off me, could you?"...

"Got that right, Bucko. What's shakin'?"

He swallowed and shook his head. "Not a damn thing. Braves are losing. That new starter of theirs is getting the shit shelled out of him."

"What else is new?" I said, not bothering to cover my yawn.

Bucky and I go way back....We worked long hours and parties and drank—and sometime slept—together....

From the other end of the counter, Tinkles, the bartender, caught my eye. I nodded and he reached into the beer box and brought out an ice-caked green Heineken's bottle....

When the foam on my beer had settled and the Braves had safely lost the game, I was ready to talk business with Bucky....

...He was occupied in trying to suck a white string of onion out of a large onion ring. That done, he inhaled the brown crust and delicately wiped his hands on the paper napkin in his lap....

"OK, Callahan. We been shooting the shit here for forty-five minutes. You wanna tell me why you came looking for me tonight, and what kind of favor you're needing?"...

Another professional house cleaner is mid-30s Lily Bard, who lives in the little town of Shakespeare, Arkansas. While amateur as a sleuth, she's expert in martial arts and known all over town for her performance at "The Fight" at a notorious sleuth hangout known as Burger Tycoon. What happened was, Darnell Glass's new car had been hit by another in Burger Tycoon's parking lot, a car containing four white teenagers who tried to beat up black Darnell. Two cops stood and watched Lily's fight, doing nothing to intervene.

The first scene demonstrates that the culprits were no match for Lily, with the help of a young Marine. In the second scene Lily and Police Chief Claude Friedrich discuss the case over dinner. Charlaine Harris's web site is *http://members.aol.com/femmesweb/harris.htm.* (From Charlaine Harris's *Shakespeare's Champion.* PB. NY: Dell Publishing. 1998.)

I'd just pulled into the parking space on the other side of Glass's [car], having picked that night of all nights to buy a hamburger....

I was tired. I just wanted to get my carry-out food and watch an old movie on television....

From the corner of my eye I finally noticed the patrol car. I saw Deputy Tom David Meicklejohn climb out of it. He did nothing but smile his mean redneck smile and extend his arms to bar spectators from joining in the brawl. A man in civilian clothes, a bag and a cardboard tray with five cups in holders bogging him down, was yelling at Tom David. I later learned this was off-duty officer Todd Picard....

"Sorry I didn't get out here earlier," he [the Marine] said. "That Tae Kwon Do?"

"Goju. For close fighting."

"My drill sergeant would love you," he said....

I caught Tom David Meicklejohn's eye. I wanted powerfully to kick him.

He smiled at me. "Keeping back the crowd," he said succinctly. By then, Todd Picard had deposited the food in his car and was standing by Tom David's patrol vehicle. Todd looked ashamed.

*   *   *

As our waitress left, Claude spread his napkin in his lap and speared a shrimp. "Tom David was there and did nothing," he said...."Todd was there and did nothing."

...I stared over at him, my fork suspended midway to my mouth with a bit of flounder impaled on the tines. "I didn't care until they all jumped him," I said after a moment's thought. "I would have done the same if Darnell had been white and the other guys black."

Lunch time in Tahlequah, Oklahoma. Molly Bearpaw, Native American Advocacy League investigator, is meeting Dave Highsmith, sheriff of Adair County, to discuss the death of an elderly Indian. Was it suicide or murder? And what is the meaning of the black stones found beside the body? (From Jean Hager's *Seven Black Stones*. PB. NY: Warner Books, Mysterious Press. 1996.)

Highsmith…pulled off his cap and stuck it in a pocket with a glove, then removed his coat and dumped it with Molly's on an extra chair before he sat. Over a sudden burst of laughter from a nearby table, he said, "Full house. The food must be good here." He picked up a menu.

"Have the chicken-fried steak or a burger," Molly advised.

He read through the menu with great deliberation, looking up to inquire of Molly about the meatloaf and pork chops. But when the waitress came, he ordered the chicken-fried steak dinner with corn, mashed potatoes, and gravy….They both wanted coffee, which was delivered immediately by a young waitress with large, bouncing breasts.

Highsmith tried to pretend he didn't notice and almost missed his cup when he stirred real cream into his coffee. "Talk," he muttered to Molly….

They fell silent as the waitress set their meals in front of them. "Anything else right now, hon?" she chirped, looking at Highsmith.

Highsmith grinned and his face turned pink. Molly laid her notebook beside her plate. "We'll need more coffee in a few minutes, hon," she said.

The waitress glanced at Molly uncertainly and Highsmith watched her bounce away before picking up his fork….

…"We can't let somebody get away with murder."

He mopped up some gravy with a piece of roll. "If you can't prove it's murder—" He let the sentence hang while he ate the gravy-drenched bread. "When all you've got is gut instinct, you compromise…."

"Seven *black* stones? Dave, you can't find black stones just anywhere. And seven of them, that's too much of a coincidence for me to swallow."

He looked at her helplessly.

We've all experienced it, pale, watery succotash, rubbery hotdogs, "elephant balls" of beef and rice that hold their shape on the bounce. Sleuths partake of institutional fare whenever necessary. Some like it more than others. Take PI Kinsey Millhone, here dining with Tommy Ryckman, jail administrator, who's housing a certain murder suspect. Kinsey's hoping the murder suspect's heretofore "death by suicide" father shows up long enough to be arrested for cheating an insurance company out of a $500,000 payoff to his wife. (From Sue Grafton's *"J" is for Judgment.* HB. NY: Henry Holt and Company. 1993.)

There was also a salad bar, featuring stainless-steel bins of chopped iceberg lettuce, sliced carrots, green pepper rings, and onions....

Ryckman still had the unruly hunger of an adolescent. I watched him pile his tray with a serving of lasagna the size of a brick, two grilled sandwiches, a mound each of corn and french fries, and a hefty side of salad with a dipper of Thousand Island dressing poured on top. He tucked two cartons of low-fat milk into the remaining space on his tray. I followed him in the line, picking up plastic flatware from a bin. I opted for a grilled ham-and-cheese sandwich and a modest log pile of fries, hungrier than I thought possible given the institutional nature of the setting. We found a free corner table and unloaded our trays....

"What's the deal?" I asked. "I don't understand what these guys are about." He squirted ketchup on his fries and passed the dispenser to me. I could tell we shared the same intense interest in junk food.

Ryckman ate quickly, attention focused on his plate as the mountain of food diminished....

"...Bankers, real estate brokers, investment counselors...anyone exposed to large sums of cash. After a while they can't seem to keep their hands off it."

"Too tempting," I remarked. I wiped my hands on a paper napkin, uncertain whether the grease was coming from the sandwich or the pile of french fries. Both were heaven to a person of my low appetites.

We're near the end of this book. Sutton McPhee, Washington, D.C., star crime reporter, is trying to keep from getting killed by meeting with the police aka Lansing and Peterson to pass along what she knows about three murders. They picked one of their hangouts, Joe's Hole in the Wall

Café. (From Brenda English's *Corruption of Justice*. PB. NY: Berkley Publishing Group, Berkley Prime Crime. 1999.)

Joe's Hole in the Wall was…a tiny, nondescript café that one easily could overlook in the middle of the other storefronts….

I walked over to join the detectives, sitting down beside Lansing when he slid over next to the wall to make room for me. By the partially eaten sub sandwiches and fries in front of him and Peterson, I judged that they already had ordered after tiring of waiting for me. At that moment, the young man from the grill appeared beside me to ask what I wanted to drink. I ordered a glass of iced tea and asked if I could get just a tossed salad. We discussed salad dressings, and after agreeing on the house vinaigrette, he returned to the kitchen….

"So what was it you got us out here on a Saturday to tell us?" Peterson asked, biting a fry in half.

The cook reappeared with my iced tea, salad, and dressing, and I thanked him. I took a couple of seconds to drizzle the dressing over the salad before answering Peterson….

I took the two of them through the whole thing, laying out one by one the articles and reports that…I had collected, filling in the gaps with my guesses. They both listened thoughtfully, between bites of their food, while I gave them the outline, my salad forgotten….

*   *   *

I looked over at Lansing, who was giving me a measuring look in return.

"What?" I asked.

"Oh, I was just thinking that you probably were one of those kids who felt compelled to poke every hornet's nest you saw, just to see how much you could stir the hornets up."

PIs and cops hear it all, see it all, murder, mayhem, madness. The best they can do is not take it personally. So when they have a place to hang, their language gets so...to the point. Here they can abandon linguistic niceties, politically correct phrases, polite innuendos. A big plus crime-wise: When conversation gets low-down, sleuths can leapfrog over oddball pieces of evidence, tie together clues, and question obscure motives. And all over workplace nirvana—a jumble of greasy fries and onion rings.

CHAPTER 5
WEIGHTY ISSUES

"Strange how one little thing, like getting fired from a job you love for being fat, can ruin your day...." (From G. A. McKevett's *Just Desserts*.)

Typically young women sleuths are slim, whether short, medium, or tall. Further, they stay slim in spite of eating Quarter Pounders, jelly donuts, cherry pies, and lots of chocolate. Their creators make them action-oriented, absorbed with their cases, and dependent on others to make sure they eat at all. They have no problems controlling their weight and they do not diet. They are definitely not like the rest of us.

What the rest of us put up with are magazines at the supermarket checkout that feature high-calorie gourmet meals next to drop-dead skinny models. We're told to eat and not eat. No wonder anorexia and bulimia plague young women. No wonder diet books will always be popular. No wonder we're never quite happy with our body image.

When police officer Jill Smith strikes a deal with her lover and fellow officer Seth Howard to give up junk food for a month if he'll stop remodeling their house, she sees no problem until hunger strikes in a house that holds only pizza, ice cream, chocolate chip cookies, and Snickers. That first night she falls asleep smelling Snickers, which Howard took into the bathroom to eat. "It must have stayed there all night—I remembered a dream in which I was buried, happily, in a mudslide—and now the whole bedroom smelled like suburban Hershey." In the following scene, she's gathering information to request a search warrant. (From Susan Dunlap's *Sudden Exposure*. PB. NY: Dell Publishing. 1997.)

Gathering enough information to support a request for a warrant is no afternoon at the beach....I must have thought twenty times in the next two hours: I'm starving; I'll run downstairs for a doughnut. A Hershey's. A Snickers. By the time I picked up the phone to call the assistant DA on weekend duty, I would have chomped through my pencil if it had been coated in chocolate. Any illusion I had about being cured of my cravings was gone. For pizza maybe; it is, after all, only food. But chocolate is the nourishment of the soul.

The ADA, just back from hiking on Mount Diablo and on his way to the Warriors game, listened as I read him the papers and answered his questions for twenty minutes. My neck, my throat, my stomach were all knotted; my head pounded. I wasn't even *thinking* of chocolate; my reaction reflected a much deeper panic. It was all I could do to concentrate on the questions and formulate sensible answers. When I hung up, I sat staring at the wall. It was the color of mint chocolate. Or pistachio. It was insane to let a bet yank the stability out of my life. I had enough real problems without creating more. If Howard couldn't see that, well, too bad. It wasn't a question of asking Howard for an out; I'd tell him. I picked up the phone and dialed the Fresno police.

Someone has been killing off the cheerleaders of PI Trade Ellis's Tucson high school graduating class of 25 years ago. Two of the remaining cheerleading Song Dogs, Charlene and Buffy, have hired Trade to find the killer. Here Trade pays a visit to her client, no longer the tall, thin, peppy cheerleader and homecoming queen of Javelina High. Charlene has a weight problem and Trade, trim and slim in her forties, has a problem with other people's problems. But we mustn't forget that her major problem is, who did it? Bobette, Binky, Charlene or Daggett? (From Sinclair Browning's *The Last Song Dogs*. PB. NY: A Bantam Crime Line Book. 1999.)

...Everything about the room signaled Serious Cook, and I remembered that Charlene had listed cooking first on her biography under hobbies....

"I hope you don't mind if I work while we talk," Charlene said. "We're having company for dinner, and I want to get the gazpacho done so it can chill."...

"Is there any news on the Song Dogs?" Charlene asked, reaching for a bell pepper. She took a boning knife and deftly stripped off long pieces of the membranes....

"Why don't you use the Cuisinart?" I asked....

"I like doing it this way," she said. Her face was flushed and I had the flash that Charlene had something sexual going with her vegetables. Kind of like me and the Twinkies....

...She retrieved a fresh cucumber from the refrigerator and replaced the boning knife with a vegetable cleaver. The dimples in her hands winked at me as she rocked the blade over the new cucumber. Chop, chop, chop.

She never missed a beat as she scooped up the cucumber and dumped it in the blender....

As her hand dropped to the side of the butcher block to remove yet another knife, I leaned over and looked at the collection.

"Holy cow, Charlene, you are serious about this, aren't you?"

"If you're going to cook, then it's important you have the right equipment," she sniffed, somewhat defensively....

*　　　　　　*　　　　　　*

…My list was getting colorful. Two red checkmarks for Bobette, Binky, Charlene and Daggett.…

Charlene had that great knife collection and knew how to use them. At least on cucumbers. And Bobette had slept with her husband [Binky]. And his cucumber.

Housewife/romance writer, now amateur sleuth E. J. Pugh of Black Cat Ridge, Texas, is a filled-out five foot eleven. She understands all too well the lure of chocolate, especially under stress. In the first scene, she reminds us of her size by commenting on the displeasure of men smaller than she, such as Detective Doyle Stewart, as well as the pleasure or displeasure she feels when she sizes up other women. In the second scene, she's just driven home from a traumatic hospital visit to the sole surviving member of a murdered family. (From Susan Rogers Cooper's *One, Two, What Did Daddy Do?* PB. NY: Avon Books. 1996.)

Stewart came back in a minute with a woman he seemed to like about as much as he liked me. She was a Chicana with short, permed dark hair and thick, dark-rimmed glasses, and she stood about six-foot in her one-inch heels. I happily decided she had about ten pounds on me, making her somewhere near 180. I'm very competitive when it comes to my weight. When I find a woman heavier than me, I gloat.

"Luna," Stewart said, "this is Miz Pugh. There's some corrections gotta be made on her statement. I gotta go." And he did.…

…"Like some coffee?"

I said, "Sure," and stood up. Detective Elena Luna looked at me, almost eye-to-eye. Then she stepped out of one of her shoes so that we were level.

"No wonder Doyle baby didn't wanna spend any time with you."…

…Luna poured us two cups of coffee and I took a tentative sip, then a bigger one.

"This is good," I said, surprise evident in my voice.

Detective Luna laughed.

*   *   *

Stress is the great enabler. I'm a secret chocoholic. I stash chocolate all over the house, only eating them after the kids are in bed....I ate the 3 Musketeers on the way home and hid the M&Ms and the Hershey's bar in the back of the freezer for later, then joined Willis, who was reading in bed.

I crawled in the bed and kissed him. When that was over, he lifted one of my lips and looked at my teeth. "You have a piece of chocolate stuck on your incisor." So much for my stealth.

You can write to Susan Rogers Cooper at *coopers@aol.com* or access her web site at *http://members.aol/com/femmesweb.cooper.htm*.

On the other hand, Reno PI Freddie O'Neal has quite the opposite reaction to a traumatic event in Catherine Dain's *Dead Man's Hand* (1997). Freddie's a typical pro who doesn't cook, eats hamburgers and pizzas on the run, and only thinks of her precious cats, Butch and Sundance, when she's in a grocery store. But in the aftermath of killing a mugger, her appetite dries up. Her stomach is in revolt. She can barely handle toast. It's hard to keep coffee down. When she does manage to eat something substantial, it comes back on her. On the next to last page—she still isn't sure she can eat! What's going on here is deep ambivalence over the killing side of the job. What better way to convey emotional turmoil than a churning stomach.

Remember Moon Pies? Hannah Malloy and Kiki Goldstein do. Sisters in their sixties, they live in Hill Creek, California, where the Rose Club is a popular venue for wealthy Marin County residents. The day after a Rose Club cocktail party, Kiki's 70-something DWM, Arnold Lempke, is found stabbed to death in his garden, by Hannah, who has an alibi, and Kiki, who does not. This fact hits Kiki square in the middle of their favorite market, the day after the day after. (From Annie Griffin's *A Very Eligible Corpse*. PB. NY: Berkley Publishing Group, Berkley Prime Crime. 1998.)

...In the Hill Creek Grocery you understood that you were someplace special....Here in this small store the local gastronomes combed the shelves for exotic chutneys, the freshest of pestos, the rarest of European cheeses....for phyllo dough, frozen demi-glacé, or perhaps ready-made crème fraiche....

...where you couldn't find Velveeta or a loaf of sliced white to save your life, but could pick from three different varieties of marscapone and four different brands of pressed seaweed for wrapping sushi....

...Kiki needed Moon Pies.

Moon Pies were hardly haute cuisine. Still, they had a certain retro appeal, so the grocery started carrying them...much to the detriment of Kiki's thighs. But this day all hungers for physical improvement had taken a backseat to the hungers of her soul.

Kiki and Hannah stood in aisle four in front of the pastry section. Kiki, disguised in a hat and sunglasses, scanned the shelves with a well-trained eye....

"You're covered with crumbs," Hannah said. "You've eaten the last two on the shelf. You'll make yourself sick. And I don't see why you can't take the stuff home and eat it there."...

..."We're not leaving until I'm sure Wanda Backus is gone."

"Why?"

"Because I can't face her, that's why. Everyone in the Rose Club must know I was at the police station this morning." Kiki shoved a last bite of Moon Pie into her mouth....

"I want a Ding Dong,"...

"They probably don't carry Ding Dongs," Hannah said…"but the chocolate-covered biscotti look good."

Kiki grabbed a package…."There's Wanda. She's headed this way," Kiki blubbered, mouth full. She then dashed around the corner…leaving a tell-tale trail of biscotti crumbs behind her.

Women writers may be reluctant to depict their female sleuths as over-weight, but they have no trouble adding flab to the guys their women work with. San Madera Homicide Detective Kate Harrod and her soon-to-get-married partner, Carl Mungers, are looking into the bathtub murder of Rebecca Symons. They stop for coffee while trying to figure out what a strange car was doing in Rebecca's driveway the day of the killing. Jeffrey is a suspect because he was spurned by Rebecca in favor of his older brother. (From Laura Coburn's *A Missing Suspect*. PB. NY: Penguin Group, Onyx. 1998.)

We'd stopped at a little corner coffee shop to get some hot brew and pool our thoughts. The place was nearly empty at this hour and I watched the blue-jeaned waitress take advantage of the slack to refill the salts and peppers.

"The car troubles me, you see," I continued. "That car may have nothing to do with the case but I've got this hunch it does…."

The waitress passed with a tray of fresh-baked Danish, on her way to placing them in a clear plastic display tray up front. Carl called her back and pointed to a plump one filled with fruit, then shook his head and waved her away.

"Can't," he groaned to me, "not with the wedding coming up. I can't have a big ol' sloppy belly hanging from that suit." Then he cast his eye longingly at the tray again….

The waitress approached with refills and Carl mumbled something only she could hear. She left, then returned shortly with the fruit-filled Danish.

"Hell, Kate, I can't resist it," he told me as he took a hungry bite. "Wedding's more than a month off yet, lots of time to lose some weight...."

"So what did you think of Jeffrey?" I asked....

"Namby-pamby sort of guy, I'd say. Seems to accept playing second fiddle to the brother...."

"So you don't think he has the passion?" I asked. "The passion needed to be a killer?"

"Frankly, Kate, I don't." Carl dabbed a crumb from his lips. "...I'm inclined to agree with what he told us—that he was content to back off without a fight. Just the man's nature, just the way he's built."

A major reason why young sleuths are trim and lean, how else would they deliver and survive those hundreds of body blows? One popular exception to the skinny rule is overweight New Orleans homicide detective Skip Langdon. Skip is six feet, physically fit, and, by her own admission, twenty pounds too heavy. In this murder investigation Skip gets to interview a rock star, Nick Anglime. Now she's come home to her lover Steve at her apartment. Dinner follows and Steve wants to know all the good stuff from Skip's brief meeting with the great star. (From Julie Smith's *Jazz Funeral*. PB. NY: Ballantine Books, an Ivy Book. 1994.)

"Hungry?"

"Exhausted, mostly. But we could have gumbo. I made some and froze it."

"But did you thaw it?"

"Well, no, but—"

"Let's go out."

She was about to protest that she was too tired, but how often did Steve Steinman come to town? You gotta get it while you can, she thought. "Okay. But low-key."

"The Gumbo Shop."...

*   *   *

But Steve wanted the good stuff. "About that last part you mentioned. Was that by any chance the part where you had a little talk with Nick Anglime?"

"Now how'd you know that?"

"Well, who wouldn't if they could? Besides, I saw the way you just happened to manage to speak to him last night."

"That was for your benefit."

They got to the restaurant.

"They do a nice gumbo."

"Good. I'll have that and the shrimp étoufée."…

*   *   *

"Are you telling me that you, Detective Margaret Langdon, are so sophisticated you weren't impressed one little bit?"

"Impressed!" She started to giggle. "Omigod. *Impressed!*" She laughed till tears ran down her face and had to be wiped by the more alert Steve. Other diners stared, and the waitress brought a glass of water.…

*   *   *

Shyly, she stroked his first two fingers. "You want dessert? Bread pudding?"

"Are you kidding? I just ate the equivalent of three meals. Anyway, we'd have to go to the Palace Café for that. You're way too tired."

"No, I'm not. I want to walk through the quarter."

As long as we're in New Orleans, let's eavesdrop on a scene prior to a Christmas Eve society wedding for which hairdresser and amateur sleuth Claire Claiborne is matron-of-honor. Leading up to this scene there's been a Family Mixer, a Lingerie Shower and Tea, and a Bridesmaids' Luncheon. No dead bodies yet but the cuisine threatens to put lots of folks out of shape. Jolene, Bobette, and Cecille are cousins of the bride and Mrs.

Cahoon is a dressmaker. (From Sophie Dunbar's *Shiveree*. PB. Philadelphia: Intrigue Press. 1999.)

"Oof!" grunted Jolene, as her sister struggled to zip up the back of her bridesmaid's dress. "I guess we shoulda tried these on before lunch!"

"Okay, Jo. Suck it in again," Bobette ordered.

Cecille Worth lifted a slim, disdainful shoulder. "Well, Jolene. After the amount of chicken you consumed, I am frankly amazed you can even get into the thing at all."…

"But it wasn't just any old chicken!" panted Jolene defensively. "See, when we were little girls, Bobette and me used to fight over the pulleybone, there being only one per bird. But then Mamma discovered Colonel Sanders and quit frying her own chicken. It was like pulleybones all at once became extinct, or something."…

"Of course, I never expected a fancy restaurant like Regina to serve up genuine pulleybones, except they called them wishbones on the menu." Her eyes took on a reminiscent glow. "…I suppose I lost my head."

"Not to mention your waistline," Cecille jabbed.…

"One, two, three. Suck in, Jolene!" Bobette's sharp command deflected her sister's angry retort. To Cecille she added, "Can't you be nice for more than three minutes at a time?"

"Probably, if I tried real hard," Cecille laughed. "But seeing as how it's only you, why bother?"…

Bobette's sudden whoop of victory at having finally coerced Jolene's reluctant zipper to do its duty was greeted with applause. The full skirt billowed as Jolene executed a triumphant pirouette; so did her full cleavage, oozing over the two-tight strapless top like melted marshmallows.…

…"Well, then, Mrs. Cahoon. Long as you're at it…insert me a little extra margin for error. That way I can party now and worry later. Like after New Year's."

"Just call 1-800-IMSOFAT!" chanted Cecille.

Emma Rhodes, 38, ex-New York City lawyer now "private resolver," has journeyed to St. Petersburg for an American investor whose gut feeling is that something's fishy with the small business he is bankrolling. Emma's a rich sleuth who numbers among her friends Prince Oleg and Princess Katrina, a couple recently returned from exile in Portugal to pick up the old life in an elegant riverbank mansion. Prince Aleksei is their son. (From Cynthia Smith's *Royals and Rogues*. PB. NY: Berkley Publishing Group, Berkley Prime Crime. 1998.)

...I hoped the dinner would be the cuisine of the country.

As though reading my mind, Princess Katrina announced to the table, "You may all thank Emma for the fact that tonight we must all forget our concern about fat and cholesterol. In honor of our American friend, I asked Raya to cook us a faithfully Russian dinner....So I give all of you permission to be totally guilt-free tonight. We have a good excuse." She smiled at me.

The first course was *shchi*, the classic hearty cabbage-and-vegetable soup served with heavy grain bread. This was followed by *bitki*, little codfish cakes with a mustard sauce. The entrée was Caucasian *shashlik*, which was marvelous....served on a bed of rice. Mushrooms in sour cream and broiled eggplant completed the course. The dessert was *sabionov*, which is the Russian version of zabaglione....Wonderful wine accompanied every course....

Everyone groaned with delight as each course reached the table....

We all struggled up from the table and went into the salon to await the arrival of tea....No one was accustomed to such a large meal and we were all sprawled out in various degrees of stupor....

"If you think this is a lot of food, wait until the Easter ball Mama is holding here next week," said Aleksei. "You'll never make it through the evening with those delightful body-hugging sheaths such as you have on tonight. I suggest you each wear a tent."

Detective Sergeant Savannah Reid is overweight, has been for years, but it was never a performance problem until now. Could it have anything to do with the fact that San Carmelita, CA's chief is her major suspect in a homicide? Captain Bloss, the chief's heavy, does the dirty work. The first scene takes place in his office; the second, in Savannah's home. (From G. A. McKevett's *Just Desserts*. PB. NY: Kensington Publishing Corporation, a Fawcett Gold Medal Book. 1996.)

NOTICE OF TERMINATION

"…Termination of what?" she asked.…

"Your job, Detective.…"

She quickly scanned the rest of the document…

"'Failure to meet physical requirements'…? What the hell is that supposed to mean?"

…"…According to the results of your last physical exam, your body fat ratio exceeds department regulations by quite a bit."

"Of course it does. I'm female.…"

…"Miss Reid, this isn't open for discussion. The decision is final.".…

"This has nothing to do with my weight.…You're kicking me off the force to cover your chief's ass.…"

…"Well, it isn't going to happen.…I'll go to my union; I'll take you to court; I'll even talk to the media if I have to.…"

In a daze of shock and fury, Savannah walked through the building, down corridors and through doors that she had grown to love over the years.…

And now?

Now what?

*   *   *

For years Savannah had struggled to exorcise all those pesky demons of guilt from her spirit....

So it was a shock to her psyche when she opened her refrigerator door and found all those vexing demons back again to torment her.

"You shouldn't eat the rest of that Black Forest cake," they said. "That's how you made yourself *fat* in the first place, you idiot, you glutton. Show a little self-control...."

"Too bad it [one little thing like getting fired] didn't ruin your appetite," one of the demons whispered.

"Oh, shut up!" She slammed the door and walked into the living room with the entire cake box in one hand and a tablespoon in the other.

Police Detective Marti MacAlister: 5'10", 160 pounds, "Big Mac" to her cohorts is always aware of poundage and body image. Husband dead, she's got two kids to raise, and she feels an obligation to maintain control in one area of her life—what she eats. It's healthy fare at home, but at the station anything goes. Vik Jessenovik is her partner, and thin, thin, thin. (From Eleanor Taylor Bland's *Gone Quiet*. PB. NY: Penguin Group, Signet. 1995.)

Marti was at her desk polishing off a Big Mac and side of fries when Vik came in. They shared an office on the southwest side of the precinct with two Vice cops who worked Saturday night and usually didn't come in on Sunday. With four desks and a table big enough for a coffeemaker, a doughnut box, and the manual typewriter they all shared, the room wasn't crowded....

Vik was frowning as he draped his coat over the back of his chair. He looked into his Chicago Bears Super Bowl mug, which was chipped but irreplaceable. Without speaking, he fed the dregs of his coffee to the spider plant. Then he looked inside the McDonald's bag on Marti's desk and extracted one of two apple pies.

"I'll bet you're missing out on a great homecooked meal, MacAlister, spinach and tofu casserole. You owe me one for not telling Joanna about this."

Joanna, Marti's fifteen-year-old daughter, had lost her father in the line of duty, and to compensate for her lack of control over that, was doing her best to keep her surviving parent healthy.

"I think things are beginning to even out, Vik. We had a turkey roast and mashed potatoes with our salad last night, and bean pie for dessert."...

"That dinner sounds almost normal after broccoli lasagna and green bean pizza," Vik agreed, holding out his mug for some of the milk shake....

Dr. Teddy Morelli, assistant history professor at Rainwater State University, is disconcerted by the death of her mentor, Dr. Dedmarsh, and by the appearance, on the orders of his wife Irene, of a very large statue of Our Lady of Guadalupe in Teddy's office. Where the statue ought to be is in the Lynden, Washington, church of Saints Peter and Paul. In the first scene, trying to get to the bottom of this minor mystery, Teddy visits the church. In the second scene twins, Marjorie and Mae, teach the ladies of Lynden how to use the Lady of Guadalupe to work on their problem. (From Linda French's *Steeped in Murder*. PB. NY: Avon Books. 1999.)

The room was packed with heavyset women. Out in the hall was an unattended card table with a signup sheet and religious books for sale: *God's Answer to Fat, More of Jesus, Less of Me*. There were foods, too—diet crackers shaped like eucharistic hosts....Free bookmarks listed wholesome Mediterranean foods that were part of a biblical diet....

The women wore pastel sweats and were very chunky. One stood among the seated crowd, deep into her testimony. Some looked away, embarrassed. Others were weeping into handkerchiefs. "...knew it wasn't a food that Jesus approved of, but I put it in my mouth anyway—my need was *that* strong. What do you think? Can you imagine Jesus coming out of the supermarket with twelve bags of potato chips, one for each disciple?"

      *   *   *

Marjorie (or Mae) was holding a cylindrical candle with the image of Our Lady of Guadalupe on the side….

…"The problem is, you have to read the whole prayer in Spanish or it doesn't work. You can't just rattle off a Hail Mary or something. I was skeptical at first, but then I started to say the prayer, especially at that terrible time, three in the afternoon: 'Dear Lord, please send your mother to help me,' then say the prayer…."

…"Votive candles are available in any Mexican grocery store. And while you're there, you might take a look at the foodstuffs, too. Our friend in Mexico City bases her diet on tortillas, beans, and fruit. She hasn't been an ounce overweight since she was thirty-five."

…"She has the most beautiful complexion."

There was skeptical silence, and finally a hand flew up.

"Yes?"

"Can we go through the prayer again?"

Our well-padded mature sleuths wouldn't dream of dieting, and our on-the-run youthful sleuths don't need to. So when dieting is a novel's theme, teenagers are a natural target.

Farberville bookstore owner Claire Malloy has an heiress friend Maribeth (nee) Farber soon to be "wallowing in it like a hog in a mudhole." An unfortunate analogy. Maribeth is a victim of her own appetites until she commits to a weight loss plan, on which she loses more than pounds.

Claire's teenage daughter Caron has been elected Miss Thunder Thighs of Farberville High School. With girlfriend Inez they search for the perfect diet, beginning with the seven-day fruit diet that promises to take off ten pounds in a week. (From Joan Hess's *A Diet to Die For*. PB. NY: Ballantine Books. 1993.)

"It doesn't sound healthy," I began in the dreaded maternal tone.

"But it is," Inez inserted. "The first day you eat nothing but bananas in order to enhance your potassium level. Then on the next day, you eat nothing but oranges...."

It lasts a day. Caron announces the next program.

"We're going on the Zen macrobiotic diet. You eat soybeans and seaweed extract and oat bran bread....Ten pounds in ten days. It's terribly healthy."

And terribly expensive. They turn to a blender diet. Caron gains two pounds. Claire asks:

"Are you sure you're mixing up the proper ingredients in the blender and using the right amounts?"

"Absolutely. We've been switching back and forth between the chocolate shake, which tastes like chalk, and the vanilla, which tastes like latex paint. Each serving has exactly three hundred calories."

..."I don't see how anyone could gain weight on nine hundred calories a day...."

..."Nine hundred calories a day?" she whispered....

In desperation, they turn to exercise.

"...Miles and miles every single day—unless it's raining too hard. Right, Inez?"

"...Did this hike take you into the ice cream store?"

"…We only had single scoops of sherbet, because everybody knows it's less fattening.…Come on, Inez; I'll bet we can already see a loss."

The wail from the bathroom was enough to drive me to my feet and propel me to the liquor cabinet.

Julie Smith reminds us of Skip's weight throughout her books. Jimmy Dee Scoggin, Skip's landlord and best friend, constantly refers to her as either "tiny one" and "Thumbelina," or as "Junoesque" and "Goddesslike." Skip herself says she's a cop because as a big broad she gets to beat up people. About Skip's size, good characters in the series have good opinions of it, while evil characters compare her to elephants and whales. Must every exception to America's ideal of the female body pay a price?

We'll end with another pop quiz. What sleuth caricatures herself as a cinnamon heart? And sees one former president as a Mr. Goodbar, another prez as a licorice whip whose wife is a frosting rose from a birthday cake? One of her acquaintances, she muses, could be a sugarplum, homemade fudge, cotton candy, divinity, or meringue. We're not quite sure how she sees her mother, father, or sister, but maybe readers with better memories can fill us in.

CHAPTER 6
AGING'S NOT FOR SISSIES

Another difference between pros and amateurs. Pros don't age happily, whereas amateurs can start out over the hill.

Angela Benbow and Caledonia Wingate are rich widows living in luxury at Camden-sur-Mer in Southern California. When a resident dies under suspicious circumstances, the two amateur sleuths do their own investigation. Here, they interview Camden's cook, Mrs. Schmitt, about the most recent death. (From Corinne Holt Sawyer's *Murder in Gray and White*. PB. NY: Ballantine Books, a Fawcett Crest Book. 1991.)

...There a grudging Mrs. Schmitt, already busy mixing meat, egg, chopped onion, milk, and bread crumbs—along with several unnamed spices and quite a lot of stewed tomato—agreed to answer a few questions. She kept on working in the giant, stainless steel mixing bowl, her bare hands stained with tomato as far as her elbows.

Angela thought she had never seen anything so disgusting in her life as the mush oozing between Mrs. Schmitt's strong fingers, slimy egg and pulpy tomato squirting upward, lumps of onion and bread rising and falling on the tide of raw meat loaf. She tried to keep her eyes on Mrs.

Schmitt's face, as red with exertion as her hands and arms were red with tomato pulp.

"I wanted to know about your visit to Mrs. Kinseth," she said....

..."I really don't remember. Did I go to see Mrs. Kinseth about something?"

"Well, yes," Angela said. "A lot of the staff did. Maybe about her diet?"

"Oh. That. I thought you meant something special. But that was just routine. I visit all the new residents. I visited you when you first came here, Mrs. Benbow, don't you remember?"

Angela was dismayed. "No. Goodness. Did you do that?"

"Sure," Mrs. Schmitt said, starting to form up the loaves of meat-mix, shaping and rolling and finally patting with enthusiastic slaps that rather reminded Angela of that fraternal little pat on the rear professional football players give one another nowadays. "I always check on diets, first thing. We get a lot of diet restrictions in here. Salt-free diets, high potassium diets, low cholesterol diets, reducing diets..." Mrs. Schmitt looked up and took in Angela's square frame. "It wouldn't hurt you to considering reducing, Mrs. Benbow."

For most of the well-heeled residents of Camden, food is a major way to fight boredom. For Angela and Caledonia, however, it comes second, after crime solving. (From Corinne Holt Sawyer's *The J. Alfred Prufrock Murders*. PB. NY: Ballantine Books, a Fawcett Crest Book. 1989.)

It was the next morning that Mr. Grogan fell down the back stairs on his way to breakfast. Angela had joined Nan and Stella over a slice of sugar-sweet cantaloupe, French toast with boysenberry syrup and a cup of excellent coffee. Caledonia, who ordinarily treated sleeping late as a sacred duty, had managed...to rouse herself this morning....

"Not much today, Dolly...two eggs over medium, bacon and sausage, four slices of whole wheat toast with unsalted butter...oh, and bring me some of those tiny pancakes...but no syrup. I'll use the marmalade today...."

Nan and Stella join Angela and Caledonia to look into the murder of one Sweetie, who left a book behind with names written in code. Was she a blackmailer?

..."Let me see...Well, there was 'The Black Knight' and there was 'The Dungeon Master' and then something-or-other from *Alice in Wonderland*. Oh, and 'Snow White'—so of course there was 'Doc' and 'Sleepy'...and there was...well, there was 'Grumpy'..."

Nan shook her head. "...Even if it does refer to us—well, we're all grumpy, day in and day out. The worse the arthritis hurts, the grumpier I get...the later the mail comes, the grumpier Emma Grant gets..."

"...It would have to be somebody who was monumentally grumpy....*Think*. If you had to choose just one person in this whole place...wouldn't that be—"

The air was split with a wild yell...a series of terrible thumps...the crash of broken glass...a stream of incredibly inventive curses in the loud and unmistakable voice of Grogan.

Technical writer Jimi Plain's been forced by finances to move into Gramma Rose's big house. Death has hit the members of the "Divorce Adjustment Seminar" for which Jimi is a volunteer helper, so there's that to investigate, at the same time that she and daughters Shannon and Chloe spend their first Saturday night with Gramma. Is this going to work out? (From Victoria Pade's *Divorce Can Be Murder*. PB. NY: Dell Publishing. 1999.)

After a dinner of to-die-for puttanesca over angel hair pasta, she'd decided Chloe and Shannon needed to know how to do the chicken dance for all the Italian weddings they'd go to in their lives....

There she was, singing "doodle-doodle-doodle-do" and dancing that nutty dance until her cheeks were the color of the fresh tomatoes she'd squeezed for the sauce....

"I know what we should do," Shannon said...."We should go rent wedding movies and stay up all night watching them. Chloe and me and Gramma could go get them and Mom could make brownies while we're gone and we could get popcorn and show Gramma how to work the microwave when we pop it."

"Did you see *Four Weddings and a Funeral,* Gramma?" Chloe asked.

"Ooh, what kind of a movie is about weddings and funerals too?"

"It's good. It's not sad," Shannon said. "And we could get *Betsy's Wedding* and *Father of the Bride* with Steve Martin, and what else, Mom?"...

"You stay up all night and watch those things?" my grandmother asked Shannon.

"And then sleep until noon. You can do it. You went to church already. We'll all put on our pajamas and lie around and eat a lot of bad stuff and drink pop, and it's really cool."...

It took my grandmother a full ten seconds to consider it. "Let me put my teeth back in and pull up my stockings. I can get a few things at the store while we're out."

PI Kinsey Millhone says of high school that she functioned at the bottom of the social heap while a chum, Ashley, was at the top. One of Kinsey's cases brings the two together after many years. Tea at four in the Wood family home on seven acres of land on bluffs overlooking the Pacific. (From Sue Grafton's *"E" is for Evidence.* HB. NY: Henry Holt and Company. 1988.)

...I heard a whisper of sound, and the maid returned with a rolling serving cart, loaded with a silver tea service, a plate of assorted tea sandwiches, and pastries the cook had probably whipped up that day.

"Mrs. Wood will be right with you," she said to me.

"Thanks," I said. "Uh, is there a lavatory close by?" "Bathroom" seemed like too crude a term....

I tiptoed to the loo and locked myself in, staring at my reflection in the mirror with despair. Of course, I was dressed wrong....

*   *   *

...Ashley helped her into a chair, pulling the tea cart within range so her mother could supervise the pouring of tea.

Ash glanced over at me. "Would you prefer sherry? The tea is Earl Grey."

"Tea's fine."

Ash poured three cups of tea while Helen selected a little plate of cookies and finger sandwiches for each of us. White bread spread with butter, sprigs of watercress peeping out. Wheat bread with curried chicken salad. Rye layered with herbed cream cheese and lox. There was something about the ritual attention to detail that made me realize neither of them cared what I was wearing or whether my social status was equivalent to theirs.

Ashley flashed me a smile when she handed me my tea. "Mother and I live for this," she said, dimples appearing.

"Oh, yes," Helen said, with a smile. "Food is my last great vice and I intend to sin incessantly as long as my palate holds out."

We munched and sipped tea and laughed and chatted about old times. Helen told me that both she and Woody had sprung from the commonplace. His father had owned a hardware store....Her father was a stonemason.

But when the palate goes, it goes. Forty-something NYC PI Sydney Sloane is looking into the murder of 92-year-old Selma Onderdonk's grandniece. Sydney goes to Greenwich Village to talk with Selma in the Treelane Nursing Home. Dismayed by Treelane's bland, meager luncheon menu, Sydney picks up super tasty lunches for office mates, Kerry and

Max, and begins to obsess about her own aging for the remainder of the book. (From Randye Lordon's *Mother May I*. PB. NY: Avon Books. 1998.)

"Oh dear." Selma sighed when a young man told her it was time to eat. "I never thought I'd say this, but, aside from jelly beans, food has gotten boring. I used to love to eat, but now..." She made a sour face....

"The older you get, the less sensitive your taste buds are. If food has no flavor, you lose interest in it. There's a gal here, maybe ten years younger than me, who loves the food here. She says it doesn't matter that everything tastes like sawdust to the rest of us because it reminds her of her mother's cooking...."

When I left, the fourth floor was assembled for a lunch of tomato soup, melba toast, and stewed prunes....

...I ordered an herbed chèvre with grilled eggplant and roasted peppers on sourdough for myself, a tuna salad with lemon sauce and capers on whole grain for Kerry, and a filet mignon with arugula, asiago cheese, and horseradish sauce on an onion roll for Max. After I tossed in a bag of chips and three sodas, the bill came to nearly thirty-six dollars, including tax. With prices like that it doesn't take a genius to figure out why McDonald's has sold more than twelve zillion burgers....

$$* \qquad\qquad * \qquad\qquad *$$

"...I know this sounds really tacky, but when I was talking to Selma, I was riveted on this one patch of hair on her chin, and I kept thinking, *Someone ought to do something about that.*"

"...I mean, if I was old and couldn't see it—or feel it—I'd want someone to yank it the hell out of there."

All's fair in love and evidence gathering. Upstate New York *Gabriel Monitor* newspaper reporter Alex Bernier is desperate to talk to anyone who remembers anything about what happened at Benson University fifty

years ago. Dr. Henry Singer is still around, living in an old-age development, when Alex drops in on him. (From Beth Saulnier's *Reliable Sources*.
PB. NY: Mysterious Press Paperback, a Time Warner Company. 1999.)

…He was eating macaroni and cheese and a fruit cup topped with
maraschino cherries that probably glowed in the dark.…

…"Dr. Singer, I'm a reporter with the *Gabriel Monitor*. I was hoping to
ask you some questions about…"

"Oh, by all means, by all means. Now tell me, dear, how was school
today?"

"School?"

"Is that Johnny Kellerman still bothering you? Now, Margaret, you
know little boys only pick on the girls they really like.…"

"Uh, Dr. Singer…" I decided to go for the gusto. "I mean, uh, Dad…"

"Are you hungry? Would you like some fruit cup? Here, have some fruit
cup."

"Er, uh, no thank you."

"But it's your favorite. You love fruit cup."…

…I took the fruit cup and the spoon that followed it, and gagged down
a couple of maraschino cherries and a piece of what I guessed was a pear.
They both tasted exactly the same, like a tin can.

"Um," I said, trying to make a convincing yummy sound.

"There's a good girl," he said, smiling beatifically and tucking into his
macaroni and cheese. Well, if nothing else, at least I was making the old
guy happy.…

*   *   *

There were a few dozen people in the picture, gathered for a group
photo.…Underneath was written, "Benson Physics Department Picnic,
Summer, 1944." I turned the picture over. Jackpot. Someone—presumably

Singer—had been anal enough to record the names of everyone in the photo....

I stayed for another hour, out of guilt or kindness or blind gratitude. I brewed us some tea, and Singer made me eat three Pecan Sandies, and he complained about how badly the Brooklyn Dodgers had been playing lately.

Sometimes you win at this game, sometimes you don't. Austin, Texas, journalist Molly Cates is convinced the death of her father twenty-eight years ago was murder, not suicide as the sheriff ruled. She knows her father's sister Harriet made an important telephone call to him a week before his death, but to this day has refused to say what it was about. Molly is making one last try, only now Aunt Harriet is in a nursing home with Alzheimer's. (From Mary Willis Walker's *All the Dead Lie Down*. PB. London: HarperCollins Publishers, Collins Crime. 1999.)

"You remember that phone call?" Molly prodded.

Harriet pursed her lips....

"You're the only one I can ask, the only one who knows. Please tell me. Please try to remember."

The line of concentration between Harriet's eyebrows deepened, as if she were making a supreme effort. "They *told* me what it was."

Molly was electrified. "Who told you? What?"

Harriet looked up to the ceiling, as if searching for the answer there....

Molly was excited because the old woman's eyes had come alive with interest and response. Talking to her about it was working. "But after that phone call, Daddy broke his engagement to Franny. He said he couldn't marry her or anyone. Why not?..."

Harriet suddenly lifted her hands in the air and opened her eyes wide, as if she were miming a person having an idea. "Oh, yes!" she said.

Molly's heart hammered her ribs. "Yes—?"

"Fried chicken and mashed potatoes. Peach cobbler. They told me and I remembered."

"What?"

"For dinner. Things you like."

Molly exhaled slowly. She could not believe this. "Dinner?"

"Stay." Harriet reached out and gripped Molly's wrist with her clawlike hand. "Please stay."

All this time the old woman had been trying to remember the goddamn dinner menu....

"Where's my ring?" Harriet demanded, holding her hands out. "I think they stole it."

There was a knock on the door. It opened and the young nurse stuck her head in. "Ladies, supper," she chirped....

"Let's go get your ring from the lockbox. Okay?"

"I'll wear it to supper," Harriet said with a smile.

"Yeah. We'll go formal."

This may be Hollywood but not all action takes place among the rich and famous. Lucy Freers, animated filmmaker and amateur sleuth, is suspected of doing in the lady across the street, Julia. After all, Julia was found in Lucy's swimming pool. In tracking down Julia's past, Lucy locates an aging former starlet, Janice Kovalarsky. They meet where Janice now works, a version of the Humane Society. (From Lindsay Maracotta's *The Dead Hollywood Moms Society*. PB. NY: Avon Books. 1997.)

She rose, a very well-padded figure in a nondescript blouse and skirt. It was hard to believe that this was the body that had, back in 1967, inspired a million wet dreams....

"Had lunch yet?" Janice asked, rummaging in the mini-fridge. From its tiny recesses she managed to scavenge an astonishing quantity of food: bagels and cream cheese, a carton of buttermilk, bags of fresh fruit and raw vegetable sticks, jars of olives and pickles and half a frozen Sara Lee Cheesecake. The entire feast she set on a table already occupied by a puddle of tortoiseshell fur. "Dig in," she cheerfully exhorted, and began smearing a bagel liberally with cream cheese....

...She paused, picked out a blue-black plum and took a bite; a tiny rivulet of black juice ran like blood from the corner of her mouth. "You know why I work here, for the animals? It's because I know what it's like to be treated like a piece of meat...."

Janice finished off the plum, sucking the last morsel of flesh from the pit, then started on a stalk of celery....

The tortoiseshell...sniffed the cream cheese, then began greedily lapping. "Bad Milady," Janice said in an indulgent voice....

...Janice scarfed down the last of the cheesecake, scraping the residue off the sides of the tin with her fork. "So that's the whole sordid little story. And now poor Julia's in her grave...."

It had been a disquieting meeting—that comfy-looking woman chatting on so matter-of-factly about drug debauches and kinky sex for hire, all the while stuffing herself with strictly vegetarian snacks.

Most of our sleuths are on the young side, in their twenties and thirties, but that doesn't mean they don't worry about growing old. Soon-to-be sleuth Jane da Silva, 37, hasn't a clue what she'll do in the future. Here she is, singing "Just One of Those Things" in a smoky little bar in Amsterdam and thinking, there's got to be a better way to make a living. One appreciative young man, Hamilton Carruthers, approaches her after her set to thank her for Cole Porter and to announce that her life has changed forever. (From K. K. Beck's *A Hopeless Case*. PB. NY: Warner Books, Mysterious Press. 1993.)

"Let's sit down and have a drink," Hamilton Carruthers suggested. "I'll explain everything."

He ushered her to his table and she asked for a cognac....

"I'm sorry to have to tell you," he said, now assuming a grave air, "that your uncle is dead." Hamilton Carruthers was, apparently, the genuine article—a true gentleman diplomat. No lower-middle-class "passed away" for him.

"Uncle Harold?"…

"Yes. I have a letter here from a firm of lawyers in Seattle. They've been trying to track you down for weeks."…

Jane took a sip of her cognac and opened it. "Poor Uncle Harold," she said. "He was such a nice man. Kind of a do-gooder type."…"He always liked me," she said, sniffing.

"I am so sorry," said Hamilton….

She blew her nose. "Well, I wonder what the lawyers have to say. Maybe he left me a little something."…

She reads the letter. She's told she must continue Harold's life's work by means of a trust if she is to receive any income.

"How bizarre," said Jane.

Hamilton Carruthers coughed delicately, and gazed into his own cognac….

"My uncle Harold's left me his money," she said. "But it sounds like I have to run his weird enterprise….My mother used to call it the Bureau of Hopeless Cases…."

Hamilton Carruther's eyebrows rose.

"…It was sort of a nonprofit detective agency."…

"Do you want to do it?"…

"It might be fun," she answered….

"To tell the truth, I've been feeling rather sorry for myself, and put out with myself too, for having led such a raffish life…." She didn't add that she would be forty in three years, and on her thirty-seventh birthday she had made a vow not to be broke anymore after forty.

San Francisco PI Sharon McCone's business takes her to Lost Hope, Nevada. She's at a vulnerable aging point when she accepts Deputy Sheriff

Chuck Westerkamp's invitation for a beer when he knocks off work. Some birthday celebration. (From Marcia Muller's *Till the Butchers Cut Him Down*. PB. NY: Warner Books. 1995.)

Deputy Chuck Westerkamp hunched on a stool midway down the bar, apart from his fellow drinkers, hands limp around a nearly empty mug of beer....He perked up some, though, when I slipped onto the stool next to him.

"So you decided to stand me a round after all."

I nodded and help up two fingers to the bartender....

The bartender set two mugs in front of us and took away the bills I placed on the plank....

..."You're a native?" I asked.

"Lived here damn near all my life. My daddy came out from Missouri as soon as the news of the silver strikes traveled back there. He never found silver, but he opened a saloon, which in those days was just as good....I got out for a while—Korea—and then I was a cop in Reno, but I came back when my mama got sick. Then...I don't know." He shrugged, his shoulders frail under his uniform shirt. "The years just went by. Couple more and I'll retire."

"And do what?"

He looked bleakly at me. "Tell you the truth, I don't know. Find some way to pass the time, I guess."

The years just went by. Like Westerkamp, maybe someday I'd look back over decades of wasted years. Here it was, my thirty-ninth birthday; tonight I should have been with Hy at Zelda's, drinking champagne and dancing to a—probably—egregiously bad country-and-western band and later going home to make love. Instead I was holding down a stool in a decrepit desert tavern, drinking watery-tasting beer and chatting up a melancholy lawman. Good god, was this going to be my life?

Forensic anthropologist Elizabeth MacPherson is visiting her lawyer-brother Bill in rural Virginia to find out why their parents are divorcing. Her own marriage is falling apart, and, as therapy, Bill and his partner hire her to investigate two of their cases involving spousal murders. Here, Elizabeth writes her husband, Cameron, who's quite literally at sea, address unknown, about her mother's transformation—new mate, new friends, new diet. (From Sharyn McCrumb's *If I'd Killed Him When I Met Him…* PB. NY: Ballantine Books, a Fawcett Gold Medal Book. 1996.)

Dear Cameron:

I have survived Mother's first postdivorce party….I'm sure Mother will be happy with her new social set.

If she doesn't starve to death….

I was wondering if I ought to slip outside and promise Bill a stop at Burger King on the way home, but then he got called away to see about one of his clients, so I was left in the—well, not the lion's den; *that* would have been an improvement—in the koala pen with the leaf junkies. That will teach me to skip lunch.

Mother and Casey served a three-lettuce salad—plain, of course; some boiled asparagus; an orange slice on a toothpick; and something that Mother called *polenta au naturel*.

"Mother, it's grits!" I hissed at her. It was. Unbuttered, unsalted *grits*.

"I know, dear," she replied serenely. "It's almost the only thing that everyone would eat. And, just think, it's so much better for you without all that butter and salt. One needs to watch one's diet as one grows older."

I wondered if she was referring to herself or to me. I trust the former, because if *that's* a sample of what I have to eat in order to reach thirty, I'd just as soon not go.

PI V.I. Warshawski is also facing the music. When her favorite bartender Sal offers her a drink and asks if she's coming down with something, V.I. moans, "Yeah. It's called middle age. I have to run the dogs and change and drive and socialize. I'll never get through that routine if I have whisky now." She notices changes in her work behavior: "Incipient middle age was making me risk-averse. I didn't like that in myself."

But she knows what it takes to feel good, if only for a moment. Here she comes through with a promise to elderly neighbor Mr. Contreras (who usually plies her with food) to fix him a meal that will transport them beyond the walls of their poverty existence. Perhaps then they will have the energy to locate a missing girl, earn a hefty fee, and regain some financial independence. (From Sara Paretsky's *Tunnel Vision*. PB. NY: Dell Publishing. 1995.)

I stopped at Mr. Contreras's before going up to my own place. "I'm running with the dogs: I need to clear my mind and straighten out my body. Then I'm going to get something nice for us for dinner—let's pretend we're plutocrats who can eat lobster and champagne when we feel like it."

"No, don't go adding any more to your debts, doll. Let's just have pizza or Chinese takeout or something."

I kissed him lightly. "Leave it to me."

On my way back from the park I stopped at the high-end grocer near Fullerton for scallops and a bottle of Taittinger. As I drove home I hummed the snatch of an old song of my mother's, about a fisherman who caught a whale and kept it in a bucket where it cried out of its blue eyes not to be eaten....

Mr. Contreras, overwhelmed by the emotions of the evening, didn't protest my extravagance in buying Taittinger's. He finished two helpings of pasta with broccoli and scallops, drained the bottle, had a grappa, and left me with the optimistic news that we'd find the girl and pay our taxes. Not that we had either money or ideas where to look, mind you, but champagne can create the illusion of prosperity and good luck.

Literary license may put off the aging process for a while. Some sleuths age at a pace far different from ours. A year may go by between books in a series, but only months in the life of the protagonist. But inevitably the worries set in. Leading to, Susan Dunlap's Jill Smith giving up donuts to lower her cholesterol? Sue Grafton's Kinsey Millhone ordering chicken salad at McDonald's? Marcia Muller's Sharon McCone substituting sugarless gum for candy bars? One thing we *don't* see them doing is learning how to cook lean green cuisine.

CHAPTER 7
COFFEE AND DONUTS

"Three plain, a couple old-fashioned, one with pink glop, two with white glop, and those colored things that look like confetti. And Smith, we still have two jellies."

I extricated a dollar. "Hand them over." (From Susan Dunlap's *Too Close to the Edge*.)

Sleuth food: Acid coffee. Maple bars. Burnt burgers. Greasy pizza. Jug wine. All fitting neatly into a carb-fat food pyramid laced with enough preservatives to immunize us all against next year's mystery flu. As for that acid coffee....

What's brewed in the typical police station is awful, but a lot of it gets drunk anyway. Billings, Montana, PI Phoebe Siegel has been summoned by her angry Uncle John who just happens to be the chief of police. The tall man Phoebe soon recognizes is the sinister Dr. Stroud, whose office she recently burgled. (From Sandra West Prowell's *By Evil Means*. PB. NY: Bantam Books. 1997.)

"I think you blew it this time, honey," Tillie said as she looked up from her desk.

"What's he on, high-grade testosterone?" I managed a nervous smile and tried to look confident.

"Aspartame. Don't push him. Ever hear of the Twinkie killer?" She giggled. "Want a cup of coffee before…"

"That sounds ominous. Got any 'real' food?"

She nodded her head toward a small cabinet that held a coffee maker and a tray of doughnuts.

"Help yourself. I only wait on people for money anymore…."

I had just poured myself a cup of coffee and taken a big bite out of a maple bar when John walked out of his office….

I stood with my mouth full of carbohydrates and watched him as he pulled open the top drawer and tore through some files. This was a new mad-on he was exhibiting, and it scared me.

"Phoebe?"

"Hmmm?" I answered as I took a drink of coffee and tried to break down the stale hardness of the maple bar.

"He wants you to wait inside his office. He'll be in, in a second."

"Thanks, Tillie," I mumbled around my mouthful. "Can I choose lethal injection?" I grinned.

"You're drinking it."…

A tall man, with his back toward me, was standing behind John's desk….A faint, sweet odor assailed my nostrils and opened one of my mental this-is-familiar files.

Before I could nail it down he turned….I took another drink of coffee, washing everything down my throat, and hoped like hell I could control the look of disbelief in my eyes.

Sonora Blair is a Cincinnati PD homicide detective and so are Molliter and Gruber. Sonora's been off in horse farm country investigating the death of a 15-year-old rider. Last night at the station had been rough, interrogating the girl's father, and Sonora had made him cry. Nonetheless, when an opportunity to do the same to a member of the office male majority presents itself, what woman cop could resist? (From Lynn Hightower's *No Good Deed*. PB. NY: Dell Publishing. 1998.)

Sonora was in at seven....

In the office, craving coffee, she found that her mug was one-third full of cold, old coffee. The cream, aged now, had gathered in the middle, forming a star shape, with streaks that stretched across the brown oily surface.

She poured the leftovers into Molliter's cup, which glistened, squeaky clean, inviting. These petty forms of revenge made her happy, a bad reflection on her character.

She made a fresh pot of coffee, washed out her mug and waited while the plastic coffee-maker bubbled three-quarters through the cycle, then filled her cup. A stream of coffee, still spewing and brewing, hissed against the brown, grungy burner and filled the bull-pen with the evocative scent of scorched coffee.

Not an unpleasant smell, to an addict like Sonora.

She eased herself into her chair very slowly, closed her eyes against the blinking lights on her answering machine, and took the first sip.

Disappointing. She hadn't put in enough cream....Might as well drink it black if it was going to taste this bad.

"Yo, *Sonora*. You make that fella cry? Molliter worked the night shift, and he said you were brutal."

Gruber....

...The city had renovated the men's bath and locker room and they were getting pretty comfortable. Sonora wondered when the women's room would get fixed up.

"Did you spend last night in the john, Gruber? What do you guys do in there for so long?"

Gruber grinned. "I could draw you a picture...."

Sonora put her fingers in her ears and turned away. Could not believe she'd given Gruber an opening like that....

Desiree Shapiro, NYC PI, wants information from Sergeant Tim Fielding. But he has insisted that she pay for his time with chocolate donuts with walnut sprinkles and coffee black, no sugar. (From Selma Eichler's *Murder Can Singe Your Old Flame*. PB. NY: Penguin Group, Signet. 1999.)

"Sit down." Fielding indicated the chair alongside his desk before taking a seat himself. And then he picked up the paper bag and peered into it, scowling. "There'd better be something here with chocolate icing and walnut sprinkles," he warned, digging in determinedly.

"Hey, I come in peace. I got four of those."

…he removed a donut, along with the Styrofoam cup that had a "B" marked on the lid. "Feel free to join me," he said, passing the bag to me….

*   *   *

"…What I started out to say is that I can't understand how you could ever have agreed to work for a jerk like that."

…I'd sooner have foregone Häagen Dazs for the rest of my natural life than admit to Fielding that I was involved in the case because I'd known Bruce before. (And in the biblical sense, too!)…All I was willing to offer by way of explanation…was "I'm self-supporting, remember?"…

"Hey, wait a second," he commanded, checking his watch. "This talk of ours was only supposed to last fifteen minutes. And not only that, but *you* were supposed to enlighten *me*….Isn't that what you said on the phone?"…

"Yes, I did….And now I'm going to tell you why you're so wrong about my client." Simultaneously we reached for the donut bag, with Fielding beating me to the punch by about a millisecond. "Before I go into that, though, I'd just like to know one more thing."

Now, I anticipated an argument....My old friend was just sitting there calmly, though, taking a bite of donut and waiting for the question. Either he'd mellowed considerably since I'd last seen him or those walnut sprinkles were sheer magic.

When a paperback cover advertises that the heroine is "junk-food loving," it's a good bet we're dealing with Berkeley Detective Jill Smith. Cops are aided and abetted in their bad food choices by the stuff they keep around the station. Witness this scene. (From Susan Dunlap's *Too Close to the Edge*. PB. NY: Dell Publishing. 1989.)

Dillingham, the Night Watch desk man, glanced up as I climbed the stairs. "Smith? I thought you'd been promoted to nine to five."

"Seven-forty-five to four-fifteen."

"So? Did you just drop by to raid our donut box again?" He grinned. He knew my reputation for junk food consumption from my stint on Night Watch. Then Dillingham had threatened me with dire intestinal consequences. "Only wine improves with age," he'd muttered, each time I'd grabbed another chocolate old fashioned on my way home. "Are you going to will your intestines to Roto Rooter, Smith?" That one he'd saved for a larger audience.

"What have you got in that box?" I asked now.

He glanced beneath the desk, wrinkling his nose....

"This stuff will kill you."

"You're wrong Dillingham. It might do you in, but I keep up my immunities. My stomach thrives on donuts the way yours does tofu."

Paper towel in hand, I walked down the hall to my office. The sugary smell of the donuts, which Dillingham had once described as "reek of bubblegum and plastic," reminded me that I had had only half a pint of ice cream for dinner. I might not have reached the level of professionalism where despair didn't faze me, but I had missed plenty of meals racing around after suspects who didn't observe the standard lunch and dinner hours. Now I ate when the chance came, regardless of the circumstances.

Bounty hunter Stephanie Plum measures success, or the lack of it, by the number of doughnuts she consumes. In *Hot Six*, she begins the day by talking old friend Carol Zabo out of jumping off a bridge. As a reward to herself, she stops at a 7-Eleven for coffee and a box of glazed chocolate doughnuts and delivers them to the office of Vincent Plum Bail Bonds. She takes a single doughnut and leaves with new assignments. This should be a slam dunk day: First, 82-year-old domestic violence offender Lenny Dale, then Moon Man Dunphy. (From Janet Evanovich's *Hot Six*. HB. NY: St. Martin's Press. 2000.)

"What'd she want?" the woman yelled....
"If you'd shut up I'd find out!" he yelled back....
...She smacked him on top of his shiny skull.
"Hey!" I said. "Stop that!"
"I'll give you one, too," Dale said....
...His mouth opened, his eyes rolled into the back of his head, and he fell over stiff as a board and crashed to the floor....
"Call 911 and I'll try CPR."...
"Honey," Mrs. Dale said, "you bring that man back to life and I'll hit you with the meat mallet until your head looks like a veal patty."...
Within seconds the room was filled with neighbors, commenting on Lenny's condition....And was it fast? And did Mrs. Dale want a turkey noodle casserole for the wake?
Sure, Mrs. Dale said, a casserole would be nice. And she wondered if Tootie Greenberg could make one of those poppyseed cakes like she did for Moses Schultz....
...This was shaping up to be an eight-doughnut day....
...Moon Man Dunphy was next on my list....

He opened the door wide and looked out at me....He had a jar of peanut butter in one hand and a spoon in the other. Lunchtime. He stared out at me, looking confused, then the light went on, and he rapped himself on the head with the spoon, leaving a glob of peanut butter stuck in his hair. "Shit, dude! I forgot my court date!"

..."Yeah, we need to get you bonded out again and rescheduled."...

"That sucks seriously dude, I'm in the middle of a Rocky and Bullwinkle retrospective. Can we do this some other time? Hey, I know—why don't you stay for lunch, and we can watch ol' Rocky together?"

Maybe a baker's dozen...

Connor Westphal runs her own weekly paper, the *Eureka!*, in Flat Skunk, California. She contracted meningitis at the age of four, which led to deafness, but by that time she had a good foundation for language and speech.

She's partial to carbs: pasties, muffins, mocha, and beer. Here, she visits Sheriff Elvis Mercer in his office to get the scoop on a recent murder. (From Penny Warner's *Dead Body Language*. PB. NY: Bantam Books, a Bantam Crime Line Book. 1997.)

In the short time I'd been in Flat Skunk, Sheriff Mercer and I had become friends for a number of reasons. One, I needed information for the weekly police blotter and he graciously supplied it, as long as I spelled his name correctly.

Two, I'd hired his troubled son to help out around my office....Three, on occasion I brought dinner to the station and we shared a pastie or corned beef sandwich....

...He lifted some papers from his desk, then catching a glimpse of himself in the window reflection, he patted his chin and neck. "Do you think I'm getting, you know kinda fat?"

"Naw. You look good...."

The sheriff, in his mid fifties, was basically trim except for the impending middle-aged spread and the beginning of a slumped and burdened set of shoulders....His smooth, even mouth was easy to read when it wasn't smoking, chewing gum, or eating the muffin he had just popped in.

"Gotta cut down on these muffins. My cholesterol's up again." He sat down at his desk, grabbed a handful of papers in one hand, and finished the rest of the muffin without even looking at it.

"You look ten pounds lighter on TV, really."

He tried not to smile. It was time to push the fat aside and chew on something solid. I sat down in the chair opposite him and leaned back, my hands folded across my chest.

"Sheriff, what happened to Lacy Penzance?"

Sleuths are into good coffee, given the choice. In Laurie R. King's *A Grave Talent*, we're introduced to San Francisco Detective Kate (Casey) Martinelli. Kate's just been promoted to Homicide, paired with Inspector Al Hawkin. She is the trainee, ergo, she does the driving *and* provides the coffee and breakfast treats. She picks up Hawkin early their first morning together. (From Laurie R. King's *A Grave Talent*. PB. NY: Bantam Books. 1995.)

...He stretched over the back of the seat for his hat. "Is that coffee?" he asked, spotting the thermos on the back floor.

"Yes, help yourself. There's a cup in the glove compartment."

"No sugar?"

"Sorry."

"Oh, well, can't be helped," he allowed, and slurped cautiously. "Good coffee. How'd you have time to make it?"

"I didn't. I have a friend."

"Must be a good friend, to make you coffee at five-thirty in the morning."

"Mmm."

"Well, he makes decent coffee, but next time have him throw some packets of sugar in for mine."

They drive to a small community outside of the city to investigate a murder. They do interviews and paperwork past midnight. She falls into bed at 1:00 a.m. At 5:45 a.m., the phone rings.

She hit the receiver, fumbled and dropped it, retrieved it from the floor, and squinted to see the luminous hands of the bedside clock. She had to clear her throat before any intelligible sound would come.

"Yeah."

"Casey, pick up some doughnuts on your way in this morning, would you? I've got the coffee on, but the place wasn't open when I came by."

"Doughnuts."

"Chocolate glazed, if they have them."

"God."

"What?"

"Chocolate glazed doughnuts."

"Yes, or whatever looks good. See you," he said cheerfully, and the line went dead.

Kate replaced the telephone with the gentle care of a hangover victim, turned to the single eye that scowled up at her from the next pillow, and pronounced the words again.

"Chocolate. Glazed. Doughnuts."

NYPD homicide detective Kathy Mallory has a secret, alternative workspace at Mallory and Butler, Ltd., where her protective friend Charles Butler resides and works. Sergeant Riker, an old friend of Mallory's deceased father, is the only other person Mallory allows into her private lair. The three are working on the murder of an artist and its tie-in with a double murder twelve years ago. (From Carol O'Connell's *Killing Critics*. PB. NY: Berkley Publishing Group, a Jove Book. 1997.)

The kitchen was Riker's favorite room at Mallory and Butler, Ltd. It was…a proper sit-down kitchen, where the best of conversations took place in the company of people he cared for, and the coffee was always first-rate.…

She set a platter of croissants and cheeses on the table. There was also a side dish of jelly doughnuts as a special concession to himself.

Charles stood at the counter, bending down to read a light display on the coffee machine. In the kitchen of Charles's apartment across the hall, he still used a manual bean grinder, and brewed the coffee, drop by drop, into a carafe. Here he dealt with a computer which organized the grinding and brewing, set the richness of the flavor, and all but fetched the mugs from the cupboard after announcing that the coffee was ready. This room was the middle ground between Charles the lover of all things antique, and Mallory the machine. Now Riker noticed the recent addition of a microwave oven sitting on the counter in company with a small television set and a radio with a CD player.

So Mallory was dragging Charles, appliance by appliance, into the twentieth century.…

"…Actually, Oren Watt could've done it."

"No, Charles, he couldn't."

Riker noticed that her attitude in dealing with Charles was the same one she might use to housebreak a pet.…

"I'll make a bet with you." Charles carried the mugs to the table. "If I can prove that Oren Watt could've done it, you pay for lunch. Deal?"…

"It's a science experiment with him." Mallory sat down at the table and selected a golden croissant.

Here's another upper class breakfast scene. Emma Rhodes, "Private Resolver," with homes in New York City, London, and the Algarve, is in none of these but on a case at the billionaire Palm Beach estate of Bootsie Corrigan for whom food became a fatal attraction. Here Emma is joined by PBPD Detective Sergeant Berkowitz who says, "May I ask if you've learned anything germane to this case?" (From Cynthia Smith's *Silver and Guilt*. PB. NY: Berkley Publishing Group, Berkley Prime Crime. 1998.)

"I was just going in for breakfast," I said. "How about a cup of coffee?"...

"I get the feeling, Miss Rhodes, that Mrs. Corrigan was one of those women who comes across as simple but is really rather complex," she said as she eyed my egg.

"...Under that delicious hollandaise-sauce-covered poached egg is a hefty slab of fine smoked Scottish salmon rather than the usual pedestrian ham. Come on, go for it. And please call me Emma.'"

She got up and put one on her plate. "I'm Deborah."

Great. She's not one of those stiffs who insist on maintaining a distance from any possible suspects in the case, which of course, I am. She tucked into the egg gustily and looked up with pleasure. "Mmm, is this delicious. I had coffee and a bagel at 5 A.M.," she said apologetically.

Lovely. She's also an enjoyer....I like people who like things. People who appreciate good eating usually appreciate all sorts of sensual experiences. Another of the "Emma Rhodes Instant People Rating Rules" is that those who scan the menu in a four-star restaurant and then order broiled salmon or steak demonstrate a low sense of adventure and limited lust for life and usually aren't much fun.

I allowed her the uninterrupted pleasure of her breakfast and then, as she picked up her coffee cup, said casually: "The fact that you're here could indicate you're not totally sold on...the alleged killer."

And now for a working class breakfast scene. Anna Pigeon, National Park Service ranger, is on fire detail on Cumberland Island off the coast of Georgia. There's been an explosive plane crash, leaving two of their tight little group dead. The morning after we're introduced to the macho world of fire fighters through this kitchen scene. (From Nevada Barr's *Endangered Species*. PB. NY: Avon Books. 1997.)

At five A.M. Anna slunk downstairs to reap the rewards of coffee beans sown the night before. Their quarters were blessed with a state-of-the-art automatic coffee maker and each evening she made it her business to load it and set the timer....

Eschewing the idea of community cooking, each member of this crew had decided to fend for himself and, burrowing through the refrigerator in search of heavy cream for her coffee, Anna could catalogue her fellows by what they ate: Vegetables and peanut butter for Al. Kraft macaroni and cheese, made in vats and eaten for days—Dijon. The beer and red meat were Rick's. A jar of Miracle Whip, three loaves of Wonder bread, and an assortment of cold cuts served Guy for breakfast, lunch, and dinner....

"Nice pajamas."

She turned to see Guy. Nearly always the second pilgrim to worship at the coffee shrine, he was dressed in Nomex and two pairs of socks....

"Do you sleep in fire clothes?" she asked.

"These ain't clothes," Guy told her as he poured himself a cup of coffee and another for her. "I just had myself tattooed green and yellow a couple of years back. Saves time."

"I believe it. You're baggy and wrinkled enough."...

...Both stared contentedly at nothing, waiting for the caffeine to turn away the night's vapors....Nobody on fire wore pajamas. It simply wasn't done. Not manly, she suspected....

Halfway down his first cup, Guy became coherent. "...They got an aviation investigator they borrowed from the Forest Service flying down from Washington today."...

"...I'm giving him you and Rick."

"What if we get a fire?"

"We should be so lucky."

Inaction was wearing on everyone's nerves, along with the ticks, the heat, and Rick's snoring.

FBI Special Agent Daveys is up everybody's nose. When he appears at NYPD's 20th precinct, Detective April Woo and her partner Detective-Sergeant Mike Sanchez are reluctant to confide what they know of a local murder.

Here, Woo, Sanchez, and Daveys are having lunch. Daveys is trying to talk them into arresting a prime suspect and finally tells them what he's learned through his own resources. Daveys may think himself better than they, but the "kids" know better. (From Leslie Glass's *Loving Time*. PB. NY: Bantam Books. 1997.)

Daveys chewed on an ice cube, staring at April's plate. "Something wrong with that?" He pointed at the uneaten last quarter of her tuna club.

"No." She watched his face twitch over the fries still piled up on her plate. He'd made a point of saying he never ate fried food....

"You going to finish it?" Daveys asked.

"No."

"Can I have it?"

"Sure."

"You guys don't talk much, do you?" he said, pulling the plate toward him.

Smiling, Sanchez nodded at the waiter for some more coffee.

"Shouldn't drink all that caffeine, you know," ....

Sanchez dumped two sugars in his fresh coffee. He didn't reply.

"Water's best, trust me on that one." Daveys took a bite of April's sandwich....

"So you're not going to trust me on this? What's with you kids?..."

Mike slammed his cup down. Coffee slopped over the edge. "Hey, Daveys, call us kids one more time—"

Daveys made a similar gesture with his glass. An ice cube jumped out and skidded across the table. "Look, I'm just being affectionate. My dad was a cop. My brother's a cop—"

"I thought your brother was a Green Beret," April interrupted.

"My other brother." Daveys caught the cube before it slid off the table, popped it into his mouth, and chewed....

Mike raised his hand for the bill....

"Look, if you pass up this opportunity, I can guarantee it'll be your ass...."

Mike sighed. "Look, Daveys. We've got our own procedures here....But, hey, we'll check it out...."

"Good man." An apparent stickler for details, Daveys nevertheless forgot to pick up his tab when he left.

Vicky Holden of Lander, Colorado, is an Arapaho lawyer in search of a valuable Arapaho artifact, a ledger book. The tribe's story teller remembers seeing it on display at the Denver Museum of the West in 1920, but today the Museum has no record of it. Why then would the curator, Rachel Foster, be able to say, "I can assure you if we owned a ledger book worth one-point-three million dollars, we would know where it is"? $1,300,000. Where'd she get that figure? Vicky's investigator friend Pat reports on the woman. (From Margaret Coel's *The Story Teller*. PB. NY: Berkley Publishing Group, Berkley Prime Crime. 1999.)

...He nodded toward the foam cups and plastic bag bulging with bagels. "Hope you brought your appetite."

Vicky reached for one of the cups, popped the tab, and took a long sip before pulling a bagel out of the bag. There was the clean, light feeling of morning in the air, with columns of sunshine and shadow lying across the sidewalk....

..."Found what you want," he said....

Vicky swallowed a bite of bagel....

"One of Denver's oldest families. Owned half the town at one time."...

..."You're telling me the curator came from a wealthy Denver family. I could have guessed as much."

"Hold on," Pat said, still peering over the glasses. "*Used* to be wealthy."...

"Real-estate crash decade ago pretty well wiped out the Wentworth fortune....

..."Rachel moved to a little apartment and went to work as a research assistant at the museum. Worked her way up to curator. She's no dummy."

Vicky washed down the last bite of bagel with another sip of coffee....

"What do I owe you, Pat?" Vicky said.

"Next time you're in town, you can take me to breakfast." The investigator crumpled the bagel bag and tossed it into a nearby trash can. "Or you could tell me what you're looking for."

Vicky leaned back and drained the rest of her coffee....

..."This got something to do with that Indian kid they found in the river?"

"I'm afraid so."...

"Good God, Vicky." The investigator was on his feet...."You get in a killer's way, you don't know what could happen."

He was wrong....She knew exactly what could happen.

There's so much good stuff out there. Muffins come in carmel-apple, blueberry, raspberry, banana-walnut, cranberry, almond, poppyseed, pumpkin, chocolate, bran-raisin, oatmeal, honey-date, cornmeal, and blackberry cobbler. Ummm. Coffee? Zimbabwe, Yukon Blend, Café Verona, Italian Roast, Guatemala Antigua, Ethopia Sidamo, Sulawesi, and Sumatra. So how come these choices are as distant from your average police station/hangout as we are from the moon?

CHAPTER 8
UNDERCOVER GRUB AND
STAKEOUT TAKEOUT

"A Dumpster is never a good place to do surveillance, unless the garbage collectors have been there very recently." (From Linda Grant's *Vampire Bytes*.)

You'd think doing exciting undercover work might be associated with adventurous cuisine. Trouble is, undercover work isn't very exciting. Ditto the food.

Usually, the undercoverer infiltrates the enemy camp in disguise. But Santa Teresa, CA, PI Kinsey Millhone has figured out a way to stay home and simply pretend to be somebody else on the telephone. Here she is phoning a high school in Louisville that her ex-husband Mickey Magruder, now lying in a coma, had called. She wants to find out why. Mrs. Magliato is no help, but Kinsey perseveres with a little help from her favorite sandwich spread. (From Sue Grafton's *"O" is for Outlaw*. HB. NY: Henry Holt and Company. 1999.)

I took a couple of deep breaths and dialed again.

"Louisville Male High School. This is Terry speaking. May I help you?"

"Uh, yes. I wonder if I might speak to the assistant principal?"

"Mrs. Magliato? One minute."...

"Mrs. Magliato. May I help you?"

"I hope so. My name is Mrs. Hurst from the General Telephone offices in Culver City...."

*   *   *

"Ah. Well, thanks anyway. I appreciate your time." I hung up the phone and thought about it for a minute. Who did Mickey talk to for ten minutes? It certainly wasn't her, I thought. I...went back to the kitchen, where I took out a butter knife and the jar of extra-crunchy Jif. I took a tablespoon of peanut butter on the blade and spread it on the roof of my mouth, working it with my tongue until my palate was coated with a thin layer of goo. "Hello, this is Mrs. Kennison," I said aloud, in a voice that sounded utterly unlike me.

I returned to the phone and dialed the number again. When Terry answered, I asked the name of the school librarian.

"You mean Ms. Calloway?" she said....

Terry was happy to oblige, and ten seconds later I was going through the same routine, only this time with a variation. "Mrs. Calloway, this is Mrs. Kennison with the district attorney's office...."

"Could you fill me in?"

"I could if I understood what this had to do with the district attorney's office. It sounds fishy as all get out. What'd you say your name was?..."

I hate it when people think. Why don't they just mind their own business and respond to my questions? "Mrs. Kennison."

PI Catherine Sayler is investigating a case of sexual harassment via e-mail at a San Francisco software company. Someone has been sending lewd messages to women employees. Catherine goes into Systech as a telecommunications consultant, allegedly to redesign the voice-mail system. In the course of her interviews Catherine has openly put down men's inappropriate behaviors to the delight of the other women. By midweek a group of them has proposed, "Let's do lunch." (From Linda Grant's *A Woman's Place*. PB. NY: Ballantine Books, an Ivy Book. 1995.)

...Mama's...an honest working-persons' restaurant, right down to the smell of onions on the grill.

It was a salad-type day, but not here. Mama's salads were a pile of iceberg lettuce with some tired tomatoes tossed on top. Fifties salads, with orange French dressing. We ordered sandwiches.

As we waited for them I asked, "Why are these guys in such a lather about Sheila's promotion?"

"Because she's smarter than they are and she doesn't take any nonsense from them," Tonia put in....

"Funny how it's always merit when a white male is promoted and sex or quotas when anyone else gets the nod," I said.

Both women laughed knowingly. "Did you hear the joke about the guy who took a year's leave and went to live in Europe?" I asked.

They shook their heads.

"Well," I said, "he had a big party when he came home, and his friends were surprised to discover that he'd had a sex-change operation. During the party a friend said, 'It must have been really painful to have your balls cut off.'"

"'Yes, it was,' he said, 'but that wasn't the worst thing.'"

"After a couple of more drinks the friend said, 'It must have been really painful having your dick cut off.'"

"'Yes, it was,' he said, 'but that wasn't the worst thing.'"

"Another couple of drinks and the friend asked, 'So what was the worst thing?'"

"'Coming home and finding my salary cut by thirty-nine percent.'"...

Our sandwiches arrived as I was telling the joke. The waiter hovered in the background waiting for the punchline. He probably didn't find it quite as funny as we did.

As "Hannah Moore," Kinsey Millhone is playing a dangerous game of undercover agent for the police, no less. She is living in the house of a gang responsible for a very big auto insurance fraud operation. The smells of the kitchen reinforce the Hispanic setting—Rosarito refrieds, cilantro, corn tortillas, Dos Equis, enchilada sauce, while outside lies a barren neighborhood of *tacquierías* and strip joints. In this scene the gang trusts "Hannah" enough to let her leave the house and have dinner with them. (From Sue Grafton's *"H" is for Homicide*. HB. NY: Henry Holt and Company. 1991.)

…Bibianna lent me some jeans, a T-shirt, and some tennies so we could go out to dinner. The four of us left on foot and headed into the dismal commercial district that bordered the apartment complex. We…went in through the rear entrance of a restaurant called El Pollo Norteño, which by my translation meant the North Chicken. The place was noisy, vinyl tile floor, the walls covered in panels of plastic laminate.…Countless chickens were trussed on a rotating spit, brown and succulent, skins crisp and glistening with sputtering fat. The noise level was battering, mariachi music punctuated by a constant irregular banging of the cleavers whacking whole chickens into quarters and halves. The menu was listed on a board behind the register. We ordered at the counter, picked up four beers, and then canvassed, looking for a booth. The place was crowded, patrons spilling out onto a makeshift wooden deck that was actually an improvement. It was quieter out there and the chill California night air was a distinct relief. Moments later, a waitress appeared with our order on a tray, setting down paper plates and plastic flatware. We tore the chicken with our hands, piling shreds of grilled meat onto soft corn tortillas, spooning pinto beans and fresh salsa on top. It was a three-paper-napkin extravaganza of messy hands and dripping chins. After, we adjourned to a bar two doors away. It was nine by then.

The Aztlan was smoky, cavernous, ill lighted, occupied almost exclusively by Hispanic men....There was, on the surface, a thin veneer of control. Under it, and unpredictable, was the boiling violence of youth.

Appetites can soar when the food is done right. Alaska native PI Kate Shugak gets a rare chance to show off her culinary skills when she goes undercover as a deckhand with what might be a murderous crew onboard the *Avilda*. Kate's been hired to find out why two men were lost at sea six months ago off the *Avilda*'s deck. The usual suspects are Ned, Seth, and Harry. Andy, a vegetarian, was hired the same day Kate was. (From Dana Stabenow's *Dead in the Water*. PB. NY: Berkley Publishing Group, Berkley Prime Crime. 1993.)

He was about to toss its contents over the side and she raised her voice. "Hold it, Ned."

"Nothing but garbage," Ned growled ....

Kate sorted through the pot's contents. "We've got four red kings—"

"Not in season."

"—a chicken halibut—"

"Which can't weigh fifteen pounds."

"—and a half-dozen Dungeness. Big ones, too," Kate said admiringly.

"What do you want them for?" Ned asked suspiciously.

..."I'm on dinner tonight."...

She busied herself in the galley as the *Avilda* beat to windward, and her crew that night sat down to a dinner of boiled king and Dungeness crab, halibut deep-fried in beer batter, a mountain of mashed potatoes and, for Andy, a tossed green salad. Ned, Seth and Harry took one look and fell into their seats. Pawing through the pile of cutlery Kate had stacked in the center of the table, each man found the pair of pliers that suited him best and began cracking crab with gusto. Mayonnaise mustachioed their mouths, melted butter ran down their chins, crab juice ran down their arms and soaked the newspapers Kate had spread on the floor, and the empty shells piled steadily higher in the emptied cooking pot she had placed in the center of the table....

When they were through, not a leg or a claw or a shoulder of crab was left, nor was a single piece of the halibut. Harry sat back and patted his belly, expressing his feelings with a loud, satisfied belch...."Jesus, that was good," Seth said, and even Ned nodded grudgingly. Overwhelmed by such enthusiastic, unqualified approval, Kate decided she could get to like these guys, given time. Say a hundred years.

As the years pile up, what's the harm in a risk or two? Seniors Angela Benbow and Caledonia Wingate are of that philosophy, going undercover for the owner of the Time-Out Inn, a San Diego women-only spa to find out who steamed one of the staff to death in the sauna.

One night Caledonia wanders down to the kitchen after everyone's asleep to leave a note for the chef. Her appetite is her undoing. (What she calls a "freezer" here she learns later is really a walk-in cooler.) (From Corinne Holt Sawyer's *Murder Has No Calories*. PB. NY: Ballantine Books. 1995.)

"If I were home now...I'd make a midnight snack. I wonder if there's something in that big freezer down there that would be good for a nibble...."

Opening the freezer was no problem....

The lunch bucket proved to be a veritable cornucopia: a salami sandwich, a chicken sandwich, celery and carrot sticks, two deviled eggs, four chocolate chip cookies, a crisp Granny Smith apple, and a thermos of coffee....the coffee was cool to her tongue....

"Maybe," she said aloud, "There's something to drink around here that would be better than coffee...."

Head down among cartons and tubs she searched. Yogurt, eggs, oranges—nothing to drink. She was all the way across the freezer in her search, and had just about decided she'd had enough of the cold and would go outside with her improvised picnic...when she felt rather than heard the door behind her swing shut....

...The heavy panel had closed completely. And not by accident, she realized with dismay....

"Hey," she shouted. "Hey...you've made a mistake...."

...Strong as she was, she could not budge the door, loud as her voice was, she could not make it penetrate the freezer's walls....

"I doubt if I can last the night," she said aloud....

Caledonia sighed and turned her attention to fashioning a bench. "No need to die standing up," she said. She dragged together two wooden fruit crates packed with oranges, placing them in the middle of the room....

"...no need to die with an empty stomach, either. That salami sandwich looked good, but I think I'll stay with the chicken for starters..."

There's a marvelous stakeout scene in *Mallory's Oracle* where Sergeant Kathy Mallory, who is on compassionate leave and conducting her own independent investigation of her father's death, is accosted by a member of the public demanding that she arrest a certain woman. Mallory denies she is a cop, because at the moment she isn't, but the woman points to irrefutable evidence, the backseat of Mallory's car—and a half-eaten sandwich, food wrappers, cardboard deli containers, sugar cubes, catsup and mustard packets, and lots of coffee cups. The woman is threatening to report her to the commissioner if she refuses to act, but fortunately the guy Mallory is tailing hails a cab, and she drives off in pursuit.

Jenny Cain directs the Port Frederick Civic Foundation, wooing the town's most wealthy and using their largess to fund worthy projects. In *Dead Crazy*, she's being driven mad by town matriarch MaryDell Paine, who is nagging her to buy a certain site as a recreation center for former mental patients. Jenny suspects MaryDell's motive is to find a place to warehouse her mentally disturbed brother. When a murder victim is found at the proposed site and the brother goes missing, Jenny plans a stakeout at MaryDell's house on a bitterly cold night. (From Nancy Pickard's *Dead Crazy*. PB. NY: Simon & Schuster, Pocket Books. 1989.)

In the kitchen, I fixed a pot of coffee. While it perked, I put together a crunchy peanut-butter-and-raspberry-jam sandwich on thick wheat bread and wrapped it in a plastic bag. I put that, along with a banana and a small bag of Fritos, into a brown paper sack, to which I added three double-fudge brownies. That gave me all the food groups: crunchy, salty, sticky, and sweet....

Now I was almost ready for camp. But what would a wise camper need for those long, boring stretches between archery and canoeing? Notepaper and pen—I stuck those in the paper sack along with the food—and a good book. I ran back upstairs and retrieved from my bedside table *Too Close to the Edge*, which was proving to be a terrific police procedural by Susan Dunlap. I figured it was just the thing to inspire me—maybe even give me a few tips—for the snooping job that lay ahead....

My plan wasn't very sophisticated—I was simply waiting for the lady of the house to leave....

At five o'clock I turned on the engine again and ate the banana while the car warmed up. I decided to save the coffee for the periods between heat. At five-twenty, I turned on the engine again and ate half of the peanut butter sandwich and one of the double-fudge brownies. At five thirty-five, even after another quarter-cup of coffee, and even though I was trying very hard to wait at least another twenty minutes—to warm up the engine, if not to eat—I chickened out again. Both the afternoon and the car were getting darker and colder.

San Francisco PI Catherine Sayler's usual undercover attire is serious office temp. In this case, however, she is trying to track down a runaway, Chloe Dorn, who may have witnessed a murder, a vampire killing. Chloe's an active participant in a live action role-playing game played on the streets of Palo Alto and it is here that Catherine hopes to catch her at the mock funeral service for her murdered boyfriend. Peter is also a PI. (From Linda Grant's *Vampire Bytes*. PB. NY: Ballantine Books, an Ivy Book. 1999.)

Several blocks away, in the park behind the Senior Center, a couple gets up and moves away rather than share their bench with a homeless woman who looks and smells like she dressed from a garbage Dumpster....

And in the bushes behind the homeless woman, unseen by anyone in the park, a young girl dressed as a boy finds a good spot from which to watch the open grassy area in front of the benches....

*   *   *

I watched the mock funeral from beneath my pile of rags and waited for the signal that it was coming to an end....

...I reached my next post, near a Dumpster, and waited for Chloe.

...This Dumpster was ripe, very ripe. Fortunately, my nose was already conditioned to rank odors. Peter, whose favorite disguise is homeless alcoholic, had outdone himself in "conditioning" my clothes. After the first fifteen minutes in them, I craved nothing so much as a long, hot bath.

The group in the park seemed to be breaking up. I waited by the side of the Dumpster, pretending to go through a big sack of stuff I'd stashed next to it....

"How about a quarter for an old lady?" I said huskily.

She shook her head and started to walk by me. When she was in range, I lunged and grabbed her by both arms....

"Stay where you are," a voice from a police bullhorn ordered us.

"You, you tricked me," Chloe said....

"No," I said, reaching out for her. My hand closed on air....

In the language of twelve-step programs, OA stands for Overeaters Anonymous. New Orleans homicide detective Skip Langdon, along with the rest of her department, goes undercover in *The Axeman's Jazz*. Skip chooses OA as her undercover group, basically to keep the guys from joking about how she *ought* to be there. Skip's relationship with her mother is as problematic as they get, and who does she spy at her first meeting, her mother. She wolfs a shrimp po'boy on the way home to await the dreaded phone call. Mom says she knows Skip must be on a case because, otherwise Skip wouldn't dream of attending OA—even if she were fat as a pig, quote unquote. Talk about cruel! But what better way to let readers feel the suffering women bear when they'd least expect it, from those they'd least expect, if they don't conform.

V.I. Warshawski's stay in a new Illinois women's prison starts out against her wishes—she's thrown into jail. But when she realizes staying there is the only way to get to the truth, she opts for *Hard Time* and refuses to let her lawyer bail her out. Her kitchen assignment has taken away her appetite—mobs of roaches, mouse droppings, the stench of overboiled food. Sara Paretsky's choice of V.I.'s prison nickname, "Cream," picks up the food theme. As do four of her chapter titles: "Crumbs from the Table," "Family Picnic," " Power Dining," and "Fourth of July Picnic." But, as a matter of fact based on chapter content, she could have used a foodie title for just about every chapter. There could have been "San Pellegrino at the Golden Globe," "Peppy Gets a Biscuit," "Smoked Salmon at Lotty's," "Mr. Contreras's Barbecued Chicken," "Tea at St. Remigio's," "Tomatoes Will Buy You An Audience with Miss Ruby," "Eat Revenge, Get Indigestion," "The Condemned Woman's Last Meal," and, finally, "Getting Rid of That Bad Taste in Her Mouth."

Undercover work and stakeouts, however boring, don't come close to the boredom of real police work. What kind of late night dinner enhances report writing? What sort of mid-morning snack peps up pounding the beat? What exciting breakfast is good preparation for sitting in court all day? And what is the favorite culinary choice while waiting for 911 calls? Does this stuff get edited out?

CHAPTER 9
LET'S DO LUNCH

To quote Sabrina, friend of amateur sleuth Jenny Cain, "We bring our tales of boyfriends and husbands and bosses and employees and politics and children and money and religion to lunch. But Ms. Cain, here, she's got to up the ante. Murder. Suicide. Bastard sons. Damn." (From Nancy Pickard's *Confession*.)

As the following lunch scenes illustrate, female sleuths' typical lunches are anything but typical. Let's consider first the matter of sandwiches. Now, no male author, as far as we know, has paid attention to the fact that women and men make sandwiches differently. On the other hand this sex difference fascinates female authors.

To start with, there is a variety of women sandwich makers. There is the traditionalist whose crustless pasty white watercress sandwiches are surrounded by radish rosettes and carrot curls. There is Mom who knows the limits for kids are peanut butter and jelly, cheese and bologna. There is the modernist who thinks high fiber, low fat, lettuce, tomato, sprouts. There's the gourmet who's into focaccia, gyros, pita with hummus, and whose fridge stocks Dijonnaise, real Swiss, deli sliced pastrami, and mixed baby lettuce leaves.

Men? Forget tradition. Ditto high fiber and low fat. Ditto baby leaves. Think Dagwood. Men want a sandwich that sticks to their ribs. Men slather on butter, mayo, *and* mustard. Men build a stack of whatever's in the fridge. Men slap down the frying pan—bacon, ham, eggs, bologna. A man may not know how to make Swedish pancakes, or how long to roast a five-pound chicken, but every man knows how to make a manly sandwich.

Children's book illustrator Calista Jacobs is mourning the death of her physicist husband Tom, who died the previous year when he crawled into a sleeping bag and found a coiled rattlesnake. He'd been doing geological testing at Rosestone in the Nevada desert. Colleague Peter Gardiner is sent to Rosestone to continue Tom's work. He too dies, same cause.

Calista's easing back into her professional life. In the first scene, she's the target of a Q&A in front of a large Boston audience; in the second, she's doing lunch with her long-time editor, someone she can trust to hear her radical views about Tom's death. (From Kathryn Lasky Knight's *Trace Elements*. PB. NY: Simon & Schuster, Pocket Books. 1987.)

Janet Weiss sighed....The inevitable question had occurred after Calista had given her slide talk...."Don't you ever have fantasies about writing an adult book or doing adult literature? I mean, maybe you could be another John Irving with your sense of fantasy."

..."Oh, yes! I do have fantasies about John Irving." She paused luridly. "All the time. I find Updike very attractive too."

*   *   *

...During the thirty-minute wait for their table at Legal Seafood they had not discussed anything about the talk that morning....

Janet Weiss, her editor for fifteen years, had shown considerable restraint up until the time she had forsaken her usual wine spritzer and ordered a martini straight up.

"You're upset?" Calista asked ingenuously.

"I'm your editor. I'm the one who first gets to look at all those letters from Looney Tunes like the Reverend Falwell and the League of Decency who complain about your drawings of naked four-year-old boys. Remarks like this morning's don't help."

"Guess not. I'm sorry." She looked down and raked the fork lightly over the oysters.

"Forget it," Janet said. "It was awfully funny."

"Maybe I'm getting horny in my widowhood."...

"Well?" Janet smiled.

"Well?"

"We could sit here saying 'well' all through lunch."

"Well, there's not much more to say."

...Calista twirled the oyster fork and looked down.

"What's wrong, Cal?"

She sighed. "I think..." She started and then stopped...."I think," she began again, "that there is a possibility that Tom's death was not accidental."...

Calista began to tell her about Peter Gardiner's death.

Just then the waiter came to take their order. Calista realized suddenly that if one had to pick a restaurant to discuss murder in, Legal's was not bad. It was rather noisy with good spacing between tables....

"I'll have grilled halibut," Calista said....

Lunches are often in restaurants, but if you're real lucky you can get a client or witness or suspect to feed you on his or her own turf. Chester Lee's in Santa Teresa clearing up after the death of his father. Chester's mad because the VA claims to know nothing about his dad's military record, so no military burial, no marble headstone. Now his dad's apartment has been tossed and he's doubly mad. Who's to blame for the vandalism? He thinks maybe PI Kinsey Millhone. Nevertheless, he leads her to the kitchen and starts making lunch. After all, it's 1:15. (From Sue Grafton's *"L" is for Lawless*. HB. NY: Henry Holt and Company. 1995.)

"You have a theory?"

"I'll get to that in a bit. Grab a chair."

At least he had my attention. I took a seat at the kitchen table and watched in fascination as he started his preparations. Somehow in my profession I seem to spend a lot of time in kitchens looking on while men make sandwiches, and I can state categorically, they do it better than women. Men are fearless. They have no interest in nutrition and seldom study the list of chemicals provided on the package. I've never seen a man cut the crusts off the bread or worry about the aesthetics of the "presentation." Forget the sprig of parsley and the radish rosette. With men, it's strictly a grunt-and-munch operation....

...The bologna was pale pink, the size of a bread-and-butter plate, a perfect circle of compacted piggy by-products. Chester tossed in the meat without even pausing to remove the rim of plastic casing. While the bologna was frying, he slathered mayonnaise on one slice of bread and mustard on the other. He shook hot sauce across the mustard in perfect red polka dots....

The air in the kitchen was now scented with browning bologna, which was curling up around the edges to form a little bowl with butter puddled in the center. I could feel myself getting dizzy from the sensory overload. I said, "I'll pay you four hundred dollars if you fix me one of those."

Chester glanced at me sharply, and for the first time, he smiled. "You want toasted?"

"You're the chef. It's your choice," I said.

While we chowed down, I decided to satisfy my curiosity as well. "What sort of work do you do back in Columbus?"

Someone tried to kill Bobby Callahan by ramming his car from behind. Bobby survived, but Ricky, son of Phil, did not. Bobby is upper-class and a light supper upstairs in his mansion presents Kinsey with such delicacies as flaky tarts filled with smoky cheese and icy tomato soup with crème fraîche and fresh dill. What we have here is the other end of the food-class spectrum, lunch with Phil in a built-in, kitchen breakfast nook. (From Sue Grafton's *"C" is for Corpse.* HB. NY: Henry Holt and Company. 1986.)

He sat down and motioned me into the bench across from him....He was already slathering Miracle Whip on that brand of soft white bread that can double as a foam sponge. I kept my eyes discreetly averted as if he were engaged in pornographic practices. He laid a thin slice of onion on the bread and then peeled the cellophane wrap from the cheese, finishing with layers of lettuce, dill pickles, mustard, and meat. He looked up at me belatedly. "You hungry?"

"Starved," I said. I'd eaten a mere thirty minutes before and it wasn't my fault if I was hungry again. The way I looked at it, the sandwich was filled with preservatives, which might be just what I needed to keep my body from going bad. He cut the first masterpiece diagonally, passing half to me, and then he made a second sandwich more lavish than the first and cut that one, too. I watched him patiently, like a well-trained dog, until he gave the signal to eat.

For three minutes, we sat in silence, wolfing down lunch. He popped open a beer for me and a second one for himself. I despise Miracle Whip but, in this instance, it seemed like a gourmet sauce. The bread was so soft our fingertips left dents near the crust.

Between bites, I dabbed the corners of my mouth with a paper napkin. "I don't know your first name," I said.

"Phil. What kind of a name is Kinsey?"

"My mother's maiden name."

And that was the extent of the social niceties until we'd both pushed our plates back with a sigh of relief.

Lunching routinely in a favorite eatery gives other people a chance to harass or confront or question a sleuth with a mouth full of food. For example, for eleven years Molly Cates, journalist for the *Lone Star Monthly*, has followed a multiple murder case, but all of a sudden her boss wants her off the story, as does the husband of the deceased, and while just trying to have a quiet meal with her daughter Jo Beth, who should appear but a witness from long ago. Who happens to be in the funeral business. (From Mary Willis Walker's *The Red Scream*. PB. NY: Bantam Books. 1995.)

…An unadventurous eater who stuck to the tried and true, Molly ordered her usual turkey on white bread and a Coors Light. Jo Beth ordered pastrami on Jewish rye and a Coors Light. Beer was one of the few things mother and daughter agreed on.

…Jo Beth said, "It may be your lucky night. Don't look now, but there's a man standing in the doorway of the bar who's been staring at you."…

…David Serrano. The McFarlands' baby-sitter-handyman….

"I hate to interrupt you," he said in a low voice, "but I wonder if I could have a word with you in private…."

…"David, are you having some second thoughts about your testimony in the McFarland matter?"

…there were several tiny droplets of liquid just above his upper lip; Molly wasn't sure whether it was sweat or Scotch. "I just wondered," he said softly. "There wasn't anything in your book about the nicks."

"Nicks?"

"Yeah. The nicks on her scalp."…

"There weren't any little cuts," Molly said.

"Yes there were. Like I've seen sometimes when our clients—you know, the departed—have been shaved by someone in the family who had a shaky hand instead of having it done by our professional mortuary barber…."

As she slid into the booth and picked up her sandwich, Jo Beth said, "He was the guy who worked for the McFarlands, wasn't he?"

Molly nodded and took a bite of the sandwich.

"Don't get coy on me, Mother. What did he want that was so private?"

"Not coy," Molly said with her mouth full, "just eating." After she swallowed, she said, "I'll tell you after I eat." She started to take another bite, then stopped. "Something's going on...."

Jenny Cain, young professional from Port Frederick, Massachusetts, does lunch weekly with four close friends. They've sacrificed the delicious food at the Buoy Bar & Grill tavern for bland Holiday Inn fare for the sake of Mary, whose husband is a Baptist minister. Reputation and all.

Jenny shares the news that her husband Geof fathered a child in his youth, David Mayer. Some months prior, David's "father" purportedly killed his mother and then committed suicide. David wants Geof to get to the truth.

The women represent a powerful network and what one doesn't know, the other one does. They're discussing David's mother Judy, who had a telephone answering service. (From Nancy Pickard's *Confession*. HB. NY: Simon & Schuster, Pocket Books. 1994.)

Marsha grabbed the salt and pepper shakers and liberally applied the seasonings to her chef's salad in a vain attempt to bring out some flavor. "Let's just say that Judy didn't quite grasp the concept of confidentiality."

"What's that supposed to mean."

Marsha made an apologetic, comical face at me. "It's confidential." But when nobody else was looking at her she mouthed a word to me. "Later."...

"I knew her too." We all shifted our attention from Marsha the psychiatrist to Sabrina the social worker. I saw that she'd ordered a taco salad. I could have told her it would taste like crumbled cheeseburger, but there wasn't any reason to spoil it for her ahead of time. Maybe suspecting as much, Sabrina poured red sauce over it. I could have told her that would only make it taste like crumbled cheeseburger drowned in catsup. She explained, "During her second marriage, I mean. They hit some rough spots and she came to us for assistance. When I heard her husband killed her, I assumed it was the second one, he was just the type!...The woman had a hell of a talent for picking the wrong men." Sabrina, suddenly aware of what that implied, glanced at me and grinned slyly. "Oops."

"Those salads taste like crumbled cheeseburger in catsup," I said in revenge and made a face at her. "What second marriage? To whom?"

Miami PI Lupe Solano is a CAP, Cuban-American Princess, and once a CAP, always a CAP. Here she meets WASP princess and close friend, Emma Gillespie, for a PI's most important meal of the day. (From Carolina Garcia-Aguilera's *Bloody Waters*. HB. NY: G. P. Putnam's Sons. 1996.)

"Emma, it's Lupe. Hi."

"Hey, girl, where have you been?"

"Busy, real busy. Listen, are you free for lunch today? I need to pick your brain on a case I'm working."

"Name it and claim it."

"Joe's at twelve-thirty."

"Great. I love a free lunch. Lucky me, I didn't even eat breakfast."...

...I knew what Emma and I would have—two orders of the jumbo stone crabs, hash brown potatoes, creamed spinach, key lime pie for dessert, and a frigid cold white wine to wash it all down. The only variable was the wine—I liked it dry and Emma favored it sweet. Today was her turn to pick....

Emma slathered a quarter-inch slab of butter on a roll....

...She reached over to the wine bucket and grabbed the bottle in a smooth motion. Four men seated at the table nearest us gave her an admiring look. Not many women today display their appetites in public....

The waiter arrived with a huge tray that brimmed over with our order. When Emma and I get together and eating is involved, there is no debate....The waiter offered plastic bibs, but we waved him away. Bibs are for tourists. We set into the cold stone crabs, alternating between the mustard sauce and the drawn butter. The hash brown potatoes were, as always, delicious and greasy. It was only when we took a halftime breather that I addressed what Emma had last said....

Emma crinkled her nose with amusement as she took another long drink of wine. "You should talk, Lupe. Have you broken any laws yet investigating this case?"

I dug into my food and didn't answer....

Another Miami Cuban descendant, crime reporter Britt Montero, isn't convinced a late-night traffic accident victim is really a victim of the traffic. She needs inside information from patrol officer Francie Alexander, who prefers the midnight shift. Leading to a uniquely sleuth version of the midday meal. (From Edna Buchanan's *Contents Under Pressure*. PB. NY: Avon Books. 1994.)

...Piercing beeps from my alarm clock roused me at Francie's "lunchtime"—3 a.m....

...She ate supper in the morning after work, and breakfast at night before reporting for duty....

Francie had picked up sandwiches, and I brought a thermos of Cuban coffee and plantain chips. "What's this, Britt?"

I was unwrapping a napkin full of herbs to liven up the fast food. "Yerba buena, it tastes like peppermint, and there's parsley and basil, from the herb garden in my kitchen window box. They're good for you."

Francie gingerly held up a green sprig for closer scrutiny. "Sure this isn't some controlled substance? Or poison oak?"

"Trust me, I'm a farmer at heart. My dad ran a sugar plantation in Cuba."

"Somehow I just can't see you behind a plow."

We dined at a rough wooden picnic table near the boat launching ramp at Pelican Harbor, under a brilliant three-quarter moon that seemed to sail across a star-swept sky....

"Most people who 'do' lunch would have difficulty with this concept," Francie laughed....

"People behave differently on this shift," she said slowly. "Not just because it's dark. It's an entirely different world, a different mentality...."

"After a while on midnights, a lot of patrolmen develop the attitude that anybody out on the street is a bad guy. Policemen tend to wolfpack. A lot of times you see them traveling together or radioing each other so they can do things in two, threes, or fours. Everyone wants to be cuter than the others."

"Why on earth do you work it?" I asked.

Dr. Celeste Braun is a principal investigator in the virology labs of Bay Area University. She also consults abroad with the biochemists at Fukuda Pharmaceuticals. On this visit, lunch is the first order of business. However, a lethal package has been dispatched to one member of the group, and this agreeable scene is not likely to be repeated. (From B. B. Jordan's *Principal Investigation*. PB. NY: Berkley Publishing Group, Berkley Prime Crime. 1997.)

"...No business today. Just lunch, then quiet drive to park. Tonight drink sake. Cure jet lag for clear head tomorrow." Sake certainly made it easier to sleep, but Celeste was skeptical about a clear head the following day.

Lunch was in a noodle restaurant in a rural town about fifty miles from the outskirts of Sapporo. The thin soba in salty brown broth tasted wonderful. It was a perfect antidote to the airline breakfast Celeste had consumed before changing planes at Osaka for Sapporo. Celeste felt comforted by the warm liquid filling her stomach. For a few minutes, noisy slurping replaced all conversation. Then Celeste realized that her companions had put down their chopsticks and were watching her eat ....

"You not like soba?" asked Minoru.

"On the contrary. This is marvelous," said Celeste.

"You must make noise, then," said Minoru, seriously.

"Like this," said Akira and sucked in a mouthful of noodles with considerable gusto and sound effects.

"Oh, I see. I *am* sorry," said Celeste, and proceeded to suck up a few noodles, but not very loudly. "I guess it takes practice," she said, embarrassed. "You all know that I love Japanese food. Especially sushi," ....

Akira, realizing that they had made Celeste uncomfortable, attempted gallantly to change the subject. "Me too," he said. "I did love sushi. Too much." He giggled.

"Yes," said Kazuko, giggling with her husband. "Three years ago Akira got hepatitis. He was greedy and ate bad sushi. He don't eat any more." Celeste was too tired to explain the immunology of hepatitis to these biochemists.... ...Akira should now be able to eat even contaminated sushi with impunity.

In Marcia Muller's *A Wild and Lonely Place* (Warner Books, 1995), San Francisco PI Sharon McCone lets an Islamic trade attaché select the restaurant where she's going to ask her questions. It's Mexican, in the Mission district, one of her favorites. They order manifold plates of tapas but Mr. Lateef pokes his fork about unhappily. How had the waiter translated this particular dish? "Old clothes" says Sharon. Why would a dish be called that, he asks haughtily. Well, it sounds more interesting than shredded beef, she replies and steers him toward chicken in peanut sauce. He pronounces it good, helps himself to a tacquito, and a relieved Sharon can get on with her interrogation.

Despite a degree in geology, Em Hansen is working as a lowly mudlogger at an oil-drilling rig in Wyoming. During Em's midnight to noon shift, she has tried to come to grips with the sudden death of the project geologist in a suspicious car accident. (From Sarah Andrews' *Tensleep*. PB. NY: Penguin Group, Signet. 1995.)

...I intended to go to town for my ceremonial mid-day bowl of chili...but as I headed out the door, I realized that for the first time, I was leaving for lunch without Bill Kretzmer. My friend. My mentor....

*   *   *

As I ate that bowl of chili in town, I began to feel better. Food is good that way. The tourists at the next table were a welcome distraction, carrying my mind to other places and other lives. The man wore pink slacks. He read the entire menu to his patient wife, regaling her with every nuance of its profound novelty. "Look here, Barbara, they have chicken-fried steak. They surely don't have that at home. I think I'll try some. And just look here at the breakfast menu. Biscuits and gravy. Have you ever. And how about these commemorative plates on the wall, you ever see anything like it? I'll bet there's one for every cow-chip tourney and pie-eating contest they've held in the state."

Barbara eyed the plates, adjusting her head to find the right lens in her trifocals. "Looks like state capitols to me, Fred. And presidents."

Even after they left I dawdled, munching down every last saltine and herding the crumbs into a pile on the Formica...as I tried to decide whether to try to talk to the sheriff....

...I sure didn't want to open myself to that kind of frustration...but I didn't know what would make it go away faster, tilting at it like a windmill by telling the sheriff what I knew, or...carrying the load of resignation that gives life its special tang.

Twenty-four-year-old Mallory has turned in her badge to the NYC police and turned up in rural Louisiana to avenge her mother's murder seventeen years ago. Like *Mallory's Oracle*, *Stone Angel* emphasizes Mallory's disquieting coldness by omitting food scenes with her in them. Behind her back colleagues call her "Mallory the Machine," and machines don't need meals. Here Mallory's friend Charles Butler has come looking for her and meets up with another vital character, an autistic savant called Ira Wooley, together with his mother Darlene, at Jane's Cafe. (From Carol O'Connell's *Stone Angel*. PB. NY: Berkley Publishing Group, a Jove Book. 1998.)

He [Charles] collected a broad array of sandwich makings, condiments and salad greens on his tray. After paying for it, he settled down at the table next to Darlene and Ira Wooley. The woman was speaking to her son in a soothing mother voice, but the young man wasn't listening. He was absorbed in constructing a tower of food on top of a slab of rye bread....

Charles determined that there was nothing wrong with any of the motor skills, as Ira laid a precise line of sardines across a bed of mustard-slathered bread....

"Forgive me for staring," said Charles. "Sandwiches are my hobby."

...Charles spread mustard on pumpernickel and then embellished it with stripes of red from a pointed squeeze bottle of catsup.

Ira reached into his mother's salad bowl and carefully picked out the carrot sticks and arranged them in a cross-hatch over his sardines.

Charles made a perfect circle of croutons on his stripes of catsup. Ira noted this and added a squared slice of ham on top of his carrots. Charles laid down two slices of bright yellow cheese, one layered askew over the other to form an eight-point star. Ira countered with a dollop of cream cheese spread over the ham in the rough smear of a triangle.

Though Darlene Wooley seemed very tired, she was smiling at the pair of them as they engaged in this conversation of sandwiches....

...Ira took up the challenge, finishing his own design first and crowning it with a slice of white bread.

Charles applauded the winner, and Ira's laughing mother joined in, taking unreasonable delight in the moment....

The Alligator's Farewell is all-Florida, the first in a series featuring Dr. Annabelle Cristina Hardy-Maratos: owner of Miami's Hardy Security and accomplished signer and lip-reader. She manages her deafness with the help of Dave the Monkeyman, wildly eccentric, a brilliant signer who fills in any communication gaps. They're investigating why a scientist at the University of the Keys Nuclear Research Reactor fell into a three-story water tank that contains the uranium core of the reactor. An autopsy shows he was glowing, filled with condoms containing radio active topazes. The investigation takes them to Key Largo. (From Hialeah Jackson's *The Alligator's Farewell*. PB. NY: Dell Publishing. 1999.)

The celebrated slow service was part of the mystique of the Ugly Pelican....

"God, I wonder if they make the waiters here take IQ tests," Dave signed. "How long can it take to find out what the soup of the day is?..."

The waiter...ambled rather aimlessly to Dave's side.

"Avocado peppercorn, with a garnish of nasturtium petals," he drawled. "it comes with warm lemon-dill bread and zucchini spears."

...He tapped Annabelle's bare arm. She opened her eyes lazily.

"Have the soup, my dear," he signed. "It's chicken barley with whole wheat toast."...

He rose from his chair and strolled to the salmon-colored stucco half-wall....

The NRC and the Metro-Dade cops and the university have all convinced themselves that Castillo threw himself from the bridge into the reactor pool....I don't believe that and Annabelle doesn't believe that. From the operator's description, I don't think Castillo was even conscious when he went into the pool....

Dave heard the waiter clinking dishes at the table, and he turned. Annabelle was sitting up, watching Einstein place huge blue soup bowls on white plates—and that's when Dave made the connection. Blue bowls. Blue. Blue....

He grabbed Annabelle's wrist....

"Christ, in a cardigan, the topaz!...This whole death-suicide-accident-tragedy hocus-pocus, dare-we-call-it-murder, has something to do with those pretty blue baubles."...

"Dave, listen to this," she said...."Say you're a scientist. Say you work with that beautiful topaz every day. What do you think about all those lovely blue stones?"

Without hesitation Dave said, "Stealing them."

He sipped his soup.

Birthday lunch, Christmas lunch. Retirement lunch, promotion lunch. Thanksgiving lunch, baby shower lunch. Anniversary lunch, reunion lunch. Project finale lunch, 4th of July lunch. Great ways to combine food as fuel with food as celebration. For a reunion lunch, turn the page.

CHAPTER 10
LET'S HAVE A DRINK

"He brought the glass over and thrust it into my hand. 'Now don't try telling me you're on duty,' he said. 'It's ninety-eight degrees out here. A girl needs her fluids.'..." (From Kathy Hogan Trocheck's *Happy Never After*.)

Authors of law enforcement and PI series are more comfortable with alcohol than authors of amateur series. Everyone who watched *NYPD Blue*, *Law and Order*, *Cagney and Lacey*, and *Homicide* knows cops, medical examiners, and PIs drink and that some of them have trouble with it. But whereas hard-drinking men are tolerated, a hard-drinking woman definitely has a problem. Perhaps that is why Chicago's and Richmond's professionals, V.I. Warshawski and Kay Scarpetta, can have full liquor cabinets and by trying to control their intake, don't antagonize their teetotalling readership.

In contrast, everyone who watched *Murder She Wrote* knows Jessica Fletcher would *never* have a problem with drink. Thus it is that the gallery owners, dry cleaners, and senior citizen center managers who play amateur sleuth in small town America apparently can't drink (and have their stories sell). Female amateur series are noteworthy for serving drinks few and far between, usually within the context of a well-behaved, upper-middle class cocktail party, with the sleuth sticking to Calistoga mineral water to keep a clear head.

San Francisco PI Sharon McCone admits to herself that she has a drinking problem. Life is flat, work mechanical, her latest affair a bust. To add to her troubles is an upcoming visit from her health-conscious sister Patsy. She hasn't seen her in three years. Is it just a social call? What should be a simple affair is turning into a crisis. (From Marcia Muller's *Eye of the Storm*. PB. NY: Warner Books, Mysterious Press. 1993.)

The last time I'd seen my sister, she'd been in a health-food stage, raising her own vegetables on a farm she owned near Ukiah. I had no reason to believe that had changed, but I know nothing about vegetarian cooking and even hate salads, unless they have ingredients like shrimp or crab or taco meat. Finally out of deference to her, I opted for a salad; out of deference to me, I put plenty of shrimp and crab in it....A loaf of fresh sourdough bread, a pitcher of iced herbal tea for her, and lots of white wine for me....

...Twelve-fifteen. Patsy was late. I felt like having a glass of wine, but I wasn't sure what she'd think when she arrived and found me drinking alone. Then I thought, Oh hell, what do I care? and went and got the wine. If she wanted to think her big sister had turned into a drunkard, let her....

...The doorbell chimed, and I went to answer it, carrying my wineglass.

When I opened the door, my mild concern about what Patsy might think of her older sister drinking when the sun was barely over the yardarm vanished. The woman standing on my front porch was not the Patsy I remembered. For one thing, she was too thin. Her skin looked dry and pale, and deep parentheses around her mouth made her look older than her twenty-seven years....Even her hair...reflected a new, brittle personality.

...Her eyes rested on the half-forgotten wineglass I was carrying.

She said, "Oh, wine! Can I have some?"...

Ex-Atlanta-cop-turned-PI Callahan Garrity is working for Rita and Vonette, two of the three voices of a 1960's group, the VelvetTeens. Callahan's original mission was to find the third member so that they can make a comeback. In the meantime, their old manager Stu Hightower serves them an injunction, claiming ownership of the group. He's dead meat within hours. Rita is found near the body, passed out, gun in hand.

Callahan begins knocking on neighbors' doors. Here she hides behind an iron gate leading to the house next door. (From Kathy Hogan Trocheck's *Happy Never After*. PB. NY: HarperCollins Publishing, HarperPaperbacks. 1996.)

"May I help you?"…

A thin, deeply tanned man wearing a brief red bikini swimsuit regarded me with a look of amusement….

"Hiding out from the men in blue, are we?" He jiggled the ice cubes in a crystal highball glass. "Naughty, naughty."…

"I'm a private detective," I admitted. "And I lied my way past the security guards at your front gate. But if those cops catch me here, they'll throw me out. And I've got a job to do…."

"Good Lord," he drawled…."Stay as long as you like. It's nothing to me. I'm just the little old house sitter."

…"You really don't know what happened?"

He shook his head. "…Now give."

He got up and padded over to a table against the wall, dropping ice cubes into a glass, adding a jigger of gin, a splash of tonic water, and a final twist of lime. His bathing suit sagged in the seat. Chronic butt deficit. God, life is unfair….

I sucked on an ice cube. My throat was dry, and I suddenly realized how thirsty I was. If I wasn't careful, I'd knock back the cocktail in one gulp and be half-tanked before noon.

"Stu Hightower was murdered last night," I said….

I rubbed the cold sweaty glass across my sweat-dampened brow. I wanted to take the whole ice bucket and dump it down my shirt. "Did you see or hear anything last night?"

"Ah, ah, ah," he said, shaking his highball glass again. "You first."

Anna Pigeon is a law enforcement ranger for the National Park Service at Guadalupe. She left a life in New York City when her husband Zach died, determined to make a break with the past.

The sun is unforgiving in the Texas desert, so no one goes anywhere without gallons of water. When Anna finds the body of a coworker in the wilderness without any kind of water jug nearby, she suspects the body was placed there after death. In conversation with Christina, one of the secretaries at the ranger station, she finally opens up about her history. (From Nevada Barr's *Track of the Cat*. PB. NY: Avon Books. 1994.)

As they approached Anna's door both women slowed. Neither had much reason to go home and the night was warm, the stars deep overhead. In common unspoken agreement they sat side by side on the curb fifteen feet from Anna's apartment.

"What happened to Zach?" Christina asked. Then quickly added: "You needn't tell me, if you don't want to."

"I don't mind," Anna said. "We were having a special supper, celebrating the fact that it was Thursday and there were no other holidays declared to infringe on ours. Zach was broiling steak on a little hibachi out on the fire escape. I wanted A-1 sauce. He was sprinting across Ninth Avenue to Goodman's to get it. A cab hit him. The cabby drove off. Nobody got the license number. Zach died. That's about it."

Christina was quiet for a while but she shifted closer and Anna felt comforted by the warmth of her shoulder in the darkness. "Such a sad thing," she said. "Is that why you are a vegetarian?"

"No. Maybe it's why I drink."

"A little wine is good for the soul."

"A lot is better."

There's a greeting card out there somewhere that talks about Christmas as a family holiday, and then it goes on to say that at least there are gifts and good food to make up for that. Too right. In the midst of an office murder mystery involving the death of CEO Carl Dorfmeyer (aka "The Downsizer"), office temp Bonnie Indermill drags herself dateless to her brother and sister-in-law's anniversary party. Her sister-in-law is one of those women who knows the difference between cream, ivory, and off-white, and cares. (From Carole Berry's *Death of a Downsizer*. PB. NY: Berkley Publishing Group, Berkley Prime Crime. 1999.)

"I'll open this Beaujolais Nouveau now so it can breathe a good long time. That way,"…"our wine will be everything it was meant to be."…
"So our wine can be what?"
"Everything it was meant to be."
No one could say that with a straight face, could they? Not about an inexpensive 1998 wine being opened in…1998!…
Never mind that the wine, which many of us know and love, has a shelf life of about six months. Never mind that it surely had been all it was meant to be the moment the bottle was corked at the winery….
"Of course you don't understand," Noreen said. "You don't often entertain. At least not formally."
I entertain plenty, and it's not always paper plates and jugs of Gallo, either, but rather than getting into a thing with Noreen, I got myself under control.
"You're right." Looking at the wine, I added, "Is that all you've got, though? Four bottles?"…
"What do you mean? One bottle is good for at least five glasses, and we have six couples."
Having said that, she turned the full confidence of her pie-shaped face to me and added, "And you. That's thirteen guests. That comes to…"

Closing her eyes, she tried doing some calculating in her head. Failing, she opened her eyes again. "About a glass and a half each. Mom will only take a sip or two of hers."

"Do you plan to pour what Mom leaves into someone else's glass?"

"Of course not," Noreen snapped. "We'll be fine. None of us are heavy drinkers. At least not that I know of," she added pointedly....

New York writer Marti Hirsch and her lover, pianist Jerry Barlow, are in Las Vegas. Jerry accompanies singer Donny Brooks at the Paradise Hotel. Until Donny gets thrown in jail for the murder of Dorothea Jones. Michael and Patricia are a couple of college kids Marti knows from the University of Nevada at Las Vegas. Neil is a has-been lawyer and Rachel is a pregnant cocktail waitress. (From Miriam Ann Moore's *Stayin' Alive*. PB. NY: Avon Books. 1998.)

The Leaning Tower of Pizza made the best pizza in Las Vegas, which was still hopeless by New York City standards. I was too ravenous to care. I was inhaling my second slice when I became aware that Michael had arrived, bringing Patricia to join the party. I needed to talk to her, but I couldn't bear the idea of one more interview that day.

I was already laden down with the sordid lives of Michael, Rachel, and Neil. I had several possible motives for the murder. I had a gang of losers looking to me for help. What I didn't have was one good reason to believe that Donny didn't do it, except Jerry's gut feeling.

Sodas were brought from the bar to wash down the feast. I needed help to prove that Donny was innocent. I took inventory of my assets. One disbarred lawyer, one scared cheerleader, a homosexual basketball player, two major league yabbos attached to a cocktail waitress, and my darling Jerry. Donny was languishing in jail, but I counted him among us in spirit. I would have preferred the Magnificent Seven, but this gang would have to do.

I raised my glass.

"Listen up, guys. I know a little bit about a lot of things, and I know more about most of you than I want to. I'm going to find out who killed Dorothea Jones, and I'm going to protect all of you and your secrets."

I was getting dubious looks....

"Do we all agree that we want to save Donny's ass?"

That got affirmative nods.

"Then we're in this together, and I want everyone to drink to it."

For an unforgettable mix of murder, blue flour tortilla chips, guacamole, and spicy bean dip accompanying flutes of champagne, dip into Valerie Wilson Wesley's *Devil's Gonna Get Him* (Avon Books, 1996). PI Tamara Hayle who hails from Newark is attending a very fancy fundraiser when all hell breaks lose. As Tamara's best friend Annie opines, you gotta watch out where beans are involved.

Even cab-driving PIs find themselves at lavish drinking parties. Boston-based Carlotta Carlyle is about to take on as client a ride named Dee, a famous, rich guitar player from Carlotta's own humble guitar-playing past. There's this late night party Dee has invited Carlotta to, instructing her to grab them something to eat. (From Linda Barnes's *Steel Guitar*. PB. NY: Dell Publishing. 1993.)

Three steps inside the double doors, Dee half screamed in my ear, "Just like old times, huh?"

"Whoo-eee," I hollered in amazed response, "wish I'd worn my formal."...

...I seized on the strategy of grabbing two of everything, wrapping the doings in cocktail napkins, and thrusting them unobtrusively into my handbag. Dee, her back against a door, champagne in one hand, and a constant parade of well-wishers squeezing the other, never had a chance to snatch so much as a crabmeat-stuffed mushroom....

It looked like Dee would be handshaking forever. I was checking around for a place to sit when I saw a long linen-covered table filled with goodies of every variety, tiny china plates, dainty silver forks. The plates seemed like a better way to stock up for Dee, so I shoved through the crowd and tried to see how many shrimps I could fit in a six-inch circle....

       *   *   *

Dee was impressed with my food haul, especially when I kept yanking items out of my bag to add to the two brimming plates....

...A bowl of fruit on an end table looked like it was posing for a still life.

We carried the fruit bowl into the living room in the interest of nutritional balance....

I stay in hotels where the management is stingy about plastic drinking cups.

Dee rejoined me, grabbing the plateful of shrimp.

"Cocktail sauce?" she said hopefully.

"Under there somewhere."

"Great"...

...She licked cocktail sauce off a finger-tip, then tried folding her hands in her lap. She seemed restless; it looked more like her left hand was grabbing the right to keep it still. "Could you find Davey for me?"

Then there are those dicey drinks with a stranger, someone you've met through the personals. Not her choice under any conditions, but Nina Fischman has volunteered to play decoy for the police to entrap the killer of her oldest friend Susan, who made the mistake of trying to find Mr. Right in the classifieds and ended up strangled on a hiking trail. All Nina knows is that he's some kind of hunk, into hiking, wears contacts. She sets up some dates, an experience that reminds her why she recently swore off men. (From Marissa Piesman's *Personal Effects*. PB. NY: Simon & Schuster, Pocket Books. 1991.)

The architect, whose name was Victor, settled in for a serious talk with the waitress.

"What do you have that's unblended?" he asked.

"Glenfiddich," she answered.

"Besides Genfiddich," he said with just the tiniest bit of impatience. As if Glenfiddich were the obvious and she should have been able to tell that he was a man who did not seek out the obvious.

"I'll have to check." The waitress went over to talk to the bartender. Victor gave Nina a small, long-suffering smile....

..."We've got Glenlivet," the waitress said hopefully.

Victor gave a tiny snort that made it clear that Glenlivet was just as painfully obvious as Glenfiddich. "What about Macallan?" he asked.

"Sorry." The waitress tilted her head in sympathy....

"Laphroag? Glen Grant?"

"No, just Glenfiddich and Glenlivet."

Nina waited it out calmly. She had never been out with a single malt freak before, but she had sat through enough similar conversations in Japanese restaurants while some sushi fetishist cross-examined the waitress endlessly about *futomaki* and reverse *futomaki* to know that all you could do was wait for it to be over.

"I'll have a Courvoisier," he proclaimed, a martyr of the highest order...."You know," he said, "you look exactly like the sister of someone I went to school with. You wouldn't happen to have a brother who went to Andover, would you?"

"Afraid not. No brother at all. Besides, we're strictly a Bronx Science family." Nina smiled. Victor did not.

"Is that where you're from? The Bronx?"

"Yup. Born and bred."

He looked at her as if she were a tumbler of Glenfiddich....

Reno PI Freddie O'Neal has figured out what works and what doesn't if she wants to do her job and stay alive. Marriage and children are out.

Long-term relationships are out. Freddie tells us: "The up side is that we get up and go to bed when we feel like it, work when the work is there, and never have to think about food because someone else is hungry...."

She likes to drink. Should she worry? "...As far as I'm concerned, drinking...isn't a problem as long as it doesn't interfere with your work or your relationships. And I didn't have any relationships to worry about. I took a sip of the beer. If it interfered with work, I'd notice." Unless the situation becomes extreme, as it does here.

It's early days, page 8 in the book. Her mother's just hired Freddie to find the father who walked out on them years ago. Freddie's ambivalent. Deke's a friend who hangs in there for her. (From Catherine Dain's *Walk a Crooked Mile*. PB. NY: Berkley Publishing Group, a Jove Book. 1994.)

I slammed the door behind me and started walking.

It was a fool thing to do. Reno is high desert country, and survival in August depends on central air-conditioning and heavy consumption of liquids....I was flirting with serious dehydration. So I compounded it by doing another fool thing.... ...I stopped at the first bar and ordered a beer. It felt so good in my throat, cool and bubbly, that I finished it in one long swallow and ordered a second....

"You ready to eat yet?"

Standing behind me was a heavyset black man....

"I don't think so, Deke,"...

"...Need help getting off the stool?"

"I can do it myself."...

...I had to grab the bar to keep my body from moving faster than my head could follow. I patted my jeans, trying to remember where I left my wallet.

Deke had it in his hand.

"It was on the bar in front of you," he said. "I used it to settle your tab."...

      *   *   *

"He left me."

"…You could ask him why he left. He might even tell you.".…

I was still thinking about it when I got home and passed out on the bathroom floor, right after feeding the cats.

Inside Atlanta is the monthly mag Amanda Roberts works for as an investigative reporter. Oscar Cates is her editor. She's deep into a story about illegal shipments to Iraq. Her source has been snuffed and she's just faced down two bribing Iraqi businessmen in her parking garage. (From Sherryl Woods' *Bank On It*. PB. NY: Warner Books. 1993.)

The only light on in the *Inside Atlanta* newsroom was in Oscar's office.…Amanda walked in and sank down.…She reached for the bottle of scotch he hadn't had time to hide, glanced around for a second glass, didn't see one, and drank straight from the bottle. The liquor burned all the way down. She shuddered.

Oscar went absolutely still as he observed her uncharacteristic behavior. "You hate scotch," he said finally, as if she needed reminding.

"Desperate women do desperate things," she said and took one more swallow of the hateful stuff. Her jittery nerves finally began to settle down.

Oscar came out from behind the desk and snatched the bottle from her, probably because it was nearing empty and he couldn't bear to part with the final shots. "Want to tell me what this is all about?"

"I was just confronted in our parking garage by two men who don't like my current investigation."

His eyes widened.…

…"Why would two Arab-Americans be so damned determined to stop me from pursuing this story? Is any of this adding up for you yet?"

Oscar shook his head. "Let's line up who we have here," he suggested.

He sat down and poured himself the last of the scotch. It filled a glass. Amanda regarded it longingly.

We're in the southern Sierras with Claire Sharples, field botanist. Loggers and environmentalists are battling over Forest Service sales. In an early scene, while breakfasting at Ma's Donuts, Claire hears a logger ordering eggs, biscuits, and some "fried spotted owl," for the benefit of the pointy heads hovered over morning coffee. There she meets up with Marcy Hobbes, wealthy, glamorous, environmentally bent. At dinner at Marcy's the topic turns to men. (From Rebecca Rothenberg's *The Shy Tulip Murders*. PB. NY: Warner Books, Mysterious Press. 1997.)

"They lie." Marcy poured herself more Chardonnay. "They can't help it. It's the Y chromosome."

"It rhymes," Claire pointed out. "'Y,' 'lie.'"…

…"Now, my first husband," Marcy went on, in what was surely the modern equivalent of "Once upon a time," "was…I don't know it's like he was wired backwards. He'd have a vanilla ice-cream cone and tell you it was chocolate; I mean, he'd lie for no reason….The whole time we were married he was seeing other women and I don't even think it was for the sex…."

She topped off her glass, and Claire covered her own with her palm….But she seemed to have discovered the nutrient medium for friendship with Marcy….The more Marcy drank—at least, the more *somebody* drank—the more personal, and the funnier, she became….

"Anyway, when I found out about the bank teller, that was it, I left him. And then afterward I kept discovering there had been *more* women, and I kept putting things together…like the Thanksgiving he had to leave dinner early, because he had to meet a client. I felt so sorry for him. Come to find out he'd actually gone to my neighbor's house and had *another* Thanksgiving dinner with her—and then *another* one with the bank teller! Sucker had to eat three dinners in one afternoon! Turkey, stuffing, the works! 'Course he was probably working up an appetite every time," she added thoughtfully….

Claire was now laughing as hard as Marcy, who filled their glasses again.

A Vintage Murder introduces us to Seattle attorney Annie MacPherson. By definition, an amateur sleuth but with a lack of culinary skills that fits neatly into the profile of the pro. She tells a friend, "...I don't feel like cooking tonight." The friend's response: "What do you mean, you don't feel like cooking *tonight*? Annie...you've *never* felt like cooking."
She's been visiting an old high school-college friend in Yakima, Washington, successful winemaker Taylor North, who's busy divorcing bad-boy husband Steven Vick. There's sabotage at the vineyard, Vick is murdered with a wine bottle, and Taylor over does it with aspirin and Tylenol, but lives. Here, Annie leaves the hospital with Galen Rockwell, winemaker and an old friend of Taylor. (From Janet L. Smith's *A Vintage Murder*. PB. NY: Ballantine Books, an Ivy Book. 1995.)

"...I'm feeling a little lonely right now. Would you want to get a drink or dinner or something?"
"Sure."...
They took Galen's truck to Grant's Brewery pub....
...Grant's pub was a combination of Old English and new Northwest....Annie ordered the fish and chips, while Galen opted for a Scotch egg...with bread and mustard. When the meals arrived, Galen took a look at his, which turned out to be a hard-boiled egg wrapped in pork sausage, then dipped in batter and deep-fried. "Hmmm, it's a good thing I drink a lot of red wine...."
Through the meal, they talked about a number of things, but the conversation kept coming back around to Taylor. Galen finished his pint of ale, and ordered them each another. After a long moment, he said, "What is this hold that she has on people...?"

"I don't know." Annie tried to think. "For me, I guess it might be the fact that she needs me for the first time. When we were in high school, I always felt like I was tagging along on her coattails...."

Galen stared into the amber liquid in his glass. "In some ways she reminds me of a cat. Totally independent, totally sure of herself....A wild animal allowing itself to become domesticated. When a cat like that walks into a room, it doesn't need anything from us, yet we make fools of ourselves trying to caress it...."

Annie looked at Galen...."How long were you lovers?" she said quietly.

Miami-based PI Lupe Solano has two partners. The first is family—cousin Leonardo who manages her office when he isn't lifting weights or munching veggies or trying to make a fast buck on the side. The second is Tommy, Lupe's personal lawyer, prime employer, and sometime lover. In the first scene, Tommy's come round the office to see how the current investigation's going. In the second scene Leonardo is personally threatened by the calamitous state of office finances. (From Carolina Garcia-Aguilera's *Bloody Shame*. HB. NY: G. P. Putnam's Sons. 1997.)

..."Lupe honey, Leonardo is telling me all about this drink he's working on. A drink that can change the world. He wants me on the ground floor, to invest in the production end."...

I stuck my finger into the thick, pinkish liquid and looked at it closely. Just as I raised it to my mouth both of them grabbed my arm, shouting for me to stop.

"What the hell's the matter with you two lunatics?" I asked, startled. "It's a drink, right?"...

"It's not for women," Leonardo explained somberly. "It's only for guys."

"Oh, I get it," I said. "So it'll only change half the world. What does it do, make you better endowed?"...

"In all ways," Tommy said mysteriously. "Physically and emotionally. It's like magic."...

…"I've had a chemist here in the Grove working on this for more than a month."

"Not the Hare Krishna guy?" I bellowed.

*   *   *

"Here," he [Leonardo] said. "I thought you might need this. It's a mango vitamin mixture—protein, carbos, even jelly for your nails."…

I took a big mouthful of mango shake, shuddering at the thickness of the weird liquid. But it didn't taste bad. I imagined I could feel my nails growing stronger….

"There's a new piece of equipment I wanted to buy," he said….

Leonardo walked over to the mirror and pirouetted around, examining his rear from all angles….

"Leonardo, cut that out," I barked. "You can work your ass on the equipment you have. Anyway, be realistic. We're Cuban. We all have big asses. It's our birthright. It's stamped on our passports. It's one of the few things Castro couldn't take away from us."

The mango shake wasn't working its magic….

There's a great scene in Barbara D'Amato's *Hardball* where free-lance journalist Cat Marsala goes drinking with Chicago police lieutenant Stan Gotchka to discuss leads. For Stan one beer leads to two, leads to three, leads to a search for real English ale, then Foster's Lager, then a Pilsner Urquell, then Dortmunder Dab. Needless to say, for clear-headed Cat it leads to calling a cab and putting him to bed.

CHAPTER 11
CRIME SCENES MINGLED WITH MEALS

"As it happened, I had to wait...for a fresh batch of bagels to be finished, and it was 11:30 a.m. before I rang Zack's doorbell. Which put me five minutes ahead of Detective Sergeant Timpkin and his search warrant." (From Margaret Chittenden's *Dead Men Don't Dance*.)

Restaurants are a favorite place to shake a tail. In the front door, out the back. More often it's a suspect dodging a sleuth, but every now and then the tables are turned. Mystery writer and K-SAGE radio announcer Jolie Wyatt is being pursued by deputy sheriff Ed Presnell who suspects her of a murder and of the shooting of the sheriff, now in hospital. The thing is, Jolie can't conduct her own investigation with this jerk trailing along. What had the dispatcher said about him? "His motherboard is missing some chips." (From Barbara Burnett Smith's *Celebration in Purple Sage*. PB. Toronto: Worldwide Mystery. 1998.)

Ed remained my faithful shadow. After two quick turns I pulled into the Sage Cafe parking lot, squeezed my car in between two minivans, and ran inside. The smell of chicken-fried steak and cream gravy engulfed me....

...It was nearing five-thirty and people were lined up for the privilege of sitting at one of the booths or tables. Only the glassy-eyed deer heads on the wall seemed placid. I edged my way toward the cashier, and when one of the owners whisked past I called her name....

..."How are you?" she asked, looking me over.

"What?"

"You know. After your night in, well, you know." She looked around. "Are you okay?"

Ah, yes, Mary Maggie knew about my time in the Wilmot County Jail, since she provided the food for the place....

"It was Ed, right?" I nodded and she added, "That boy's not bright."..."I'm sorry but it's going to take at least twenty minutes for a table."...

"No, thanks. I'll move on."

"Sorry. See ya." And she was weaving through the crowd with the grace of a belly dancer.

I made it back to the window only to discover that Ed was standing beside his car, patiently cleaning his fingernails with his knife. Now there was a view to quell anyone's appetite.

A large party of people was leaving, and I took the opportunity to slip in among them. I stayed in their midst all the way out the door, and through the lot until they passed my car. Then I jumped in the Intrepid, thinking it had better live up to its name.

Virginia State Medical Examiner Kay Scarpetta is an exception to the rule that professional sleuths don't do gourmet. She loves to cook. It's an escape from a profession that forces her to confront death daily. It's ironic and macabre that on the job she finds herself using the same equipment she would use with great enthusiasm in her kitchen. In *Point of Origin* (G. P. Putnam's Sons, 1998) she prepares a body for boiling to clean the bones.

She fills a forty-quart pot with water and sets it on an electric burner, pours in laundry detergent and bleach to speed up the loosening of membrane, cartilage, and grease. In go the femurs and tibias, the pelvis and part of the skull, the vertebrae and ribs. Her silent observations are reminiscent of a scene from *The Conversation*, where Gene Hackman listens to two people, unaware that they are being taped, talk as they walk through a park. The woman observes a homeless man on a bench and says to her male companion in the saddest voice imaginable that in the past he had been somebody's baby boy. Likewise the sentiments of Kay Scarpetta, who knows that somewhere someone loved this woman who had no doubt accomplished something in her life before her body was stripped away by the bubbling broth. For more about Patricia Cornwell's books and about her life, visit *http://www.patricia-cornwell.com*.

We thought nobody could bring it together—food and death—like Kay Scarpetta, but Orange County forensic specialist Smokey Brandon is up to the challenge. Take knife wounds. What better way to figure out the kind of damage a kitchen knife can do to human flesh than to try one out on a compliant lump of raw beef? Joe is Smokey's boss and sometime-lover. (From Noreen Ayres's *A World the Color of Salt*. PB. NY: Avon Books. 1993.)

He was in a lab coat, standing near a slab of roast on butcher paper....I knew what he was doing....I knew he had to skewer pork fat onto the roast too, because meat comes trimmed nowadays and the human body's muscle-to-fat ratios have to be matched. But human fat is different, spongier, and yellow....

"Are we having a cookout?"

"What we're having here is Sanders's unsuccessful attempt to learn what kind of hole a kitchen knife makes. As opposed to, say, a jackknife."

"Seems straightforward to me."

"Not this one. This one happened when you were off."

I moved in closer to see what damage Joe had performed on the roast. Behind him on the counter was his notepad....Next to the notes was a magnifying glass. He said, "We have the knife, with the victim's blood on it. So we *know* that's the goddamn murder weapon. But the wound doesn't match the characteristics of the knife."...

"Maybe I'm slipping. I can't figure this one out," Joe said. He whaled at the piece of meat again.

I said, "The wound gets wider when there's a struggle."

"Yes, I know that." He stood away from the table and turned to point at his notepad with the knife...flipping it over to reveal a drawing meant to depict the vertical wound...."This peculiar little edge here, this quirk. Why is it there?"

"Is it important?"...

"Evidence has to be interpreted...."

"Maybe you should use flank steak," I said. "It's tougher. How old was this lady?"

Noreen says check out *http://authorsontheweb.com/*.

We think we may have discovered another sex difference here—*where* men and women are willing to chow down. Like the unfussy sandwiches they construct, men are less fussy about *where* than women. What's wrong with the morgue? In Linda Fairstein's 1998 *Likely To Die*, homicide detective Mike Chapman is perfectly comfortable unpacking a bag full of over-stuffed turkeys on rye with Russian dressing, potato chips and root beer, while hanging over a body watching a medical examiner do his thing. Appalled, Alexandra Cooper, NYC assistant district attorney, muses on his behavior hours later when, starving, all she gets before giving a talk are a couple of miniature crustless watercress on seven-grain.

Sleuths spend a lot of time in hospitals. The people they deal with tend to end up there. But think about it. Hospitals are the last place you'd go for comfort food. What's needed is a comfy café with a menu featuring Kraft macaroni and cheese. Tea and toast. Pot roast. Campbell's chicken noodle. Not a dysfunctional vending machine.

PI Catherine Sayler once again has teamed up with her lover, PI Peter Harman, to crack a case before a flawed computer system loses First Central a huge transfer of funds. A stakeout goes wrong and Peter is badly wounded. Here Catherine has just received news that the bullet has been removed from his lung, and he's not going to die. (From Linda Grant's *Blind Trust.* PB. NY: Ballantine Books, an Ivy Book. 1991.)

I sank into the chair with a sense of immense relief. The nurse eyed me with concern. "You donated blood, didn't you?" she asked. I nodded and found I could hardly keep my eyes open.

She left me but returned a few minutes later with a soda, a sandwich wrapped in clear plastic, and a candy bar. "You need to eat," she said, "especially after donating blood. You're getting faint."

…My system was so pumped with adrenaline that I felt vaguely nauseous and light-headed, and my stomach had been tying itself in knots for the last two hours. I forced myself to eat the food she'd brought….

Finally, the nurses chased me….

…The nurse had said Peter was stable, but he looked terrible, and I didn't want to be away from him. There wasn't anything I could do, but I didn't want him to be alone. Truthfully, *I* didn't want to be alone.

Finally, I drove back to McHenry and found a restaurant that looked like it might serve soup. Soup and tea always seem like comfort foods, maybe because that's what my mother used to feed me when I was sick.

I was hungrier than I'd realized, and after a second bowl of soup…I found a phone and called the office. Amy was still there. I realized with some guilt that she was waiting for my call.

When your family's as rich as Wyoming federal marshal Lilly Bennett's is, that hospital kitchen can rustle up some pretty good grub. In this scene everyone is waiting to see if Lilly's brother Elias, hit by a bullet meant for Lilly, is going to make it. Duke Fletcher is a former senator from Montana. Mr. Jerome is the father of Lilly's betrothed, Richard. (From Marne Davis Kellogg's *Nothing But Gossip*. PB. NY: Bantam Books. 1999.)

An orderly rolled in a covered table that looked like a body on a gurney....

He removed the cover, and when I saw the luncheon spread—a mound of turkey, ham, and chicken-salad sandwiches, large baskets of Fritos and potato chips, a stacked-up pile of fudge, and squares of white cake with pink icing that looked as if they might have been left over from a reception on the pediatrics floor because they had little yellow icing ducks marching around the edge—I was suddenly so hungry I thought I would faint. Mother was chairman of the board of Christ & St. Luke's and, thankfully, had flexed her muscles.

"They get so bored down there in the kitchen boiling all those briskets all the time," she explained....

*   *   *

Ever since he'd arrived, Duke had had his eye on Mr. Jerome, waiting for the right time to hit him up for a donation to his presidential campaign....

"I was very surprised to see your name on the SIBA list," I said to Duke once I'd finished my second piece of cake....I have never in my life been too upset to eat, and the longer Elias was in surgery, the hungrier I got....

"Now, hold on there, Lilly girl. Is this a joke?" He glanced nervously at Mr. Jerome—who could open the door to millions....

"Well, that's some kind of damn mistake. The SIBA Fund stands for everything I detest, and I would not put one penny of my money toward their efforts...."

I believed him, but I'm not so sure about Richard's father, who ripped into a celery stick like a lion devouring a bloody leg.

Is there a PI out there who hasn't come home to her front door hanging open and the place torn apart? And where the trasher puts his or her best efforts is invariably the kitchen. Flour and sugar sacks rent apart. Egg-splattered walls. Broken jam jars. Smashed microwave. Melted ice cream mixing with fresh spinach fettucini. Trashed food can take on many meanings, but usually it's (1) Revenge: I didn't find what I was looking for, so this is what you get; or (2) Warning: Back off or you're next.

This scene involves Emma Victor, amateur sleuth who works for Boston's Women's Hotline, who has invited her lover for dinner at eight. At six we find Emma in the Star Market for the fixings. Just enough time for mischief back home, and ultimately dinner elsewhere. (From Mary Wings's *She Came Too Late*. PB. London: Women's Press. 1995.)

...At six o'clock Star Market had a population of people making traffic situations with shopping carts. All the meat and dairy counters had knots of people before them, and minor collisions occurred on every aisle corner....

I turned into the lane of cart traffic going towards the produce section. I picked up an eggplant for no reason at all, some green peppers joined it and I tried to swim over the crowd to the cauliflowers but gave up....Whatever I had, it was food, and some of it would go with some of the rest; I just couldn't think of how. Eggplant and eggs? Chicken and cheese?...

*   *   *

...I had to walk carefully in the kitchen. A large can of honey was covered by a milk puddle, the refrigerator door hung open, swinging to and fro; it had been tipped over enough to let all the contents spill out, a cabbage was covered with blueberry yogurt....

The someone who had invaded my house was actually motivated to do this, not just rip me off, feeling anger or perhaps contempt for reasons I couldn't understand. I was hated. I thought about this and was glad that it was only food to clean up, no smeared faeces, or spray paint graffiti, suggesting ways to die....A bag of sugar was still streaming on to the floor, making a small pyramid of white refined on the tiles. The next thing that happened was that someone must have hit me...because I just saw the whole kitchen melt before me....I felt my face hit a swamp of jelly and milk before I gave up and sank into the big darkness.

How can food possibly play a role in a search warrant scene? How about the detective arrives at mealtime and says, Oh, carry on. I'll just be upstairs going through your underwear. Or a cop agrees to let a PI come along to observe and, unobserved, she "does the kitchen." Or perhaps an amateur sleuth just happens to be on the premises, and she says, Oh, go on up. We'll just be down here having breakfast. As in the following.

Charlie Plato, 31, divorced, is part-owner of CHAPS, a country-western dance hall in Bellamy Park on the San Francisco peninsula. She has invited herself for breakfast at another part-owner's house, namely, that of Zack Hunter, ex-TV actor and suspected murderer. Winston Jermaine is a friend of Zack's; he recently paid Zack a visit and left a little something incriminating behind. (From Margaret Chittenden's *Dead Men Don't Dance*. PB. NY: Kensington Publishing Corporation. 1998.)

Zack and I had barely finished greeting each other and setting the bagels on the plate, the coffee cups on a tray, when the doorbell rang. Zack opened the kitchen door to the nattily dressed Sergeant Timpkin and three officers....

"Let's eat," I said to Zack as cheerfully as I could manage. "We know they aren't going to turn anything up, so we might as well fortify ourselves against whatever the day is going to bring."

We climbed up on stools at Zack's kitchen counter and started munching, the officer having declined Zack's offer of hospitality. Having a police officer with a gun on his hip keeping an eye on you tends to kill the appetite. We managed one bagel apiece and a couple of cups of coffee....

After a long time, during which Zack prepared and perked another pot of coffee, it went quiet in the far reaches of the house....

*   *   *

"Winston [Jermaine] came by," Zack offered abruptly.

"When?" Timpkin and I said at the same moment....

"We sent out for a double-cheese and pepperoni pizza, had a couple beers," Zack continued.

Had he ever had his cholesterol levels checked? I wondered.

"Was Jermaine unattended at any time?" Timpkin asked.

Police officers never seem to talk like real people when they're on police business.

Zack shrugged. "When I called out for pizza, I guess. I used the kitchen phone. He was sittin' by the pool. Hot last night."

Her Chicago futures market client is dead and lawyer Katharine Millholland is suspected. She shares an apartment with another professional, an ER surgeon, Dr. Claudia Stein. The two decide to stick close to the cops searching their apartment for evidence. (From Gini Hartzmark's *Final Option*. PB. NY: Ballantine Books, an Ivy Book. 1994.)

"I don't like this," began Claudia. "They're not going to look in the freezer, are they?"

"I'll handle it," I broke in grimly and followed the low rumble of male voices into the kitchen. Ruskowski had taken up a supervisory position, lounging against the kitchen sink as two plainclothesmen went through the cupboards.

"Not much of a cook, are you Katie?" Ruskowski needled. "These cupboards are pretty bare."…

"Holy mother of God will you look at this!" exclaimed one of the policemen, his hand resting on the handle of the freezer door, his face stretched into a caricature of amazement. "What the fuck? Come and look at this, Rusty! Jesus!"

Ruskowski walked over to the freezer and looked….

"You want to tell me what this is?" demanded the detective angrily.

"What do you think it is? It's an arm."

"A human arm?"

"No," I replied. "It's the arm of a giraffe. Of course it's a human arm."

"So what's it doing in your freezer."

"My roommate, Dr. Stein, is a surgeon. She rotates between the University of Chicago and Michael Reese Hospitals. Sometimes she gets a dissection specimen at one hospital and she takes it to the other hospital to work on the next day. In the meantime, she stores it in the freezer here overnight. Let me show you."

I took the gruesome parcel from the freezer—a human arm, folded neatly at the elbow, hard as a frozen pot roast and wrapped in plastic. I passed it to the plainsclothesman with a little toss….

"Put it back, you joker," exclaimed Ruskowski in disgust…."No wonder you don't do much cooking," he said.

Behind homicide detective Kate MacLean's back—and sometimes right in her face—Eastside Lake Washington Police Department male colleagues call Kate "Mother MacLean" or "Earth Mother"—the price she pays for sometimes caring too much. This scene is doubly unique to the female sleuth. First, because police are the number one bearer of bad news on the doorstep, and second, because who else but a woman would head next for the tea kettle? Here Kate has just informed a couple that their daughter has been murdered. (From Noreen Gilpatrick's *Shadow of Death*. PB. NY: Warner Books, Mysterious Press. 1996.)

Instinctively, Kate rose and slipped the afghan from behind the woman…wrapped the woman warmly, patted her hand, then headed for the kitchen. Her New England mother always said there was no problem too big that a nice cup of tea couldn't handle. Of course, her mother had never worked Homicide….

After a moment, Pastor Matt followed her and got busy on the phone hanging on the dinette wall….The detritus of death, Kate thought, openly listening as she put water on to boil. After about the third call, he said to Kate, "We'd better get some coffee brewing, too. Would you mind?"

…Kate started searching cupboards for a group-sized coffee urn…and she went looking in the adjoining garage. It was as neat and tidy as the house…shelves all along one side wall that held enough jars of canned fruits and vegetables to feed the homeless for a year….Beneath them was a chest-style freezer filled, Kate assumed, with the bounty of the hunt. The coffee urn was in a niche below the canning shelves, in its own box, protected from dust….

When she'd judged enough time had gone by for the parents to move from shock into some semblance of numbness, she loaded up the tray she'd finally found and brought the tea into the living room….

Kate placed the last teacup next to Matt, back sitting in the wing chair again. Then she took a seat at the far end of the sofa, on the edge where she could see both parents. "I have to ask some questions now," she said quietly.

Bounty hunter extraordinaire Stephanie Plum defines her world in terms of food. She tells us in *Four to Score* that living in Trenton in July is like living inside a big pizza. She's on a search at the Jersey shore for someone who's jumped bail, but the beach seduces her, not the beach exactly. The food. (From Janet Evanovich's *Four to Score*. PB. NY: St. Martin's Paperbacks. 1998.)

And the best part is the smell. I've been told there are places where the ocean smells wild and briny. In Jersey the ocean smells of coconut-scented suntan lotion and Italian sausage smothered in fried onions and peppers. It smells like deep-fried zeppoles and chili hot dogs....

When I was a little girl, my sister and I rode the carousel and the whip and ate cotton candy and frozen custard. I had a stomach like iron, but Valerie always got sick on the way home....When I was older, the shore was a place to meet boys. And now I find myself here on a manhunt. Who would have thought?...

I worked my way down the boardwalk, showing the picture, distributing my cards. I ate some french fries, a piece of pizza, two chunks of fudge, a glass of lemonade and a vanilla-and-orange-swirl ice-cream cone. Halfway down the boardwalk I felt the pull of the white sand beach and gave up the manhunt in favor of perfecting my tan.

You have to love a job that lets you lie on the beach for the better part of the afternoon.

The cover of this book sets the scene—kitchen tiles, a kitchen knife, lots of red blood. L.A. homicide detective Kate Delafield is collecting evidence for the murder of Teddie Crawford who co-owned with Francisco Caldera a restaurant known as Tradition. Again, we ask, would you find a male sleuth behaving like this? (From Katherine Forrest's *Murder by Tradition*. PB. Tallahassee: Naiad Press. 1998.)

On the Saturday two weeks before the trial...Kate sat in her Nova in front of Tradition at one-forty-five in the morning. Wearing jeans and sneakers and a gray LAPD sweatshirt, sipping from a carton of coffee she had bought at the 7-Eleven on the corner, she contemplated the shuttered restaurant....

The last time she had been here was six days after the murder of Teddie Crawford. In a follow-up interview with Francisco Caldera, he had confessed that he could not enter the restaurant because the kitchen was filled with Teddie's blood; he could not bring himself to clean it up, nor could he ask anyone else to do so. "Do you have a wet mop in the restaurant?" she had asked. She had gone into the place that evening, swabbed the blackened floor, wiped down the spattered cabinets and walls, made the kitchen spotlessly white once more. This homicide was not the first time she had performed such an act....

To speak with total authority to...a jury, she needed to add one final piece. She needed to see—to understand—what had happened in the kitchen at Tradition. To understand it in her bones.

She drove down the dark alley behind Tradition, got out of the car. Restaurant keys in hand, she closed her eyes briefly. "I am Teddie Crawford," she whispered.

A more lighthearted take on a common detective scene, the office. Burton Kimball, defense attorney, has come to visit Cochise County, AZ, Sheriff Joanna Brady. The lobby of her building displays black-and-white formal photos of all the previous sheriffs in cowboy getup, sometimes with their horses. In contrast, Joanna's picture shows her as a kid, dressed in a Brownie uniform, with a wagon full of Girl Scout cookies. Vive la difference. (From J. A. Jance's *Skeleton Canyon*. PB. NY: Avon Books. 1997.)

"The Women's Club did a great job of putting this display together, but how come most of these guys look like they have a corncob stuck up their butts?" Burton asked Joanna when she walked up beside him.

..."Probably because they did," she replied....

..."Tell me," he said. "How's Ruby Starr holding up? Is she still cooking up a storm around here?"

...She and her husband had come to Bisbee with the intention of opening a fine dining establishment. The husband had been supposed to provide the business expertise while Ruby was expected to do the cooking. Their partnership and marriage both had come to grief in a domestic dispute that started with Ruby going through the house and nailing her husband's discarded dirty clothes to the hardwood floor. The battle had escalated into a sledgehammer-to-windshield finale that had put Ruby Starr in the county jail charged with criminal assault.

She just happened to be there…when the jail's previous cook made off in the middle of the night, taking with him all the fixings for the jail inmates' Thanksgiving dinner. In an act of civic generosity, Burton and his wife had provided dinner, replacing the missing turkeys and other necessary ingredients as well. Ruby Starr had been drafted out of her jail cell to do the cooking. She had done such an admirable job that, upon her release, she had been offered the jail cook's job on a permanent basis. Seven months later, she was still there.

Joanna smiled. "Ruby's doing fine," she answered.

Now for a more somber jailhouse scene. Boulder, Colorado's Rape Crisis Center director, Lucinda Hayes, is also a lawyer who has been asked to prepare an appeal for Jason Smiley, Boulder's most notorious rapist-killer, now on Colorado State Prison's death row. On her first visit to Jason, Cinda only had $3.84 in change with her. No paper bills are allowed in the prison, but visitors can bring along as many coins as they want for the vending machines in the visiting room. This is Cinda's second visit. (From Marianne Wesson's *Render Up the Body*. HB. NY: HarperCollins Publishing. 1998.)

…I was prepared with nearly twenty dollars in change; Jason and I could eat like junk-food royalty.…

"What a great deal. Okay, I'd like some M&Ms, some beef jerky, chicken noodle soup, a ham-and-cheese sandwich. Maybe some ice cream after that."

"Okay. Are you really that hungry? I mean, is your food here that much worse than beef jerky?"

"Look, Cinda. One, I grew up in Rahway, New Jersey. My old man worked in a machine shop. We didn't eat very fancy when I was a kid. When I discovered beef jerky as a teenager I thought it was pretty special. Two, anything tastes good when you don't have to eat it two feet away from a crapper. Excuse me, john."

I laughed. "Okay, do you want to go get the stuff? Here's the money. I'd just like a Coke, please."

"Nope. New rule since last week. Inmates are not allowed to handle money in the visiting room. You'll have to be the waitress. I want you to know right now that I'm not going to be in a position to leave you a very good tip, either. Sorry."

So I poked coins into slots and collected his order. When I started to cook his soup in the microwave he came over to join me at the cart; apparently he was still allowed to employ his cooking skills. "Set it on high, Cinda; this machine is stone feeble." We laughed together at how tepid the soup was even after ten minutes on high, a dose of waves that should have triggered the China Syndrome....

How could a sleuth possibly avoid the temptation of junk food vending machines? They're everywhere. Police station lunch room. Supermarket. Strip mall. Bus terminal. Airport. Court house. Community health clinic. Gas station. But Death Row takes the cake.

CHAPTER 12
JUNK FOOD ON THE RUN

"…I decided to forsake a downhome western breakfast and opted instead for my regular: a cup of coffee, a bag of barbecue chips, and a Snickers bar to go. If possible, my eating habits have gotten worse: my idea of good nutrition now is Taco Bell Lite…." (From Jessica Speart's *Tortoise Soup*.)

PIs and cops are reknown for loading up on all the major food groups—grease, sugar, chocolate, salt, caffeine, and alcohol. They aren't exactly dainty when it comes to stuffing themselves, so there's a lot of chomping, dripping, slurping, and, in the case of Kinsey Millhone, moaning. Remember that endearing scene from the Coen brothers movie, *Fargo*, where the sheriff loads up her tray at one of those eat all-you-can-eat places? True, she was eating for two, but the typical pro has no such excuse.

Maybe amateurs make more healthy choices overall, but when it comes to junk food, all sleuths are pretty outrageous.

When Kinsey Millhone drives through an unfamiliar town, she's likely to first take a count of the fastfood restaurants. Kinsey's kind of town boasts Kentucky Fried Chicken, Pizza Hut, International House of Pancakes, Sizzler, Taco Bell, and her personal favorite, McDonald's. Here we're out in the Mojave in the little town of Brawley where Kinsey is searching for a client's mother and must make do with a franchise-less, no-name roadside, country café. Ah, well. (From Sue Grafton's *"G" is for Gumshoe*. HB. NY: Henry Holt and Company. 1990.)

...As I was starving, I decided I might as well grab a bite of supper. I zipped on a windbreaker, effectively concealing the shoulder holster and the gun.

On the far side of the road was a café with a blinking neon sign that said EAT AND GET GAS. Just what I needed. I crossed the highway carefully, looking to both sides like a kid....

The café was small. The lighting was harsh, but it had a comforting quality. After years of horror movies, I'm inclined to believe bad things only happen in the dark. Silly me. I elected to sit against the rear wall, as far from the plateglass window as I could get. There were only six other patrons and they all seemed to know one another....I studied a clear plastic menu with a slip-in mimeographed sheet reproduced in a blur of purple ink. The items seemed equally divided between cholesterol and fat. This was my kind of place. I ordered a Deluxe Cheeseburger Platter, which included french fries and a lily pad of lettuce with a gas-ripened tomato laid over it. I had a large Coke and topped it all off with a piece of cherry pie that made me moan aloud. This was the cherry pie of my childhood, tart and gluey with a lattice top crust welded in place with blackened sugar. It looked like it had been baked with an acetylene torch. The meal left me in a chemical stupor. I figured I'd just consumed enough additives and preservatives to extend my life by a couple of years...if I didn't get killed first.

When the *Baltimore Star* shuts down, 29-year-old Tess Monaghan loses her job as a writer. No one appreciates the dark side of Baltimore better than Tess. The mayor calls Baltimore the City That Reads, but Tess knows it as the City That Bleeds, a tribute to its unprecedented murder rate.

Her sometimes-lover Jonathan Ross is a reporter for the *Beacon-Light*. She knows he's engaged to be married, but it suits her. (From Laura Lippman's *Baltimore Blues*. PB. NY: Avon Books. 1997.)

Tess experienced Jonathan only at his extremes—cocky and in need of affirmation, or depressed and in need of affirmation. Once, in conversation with Whitney, she had compared her Jonathan encounters to eating Oreos without any filling.

"Well, that's what you sign up for when you keep company with men who are virtually engaged to other people," Whitney had said in her blunt way. "Licked-clean Oreos."

Tonight, the plain chocolate cookie in question had brought, along with the harmonica, a bottle of mescal, a Big Mac, and a large order of fries. He pressed the warm, grease-stained bag into Tess's middle as he hugged her, giving her a wet kiss tasting faintly of salt and Hohner Marine Band steel.

"Oh, you shouldn't have," Tess trilled in falsetto, cradling the brown paper bag. "Let me get a vase for these fries."

He grabbed the bag back from her, growling deep in his throat, and began to cram French fries in his mouth by the fistful. When obsessed at work Jonathan sometimes forgot to eat until his need for food became so acute he almost fainted. Once he did find sustenance he guarded it as jealously as a dog. Tess knew what a hunger like this meant.

"Big story?"

"Huge," he said around a mouthful of fries. "Enormous. Gargantuan. Pulitzer material...."

Jonathan held up his hand as if he were a traffic cop, motioning her to wait while he worked his way through the last handful of fries. "Better. Much better than any dead lawyer."

Vejay Haskell, 32-year-old divorcée, has left San Francisco for the little Rogue River town of Henderson. She's looking into her second suspicious death, this one of Michelle, niece of a fellow meter reader. Vejay proves that the same meal—whether taken as breakfast, lunch, or dinner—can be equally stimulating to the little gray cells. Says Sue Dunlap: "Eggs, sauerkraut, and chorizo—better than it sounds. Trust me!" (From Susan Dunlap's *The Bohemian Connection*. PB. NY: Dell Publishing. 1994.)

...Recently I had discovered I'd become enough of a regular to call ahead and have my eggs and kraut waiting as I rushed in, which solved my problem on those days when I had neither time nor ambition. By now it never occurred to the cooks that I ate anything else....

My eggs, sauerkraut, and chorizo arrived with a slab of heated black bread. A non-meter reader might have been too depressed to eat, but I dug in.

What *did* I know had happened? ....

I dunked a forkful of sauerkraut in egg yolk.

Who else benefited from Michelle's death? Craig?...

I piled a forkful of sauerkraut atop a piece of chorizo and managed to balance an inch of egg on that before I brought it warily to my mouth....

I bit into the warm black bread.

Alison? Alison had gone to a lot of trouble to get a job in Henderson. Why?...

I finished the sauerkraut and chorizo and mopped up the last drops of yolk with the black bread. It was clear to me that before I came to a decision, I would have to be sure Sugarbaker was telling me the truth about Michelle's departure—that he hadn't left with her—and I would have to see if Alison was the woman he saw at the bar. I paid for my dinner and headed outside.

...Fischer's Ice Cream was still open. There was still a line. Otherwise, the only populated establishment was the bar. It was amazing how quiet the town proper was.

And then there's Ted Drewe's. Author Eileen Dreyer's sleuth Molly Burke is never more than a thought away from food. She lives in St. Louis and it's summer: The air was "close, hot, sticky as warm donuts." But this is a story about lawyers and people who hate them, including Molly, who's a hospital death investigator and ER nurse. Five local attorneys who supposedly didn't know each other commit suicide. Molly begins to investigate the coincidence, but is ambivalent. She's still recovering financially from a malpractice lawsuit won by ambulance chaser Frank Patterson. He shows up at her elegant home which was protected from his avarice by an unbreakable family trust. (Dreyer can be reached at *kdreyer@mvp.net* .) (From Eileen Dreyer's *Bad Medicine*. PB. NY: HarperCollins Publishing, HarperPaperbacks. 1995.)

Frank smiled at her…and he dug a pink plastic spoon into his cup of Ted Drewe's frozen custard….

There in her backyard. Breaching her sanctuary. Tempting her with the sight of Ted Drewe's….

…"So this is what I missed out on," he said…."It really screwed up the size of the settlement, ya know."…

Not only that, but he was taunting her with one of the greatest sins in life. Ted Drewe's frozen custard. Heart attack in a cup, a St. Louis tradition more cherished than the Cardinals….

Then she saw the avarice in his eyes….

"Would you like to see it?" she asked.

He damn near did a double take….

…"You can't take that in here," she said.

Still grinning, Frank lifted the cardboard cup. "Want some?"

Molly had seen sexual innuendo before. Frank went right to the head of the class.

"You can leave it in the freezer," she said, which made him laugh.

He had no idea what it cost her to say that. Not because she wanted sex—at least not with him—but because she wanted that damn custard. Hawaiian special, if she was any judge. Pineapple, macadamia nuts, chocolate, and butterscotch….

She takes him on a tour of the house, showing him the Waterford chandelier, Persian rugs, gilded mirrors, a Rembrandt sketch, a fabulous jade collection. He's impressed, finishes the tour, walks out the door.

"Hey!" she yelled…"You forgot your Ted Drewe's!"

"Think of me when you lick the spoon!" he called over his shoulder.

…By the time she heard the throaty roar of his engine, she was scraping the bottom of the ice cream cup to get the very last of that pineapple and custard.

What is it with rich folks and rich ice cream? San Diego deputy district attorney Judith Thornton and homicide detective Pike Martin have gone to the palatial home of billionaire land developer Frank Talbot. One of Talbot's henchmen was found dead with an envelope containing money with the name of a recently murdered field hand written on it. Talbot can't help himself—grabbing raw land any way he can is his obsession. Here Talbot has asked his housekeeper to bring them ice cream. (From Patricia Benke's *Above the Law*. PB. NY: Avon Books. 1997.)

…On a tray she carried three bowls of Neapolitan ice cream. One she set perfunctorily before Pike; another, before Judith. The third, containing four times the amount in either of the other bowls, an inedible portion, she set ceremoniously before Talbot. The disparity, embarrassingly noticeable, was ignored by the host.

"Now, where were we….Ah, yes, you were talking about a field hand who's met…an untimely death. A Mister Carras."

"Carrasco," Judith corrected….

…He pushed a spoonful of the ice cream into his mouth and pulled the spoon out half-full. "Felled by one of his own kind. That's a truly fucked up end to a brilliant career."…

"...You wouldn't know of any reason why one of your lobbyists might be paying money to a field hand?"

Talbot's face was expressionless as he lifted another spoon of ice cream into his mouth and pulled it out, still half-full. He smacked his lips and pointed the spoon at Pike....Another spoon of ice cream slipped into his mouth and was drawn out half-full. Neither Judith nor Pike had touched their dessert. Talbot addressed his comment to them both. "You'd better eat your ice cream there; it's melting."

Pike looked down at the softening mound and shook his head. The information Pike hoped would shake him seemed only to stimulate his appetite....

Talbot swallowed several spoonfuls of ice cream and pushed the still half-full bowl away. "I'll tell you what, folks. I don't know anything about this Carrasco...."

Sutton McPhee, reporter for the *Washington News,* has returned to her apartment in Alexandria with two murder stories in her head. Dead are Ann Kane, a young Senate aide, and Janet Taylor, wife of a county supervisor. Detective Noah Lansing is in charge of both investigations and he has already taken an intense dislike to Sutton. Who was it said that food is just something to keep your fingers busy while your mind gets down to work? (From Brenda English's *Corruption of Power.* PB. NY: Berkley Publishing Group, Berkley Prime Crime. 1998.)

I turned from the window and went to my small galley kitchen to find something to eat. From the freezer, I took a boring but convenient frozen dinner—sliced turkey, carrots, and green beans—and put it in the microwave to heat. While that mainstay of the overworked single professional was warming, I...ducked into my bathroom long enough to clean the makeup off my face and then went back to the kitchen to pour myself a glass of Burgundy. To hell with white wines with fowl, I thought. I prefer a decent dry red....

The microwave dinged behind me as I put the wine bottle back on the counter. I took out my dinner, peeled off the cover, set the little plastic tray on a real plate, grabbed a knife and fork from the drawer, and took all of it and my glass of Burgundy out to the teak dining table....

First I thought about Ann Kane and what could have happened to her....

From there my thoughts went on to Janet Taylor....What in her life could possibly have called such a fate down on her?...

And from Janet Taylor, it wasn't very far to Noah Lansing....

"Okay, that's it," I said loudly into the quiet room, throwing my fork down on the plate. I...gathered the remains of my dinner, eaten mostly unconsciously. Back to the kitchen I went, tossing the disposable tray into the garbage and putting my glass, plate, and utensils into the sink. I was angry, at Noah Lansing for judging me so swiftly....But it was more than that. I didn't want him screwing up my story.

Santa Fe forensic psychologist Sylvia Strange testifies in court about an interview she had with a man who beat and raped a young girl and then recanted his confession, blaming drugs. He gets off. She's pissed at herself and the system. State police criminal agent Matt England, aka Sylvia's lover, hustles her away from the courtroom and reporters. Here we're introduced to the power struggle in their relationship over a chile cheeseburger. (From Sarah Lovett's *Acquired Motives*. PB. NY: Ballantine Books, an Ivy Book. 1997.)

"I don't always understand your career choice."

"Is this the I-work-like-hell-to-put-them-away-and-you-let-them-off speech?" They were on opposite sides of the fence when it came to professional issues....

..."Where are we going?"

..."I thought you said the Zia for lunch."...

"I can't go back to work without my chile fix."

…Matt cut the wheel to the left, and the Caprice swerved across the curb into the parking lot of Bert's Burger Bowl. It was a fifties-style take-out stand where locals had been ordering chile-cheeseburgers for forty years….

…At eleven-thirty, the lunch rush had barely begun….When the order was ready, Matt carried out iced tea and burgers wrapped in wax paper. Tin umbrellas provided tiny islands of shade….One bird hopped across the table where Sylvia waited.

She tore off some bun for the sparrow and then she took a bite of burger….

…"Why did you agree to evaluate Randall?"

She set the burger on the paper plate and wiped mustard from her chin…."…Bottom line, the man had the right to a competent psychological evaluation."

Matt nodded slowly. "That didn't have to be you. There are other shrinks out there….Why didn't you just let this one go?"

She tipped her head; her look said, *You're out of line.*

…"…Can we go?…"

Instead of a verbal response, he pushed her against the Caprice and kissed her….

…They kissed until the teenagers began to honk the Buick's horn in appreciation….

…"I think you should lighten your caseload…."

"My schedule's no worse than yours. You want me to stay at home with an apron on?"

Amateur U. S. Fish and Wildlife Agent Rachel Porter is working in the desert near Las Vegas. Everyone hates her. The ranchers, the miners, the land developers, local government officials. She represents the Feds and they all want her off their back. She goes into the Gold Bonanza which has a $1.99 breakfast special. (From Jessica Speart's *Tortoise Soup*. PB. NY: Avon Books. 1998.)

I received my usual friendly greeting. "We're full up."

And as usual, I looked out at a sea of empty tables....

The Mosey On Inn was a pit stop on the road to nowhere....

"What'll it be today, sweetie?" ....

"A slice of lemon meringue pie and a jolt of black coffee would be perfect," I replied.

Ruby waddled back and forth filling my order, her ample rear end threatening to burst her uniform at the seams....

"Listen, sugar. You want to find out what's going on in these parts? You head over to see old Annie McCarthy," she said, shoving a paper bag into my hand....

..."She's a miner?" I asked, glancing inside the bag.

A ham and cheese sandwich was accompanied by a shiny red apple....

*   *   *

It looked like a white sheet had been thrown over Annie's remains....

...I realized the crudely made shroud was nothing but maggots....They wriggled between Annie's bare bones as the last witnesses to death, forming a living blanket of squirming, well-fed bodies....

...I tore down the hall and out the front door, where I leaned...throwing up my breakfast along with the sandwich and pie. I was still shaking as I staggered to the Blazer and rinsed out my mouth with a swig of warm Coke....

It's two o'clock in the morning and detective Seth Howard has waited up for detective Jill Smith with prawn satay in the microwave. These do this all the time, junk food in the living room, junk food in bed. Susan Dunlap doesn't call this tenth in the series *Cop Out* for nothing. Jill is getting closer and closer to suspension and her relationship with Howard more and more tenuous. (From *Cop Out*. PB. NY: Dell Publishing. 1998.)

Howard swallowed. Once when he was a child, he had told me, he'd stared at a glass of castor oil and orange juice for two hours before forcing it down. How hard to swallow was what he couldn't quite bring himself to say now?

"You were doing me a favor?" I forced out.

"Keeping my ears open—for you. Went to dinner…with a couple of the guys….Came back to…finish up some paperwork." He swallowed again…."You want to hear what the word is around the station?"

"I just left Doyle's office. I already know." Balancing rice carton, spoon, bowl, and chopsticks in my arms, I headed for the coffee table.

"You sure?" He plunked the satay carton on the *Chronicle*. "Is this what you know? You don't find Herman Ott, you're either incompetent or sleeping with the enemy."

"They said that to you?"

Howard nodded.

My throat constricted. It wasn't so much the comment that frightened me as the realization that my fellow officers—my friends—viewed me as so suspect they felt free to damn me to my own lover….

"I *said*, Jill, that you knew Ott, you'd find him."

"But not that they could count on me."

It was a moment before he answered. "That wasn't the question."

I yanked his arm around. His chopsticks shot onto the floor. "It wasn't *not* the question."…

On the table the peanuty smell of satay mocked us, too sweet, too oily. Howard spooned rice onto plates, satay over the top. It was cold, of course, the way the room was cold, the way I was cold, down to my marrow.

Cincinnati homicide detective Sonora Blair has an ulcer. She's also got on her hands the tall, dark, and handsome brother of a murder victim. Sonora's asked the brother, Keaton Daniels, to meet her at the Dairy Queen. Keaton's an elementary school teacher and the game is "Can You

Top This for Sex Discrimination?" (From Lynn Hightower's *Flashpoint*. PB. NY: HarperCollins Publishing, HarperPaperbacks. 1996.)

...Keaton was inside, studying the menu. He moved close to the cash register. Ordered fries, a barbecue, a Sprite.

"For here," Sonora told the girl behind the counter. "Chili dog, onion rings, and a Coke. Yeah, I want chili on it. That's usually implied, with a chili dog, right?"...

Sonora looked at the chili dog, wondered how the ulcer would handle it, toyed with an onion ring....

Keaton stacked three french fries and ate them in a wedge, sans catsup....

"I used to be the only guy at my school, my old school."

"You were the only man there?"

"Only. Custodian, principal—all female."

"Is that good or bad?" Sonora started getting serious on the chili dog....

*   *   *

They were eating ice cream....She felt pretty good. No ulcer pain and a hot fudge sundae....

He poked the bottom of a frozen lime push-up. "At my school there *was* no men's room."

"They plant a tree in your name?"...

*   *   *

Sonora stuck a straw in the milkshake. "The men are way overprotective...."

Keaton peeled a piece of chocolate topping off his ice cream cone. "Try this. The first teaching job I got offered I lost, because I wouldn't coach the basketball team. I guarantee you the women don't have to coach."...

*   *   *

Sonora picked up a chicken finger, then laid it back on the paper box. Keaton Daniels picked up a pork fritter and chewed halfheartedly....

"What's so funny?"

"Nothing. I think I have a junkfood hangover."

Keaton started stacking trash. "You know, at home and stuff, I eat salads. Fruit and cottage cheese."

"I hear denial."

The words "diner," "restaurant," "lunch," "dinner," "bar and grill," and "supermarket" grace the pages of Marcia Muller's *A Walk Through the Fire* (Warner Books, 1999). But since it's San Francisco PI Sharon McCone who is doing the walking, she sits down once only for a proper meal at the Bali H'ai. She's on Kauai so there's plenty of edible vegetation around— breadfruit, ginger, taro, papaya, bananas, sugar cane. But Sharon samples none of it. Drinks and drinking scenes abound. Martinis, Scotch, beer. Gin and tonic, lots of gin and tonic. Coffee, lots and lots of coffee. And there are a couple of ravenous scenes involving sushi and canapés, pastrami sandwiches and soda pop, following the prototypic sleuth's habit of forgetting to eat. Sharon eats lunches and dinners, but we seldom learn what exactly she's eating. *What* is not important—what's going on in her head is. That's how Sharon McCone has been defined by food for over twenty years.

By page 138 of Nancy Pickard's *Twilight* (Simon & Schuster, Pocket Books, 1995), amateur sleuth and organizer of Port Frederick, Mass's autumn festival, Jenny Cain, has been bloodied by a protester's sign, bruised by a run-in with a wine red Jaguar, and finally, battered by a tumble into the trees. She's seriously worried about whether the festival will come off when, fortunately, right in front of her is the Beantown Diner, a major mode of dealing with her growing anxiety. She tells the waitress, later, later there will be time for vegetables, but tonight it's comfort all the way with a double cheeseburger, fries, a malted, and by damn, hot cherry pie à la mode. Will she leave the Beantown feeling lighter or heavier? Will the festival be a victory or a failure? Can she get to the bottom of those murderous twilight accidents?

Last question: Do you think Jenny Cain is serious about those vegetables? Given that crime work turns days into nights and a sleuth's mind is focused on externals, the chance that she'll opt for a spinach and mushroom salad at midnight, or a cottage cheese and fruit platter at 3 a.m., or a tricolore salad mix at dawn isn't very likely. Especially if she's trying to locate it between displays of salt-laden popcorn and blackened, day-old hotdogs at the local gas station.

Chapter 13
What Do You Know About Country Cookin'?

"The generous luncheons that came afterward were as much a custom in Waters County as the funerals....Through hamburger casseroles and gelatin salads, sadness was transformed into a philosophic acceptance of death...." (From Jo Dereske's *Cut and Dry*.)

Amateur sleuths are more comfortable working in small town settings. On the one hand, country cookin' is limited in variety, traditional in recipe, and plain in delivery. On the other hand, it reflects regional differences, large and small. Did we say plain in delivery? Not when it comes to funeral lunches. Nor when it comes to a prayer meeting following the flight of a fugitive. PI Kinsey Millhone in Sue Grafton's *"F"* (1999) finds herself in a church kitchen arranging Pepperidge Farm cookies on paper doilies, where she muses there must be a section of the ladies' auxiliary church cookbook for Sudden Death Quick Snacks that teaches how to get Jell-O molds of cherry with fruit cocktail and lime with grated carrots to set in an hour and a half. Tricks with ice cubes, no doubt.

On the Arapaho reservation where attorney Vicky Holden turns up to solve crimes, food streams into the St. Francis Mission before a body is even cold. What do native Americans on the res serve at funeral lunches? Same as the rest of us. Roast beef, ham and scalloped potatoes, casseroles, potato salad, cakes and brownies, bologna sandwiches, potato chips, and endless coffee. In Margaret Coel's 1999 *The Lost Bird*, as in most novels set on Indian reservations, fears of alcoholism are drowned by the never-ending output of a gargantuan stainless-steel coffee urn. So if you're into coffee, there's a lot to savor in this book besides the conflicted and complex characters Coel is known for.

Ruby Crane, forgery detector, has moved back to the family cabin near the small town of Sable, Michigan. She recalls her high school days and finding on the hood of her boyfriend's car a Bible, a dozen chocolate chip cookies, and a note saying turn away from the cheap pleasures of the flesh. The cookies were baked by one Enid Shea. Here, Ruby first visits Mina who has just lost her husband Corbin in a grisly sawmill accident. Later, she meets up with consulting forester Hank Holliday for a thermos of coffee and Enid's cake in the woods. (From Jo Dereske's *Savage Cut*. PB. NY: Dell Publishing. 1996.)

Mina carried a tray into the living room that held two cups of poured coffee and a glass plate of cookies and chocolate cake. "My freezer's full of food," she said. "Enid Shea brought over a carrot cake; she said she knew it was Corbin's favorite—isn't *that* weird?"

"Not from Enid," Ruby said....

..."Enid...she tries. At the lunch after the funeral she told me it was a shame I'd already gone through two husbands when I wasn't even forty. 'It doesn't look good,' she said."...

Mina offered a foil-covered plate to Ruby. "It's Enid Shea's carrot cake. I can't eat it."

Ruby protested but Mina said, "Please. I'd like you to have it. Enid's a good cook."

"I know. She left me chocolate chip cookies once," Ruby said, taking the plate....

*   *   *

Hank wiped frosting from his mouth with the back of his wrist. "This is great. Did you make it?"

Ruby shook her head. "Enid Shea did. She gave it to Mina Turmouski."

"Funeral food."

"Does it still taste all right?"

"Worth dying for." He hit himself in the forehead with the heel of his hand....

...The truck pulled behind her car and momentarily stopped. Silas wasn't alone. His wife, Enid, sat in the passenger seat, avidly peering out the window at Ruby and Hank in their sugar maple bower....

Enid leaned out the window and called over the truck's shifting gears, "You didn't even come home for your mother's funeral, Ruby Crane."

Hank looked after the departing truck, his mouth open. "Subtle," he commented.

"Enid's always spoken her mind," Ruby told him....

In Chapter 1, the town of Sable loses Alice, owner of its only beauty shop. Strangled by a hair dryer cord. Chapter 2 is necessarily devoted to funeral luncheon organization. Here, Enid Shea is on the phone with Ruby. Desperate to shake off Enid's scathing criticism of the sheriff, Ruby declares she's driving into town and has to hang up. Mary Jean is Ruby's best friend. (From Jo Dereske's *Cut and Dry*. PB. NY: Dell Publishing. 1997.)

"Oh. That reminds me why I called," Enid said loudly...."I've taken charge of Alice's luncheon....Could you make a nice Jell-O salad? The grocery store's having a sale on that good chunky canned fruit cocktail, the kind that has sliced bananas in it, so you could pick some up while you're in town."...

*   *   *

Ruby...arrived at the luncheon in time to pay her respects and eat a piece of cherry cobbler....

"And the insurance," Mary Jean went on softly. "Nothing to sneeze at....That's great cherry cobbler, isn't it? Enid Shea made it." She waved her fork at Enid, who bustled between tables, dishcloth in one hand, dirty cups in the other. "Being a great cook is almost compensation for having the meanest mouth in the county."

"Green is more traditional for funerals," Enid had told Ruby when she'd delivered her salad to the church kitchen, doubtfully eying Ruby's fruit-studded peach Jell-O. "I wish you would have used lime. I thought you knew."

*   *   *

Mary Jean beckoned Ruby farther into a corner....They stood behind two older women who were sharing a piece of pie....

"And she did it," one of the elderly women in front of them was saying gleefully, sotto voce. "She went out there after dark and peed right on his grave," and the two broke into muffled laughter....

"Here," Mary Jean said, shoving a napkin in Ruby's hand. "Wipe your face. Oh God," and she clutched her chest.

In addition to the funeral lunch, holiday fare is a surefire way to convey sleuthing in small town America. Christmas is America's favorite, starting as it does around Halloween. On an East Coast barrier island, Josie Pigeon's into construction, and a rush remodeling job is threatened because, not only has carpenter Caroline been murdered, but carpenter Betty is in jail, accused of the crime. The following conversation takes place between Josie and Betty's lawyer, John Jacobs, at the jail. Valerie Wolzien can be e-mailed at *valerie@wolzien.com* or at her web site: *http://www.nmomysteries.com/main.htm*. (From Valerie Wolzien's *Deck the Halls with Murder*. PB. NY: Ballantine Publishing Group, a Fawcett Gold Medal Book. 1998.)

"I brought Betty some lunch." Josie held up the bag. "It's a hoagie from the deli."

"Let's see, she already has a pan of lasagna, a pot of baked beans with hot dogs, a good-sized bowl of tuna salad and a loaf of rye, cheese and crackers on a bread board, three jello molds—or molds of jello and fruit to be more exact—at least four thermoses of homemade soup, one of which is clam chowder, my very favorite and which I may sample sometime soon, and too many plates of homemade cookies to count. I feel like I've stumbled into the middle of a lavish church supper."

"Are any of the cookies Christmas cookies?"

"All of the cookies are Christmas cookies as far as I can tell. And the few I've snitched have been wonderful."

"I wonder if anyone would mind if I took some home with me," Josie said, thinking of her son and his friend and the bag of Oreos sitting in the truck. The kids would certainly prefer the best that the best bakers on the island had produced—and so would she.

"Don't see why not. They're just going to waste here."

"Has Betty eaten anything?"

"She was refusing all food this morning. And then, about an hour ago, this extraordinary-looking woman sort of swooped in the doorway, clothing and hair flying out in all directions. She was carrying a casserole which smelled irresistibly delicious and garlicky. Apparently Ms. Patrick had the same impression because that casserole was accepted immediately."…

Amateur sleuth Molly Masters had lived in her new home outside Albany, New York, just three months when a neighbor gets shot dead while digging in Molly's garden. Not much later, another neighbor dies, electrocuted. There is a host of suspects and in this scene, one of them, after kidnapping Molly, releases her on a back country road. Molly runs to the nearest farm house to phone the police. (From Leslie O'Kane's *The Cold Hard Fax*. PB. NY: Ballantine Publishing Group, a Fawcett Gold Medal Book. 1998.)

…Then, next thing I knew I was seated at a table with a soup spoon in my hand, a bowl of homemade chicken soup in front of me along with an entire loaf of fresh-baked corn bread, and a pitcher of lemonade.

…"Look at you. You're half starved to death. Now you eat something, 'fore you fall over."

"First I need to call my mother and let her know I'm all right."

"You let me make the call." She pointed a chubby finger at me. "Meanwhile, you eat. Now what's the number and your mama's name?"

…Soon the woman was saying on the phone, "Don't you ever feed your child? She's all skin and bones!"…

There was a knock on the door and some deep-voiced officer began to speak to my food Nazi.

"I don't know where I am, Mom, but don't worry. I'll get a ride home from the police."…

The woman snatched the phone away from me. "She needs to speak to the police now," she told my mother. "You feed her a good meal when she gets home."…

…As I got into the backseat of the patrol car, the woman hollered, "Wait," from the porch, and soon puffed her way down the stairs with a grocery bag clutched against her enormous bosom. She shoved the bag into the seat next to me, wagged her finger through the window at me, and said, "It's your leftovers. You eat every bite of this."

I nodded and smiled wanly at the woman. If she had owned Lassie, the collie would have been dragging her tummy on the ground en route to rescuing Timmy.

Sydney Teague's a businesswoman in Charlotte, North Carolina. Two people she greatly admires have been murdered and she needs both fuel and comfort. The two victims were working on a safe synthetic-nicotine substitute. But in Wade County where tobacco is king? Not a good idea. On her way back to Charlotte from investigating, Sydney can't resist the hickory smoke emanating from a country family restaurant. (From Anne Underwood Grant's *Smoke Screen*. PB. NY: Dell Publishing. 1998.)

…The special today was smoked pork chops. I ordered it along with turnip greens, cabbage, and a sweet potato. The smiling young woman put a basket of homemade biscuits, a plate full of butter squares, and a jar of fruit preserves on my table.…

I overheard two men discussing hog production in detail and the problems they were having with state inspectors. The whole time they talked, they were eating the smoked pork chops. I was jealous of lives so neatly compartmentalized.…

Almost all of them were smoking, so I did too. I couldn't think of a single restaurant in Charlotte where the practice was still tolerated. The busy but attentive waitress brought me a glass ashtray. The coffee, the cigarette, the clang of plates and the buzz of people enjoying each other was a comforting combination. I settled back in the booth and relaxed for the first time in two days.…

…The pork chops were laced with fat that bulged when it cooked and moistened the meat to mouthwatering perfection. Totally unlike the cardboard that passes for pork these days. I smothered the potato in four or five patties of butter, then set it off with several shakes of both salt and pepper. Its sweetness lightened the heaviness of the pork and piqued some taste buds I hadn't used in years. Since the cabbage and greens were both cooked in fatback, they would have tasted the same had I not dribbled vinegar onto the turnips. The vinegar was just enough tart to cut through the fat of all else. I punctuated each bite with biscuit smothered in what I finally decided was plum preserves. After thirty minutes of nonstop eat-ing...a nap would have been nice.

In Grace F. Edwards' *A Toast Before Dying*, we're introduced to Mali Anderson, born and raised in Harlem, who joined the NYPD only to be fired three years ago for hitting another officer. Details vague.

As many cops do, Mali neglects her three squares when there's crime afoot. Right now she needs to break into the apartment of murder victim Thea, who was shot in the alley behind the Half Moon bar shortly after raising a toast with the crowd to her own birthday. Mali's also hungry. And seeks out down home country cookin' on the streets of NYC from an ex-burglar and ribsman extraordinaire Old Man Charleston. (From Grace F. Edwards' *A Toast Before Dying*. PB. NY: Bantam Books. 1999.)

...."Mali, Baby. Long time to see. Whassup?"
"Nothing and plenty." I laughed. "I need an order of ribs and a favor."
"The ribs you got. Name the favor."
"I need your picks."
"Locked out again?"
"Again," I said. He reached under the counter and pulled a palm-size case from the shelf....
...."I've been meaning to ask you why you keep them."...
"Listen, I keep 'em to look at every now and then. Specially when things git a little tight, what with the rent and all the other bills....I pull this box out and gaze long and hard at my used-to-be life....Me, I'll take the cradle—die—before I see the slammer again. I keep this box to remind me how I got there...."
As he talked, he filled a take-out carton with coleslaw, red rice, and yams, and left enough space for the ribs. He moved quickly and I mar-veled how someone so large was able to maneuver in such a small space: like the night I wanted a rib sandwich and walked in on the two stickup men who had him pressed to the wall.

I had been on the job then, and when I'd yelled "Freeze! Police!" Charleston slid out of sight so fast behind the counter I thought the wall he'd been leaning against had been oiled....

My nerves got the better of me, and before I reached 116th Street I donated my dinner to a street person. It wouldn't do to have Charleston's secret sauce lingering in Thea's elegant apartment, even though she was no longer there.

Vejay Haskell, 32, small town meter reader, currently suspected of murdering the owner of a bar, is running all around town doggedly questioning townsfolk. Usually in places where she picks up a little something to eat. Tonight she veers from her usual haunts into a genuine restaurant. Now, what can Skip, a real estate agent, tell her about the murdered man? (From Susan Dunlap's *An Equal Opportunity Death*. PB. NY: Dell Publishing. 1994.)

The bakery, the drugstore, the normal places I grabbed something to eat, were closed. The only place still open was The Pines, a restaurant with tablecloths. It was more formal than I had in mind, more so than I was dressed for, and likely to cost more than I wanted to pay. The hostess, apparently sharing my assessment, sat me at a table next to the kitchen door....

Taking a final large bite of salmon, I got up and made my way to Skip's table.

As he recognized me approaching, Skip sighed.

I sat down across from him. "I'll only be a minute."

He put down his fork and waited.

"Do you remember telling me Frank asked you about restaurants for sale? When was that?"

"A month and a half, maybe two months ago. Why?"

"Was he only interested in restaurants?"

"Restaurants or stores that could be converted to restaurants, like butcher shops or groceries."

"Was it just places along the river?"

Skip smacked both hands down on the table. "Look, Vejay, you used to be a nice enough young woman, but you're getting to be a pest. I can't eat breakfast out without being observed by you. I can't dine out without you barging in. And what kind of foolish questions are you asking me? 'Was it only restaurants by the river?' This is the 'Russian River Resort Area.' The attraction here is the river...."

I wanted to apologize for making such a nuisance of myself, but I couldn't. I wanted to finish my dinner, but I didn't do that either. I paid the bill and left.

Atlanta newspaper columnist 50-something Kate Mulcay lives in the woods outside of town. A new Episcopal preacher has come on the scene, Jonathon Craven. But he's familiar with hog head cheese, tater pone, jelly cake, and stew that just ain't right without a squirrel or wild rabbit in it. Here Kate introduces her neighbor, Miss Willie, to Jonathon. (From Celestine Sibley's *Spider in the Sink*. PB. NY: HarperCollins Publishing, HarperPaperbacks. 1998.)

"A reverent, huh?" said Miss Willie, her wrinkled face wreathed in smiles. "Well, that's a change from them police and newspaper folks you usually have. I'm glad I brung you some pot likker for the reverent to eat. You do like pot likker, don't you?" She examined Jonathon's face to make certain of an honest answer....

"Sit down, Miss Willie," said Kate, pushing a rocker toward her.

"No, much obliged. I best be a-going home. You can make a hoecake to go with this, I know," she said, handing Kate the basket, which held, wrapped in a clean flour sack, a fruit jar full of the dark-emerald liquid in which turnip greens had been cooked.

I can do better than that, Kate decided. I'll make little corn cakes. Suddenly it felt good to be cooking something for Jonathon, who walked Miss Willie to the road and came back dusting his hands....

A while later, they sat by the fire, sipping hot pot likker from cups and eating thin, crisp corn cakes.

"You know," Jonathon offered after a time, "you live well."

"Hmm. Good neighbors," murmured Kate.

"I heard that you saved Miss Willie from going to prison for killing her son."

"She wasn't guilty, and I knew it," Kate said....

A country-western bar in rural Alabama. Closed. Ed, the owner, has been murdered. Ed, whom the whole staff saw forcing himself on Doris, who has quit and disappeared. The evidence says maybe the handsome, young cook is the murderer. Bonnie Blue, who helped in the bar kitchen, now works at a truck stop. She's asked retired teacher Patricia Anne Hollowell to prove the cook ("that precious child") innocent. Patricia has come to report to Bonnie—too bad she's never been inside a truck stop before. (From Anne George's *Murder On A Girls' Night Out*. PB. NY: Avon Books. 1996.)

"Yo," said a burly, whiskered man who turned to look at me. He was sitting at the counter eating a hamburger, and he held up a French fry in salute....

I took out the plastic menu that was stuck between the sugar and the salt shakers and which felt slightly greasy. I had been planning on some dessert, but maybe I would just have coffee.

I wasn't the only woman in the restaurant, but I was the only one in a red suit. The others seemed to be lady truckers. Truckettes?...

The truck stop was a male bastion, though. The women were outsiders, even sitting together away from their male counterparts....

Bonnie Blue pulled out the chair next to mine and sat down....

"Is that precious child all right?"

"That precious child is fine. And Doris Chapman is in Florida."

"I figured that."

"But, Bonnie Blue, I found out something else. You know when Ed tried to rape Doris?"

"Sure, I was there."

"Well, he probably wasn't trying to rape her. He had a cut weenie."

"A what?"

"His penis! He cut his penis that morning and had to have it sewed up!"

I had spoken louder than I realized. Suddenly, except for the corner where the truckettes were eating, there was silence. The words "penis" and "cut" had been amplified in the testosterone-laden air.

"Oh, Lord, Patricia Anne." Bonnie Blue looked upset. Some of the men were pushing their plates back, preparing to leave.

"But they sewed it up!"

There was a general rush for the door. Bonnie Blue groaned....

I got up and stomped out. Several of the truckettes waved at me and smiled.

Sage Rock in Modoc County, CA. PI Sharon McCone and her lover Hy Ripinsky are trying to trace the circumstances surrounding Sharon's birth. They need to question the owner of the Cattleman's Café. What better time than over breakfast. What better way to think up a cover story than by listening to the locals. (From Marcia Muller's *Listen to the Silence*. HB. NY: Warner Books, Mysterious Press. 2000.)

The café was small—six tables....Sloppily hand-lettered signs were tacked helter-skelter on the walls:

DON'T ASK FOR CREDIT. YOU DON'T DESERVE IT.

ALL OUR ROADKILL GUARANTEED FRESH.

BURGERS COOKED TO SATISFACTION—JIMMY D'S.

NO FRIES SERVED HERE. JIMMY D DON'T LIKE THEM.

YOU GOT A COMPLAINT, TAKE IT OUTSIDE....

…"Hey, Ed," he called over his shoulder, "you're here pretty late. Got a hangover again?"

"Screw you, Jimmy D," Ed, a diner in mechanic's overalls, said.

Jimmy D. Bearpaw was short and built like a fireplug, but his movements were as quick as a man half his girth. He dashed from the eggs to another griddle covered with frying bacon and sausage, tended to them, then darted back to the eggs and slid them onto plates....

"Jeez, Ed, you oughta leave the Green Death alone...."

"Screw you, Jimmy D," Ed said....

…Hy stared at me in astonishment as I asked for corned beef hash with fried eggs and toast and a side of biscuits and gravy. After he'd ordered a cheese omelet, he said, "I've never seen you eat a breakfast like that McCone."…

"Highway department's got its head up its butt, giving us somethin' like that. Where do they think this is, anyway? L. fuckin' A?" The waitress picked up three plates for one of the window tables and he added, "Christ, Angela, you get any slower, I'm gonna have to buy you one of those motorized wheelchairs! You're almost as slow as Ed over there, and that's slower'n a snail. You don' believe Jimmy D, just ask Ed's missus."

…"Screw you, Jimmy D."

As before, Bearpaw ignored him. "Hey, any of you hear about that woman lawyer, Blackhawk, almost got whacked in Boise...."

At last—something interesting.

For a taste of Lickin Creek, Pennsylvania, seek out Valerie Malmont's *Death Pays the Rose Rent*. Tori Miracle, 30-year-old NYC ex-crime reporter and current novelist, has a dinner date, if you can call it that, with the Police Chief Garnet Gochenauer. Hog maw, slippery pot pie, gravy the color of dandelions, heaping spoonfuls of sauerkraut, green beans, potatoes, ham chunks with a bright red, peeled hard-boiled egg on top and shoofly pie for dessert. Hog maw? The local favorite. When it's served at the Moose, there's a line out the door. All for pig's stomach, stuffed and baked.

Traveling further south to the Inland Waterway of North Carolina you can meet Dr. Michael Stone, female forensic psychologist, while she visits her family in Anna Salter's *Shiny Water*. Here the local favorites are piles of fried chicken, sweet potatoes, collard greens, sweet peas, butterbeans, sweet corn, black-eyed peas, cornbread, shrimp, scallops, and a host of other sea critters, which critters Michael has never considered edible.

Or go west as far as Kansas where San Celina, CA, amateur sleuth Benni Harper is visiting the in-laws and old friends of San Celina's chief of police, Gabe Ortiz, her new husband. Earlene Fowler has them all meet up in Buffalo Barney's Hoof and Fin restaurant for Mid-western cornfed, thick, and juicy steaks and broiled Alaska salmon served by a cowboy waiter. As for the *Kansas Troubles* Benni and Gabe find themselves in, they're thick and juicy as well.

Authors are equally adept at describing big city food scenes—chowing down at a Chicago steak house, loading up on New York City Italian, or savoring blackened anything in New Orleans. But to capture the true flavors of America, you have to go country.

Chapter 14
The Truth About Sleuths
and Pets

Why does a sleuth, against all reason, take on a pet? Because no matter how messed up her personal life, no matter how crazy her work, this animal will be there, dogging her steps worshipfully, nosing her feet, licking her hands and face, purring in her ear from some deep well of contentment. Susan Dunlap's detective-for-hire Kiernan O'Shaughnessy's Lab-Irish wolfhound knows that if he presses his wiry muzzle against her stomach, he'll get a scratch behind the ears.

Unlike Mom, a pet is nonjudgmental and cheap therapy. Under great stress, V.I. tells her neighbor Mr. Contreras in *Tunnel Vision*: "I'm running with the dogs: I need to clear my mind and straighten out my body." Over time, a kind of ESP develops between pet and keeper. Stephanie Plum's hamster Rex's sensibilities are finely tuned to her own, even when he's buried in a bowl of popcorn. If someone's at their front door, both heads swivel toward the tapping.

The pets they acquire are often strays, the more waif-like, the better. Laura Lippman sets the stage for a "rescue" when newspaper writer-turned-PI Tess Monaghan finds herself at Baltimore's Inner Harbor.

Somebody's handing out free hotdogs (foreshadowing?). She grabs one and heads for home, only to learn Uncle Spike has been robbed and is in the hospital. (From Laura Lippman's *Charm City*. PB. NY: Avon Books. 1997.)

…Uncle Spike looked like a plum gone bad….Who did this to an old man?…

Tommy [the dishwasher]…insisted on walking Tess to her car….March…suddenly seemed as bitter as baking chocolate.

"He has something for you?" Tommy began…."Back at the bar?…"

…Tommy took Tess in the back way, through the kitchen—the kitchen where she had eaten her first french fry, her first onion ring, her first mozzarella stick, even her first stuffed jalapeno. Those had been the base of Spike's food pyramid, and who was Tess to disagree?

"There," he said….

…"What the hell is it?"

It was a dog, a bony, ugly dog with dull black fur and raw patches on its hindquarters. The brown eyes were…vague…the shoulders hunched in an uncanny impersonation of Richard M. Nixon.

"It's a greyhound? Spike just got it this weekend?"

"But it's *black*."…

The dog looked up at Tess….Tess looked back. She was not a dog person. She was not a cat person, fish person, or horse person. On bad days, she was barely a people person….

"Can't keep a dog in the bar…? Name's S. K.?"

"What do the initials stand for, S. K.?"

"No. *Esskay*. Like the sausage?"…

Five minutes later, Tess was in her twelve-year-old Toyota, the kibble was in the trunk….

            *   · *   *

…It was not Crow's long, warm body next to her this morning. She rolled toward the middle of the too-soft bed and found herself staring into the faintly cross-eyed gaze of Esskay, the dog's untrimmed toenails digging in her arm, her hind legs twitching spasmodically….

"Don't take this personally, but you are the ugliest dog I've ever seen."

Cincinnati homicide detective Sonora Blair is in possession of a cassette tape made shortly before a young woman's dismemberment. Sonora and her partner Sam Delorosa have gone to Sonora's to hear what murdered Julia Winchell had to say. Clampett is a very large three-legged dog. (From Lynn Hightower's *Eyeshot*. HB. NY: HarperCollins Publishing. 1996.)

…The boom box slipped out of Sam's hand and he dropped Julia Winchell's cassette.

Clampette had it in his mouth before Sam or Sonora could move.

"*No.*" Sonora set the beer on the floor, grabbed the dog by the mouth. "*Drop.*"

Clampett looked at her, brown eyes apologetic. But his jaw muscles were tight, and he clamped down harder….

"Get him a cookie….Get the chocolate chip ones in the top of the pantry."

…Clampett gave her a sad look. He was a retriever. He was retrieving. His expression begged for understanding.

"*Drop,*" Sonora said. "Sam?"

"No cookies."…

"…Okay, there are sausage biscuits in the freezer…."

"Empty box in the freezer. Want me to throw it away?"…

Drool slid down the side of the dog's muzzle and hung in a line of saliva.

"Sam? Meatballs?"

"Nope."…

"Don't you have any dog biscuits or treats, or did the kids eat those too?"

"Go back in my bedroom, and look in the shoe box on the back left-hand side of the closet."...

"I'm not going to even ask, Sonora, why you keep Oreo cookies in a shoe box in your closet."

"For emergencies, obviously. If it isn't nailed down or healthy, the kids inhale it. Clampett's lucky he can run fast."

Sam looked at the three-legged dog. "Looks like they've been snacking on him."

"Cookie please. No, hold it up."...

"Drop for a treat," she said.

Clampett opened his mouth and the cassette hit the floor. He jumped for the cookie and snapped it out of Sam's hand....

Sam held up the tape. "Specialist Blair, please explain to the jury why there are tooth marks on Exhibit A?"

"Shut up and play the tape."

While there's a dog named Champers in this and future novels, the most important sub-human animal in Charlie Plato's life is a bunny named Benny. Charlie owns an interest in a California country-western joint called CHAPS, along with a TV movie star, Zack Hunter, who is the most important human animal in Charlie's life. At least, that's what we think. A lady named Estrella has been murdered and Zack and Charlie meet up in Charlie's loft after interviewing a major suspect. (From Margaret Chittenden's *Dead Beat and Deadly*. PB. NY: Kensington Publishing Group. 1998.)

Apparently he took for granted that he was invited to lunch. He got out of the pickup with me when we arrived at CHAPS, accompanied me up to my loft, took his hat off, let Benny out of his cage, and sat down with him in my flea-market rocking chair....

...If a child were to draw Benny, she'd first make a small circle for his head, then a much larger circle for his body and a tiny cotton-ball circle for his tail, then add a few whiskers to his cheeks and put two ears on top of his head, close together and sticking straight up, though not as far up as those of bigger rabbits.

Benny always looked relaxed when Zack held him. His nose didn't even twitch, and I'm here to tell you a rabbit's nose twitches a *lot*. Let's face it, our man-in-black is loaded with far more than his share of charisma; everybody falls under his spell. I could feel my own chemistry perking like a coffee commercial as I put some turkey sandwiches together and tossed a salad, and Zack wasn't even looking at me.

While we ate, and Benny hopped around my loft, we discussed everything we'd found out about Estrella so far....

Zack helped me clear the dishes from my rickety table to the sink. When we both reached for a plate at the same time, our hands met. And paused.

Whomp! Went my stomach.

Pets can help get those synapses firing even when life is not kind. Psychotherapist Cassidy McCabe's been receiving threatening calls from someone who wants to locate her ex-husband. One of her patients kills himself. Someone who was not suicidal. He leaves a note blaming her. The family threatens to sue. She and the patient's brother, Zach Moran, who also doubts suicide, team up to find out the truth. Cassidy proves you don't need a *homo sapiens* to converse about what's happening. (From Alex Matthews's *Secret's Shadow*. PB. New Mexico: Intrigue Press. 1998.)

She got back from Martin's and realized she was hungry. Looking for something to eat always depressed her. It forced her to notice how broke and disorganized she was, how lax about shopping, meal planning, and cleaning out the refrigerator....

She filled a tray with snacks and headed for the front porch, assisted by the cat who bobbed along beside her, chirping encouragement. She sliced moldy edges off the cheese and piled them on the rough wooden picnic bench. The cat pounced, finishing off every crumb before Cassidy was done arranging her own plate of cheese, crackers and fruit....

"Cheese is a special treat. You do not get to stuff yourself on it...."

Cassidy broke off another bite and handed it to the cat. "Now that Zach's back on the scene, we have this one slight problem...."

"You see, there're a few details I've neglected to mention. The drawing I found in the attic. The consultation with Honor. The gas leak. My little chat with Yvonne. And of course the tidbits I picked up from Jerry and Martin...."

The cat reached out, tentatively touching her plate.

"Get your paw off my food. Cheese costs as much as steak. At least it did when I used to buy steak...."

The cat made a swipe at one of the slices. Cassidy barely succeeded in snatching it out of her reach.

"This is important. Why can't you get your mind off your stomach long enough to hold a decent conversation?"

Retired office manager Betty Trenka of East Moulton, Connecticut, coexists with a plump cat named Tina. They meet mainly over Tina's food bowl and at bed time, even more so here as Betty takes on a temporary school secretary job. But Tina's doings are a touching way to hold together this story of a new job amidst a host of evil characters. We said pets were nonjudgmental, but here's a possible exception. (From Joyce Christmas's *Mood to Murder*. PB. NY: Ballantine Publishing Group, a Fawcett Gold Medal Book. 1999.)

Tina...did eye the full dish of dry cat food with some dismay. She preferred tuna.

"You'll be glad of it when I'm not around all day to cater to your every whim," Betty said. "And you'll miss not having me to kick around." Tina condescended to nibble at the dry food, and even went so far as to bat a nugget around the kitchen floor in an uncharacteristically playful manner. Betty understood cats less than she understood children.

*   *   *

Betty was pleasantly tired when she finally got to bed around ten. Even Tina appeared to have mellowed out....The bowl of dry cat food was empty, so she'd been given a hefty spoonful of tuna to let her know she hadn't been completely abandoned. Betty nodded off, with the faint odor of tuna breath floating up from the foot of the bed.

*   *   *

...the robbery, the stolen gun, the stolen jewelry....
Betty did not sleep well that night. Her mind was too full of thoughts. Tina, however, sacked out at once, curled up on her feet, as though she'd genuinely missed Betty since she'd gone back to work.

*   *   *

But where was Tina? In spite of their often testy relationship, Tina was a constant of Betty's life, and she hated to think that any harm had come to her....Then she came to her senses. Missing cat or not, Betty was facing a suspected intruder in her home....
Finally she stepped boldly into the house and called out, "I'm here. What do you want?"
...she heard someone moving in the living room. Then Tina sprinted into the kitchen faster than she'd ever moved in her life and twined herself affectionately around Betty's ankles. Also unheard of.

Some dogs are formally trained as sleuths, the better half of a K-9 unit, some say. There is the search dog, who tracks and then bites its prey (leading to very expensive settlements), the drug dog who unerringly sniffs out every kind of narcotic, and, here, the accelerant dog, who's working beyond her job description. Durham, North Carolina, PI Casey Jones is only hours into bodyguarding a harassed tobacco researcher when he turns up dead, an apparent arson victim. Casey's background is rough, low-down, and dirt-poor where the major food groups are grits, possum, syrup, and bacon grease. Even so, identifying the guy's crispy remains is too much. (From Katy Munger's *Money to Burn*. PB. NY: Avon Books. 1999.)

"Well, hello there," I said to the dog. It looked up at me without interest, then returned its gaze to the fire.

"Annie's only interested in fires," the owner explained apologetically. "She's an accelerant dog."…

…"This gal's got two hundred twenty-five million nerve endings in her nose alone. You and I have five million at best."…

"She's trained to sniff out five different kinds of accelerants used to start fires, from petroleum to acetone and alcohol-based products. If she finds something, she bows over the spot and waits until I arrive. I mark the spot and give her something to eat." She patted the pouch hanging around her waist.…

*   *   *

Charred remains that had once been a face stared up at me, the flesh on the left side burned away so that the skull and teeth gleamed in a death grimace.…

…I had to get the taste of fire out of my mouth. I bent over and coughed so violently that I finally threw up, losing the contents of my stomach on the edge of the grass and not giving a shit who saw it.…

…Something wet and cold touched my arm. I opened one eye tentatively. A narrow dark nose was in my line of vision, pointing obediently at the pool of vomit at my feet.

I looked up to find Annie the accelerant dog bowed at attention, her front paws daintily crossed and her hind-quarters thrust into the air as she pointed her nose at the pile at my feet. One of her two hundred and twenty-five million nose nerve endings had detected one of my three gin-and-tonics of the night before.

Some breeds of dogs are better than others as stalkers. Here we have that unique man-trailer, the bloodhound. To be more exact, we have a kennel full of them, all ages and sizes. Jo Beth Sidden is their breeder and trainer and can't help but be led by their leashes into investigating crimes deep in the Okefenokee Swamp. If Jo Beth is what she eats, so are her drooling four-footed friends. Jonathan is Jo Beth's lover. (From Virginia Lanier's *A Brace of Bloodhounds*. PB. NY: HarperCollins Publishing, HarperPaperbacks. 1998.)

"Whoever served breakfast this morning must be an excellent chef," Jonathan noted. "I see every bowl is licked clean."

"Donnie Ray Carver and Jasmine Jones had the honors," I said. "It's good there're no leftovers. If a crumb was left, I'd start yelling for the vet….If they don't eat, they're sick. It's also good for me that they eat every bite. The cost of feeding this mob has me teetering on the edge of bankruptcy…."

…"Just how much can—oh, let's say, ten fifty-pound sacks of good dog food cost? Surely that would feed all the dogs for a week."

"Ho, ho, ho." I chuckled….

"…Each adult bloodhound, after turning one year old, eats the following each day: six cups of top-grade commercial dog meal; a pound of ground beef with less than fifteen percent fat…a boiled egg—they can't digest raw ones; a cup of cottage cheese; a tablespoon of corn oil; a teaspoon of baking soda; vitamin B-twelve; plus a good vitamin supplement just like adult humans take. All this is combined and moistened with skim milk. Two times a week we mix in tomato juice. Three times a week we add honey, and three times a week we add yogurt...."

"...Did I mention that they're fed twice a day and the meals have to be mixed individually? Some bloodhounds have quirky digestive systems...."

"...I haven't yet enlightened you on the feeding schedule for the puppies. Even at three months they're fed four times a day, and they consume more food than the adults! The puppies gain four to five pounds a week....I won't bore you with any more details, but we boil more eggs than the Easter bunny...."

San Diego child abuse investigator Bo Bradley has been invited for dinner by her lover Andy LaMarche. Andy is trying to cope with the surprise visit of his second cousin, cajun Teless, from Louisiana. Molly is Bo's dachshund puppy who is dropped off at an elderly sitter's when Bo goes to work. In Cajun, T before a name means "little." (From Abigail Padgett's *The Dollmaker's Daughters*. PB. NY: Warner Books. 1998.)

"*Cher pacan!*" Teless Babineaux muttered, banging a skillet Andrew LaMarche had found perfectly adequate until now against his new cooktop. "Dis *moodee* thing give me *de chou rouge*, Nonk Andy. Ain't you got a iron pan?"

"I'm afraid not," he answered, studying the orange-mango salsa he was mixing in a white ceramic bowl. "And please try to speak English when Bo arrives, Teless. She tends to pick up speech patterns from people around her. It wouldn't do for her to latch on to some of your more colorful phrases."

"Now *you* givin' me *de chou rouge*," the teenager grinned, stirring a mountain of shrimp, butter, and spices in the less-than-adequate skillet....

"Young ladies don't say "You're giving me a red butt' every time they're irritated," he smiled while inhaling the spicy smells.

"Sounds all wrong in English, don't it?" the girl agreed....

...The doorbell announced Bo's arrival.

Teless got there first, her wooden spoon dripping roux on the flagstone entry floor...

"Teless has made a sort of shrimp gumbo," he explained as the girl played with Molly. "Popcorn rice, yeast biscuits. My contribution is the appetizer and a chocolate raspberry torte for dessert."...

"...I love gumbo, but what's popcorn rice?"

"Louisiana special rice. Smells like popcorn," Teless explained. "I brought five pounds for Nonk Andy. Wouldn've brought crawdads, too, 'cept the bus man said they had to be froze with dry ice an' I didn't have no dry ice, me. This puppy is like a boudin sausage on legs, Bo. T-Boudin!"

Miami's working women are being stalked by the Downtown Rapist who attacks in women's rest rooms. At her kitchen table, Britt Montero, ace crime reporter, is reviewing her notes on the predator. Her mother, who manages a fashionable boutique, interrupts Britt's reading with a phone call to set her up with yet another eligible young man. (From Edna Buchanan's *Miami, It's Murder*. PB. NY: Avon Books. 1995.)

..."The Fine Arts Center is opening a wonderful new show, the Headache Art Exhibit."

"The what?"

She laughed. "It was written up in your own paper. It's the work of artists with headaches, exposing their pain."...

Exactly what I need after a hard week's work, I thought. My lower right eyelid had begun twitching almost imperceptibly. It does that occasionally. I pressed my fingers against it, squinting....

"What's wrong?"

"Nothing. My eyelid is twitching."

"Lack of potassium. Eat a banana, dear. Or bake a nice sweet potato. You don't eat or sleep right."

"I don't know about Friday."

"He's an ophthalmologist, Britt."…

I sighed, holding my eyelid tight as something inside it did the polka. With the other, I saw Billy Boots boldly force his whiskery face into Bitsy's dish. The dainty little dog stopped eating and politely sat down, watching the cat devour her beefy food.

"Britt, I hope they find the rapist, but why are you always so fascinated by the dark side.…"

Stretching the phone cord and my right leg to the max, I tried to move Bitsy's dish to safety with my foot, but the greedy cat moved with it, picking up speed, wolfing the dog food with amazing speed.

"None of us is young forever," my mother said. My attention wandered back to my notebook. "Opportunities don't always come again," she warned.…

"Uh-oh, something is boiling over in the kitchen," I said. "Have to go now. Call you tomorrow. 'Bye."

Burdened by guilt, I glared at poor Bitsy, who was sniffing at her empty dish. "What's wrong with you?" I scolded. "Why don't you ever stick up for yourself?"

Vegetarianism in sleuths is rare. Perhaps what motivates it in Natalie Gold is identification with Brenda Starr, her horse. Natalie writes fashion news for *The Charlotte Commercial Appeal* to support her riding habit. She boards Brenda at February Farms, and when a pricey show horse and trainer are brutally murdered at the Farms, she pairs up with *Appeal* writer Henry Goode to get to the bottom of things.

Here, Natalie and Henry are driving back to town after checking out the dead horse and trainer before the law arrives. (From Jody Jaffe's *Horse of a Different Killer*. PB. NY: Ballantine Books, an Ivy Book. 1996.)

"I'll bet someone finds an extension cord with two alligator clips in that stall," I said. "It's gruesome, but it works. You turn the horse into a giant filament....then the killer slams a leg or two to make it look like the horse was flailing around in his stall and broke his leg."

"Are horses really that stupid?..."

..."Dumb to our ways is more like it. Horses are supposed to live outside, in the open. They're grazers....If a horse lies down too close to the wall, he can get wedged. In. He doesn't have enough room to roll over into a stand—that's what happens when a horse gets cast in its stall—he panics and starts smashing all around. Leg bones can snap just from the percussion of running. And a stomach ache can kill a horse...."

...I was hungry and thought about asking him to stop at the Circle K for a package of Cheetos. But I didn't want to interrupt his internal debate of whether or not to tell the deputy. Plus, I'd let my father corral me into trying his latest miracle cure-all, the Fit for Life diet, which meant nothing in my mouth before noon except fruit. The Fit for Lifers, an ascetic band of vegetarians who eat nothing but uncooked plant products, contend the human body stays in the "elimination process" until noon and can't digest anything before that without dire consequences—everything from gas to cancer. Fruit doesn't count because it goes right through you.

Another vegetarian is small town New York newspaper journalist Alex Bernier, who has a lady dog named Shakespeare, part German shepherd, part beagle. Two young women have been murdered and Alex is receiving threats. Which is why Detective Brian Cody is trying to teach Alex not to open her door before she knows who is there, because if it were a rapist, Shakespeare would likely play fetch with him. (From Beth Saulnier's *Distemper*. PB. NY: Mysterious Press Paperback, a Time Warner Company. 2000.)

When you're feeling all freaked out, nothing returns you to your right mind like banana bread. I mean the baking of it, not necessarily the eating, though that's pretty satisfying too. There's something cathartic about the process, all the mashing and pureeing and sifting and egg-cracking. It allows you to be both destructive and creative at the same time, and your friends thank you afterward....I was home in the midst of a baking orgy when the doorbell rang. I wiped the fruity sludge off my hands and opened up to find a very irked Detective Cody on my front steps.

"What the hell is wrong with you, Alex? Do you have a death wish?"...

I went into the kitchen and when I got back to the living room I could see him casting about for a place to sit that didn't look like it was going to sprout a tail. He finally settled on the arm of the couch next to Shakespeare, who looked up long enough to see if he happened to be carrying a steak....

"Smells good." He reached into his jacket pocket. "Mind if I smoke?"...

"Outside. It's a nonsmoking house...."

"Are you serious? Look at this place. I've never seen so much dog hair that wasn't connected to a dog. I've got clumps on my tongue. And I can't smoke in here?"...

I got up and went to the coat closet, pulled a beach towel off the top shelf, and spread it out on the couch to cover the dog hair....He moved over and Shakespeare promptly stood up, turned around, and settled with her head on his lap.

"Nice pooch."

"Love of my life."

One of the perks of enforcing the law in a national park is the wildlife. The deer who eats your front yard, the bear who dines in your garbage can, and the critters who pig out in your dormitory where pets are not allowed. Here Anna Pigeon, Mesa Verde park ranger, sits with a glass of burgundy in the dorm kitchen trying to figure out what's felling tourists visiting the ruins. (From Nevada Barr's *Ill Wind*. PB. NY: Avon Books. 1995.)

A pretty little mouse with ears Disneyesque in their cuteness and whiskers Gus-Gus would have been proud of poked her nose out of the kitchen and contemplated crossing the risky expanse of carpet in the living area.

"You're getting fat," Anna warned. "One day you won't be able to squeeze under the door."

The mouse looked up at the sound of her voice but was otherwise unmoved. When Anna had first arrived at Far View there'd been no mice. With the largesse left on countertops and on dirty dishes by her room-mates, the little creatures had come to stay. This one was so plump Anna was put in mind of an ink drawing in her childhood copy of *Charlotte's Web*; a very round Templeton the rat lying on his back at the country fair saying: "What a gorge!"

Early on Jennifer and Jamie had set out d-CON. Dying mice had stag-gered out with such regularity the living room began to resemble the stage after the final act of *Hamlet*. Disgusted, Anna'd thrown the poison out. "Not cricket," she told her housemates. "You can feed them or kill them. Not both."

Since then they'd all come to terms with one another and the dorm no longer had pests but, as Jennifer had dubbed them, politically correct pets.

Anna's wristwatch beeped. The mouse squeaked on the same frequency and ran behind the refrigerator. Three A.M. on the nose.

Yet, pet ownership runs contrary to a sleuth's life. Pets must be fed daily, dogs walked, horses ridden. These needs don't go away just because our sleuth is on a hot case or, worse, must travel. Marcia Muller's Sharon McCone too often finds that her cat Watney has not been fed as promised. And pets cost money. In Jody Jaffe's *Horse of a Different Color*, Natalie Gold admits that she can only afford a $200/month apartment because board for her horse is $350/month.

You'll want to check out the recipes for Jody Jaffe's grandmother's kugel, Betty Trenka's bean soup with dropped noodles, and Charlie Plato's killer turkey sandwich in Jo Grossman and Robert Weibezahl's *A Taste of*

Murder (Dell, 1999) where other sleuths will fill you in on bluefish pate, spinach soup, green chile stew, crispy hacked duck, seafood gumbo, and much much more.

CHAPTER 15
PARTNERS R US

Homicide detective Skip Langdon's partner was Jim Hodges. She's young, he's middle-aged. She's white, he's black. He's from one part of New Orleans, she's from another. But still, "working with him was like having a twin, a part of yourself that knew what you needed before you did. She hoped she was as good a partner as he." (Julie Smith's *House of Blues*)

Patricia Cornwell has created one of the most engaging partnerships in sleuth fiction, that between Virginia State Medical Examiner Kay Scarpetta and Richmond Police Captain Pete Marino. Even though they're outrageously different, together they make a good cop. She's compulsively neat, he's a slob. She's into control, he's into effrontery. She pampers her digestion. He drowns in Wild Turkey. But when one is down, the other's up. When one is blinded to the truth, the other acquires a kind of laser vision to compensate.

Some of their best conversations take place over food and drink. In *Black Notice* (G. P. Putnam's Sons, 1999) Kay is preparing pizza for the grill. She fetches garlic and yeast from the refrigerator, locates crushed tomatoes and high-gluten flour. She offers Pete some peanuts to nibble on, but he's thinking about going on a diet. About as far as he ever gets to actually going on one, she reminds him. Their tastes booze-wise clash, but then so do their histories, motives, personalities, prejudices. In an early scene from *Cruel & Unusual* (Avon Books, 1994), Kay, who's had her share of performing autopsies on people executed in the electric chair, wonders why Marino was so eager to attend the execution of a man he'd sent away ten years ago for the killing of a young woman. It's the middle of the night; they're drinking in Kay's kitchen after the autopsy. Kay is out of Marino's bourbon, so he has to make do with Scotch. He asks her to cut the flavor with lemon and soda water, which in her view will be its ruination. As he so often does, Marino hides behind small talk to avoid answering the big questions. Kay persists, and learns that Marino blames the man for the suicide of his partner. This was get-even time.

In *All That Remains* (Avon Books, 1993), Kay and Marino team up to interview a witness, but they must fly, which neither enjoys. She brings breakfast coffee and cream cheese bagels, comfort food to take their minds off the fact that there's very little between the thin skin of the commuter prop plane and what's outside. They fly into turbulence, in and out of fog above the mountain tops. Twice the plane dips precipitously, rearranging all that good food up and down the digestive track. Sometimes motherly instincts are better off left alone.

San Francisco PI Sharon McCone has discovered the body of client Jake Kaufmann, blunt trauma to the head. He'd asked her to meet him at one of the Victorian houses he was renovating. She calls friend Greg Marcus, head of homicide, to report the murder, then her boss Hank Zahn, head of All Souls Legal Cooperative. Greg wants a statement, and sends her to a local restaurant to wait for his escort. Hank goes along. In talking with the chef, they learn just how unwelcome the trendy renovations are. (From Marcia Muller's *The Cheshire Cat's Eye*. PB. NY: Warner Books, Mysterious Press. 1990.)

The sign in the window of Johnny's Kansas City Barbecue said OPEN, but there were no customers at the oilcloth-covered tables. When Hank and I entered, a big black man with grizzled hair emerged from a swinging door at the rear, wiping his hands on his stained chef's apron.

"We're not serving anymore," he said, "but the bar's still open."

Hank looked questioningly at me. I nodded. A drink sounded like a good idea....

..."You folks ain't been in before."

"First time," I replied.

"Thought so. I got a good memory for faces. 'Course I don't get too many white faces here."

I looked at him to see if it might be a warning, but his dusky features were bland....

"You the owner?" I asked.

"Yeah, Johnny Hart's the name."

"...Have you been in this location a long time?"

"Ten years this coming October...."

"Tell me something: that block of empty Victorians on the hill above Steiner Street, are they being restored?"

"That's what I heard."

"Who owns the big house on the corner? The one with the tower."

"Same people as own all the others. Wintringham and Associates, they're called."

"What do they do, buy up old wrecks and restore them?"

"Yeah. They'll spiff them up and make a killing selling them to middle-class whites...."

I sipped my drink. "Can they get much for the houses, even fixed up, in this neighborhood?"

"Sure can. You should see what's buying in here: fairies like Wintringham, young families, rich white lawyers." Hart's voice dripped scorn.

A partnership can be created on the spot. Thirty-something Nantucket police detective Merry Folger was looking into the death of a middle-aged woman killed eight years ago. However, shortly after the woman's bones were found, a serial killer appears to have struck down his sixth young victim, also in Nantucket. This means Merry's case is sidelined and mobs of state police and FBI are running about. Special agent Dana Stevens is in charge of the serial killer case and Merry has found herself playing chauffeur to the bigwigs. She's pissed and that's why she withholds information that might link the long-ago death with the fresh one. Dana confronts Merry on her doorstep. (From Francine Mathews's *Death in a Mood Indigo*. PB. NY: Bantam Books. 1998.)

"Dana—"

"Can we have this conversation somewhere else? Like inside?"…"I brought us take-out Chinese. From Chin's. I hear it's the best."…

"I'm sorry," Merry said.

"About the extra trip?" Dana asked casually as they mounted the steps. "Or about lying through your teeth? Wait—I didn't mean that. What I should have said was 'withholding information.'"…

"Where do you want the food?" Dana asked. "Here on the counter?"

"You don't have to stay." Merry dropped her purse onto the floor and slumped into a chair.…

"What are you trying to do?" Dana was pulling white cardboard containers of Chinese food from the brown bag. "One-up the Bureau? Or the state guys? Or just me?"…

…"It's happened before, believe me. Half my time in every investigation is spent soothing the feelings of the local force.…"

"And do you always build bridges with Chinese food?"

Dana's eyes were tinged with amusement. "Call it the feminist management style of the nineties. A guy would have hauled your ass before the assembled ranks.…"

Dana pulled up a stool to the kitchen counter and kicked off her shoes.…

"…Want some sesame chicken?"

"In a minute. Thanks."

"So why was it so necessary to buy yourself time?"

Merry picked up an egg roll for something to do. It was already cooling and greasy. She dropped it back onto the plate....

Merry started and slid off her seat. "There's wine...."

"Water's fine."

"So what are you planning to do? Have me fired?"

..."That would hardly be in keeping with feminist nineties management, now, would it?..." She patted her lips delicately. "No, Merry, I've got a better idea. I'm putting you on the case."

Carlotta Carlyle, PI, and lieutenant Joseph Mooney, Boston Police, are midway through a case of illegal aliens, the INS, a serial killer, and the disappearance of Carlotta's "little sister," Paolina. It's just as well their conversation sticks to business, otherwise they would end up asking each other who they're dating, hoping the answer is "nobody." (From Linda Barnes's *Coyote*. PB. NY: Dell Publishing. 1991.)

We wholeheartedly agreed to eat at Mary Chung's in Central Square, each of us pretending the other had pulled a fast one and picked the restaurant. I can go without a hit of Mary's Suan La Chow Show for a week before I start getting withdrawal symptoms. It's a bowlful of plump wontons resting on beansprouts in a hot, spicy sauce that will cure whatever ails you. Sometimes I order two bowls. If the government declared it a restricted Class-A substance, I'd go outlaw....

Mooney does not eat Suan La Chow Show. It's too spicy for him. He ordered spring rolls. I've tried to educate him, but there it is.

We compromised on the rest of the order because I like everything spicy and Mooney likes everything bland—except he wouldn't call it bland, and he'd describe my taste as fiery. Lemon chicken, mostly for him; and hot stuffed eggplant, batter-fried and hot-pepper-sauced, mostly for me....

"Just how much are you cooperating with Immigration on this investigation?" I asked....

"A hundred and ten percent," Mooney answered disgustedly. "Word came down from on high...."

The appetizers arrived, and we dug in like starving orphans....

Mooney said, "Jamieson is the fastest paper-pusher I've ever met. He's filed so many goddamn interagency request forms, I could use a full-time liaison just to keep up with him. I don't have time for that crap...."

He stopped, shook his head like a wet dog, forked a bit of spring roll, and...said, "And how are you?"

Cincinnati homicide detective Sonora Blair and her sidekick Sam Delarosa are after a dangerous sociopath who has wiped out a family in debt. Sonora lost her brother Stuart to an equally dangerous sociopath. Here we find Sonora and Sam in the aftermath of a visit to McDonald's. (From Lynn Hightower's *The Debt Collector*. PB. NY: Delacorte Press. 2000.)

"Sam, something's bugging me."

"Something's bugging me too, Sonora, which is what did you do with that cherry pie thing?"

"I'm saving it."

"For what?"

"Sam, you know my brother loved those things."

"I know Stuart is dead and he can't eat it. I know you owe it to me."...

"Give me the damn pie."

"I told you I'm saving it. I'm stopping by the cemetery on the way home. I haven't been in a while...."

"...Listen, I'll make you a deal."

"What?"

"Split it. Half for me, half for Stuart. It's not like he'll care, since he's dead. It's the thought that counts, right? Like flowers, except you take weird stuff. Is it that you can't afford the flowers?"

"No, Sam, it's that I want to take him stuff that he liked."

"Very Buddhist of you."

"Okay, we split the pie, but we have to stop by the cemetery now, on our way back to the office."

"It's a deal only if you promise to be quick, Sonora. Zip in, zip out—no big tears and shit."...

*   *   *

The black iron gates were wide open in welcome. Sam turned right....In one hand he held a little more than half of a fried cherry pie. Syrupy red filling oozed over his fingers.

"I still don't know why you couldn't give me the little cardboard holder."

"I'm not going to just leave the pie out there naked on the stupid headstone."...

Sonora checked the row of McDonald's...three cardboard boxes side by side. The rolls were gone. They always were. Squirrels? The homeless? She set the portion of pie next to the boxes, adding the leftover French fries that had been in the bottom of the bag.

Jill Smith, Berkeley beat cop, has been careful, thus far, to keep her relationship with her partner, Seth Howard, "just friends." She doesn't want to get involved with men at the moment. So why can't ex-husband Nat leave her alone? Why come asking, "as a favor," if Jill would find a disappeared co-worker? However, the following meeting is to work on Seth's biggest problem. Someone keeps vandalizing his patrol car to the point where the lieutenant threatens to take it away. (From Susan Dunlap's *As A Favor*. PB. NY: Dell Publishing. 1991.)

I finished my burger. "Did the lieutenant say anything else?" Howard's burger lay barely touched.

"Oh, yeah. He said, one more day. Then, no thief, no car. And definitely no hope of making detective."

I put my hand on his arm…."We'll get your thief. Come on, have a little confidence in us. And in the meantime, eat some of that mound of food you ordered…."

Now Howard asked, "What did you ever see in Nat? Take your time. I've still got salad and dessert to eat…."

"…He was going to be a professor, which to a college senior like me was virtually next to God. He knew exactly what he wanted and it sounded fine to me."

Howard started in on his salad.

It was the job that had changed me, that and growing four years older. We'd moved to Berkeley when Nat started graduate school and I'd taken the Patrol Officer's test hoping for a job to support us during that time. Our stay in Berkeley was to be temporary, a necessary period until Nat graduated and our real life began.

But I had come to love Berkeley….

"You can eat and talk," I said. "Tell me about your plan."

"Okay." He chewed the remains of the salad and shifted a slice of cherry pie in front of him….

…"I'll cruise down Telegraph twice…and leave the car just long enough for him to salivate. Then I'll snatch it [the car] away….By the time I get to College Avenue his tongue will be hanging out and I'll grab it [the tongue]…."

Los Santos, Texas detective Elena Jarvis has been given help in her murder investigation in the person of handsome, young detective Jaime Sandoval. The setting is the campus of Herbert Hobart University where student Graham Fullerton was the campus Casanova until someone got into his medicine cabinet. Graham Fullerton was HIV-positive and not telling his dates a thing about it. Early in the case Elena and Jaime do lunch in typical cop fashion. (From Nancy Herndon's *Casanova Crimes*. PB. NY: Berkley Publishing Group, Berkley Prime Crime. 1999.)

"You like McDonald's?" Elena watched his face light with enthusiasm....

"...Mom used to send me to school with tamales and rice. I never have got over thinking a Big Mac's an exotic treat."...

*   *   *

She paid for her cheeseburger, Coke, and fries, carried the tray to a window table, and sat down to look at her notes....Grimacing at the uselessness of her calculations, she took a bite of her burger.

"That bad?" asked Sandoval ....

"The case, not the food," she replied and dipped a French fry in ketchup. "What did the pharmacist tell you?"

Before answering, Sandoval had spread his lunch—two Big Macs, a large order of fries, and a Sprite—out in front of him and admired it with a happy smile....

"...This guy was really upset at the idea that his AZT supplies might be poisoned. 'How am I supposed to tell?' he asks me. 'If my customers start dying, I'll be open to law suits.'"...

...Sandoval started on his second Big Mac. "This is really a depressing case. I hate to start interviewing co-eds."...

"...I got four sisters, real sweethearts, all of them, and I guess I'd want to kill anyone gave them AIDS. Not that they're out screwing around or anything, but still—"

"So you think you'd pull apart some capsules and stuff them with cyanide?"...

"Nah. I'd probably just shoot the son of a bitch." Then he looked embarrassed. "Sorry about the language."

She grinned. "Hey, you're SWAT. You're supposed to be macho and foul-mouthed."

Sandoval looked shocked. "I am not. That's a real great bunch of guys. In fact, we've got a girl now too."

"Really? Girl? She's what—twelve, ten?"

Two young Native American men have been killed in Billings, Montana, one left hanging in PI Phoebe Siegel's backyard. It's the evening of the next day and Deputy Sheriff Kyle Old Wolf has come round to commiserate. (From Sandra W. Prowell's *The Killing of Monday Brown*. PB. NY: Bantam Books. 1996.)

…The glass of lemonade, the wicker chair I settled into, and the summer evening became a meditation. I hadn't felt brave enough to go into the backyard yet. It would be a while before I could envision the cottonwood tree without the swinging body, so I purposefully positioned myself on the porch on the opposite side of the house.…

"Tell me this visit is friendly. I'm on overload," I said and frowned. "Lemonade? Oh, thanks for getting my truck back here."

"No problem. Beer?"

"Lemonade."

"Why not?"…

I pulled the pitcher from the fridge, grabbed a glass, and filled it to the brim. "Let's take this outside; this place gets a little hot this time of day."…

"Tough day?"

He turned toward me, his expression intense but curious. "What?"

"Tough day?" I repeated.

He stared at me, through me, a storm played out in his eyes. It was his turn.

"Tough day?" he asked. "You're asking me if this has been a tough day?"

"We're getting redundant here."

He lasted less than a minute. A cynical smile broke out on his face. "Do you believe this shit?"

"Could you be more specific?"

Kyle took a long, deep drink. No sooner had the glass touched his lips than a great spray of liquid flew from his mouth as he lurched forward and stood.

"What the hell is this?" he asked as he brushed off the front of his shirt.

"Lemonade," I said defensively.

"Last year's?" He set the glass on the rail of the porch. "What do you make this shit out of?"

"I buy those little yellow plastic lemons and add a little water. No one's complained so far."

You can write to Sandra Prowell at *scribe@wtp.net*.

Cops, as a matter of course, usually have a working partner, but where do PIs and amateurs go for help? Where better than to Officer Friendly? Take Helma Zukas, perhaps the most serious and cerebral of amateurs. One of her partners is Bellehaven's police chief Wayne Gallant. Here, in an attempt to help her best friend and other "partner," Ruth Winthrop, currently a murder suspect, Helma has invited the chief for lunch. (From Jo Dereske's *Miss Zukas and the Stroke of Death*. PB. NY: Avon Books. 1995.)

The interior of Sam and Ella's was determinedly Italian: red and white and green, accented by artificial vines, bunches of grapes, and squat wine bottles....

...At the far end of the restaurant the chief was already seated beside a window too shaded by the awning to see the street—or to be seen....

They paused while the waiter set salads in front of them. "Excuse me, sir," the waiter apologized after clumsily tipping the chief's plate so a cherry tomato rolled onto the table. The waiter caught the tomato at the end of the table. "I'll bring you a fresh one."

"No need," Chief Gallant told him.

When the waiter was gone, Helma said, "You seem to make our waiter nervous...."

"There's enough circumstantial evidence for us to be interested in Miss Winthrop," he said.

"Such as?" she asked.

"Haven't we been through this type of conversation before, Helma? You know police information is confidential."

"What about the murder weapon?" Helma asked as she cut her tomato into four equal quarters. "You didn't find anything in Ruth's house...."

Yet another waiter delivered their entrees: a turkey and havarti sandwich for Helma and a dish called "meatball mania" for Chief Gallant. Helma checked her sandwich to be sure there wasn't any mustard on it....

"Did he [the bartender] tell you about Lotz's friend Stereo?" Helma asked, carefully watching Chief Gallant's face.

"You mean Radio..." The chief stopped, a forkful of pasta and meatballs halfway to his mouth. "I believe you just tricked a piece of information from me, Helma Zukas."

This time Helma's asked the chief if his dinner invitation is to discuss business, i.e., death, vandalism, and arson. No, he just wanted to enjoy an evening together, which pleased Helma no end. Until Gallant began talking about his recent divorce. (From a chapter titled "Dinner Talk" in Jo Dereske's *Miss Zukas and the Raven's Dance*. PB. NY: Avon Books. 1996.)

"How does seafood sound tonight?" Chief Gallant asked....

"Delicious," Helma said....There was an element to seafood that reminded her of sunshine and cloudless skies, the clean uncomplicated succulence of the pale tender meat.

They drove to a restaurant at the tip of a long spit....She blushed and glanced away from the now bare and sandy carnival site, remembering the Tilt-a-Whirl ride she'd shared....

"When's the last time you saw a sunset?" Wayne Gallant asked.

Helma laughed. "My head says it was only a month ago but my heart thinks it's been years."

The restaurant was circular, with tall windows that on fair days overlooked the marina with a long view of the bay and the islands beyond.

But now it was dark outside and in the window beside their table, all that could be seen were their own smoky images....

"I value your friendship more than I can tell you, Helma," he said, leaning toward her across the table, his eyes now intent on her face.

She unclasped her hands; the bite of her nails into her palm was growing painful. "And you'd like us to remain friends," she said, "with no mistake about our friendship developing any further."

He pulled back, visibly uncomfortable again. "That's not what I mean at all. It's just too soon. My life…"

"I know exactly what you mean," Helma said, feeling the slow, somber beat of her heart. "I understand completely." A gust of wind dashed rain against the window and the water ran down the glass like tears.

We forget how big the portions served by Indian restaurants. We say, oh, let's get one lamb, one chicken, one prawn, and we'll share. Of course, rice. Of course, naan, and we got to have papadums. Then it arrives and we think, oh, jeez, why can't we ever remember?

Anneke Haagen is a computer consultant engaged to lieutenant Karl Genesko of the Ann Arbor PD. They are working on the murder of dismissed researcher Gerald Swann in a dorm at the University of Michigan. It's been a hard day, and when a sleuth needs to load up, sometimes she also forgets when to stop. So the meal ends when Karl's beeper calls him away, with Anneke trailing. (From Susan Holtzer's *Black Diamond*. PB. NY: St. Martin's Paperbacks. 1998.)

"We probably shouldn't have ordered the samosas." Anneke looked dubiously at the heaping platters of chicken tikka masala, lamb vindaloo, and biryani rice, flotillas of food surrounded by outriders of naan, papadum, and raita.

"What we don't eat, we'll take home and have tomorrow night." Karl spooned rice and chicken onto his plate.

"True." Anneke tore off a chunk of naan and dipped it into the masala on her plate. "I'm glad you got through in time for dinner," she said around mouthfuls of the chewy bread....

"I didn't think I was going to make it," he said. "The Missaukee County sheriff didn't return my call until nearly six o'clock."...

"What was he [Gerald] doing up there?" Anneke reached for the lamb vindaloo.

"The sheriff wasn't really sure what he did when he was in town. Are you all right?" he broke off.

"Barely," she choked, grabbing for water. "My God, does this stuff come with a fire extinguisher?" She gulped water for several seconds. "Thanks for the sympathy," she said, grinning in response to Karl's laughter.

"That's authentic vindaloo." He helped himself to a serving. "You wouldn't want them to water it down for midwest sensibilities, would you?"

"Damn right I would."...

...Karl made a face "...But no one admits to having any idea what he was researching....One of them said he was, and I quote, 'such a fruit loop that he could have discovered the Cosmic Egg and no one would have believed him.'"...

        *   *   *

..."You can come along—it shouldn't take much time. Assuming you're finished eating?"

"God, yes." She looked at the nearly empty platters with mild dismay. "There isn't even enough left to take home."

When Seattle-based amateur PI Jane da Silva begins to investigate the disappearance of a reclusive news clipping employee, it turns out the employee was blackmailing an untold number of people. No one knew who she was until she exposed herself on national TV as a *Jeopardy!* contestant. Jane is tracking down the victims, much to their dismay. She's in Eastern Washington, staying the night at Coulee Dam, where one of the victims goes so far as to hire a tough to follow and threaten her.

She calls Bob, a 300-pound Samoan who charges $50 an hour for protection. When he flies in from Seattle to meet with Jane, we learn his dietary secret. (From K. K. Beck's *Electric City*. PB. NY: Warner Books, Mysterious Press. 1995.)

...."I want him to be scared."

"No problem," said Bob. He was rummaging around a little in his satchel....

"And I want him to tell me who hired him to scare me," Jane continued....

"Okay." Bob looked thoughtful and produced a can of Spam and a loaf of bread from the satchel. "You can ask the question. But if you think he might lie, the thing is to go slow. Make him real eager to tell you. Like you don't care if he gets hurt instead of telling you." Bob was now wielding a can opener. "They never have the kind of food I like in places like this," he said.

Jane watched as he made himself a sandwich. Pacific Island people were notoriously crazy about Spam. Maybe it went back to prerefrigeration days when boats brought this stuff to them and weaned them off taro root...."Want some?" he asked.

"No thanks," she said....

"Anyway," said Bob eating contentedly, "I figure we can muscle him down to that creek bed. As good a place as any."…

Just then, a huge voice boomed through the window.

Bob killed the lights, went over to the window and pulled back the curtains.

"Wow," he said. "Take a look at that."…

The spillway, which had been bone-dry earlier, was now gushing a wall of white water….

"I am the Columbia," intoned a godlike voice, as images projected on the rushing white water depicting stylized waves and fish and animals of monumental proportions….It was the sort of thing, reflected Jane, that they would only think of doing here in America….

"That should keep everyone in town busy," said Bob. "Let's go."

"No marks," said Jane.

"No marks," he agreed.

Kate Banning's given up Boston and work as an investigative reporter for a publications job in Tennessee that's boring but pays. Luckily she didn't have to give up her partner in crime detection, Sam Powers, a pilot of corporate jets who flies in and out of her life often enough to help her think through her latest case. The victim is country western singing sensation Brandi Burns. Was it an accident, or did someone cut her car's steering fluid line? And what's so special about her music notebook that someone wants to torch it? (From Cecelia Tishy's *Jealous Heart*. PB. NY: Penguin Group, Signet. 1999.)

The mussels came in a net bag at Kroger. Three pounds. To which add garlic, linguine, virgin olive oil, the last real tomatoes of the season. Kate slit the net. Beard the mussels, as every recipe began….

"Sam!"

"Got a ride in. Guy at the maintenance hangar—"

"Don't explain just—get in here."…

…She…pulled out a plastic grocery bag. Sam pulled out a chair to sit down….She must not be lulled into normality, even if Sam exorcised the menace from her world…."Exhibit A, the notebook."

…"Been in a fire?"

…"Open it."…Kate went to the refrigerator, opened a bottle of Amstel, put it in front of him. She poured herself a cranberry juice and soda and stood sideways at the sink to resume the mussels and tell him about the fire…

"And all these numbers."

"They're chords. That is, they correspond to notes. It's a local Nashville notation system for musicians who don't read music."…

"The boyfriend?"

"Wade Rucker. Prime candidate…."

"…What I mean is, if Wade killed Brandi, he seems like the type to personally strike the fatal blow…."

She reached into the sink. Another six mussels….

He paused to drink. This was the junction of their mutual worry—of her flights of crime, of his flights at thirty thousand feet…."I'm thinking the obvious—an empty steering fluid reservoir is not a car bomb. Now, if Brandi had a steering failure—"

A great delight found in a typical female sleuth series is yet another great partnership. Crime investigation is still male-dominated so most of the partners are men.

No matter how different partners are, no matter the flaws each brings to the relationship, it works because of mutual trust and respect. It has to work. Their lives depend upon it.

Maybe half of partners are lovers as well. Sex isn't essential to team success and probably is not a great idea in any event—with the little head thinking for the big head?

CHAPTER 16
KIDS R NOT SOME OF US

A big difference between pros and amateurs is kids. Amateurs have them, pros tend not to. Kids are probably the worst kind of dependent in terms of responsibility, and pros don't want dependents of any kind. In contrast, in Susan Rogers Cooper's suburban Texas mom E. J. Pugh series, you can't keep track of the kids, let alone the hours E. J. spends on the road driving them to daycare and school, soccer practice, park, pool, mall, movies, and their grandmother's. *A Crooked Little House* (1999) is a prime example. There we meet Brenna, Bessie, Megan, Graham, Garth, Trent, Puddin, Bert, Ernie, and Axl Rose. Admittedly, the last four are three cats and a dog, but still, they must be fed, as must the kids even if it's only juice, canned soup, bologna and white bread sandwiches. Kids also mean putting up with an ever expanding house to accommodate their numbers, and here we could identify. At the same time as we read about E. J.'s house remodel, ours was going on as well. The same thump, crash, screech, boom, tinkle, rip and tear. The same disappearing work persons. And in the end, a ball on the floor tends to roll off to a far corner.

In contrast, the only family PI Carlotta Carlyle has is a "little sister," Paolina, for whom in her Big Sister role she actually cooks. In *A Trouble of Fools* we find Carlotta in white painter's pants streaked with egg yolk because she doesn't own an apron. She's messing about in the kitchen making chocolate chip meringue thingies colored loden green and bright pink because that's how Paolina's fifth grade likes them. A rare event, Carlotta shoving cookies into the oven.

Here we'll trace the impact of kids on sleuths' lives from childhood through young adulthood. It generally gets better, maybe not for E. J. Pugh or Carlotta Carlyle, but for most folks.

Child abuse. In sleuths' lives this usually means being abused by your own kids or your own mom. As a break from forensic psychologist Portia McTeague's current murder investigation, PI Alan Simpson, Portia's lover, thinks he'll kill two birds with one stone. (1) Dinner out. (2) Dinner out at Charlotte's newest McDonald's—to try to worm his way into the heart of Portia's adopted 7-year-old daughter, Alice. (From Faye Sultan's and Teresa Kennedy's *Help Line*. HB. NY: Doubleday. 1999.)

The excursion that evening had been Alan's idea, his latest attempt to woo Alice's affections. Now he stood with his muscled arms akimbo, that bright fake smile still plastered across his features, begging the recalcitrant little girl to come out from the farthest reaches of a red plastic tunnel.

"C'mon out, honey," he coaxed. "Your McNuggets are getting cold."

"I'm not hungry," Alice said belligerently. "And stop bothering me!"

Portia ducked her head to hide a smile....

"Leave her alone and come and eat something," she instructed him, not unkindly. "She'll come out when she's ready."

He slid into the booth beside her. "I just thought it would be nice," he said...."I thought she'd enjoy herself."

"She is enjoying herself, Alan. In her own way."

He turned to her, startled. "But her Happy Meal is getting all cold."

This time, Portia couldn't hide her grin...."She loves cold food," she said. "Believe me, to her, cold french fries taste just as good as hot ones."

Alan sighed and began to tear the box away from a double cheese-burger. "She hates me," he said miserably....

       *   *   *

Alice sidled up and slid underneath Portia's elbow as they watched Alan's broad shoulders disappear through the doors and into the street.

"Mom?" she inquired.

"What?"

"Did you guys have a fight?"

Portia glanced down at her...."Not a fight, really," she answered. "A discussion."

Alice skipped ahead and held the door open as Portia passed through. "It was a fight," she said confidently....

Against her better judgment NYC PI Blaine Stewart has taken on a missing persons case, the Marsden case. She is partners with her sister Eileen in a firm that handles white-collar crime. The missing person is a surrogate mother-to-be who has decided to keep the baby. Blaine, Eileen, and Sandy, Eileen's 5-year-old daughter, are together at a typical Upper East Side Chinese restaurant because the kid's latest food kick is Chinese. (From Sharon Zukowski's *Leap of Faith*. PB. NY: Penguin Group, Signet. 1995.)

The kid rolled pancakes around pieces of beef. She didn't pay attention to the dull conversation going on around her. I poked around in the pile of vegetables on the platter in the center of the table and speared a shrimp that was hiding under a snow pea. Before popping it into my mouth, I casually asked, "What are you going to do?"...

Sandy's fragile grip on her moo shu beef faltered. The mess dropped into her plate with a soggy plop. She impatiently jerked on Eileen's arm for help and ended our conversation. As Eileen made a child-sized bundle out of the pancake and meat, she cautiously said, "There's something else I want to talk to you about. People who go to fertility clinics are usually pretty desperate...."

"Sandy never would have been born if we didn't go to a clinic."

My sister and I had been working side by side for the past ten years. Forty, fifty, sixty hours a week. I thought I knew everything about her. I was wrong....

...I leaned forward for a closer look at Eileen's eyes. "Does the Marsden case make you feel uncomfortable? Would you like me to find a graceful way to withdraw from it?"...

..."Graceful? You? Don't worry, Blaine, we used a different clinic. There's no conflict of interest here."

I wanted to ask about emotional conflicts of interest, but never got the chance. Sandy decided it was time to go....

...Before Eileen climbed inside [the cab], she stopped, put her hand on my arm, and issued her standard warning.

"Blaine, be careful tomorrow."

What's happened is that an orphaned niece and nephew have upset the lives of Jimmy Dee Scoggin and his tenant, homicide detective Skip Langdon. The kids must be clothed, schooled, looked after, and fed nothing but healthy, homecooked. Not surprisingly, Sheila, the 13-year-old niece, has run away and here she is found by Skip and a friend, Darryl. How to get her to come back? Certainly not with healthy, homecooked. (From Julie Smith's *New Orleans Beat*. PB. NY: Ballantine Books, an Ivy Book. 1995.)

Skip knelt. "This is my friend Darryl."

"Hi, Sheila." He held out a hand to shake. She stared at him for what seemed like a long time, and finally shook.

"At least let's go get something to eat.'"

"I'm not hungry."

"Well, I am," said Darryl. "I'm having a major Big Mac attack. You don't want fries or anything?"

Sheila's eyes got round. "We could go to McDonald's?"

"Sure. Or maybe we could get pizza. You want some pizza?"

She shook her head. "McDonald's."...

When they had reached the house, she...gave Jimmy Dee a call. "She's fine; we've got her. She can stay with me tonight, okay? And no school tomorrow, I think."

She hung up, feeling beat. "Does everybody really want to go out? What about some sandwiches here?"

Sheila teared up. "You mean we can't go?"

Darryl said, "I want to go."

"I'm outnumbered." Trying hard to smile, she picked up her car keys. "Wait. What if they're not open?"

She made a couple of phone calls—and got no answers. But the look in Sheila's eyes said she'd better come up with something.

"I know," said Darryl. "The Clover Grill's open all night."

"Have they got fries?"

He nodded soberly. "And shakes."

Sheila meant business. She got a burger, chocolate shake, and fries. Not to be outdone, Darryl did too, Skip made do with a Diet Coke and bites of theirs.

As soon as Sheila's mouth was full, which assured Skip the floor, she said. "I'm getting the idea you aren't happy with Jimmy Dee and me."

"I'm afraid of Uncle Jimmy."

Anna Peters, Washington, D.C., PI skilled in corporate blackmail, and her artist husband have arrived in Branch Hill, Connecticut, for an exhibit of his paintings. They are houseguests of the Brownings where they meet two young women, the Browning's daughter Angela and her friend Lindsay. The girls leave for pizza. Lindsay's mother to Anna: "Lindsay'll be as fat as a pig. Angela, now, was born thin. Hardly fair....Singers can carry a bit of fat. But Lindsay's a gymnast. Bone thin or no hope." Lindsay is fourteen. That night she is brutally murdered on her walk home.

Anna interviews an Angela both afraid to talk and eat. (From Janice Law's *A Safe Place to Die*. PB. NY: Worldwide Mystery. 1995.)

"Have you had lunch?"

Angela shook her head. "I'm not very hungry."

She was thinner than ever and rather pale. "I thought that the singer had to feed the voice. I'll treat, if money's a problem."

"All right," she said, but she didn't look very happy. "Maybe some yogurt."

"I thought it was pasta for the voice."

"Then you want Luigi's." She pointed across the street to a tiny one-story restaurant with awnings and windowboxes filled with chrysanthemums. It turned out to be as pretty inside as out and twice as refined. "I don't suppose they have plain spaghetti and meatballs," I said.

"The pasta with seafood is very good."

"We'll have that, if you'd like."

"Yes, all right," she said. She moved her fingers nervously as if food were an occasion for upsets and tensions. "Do you know what Maria Callas said?" she asked after we had ordered.

I shook my head.

"She said "I lost my fat, then I lost my voice, then I lost Onassis.'"

"A lesson for you. Eat up."

Lucy Stone, mother of four, is trying to track down the killer of a Tinker's Cove, Maine, school teacher. Lucy's preoccupation with her kids slows her down, as on this day when the eighth grade visits a state university library to do research on their term papers. As Elizabeth's mother, Lucy has gone along as a parent volunteer in order to do some library sleuthing of her own. Lance is Elizabeth's boyfriend. (From Leslie Meier's

Back to School Murder. PB. NY: Kensington Publishing Corporation. 1998.)

Entering the crowded snack bar, she kept an eye peeled for Elizabeth, but didn't see her. Come to think of it, she hadn't seen her in the library either. She did see Elizabeth's buddies, Emily and Melissa, and made her way over to them.

"Do you know where Elizabeth is?" she shouted over the lunchtime din.

They exchanged a conspiratorial glance and shook their heads....

...She'd like to wring their necks. And if anything had happened to Elizabeth, that Lance would get a piece of her mind.

*   *   *

"Mom—what are you doing? You're going in the wrong direction!" Lucy looked up from the asphalt path, straight into Elizabeth's puzzled face.

"Are you okay?" she demanded.

"Sure, Mom. But we've got to get back or we'll miss the bus."

"I know that. Why do you think I was looking for you?"

"Calm down, Mrs. Stone. Everything's under control," volunteered Lance....

..."You gave me a terrible fright. Are you sure you're okay?"

"I'm sure," sighed Elizabeth. "But I'm not so sure about you. You look awfully pale. Have you eaten?"

"No—I was looking for you."

"Don't you think you're overreacting?" asked Elizabeth, reaching into her backpack and producing a packet of cheese and peanut butter crackers. "Here. Eat these. You'll feel better."

How did this happen, wondered Lucy....

She opened the packet of crackers and ate one as she walked along, a step or two behind the kids....Probably laughing at her expense, she thought with a flash of paranoia, then shrugged the idea away. When she was a teenager, her mother was the last person she thought about.

Fortunately, kids grow up and one of the ways writers let them show it is by their cooking for themselves, and if they're really good, cooking for weary female sleuths.

The sound of a doorbell wakens San Francisco homicide detective Kate Martinelli. It is Jules Cameron, precocious daughter of her partner's fiancé. Martinelli is exhausted and can barely be civil to the twelve-year-old. She leads Jules into the kitchen. (From Laurie R. King's *With Child*. PB. NY: Bantam Books. 1997.)

"...Look, Jules, are you just here for a friendly visit? Because if so, I'm not very good company."

"No. I need to talk to you. Professionally."...

"Okay, Jules, I'm not going to throw you out. Just give me ten minutes to jump-start the brain...."

A minute later, Jules heard the shower start....She found half a loaf of rock-hard French bread and some eggs in the refrigerator, a few strips of bacon in the freezer compartment, a bowl and a frying pan behind the low doors, then began with deliberate movement to assemble them into breakfast. She had to lean her entire weight against the Chinese cleaver to chop the bread into something resembling slices, and substitute frozen orange juice concentrate for the milk....She found a sugar bowl and added a large pinch to the beaten eggs.

Kate bounded down the stairs a few minutes later and burst into the kitchen.

"God, it smells like a Denny's in here. What have you been making?"

"There's a plate of French toast for you, if you want it, and some bacon. I couldn't find any syrup, but there's warm honey and jam and powdered sugar."

Kate swallowed five thick slices and more than her share of the bacon, stopping only because Jules ran out of bread. She ran the last corner of the eggy, buttery fried bread through the pool of liquified honey, put it into her mouth, and sighed.

"I take back the insult. It smells like heaven and tasted like paradise, and what do I have to do to pay you back for it?"

PI Kate Shugak has stolen off to Bering, Alaska, to work through a difficult time in her life. She meets up with an old school friend, Alice, who invites Kate home for a dinner of broiled salmon, boiled salmon eggs, and sticky rice. Kate is drawn to Alice's 10-year-old daughter Stephanie who retreats to her room decorated with *Challenger* and *Star Wars* posters and a ceiling dripping with model airplanes. She is reading *Beginning Physics*. Here we get some insight into why two precocious native Alaskans will never quite fit in. (From Dana Stabenow's *Midnight Come Again*. HB. NY: St Martin's Minotaur. 2000.)

She [Stephanie] set the table before dinner, she did the dishes and took out the garbage afterward, but she displayed no interest in Kate and very little in the conversation around the table. She ate her dinner with no real enjoyment, as if she was merely taking on fuel. She was waiting, Kate realized, waiting to be dismissed from the family circle so she could take up her own life again....

            *   *   *

Alice was pouring out after-dinner coffee in the kitchen. "That girl of yours is up there in her room studying beginning physics," Kate said. "It is July, isn't it? School has been out for two months, right?"...

…"I can't offer her too much encouragement, at least not where anyone can see, you know how it is with us."…

Alice put mugs on a tray. "You take milk? Good, so does everybody else." She poured a healthy dose of Carnation Evaporated Milk into the bottom of all the mugs. "It's a Yupik thing, I guess. She has to get good grades to get into college, but the way we do things won't help her."…

The coffeemaker burped its way to a finish and Alice poured out. "We don't act alone, independently of each other. We're a *tribe*. When we do something well, it doesn't reflect on us personally, it reflects on the tribe as a whole. We're not supposed to be singled out, to be set apart, to be praised for something we do on our own."

"To be individuals?"…

"She'll manage," Alice said. "To get what she wants, she'll have to."

But she would leave the village, Kate thought, and unlike her mother, she would very probably never come back.

It's the morning after the murder of Oliver, Indiana, Judge David Putnam during a rehearsal of *Ruddigore*. Joan Spencer, symphony violist, was at the scene. Boys may not do as elaborate meals as girls, but at least they do their own dishes. Andrew is Joan's teenage son. (From Sara H. Frommer's *Murder & Sullivan*. PB. Toronto: Worldwide Mystery. 1998.)

"I thought you'd never get up," he [Andrew] said when she yawned into the kitchen around ten in her robe and slippers. "David Putnam's all over the front page. I brewed a pot of coffee."

"Thanks." She dropped a couple of slices of whole-wheat bread into the toaster, poured herself a cup of coffee, and looked at the paper. It was true….The obituary must have been ready and waiting for whenever and however Judge Putnam died. She scanned it, inhaling the smell of the coffee while she waited for the toast….

She skipped the quotations from Mayor Deckard and other prominent Oliver politicians and laid the paper on the table in time to catch the toast before it hit the floor. Their toaster had a mind of its own.

"Pass the butter, Andrew." He did, and pushed the jam jar across the table. She buttered the toast while it was still hot. The jam could wait.

"Tell me all about it, Mom." He propped his chin on his hands and his elbows on the table, across from her....

"He had to stand still in a picture frame....He looked asleep, and he'd fallen asleep in rehearsal a couple of nights before...." Between bites, she drew the picture frames on the kitchen table with her finger and explained how David had been vulnerable to anyone behind him...

"The plot thickens." Andrew snitched a piece of her toast and slathered jam on it....

He stood up. "I'd better get busy."

She washed her plate and cup, glad to find Andrew's supper and breakfast dishes in the drainer, instead of waiting for her in the sink.

A serial killer is Joanna Brady's biggest challenge in her new career as sheriff of Cochise County, a job she was elected to after her husband Andy, previous sheriff, was slain. She's changing every day in ways that surprise her: "Without realizing it, she had turned into a real cop, into someone for whom a homicide investigation became paramount and took precedence over everything else."

But it takes her daughter's being away, visiting grandparents, to savor how she'll change when the daughter's gone for good. For the first time in memory Joanna is really alone, physically and emotionally unconnected for an extended period. It's dinner time, a time ripe for more self-revelation. (From J. A. Jance's *Rattlesnake Crossing*. PB. NY: Avon Books. 1998.)

The CD was new, a birthday gift....It was a never-before-released recording of a concert Patsy Cline had given shortly before the plane crash that had taken her life. Listening to Patsy sing from across all those years was like hearing from Andy as well. Patsy Cline was dead and yet, through the magic of her work, she lived on in much the same way Andy was still a part of High Lonesome Ranch and of Jenny's and Joanna's lives as well.

Joanna had been taken aback by her strong emotional reaction to the music....

With the music still swirling around her, Joanna opened the refrigerator door and stared at the contents, wondering what to fix for dinner. It came to her all at once. Closing the refrigerator door and opening the cupboard instead, she plucked out the box of Malt-o-Meal. She had always wondered what it would be like to have hot cereal for dinner.

That night, with no one there to criticize or complain—with no one to consider but herself—Joanna Brady found out. She cooked the cereal in the microwave, covered it with milk and brown sugar, and then ate it standing there by the counter....

For the first time, a fragile thought slipped across Joanna's consciousness...that maybe living alone wasn't all bad.

Walter Demming, school bus driver, and eleven children are being held hostage in a school bus buried beneath the floor of a barn. For forty-seven days their only food has been cereal and milk, with an occasional peanut butter sandwich. Walter shortly will be released and have one minute to deliver messages from the children to their families. Unless somehow the messages convey to the FBI where they are held, death will come soon. The children's memories of beloved foods is an awesome metaphor for the total deprivation they have suffered. (From Mary Willis Walker's *Under the Beetle's Cellar*. PB. NY: Bantam Books. 1996.)

"My mom doesn't cook," Heather said. "We take home from McDonald's or sometimes Chinese." When she spoke the word "Chinese," her face glowed, as though just saying the word had filled her mouth with juicy, succulent bliss. Walter's mouth watered in response, and for an instant he tasted and smelled the chicken in hot garlic sauce from China Sea....

"I love Chinese food." Sandra closed her book and abandoned all pretence of not listening. "Egg rolls, fried rice, sweet-and-sour pork. There's a place near us that delivers."

"My mom cooks really good," Hector said. "The best tamales. The *best*. Everybody says so...."

"My dad cooks," Josh said, "and I help him. We've got a couple of those vegetable peelers. We use them to peel potatoes when we're making mashed potatoes. But we leave a little skin on because my dad says it makes them more interesting. We put lots of butter and milk in them...."

"What I love even better than mashed potatoes," Josh said, "is fresh bread. My dad got this machine, a bread maker, for Christmas. So we make bread and we cut it while it's still hot even though you're not supposed to, and we put butter and sugar on it and it smells better than anything in the world."

A reverent and hungry silence followed.

Walter felt his stomach doing flips of desire....He looked around at the kids and thought if you could look into their heads and see what they were picturing, you would have some delectable illustrations for a cookbook.

"One sure thing," Sandra said softly, "I'm never, ever gonna eat cereal again."

"Me either," Conrad said.

Why are girls overrepresented in these sleuths' lives? Easier for the sleuth to identify with? Communicate with? Easier to understand than boys? Easier to get understanding from girls when it comes to the demands of the sleuth's job? Easier to integrate into a female sleuth's life from a female author's POV? A good example of a "mother-daughter" relationship is that between Patricia Cornwell's Kay Scarpetta and her niece Lucy. Kay relishes cooking and playing the surrogate mother to Lucy, in memory a bright, pesky child, but in the present in *Unnatural*

Exposure (G. P. Putnam's Sons, 1998) a computer whiz and technical specialist for the FBI's Hostage Rescue Team. Their work begins to overlap when Kay receives e-mail from someone with the user name of deadoc who sends her photos of a murder victim. Lucy's maturity is further demonstrated by greeting Kay with dinner—grilled fillets, baked potatoes, spinach sauteed in garlic and oil. They sit out in the cold on the deck sipping a bottle of good red wine, while Kay reflects on how their relationship has evolved into that of friends and partners in crime detection.

CHAPTER 17
I LOVE YOU, NOW TELL ME ABOUT IT

"'…I can't face how out of control things sometimes get.'" Maggie pushed the bread basket in front of her. "'C'mon, you've got to eat. I'll bet you've been starving yourself.'" (From Alex Matthews's *Satan's Silence.*)

In addition to her partner in crime, every sleuth needs significant others, friends and family who nourish her via food designed to console and sooth and sometimes celebrate. San Francisco's PI Sharon McCone depends on her neighborhood tavern, Ellen T's, to provide more than her usual comfort food, a glass of the house white. In *Ask the Cards a Question* since it's dinner time, she also orders a roast beef sandwich. Motherly Ellen and fatherly Stanley constantly try to get her to eat better, this time saying that the sandwich comes with a tossed salad, free of charge. Thank heaven, because the only thing in Sharon's apartment is a case of cat food for Watney, adopted due to the untimely demise of his owner.

Sara Paretsky has written about the conflicts that beset PI V.I. Warshawski, the need to be alone and the need for intimacy. These needs war with each other, particularly when V.I. is under pressure. Her well-meaning neighbor Mr. Contreras expresses constant concern for her health and sees food as the remedy, to be fixed by him, of course. Sometimes it translates into company when V.I. would most like to be alone. (From Sara Paretsky's *Blood Shot*. HB. NY: Dell Publishing. 1989.)

...Behind Mr. Contreras's door, Peppy gave a welcoming bark....

"That you, doll? You just getting back? Your friend's funeral was today, huh? You haven't been out drinking, have you?"...

"No," I said, forcing a smile, holding my hand out for the dog to lick....

"Well, you go on upstairs and take a hot bath, doll. By the time you've done that and had a chance to rest, I'll have some dinner ready. I have me a nice steak I've been saving for sometime special, and that's what you need when you're feeling this low...."

"Thanks," I said. "It's very good of you, but I really don't—"

"Nope. You think you want to be alone, but believe me, cookie, that's the worst thing for you when you're feeling like this. Her royal highness and I'll get you fed, and then if you're ready to be on your own again, you say the word and we'll be back down here on the double."

I just couldn't bring myself to bring the cloud of hurt to his faded brown eyes by insisting on being alone. Cursing myself for my soft heart, I trudged up the stairs to my apartment. Despite my neighbor's dire words, I headed straight for the Black Label bottle, kicking off my pumps and pulling off my panty hose while I unscrewed the cap....

...By the time Mr. Contreras showed up with the steak, I was a little drunk and much more relaxed than I'd have thought possible a half hour before.

...After a few bites I grudgingly admitted—only to myself—that he'd been right about the food: life did start to look better.

It's tough to pick a best food scene in anything by Elaine Viets. Francesca Vierling, writer for the fading *St. Louis City Gazette*, has her eggs and toast each morning at Uncle Bob's Pancake House which also serves up yummy gossip for her column. For lunch there's always the suspicious pale and gray stuff in the *Gazette* sandwich machine, and for dinner "Francesca's Top Five Food Delivery Phone Numbers." Here are two wonderful scenes from Miss Lucy's Lunchroom. Prior to the first, Francesca phoned Georgia, her features editor boss and best friend, complaining about the managing editor's demand that she write a feature on a murdered woman—at the same time shackling her with more time-wasting committee work. To her surprise Georgia quickly shushes her up. What's going on? (From Elaine Viets's *Rubout*. PB. NY: Dell Publishing. 1998.)

...This didn't sound like my funny, foul-mouthed mentor. Had she been taken over by the pod people? "Your blood sugar must be low," she said, much too sweetly. "I want you to have a relaxing cup of tea at Miss Lucy's Lunchroom. Promise me you'll be there in ten minutes."...

...I ordered oolong and cress sandwiches for two, because I'd read about them in English novels. The oolong tasted like ordinary tea and the cress sandwiches tasted like buttered grass.

"Your ass would have been grass if I hadn't shut you up," Georgia bellowed....The tearoom was empty, but the sweet pink lady pouring the oolong looked so shocked, she slopped tea into my saucer. She apologized and fluttered back to the kitchen to get me another cup....

"I couldn't talk to you because the fucking phones are bugged," she [Georgia] said....

"*Gazette* management specializes in divide and conquer," Georgia said. "If the staff is at one another's throats, they won't notice management is reaming their asses." The sweet pink lady had returned while Georgia was making that speech. She was so startled she oolonged on my wrist.

"I'm so sorry," the tea lady said, and pulled out an embroidered handkerchief to mop up the spots on my sleeve....

When the pink lady went back for another fresh cup for me, Georgia said, "Now, what's the problem?"

       *   *   *

…"Georgia, is there really no hope for the *Gazette?*…"

She looked at me with pity…."You know what our former mayor said about the *Gazette?*"…

"Hizzoner said 'That newspaper couldn't sell whores on a troop ship.'"

There was a resounding crash as the pink lady dropped my teacup on the floor.

The second Miss Lucy's scene sets the stage for a plot about medical murders. (From Elaine Viets's *Doc in the Box*. PB. NY: Dell Publishing. 2000.)

…Georgia and I stood out there like a couple of streetwalkers at a finishing school, and it didn't help that Georgia sounded like one.

I arrived first, sat at a dainty pink table, and felt like the Incredible Hulk. The pink ruffled waitress brought a pot of cinnamon orange tea and a plate of cookies that tasted like ceiling insulation dipped in powdered sugar….

When Georgia charged through the tearoom door…I wanted to pour her a stiff Scotch, her usual drink. Instead, she swallowed some tea, made a face, and said, "Might as well get used to this swill. I can't drink booze for eight months. I've got the Big C, Francesca."

"Cancer?" I was almost too frightened to say the word….

"How do you feel?" I said, sounding like a talk-show shrink.

"Like shit," she said, and the two women in Laura Ashley at the next table looked up like startled deer….

"Breast cancer," she said, in a voice loud enough to be heard over the roaring web presses, except it was perfectly, pinkly quiet in Miss Lucy's, so quiet I could hear one of the ladies at the next table pouring, and I knew both were eavesdropping. "Can you believe it? Tit cancer. Isn't that a joke? I finally get a lump on this flat chest of mine and they want to whack it off!"

I heard a teacup hit the floor and knew the ladies had been shocked to their Pappagallos. I called for the check, and drove Georgia home to her penthouse, stopping first for a bottle of Dewar's for medicinal purposes.

Newspaper types seem as eager to escape their workplace as police officers. Robin Light runs a pet shop in Syracuse, New York, and privately investigates in her spare time. Her best friend, newspaper reporter Calli Cornfeld, provides Robin with background articles on crime victims. George is Robin's lover, Murphy is Robin's deceased husband, and Calli is lately returned from California. (From Barbara Block's *Vanishing Act*. PB. NY: Kensington Publishing Corporation. 1999.)

Calli took a sip of her latte and pushed an envelope containing the articles I'd asked her to get…across the table with the tip of her finger. "What would you do if I were still in California?"

"Pay the fee."

Calli laughed. I suddenly realized how much I'd missed not talking to her. "You didn't have to bring them. I would have picked them up."

"I know. But this gave me an excuse to see you and have some coffee."

We were sitting in the café at Barnes & Noble.

Calli looked around. "I know we're not supposed to like the big chains, I know they're driving out the little bookstores, but it's still nice to have a place like this in Syracuse. It gives me the illusion of being au courant."

"Sorry you've come back?"

She ripped open another packet of sugar and poured it into her coffee. "Well, this isn't exactly the center of the universe. Especially if you're single."…

"Too true."…

"Of course, you have George. If I had somebody, maybe I wouldn't feel this way."

"I wouldn't be too sure." I told her what had happened earlier….

"The man is an asshole."

Calli took another sip of her latte and scraped the last crumbs of icing from her chocolate cake from the plate with her fork. "They all are, but at least yours is good in bed," she said, licking the fork.

"I'm not sure that's enough."

"You used to say it was with Murphy."

I finished off my cake. "I'm changing my mind. Talking would be nice too."

"You must be getting older."

"That's probably it."

Psychotherapist Cassidy McCabe has been working with Zach Moran, investigative reporter and lover. She's worried because he's been retreating from her life, calling less, cancelling out on Saturday nights, and now seemingly is gone forever. She's also worried about one of her more disturbed patients, who might be a ritual abuse survivor. What better way to figure things out than over a birthday dinner for her good friend Maggie. (From Alex Matthews's *Satan's Silence*. PB. Angel Fire, New Mexico: Intrigue Press. 1998.)

"Over a week now since the grand exit." Cassidy pushed pieces of lightly oiled romaine around a sleek white plate. *Chocolate, I want chocolate....*

"I've been eating okay. Two full bags of peanut butter cups in the past week." Cassidy dutifully took a chunk of French bread....

"Why so quiet?"

"I'm eating. You told me to eat so that's what I'm doing." Cassidy clinked her glass against Maggie's. "By the way, happy birthday, I'm in such a lousy mood, I almost forgot that's why we're here." She sipped her wine. "There's something else I wanted to ask. You ever had any experience with ritual abuse survivors?"

"Cult victims? One of the trendy types, like multiples and post traumatics? Nope, can't say that I have. Not sure I even believe it's for real."

"I've had a few doubts myself. Anyway, I've been researching Satanism this week—trying to get my mind off Zach. And it reads like a Stephen King novel. One woman claims she was used by the cult to breed babies for sacrifice."…

…"Why're you telling me this before dinner?"

"I can't seem to get it out of my head. You remember that subpersonalities method I told you about? I'm starting to think maybe everybody has an evil part…."

"I suggest you go back to Barbara D'Amato and Nancy Pickard and lay off that horror stuff."

The first time she had sex, at age sixteen, she celebrated with blueberry pie and vanilla ice cream. To this day, she claims, blueberry pie makes her blush. Now she's thirty and still the association of men and pie goes deep. She misses Crow. Sure, she kicked him out, but he didn't have to go. Now he's in Texas, but where? Baltimore PI Tess Monaghan consoles herself in the company of her favorite women friends who give her a fresh spin on men and food. Kitty is her aunt, Jackie, a former client, Laylah, Jackie's adopted daughter. (From Laura Lippman's *In Big Trouble*. PB. NY: Avon Books. 1999.)

…The girls stayed in, with Tess bringing pizza from Al Pacino's and Kitty relying on Chinese or Japanese carryout. Jackie was the experimental one, arriving with Styrofoam boxes from whatever Baltimore restaurant struck her fancy. Tonight it was Charleston's, which had meant cornbread, she-crab soup, oysters fried in cornmeal, a rare steak for fish-averse Tess, and pureed vegetables for Laylah. At least everyone could share the dessert, a pecan pie that Kitty was now slicing.

Tess watched the knife sinking into the sweet pie and suddenly thought of Crow. The connection was probably worth analyzing—was it the nuts that reminded her of Crow, or was she still on that pie-sex jag?…

"Who wants whipped cream on their pie?" Kitty asked….

"So what do you think?" Kitty asked Jackie as soon as Tess's mouth was full. "Is Tess really interested in Crow, and pretending not to be? Or do you think she's in love with him and being stubborn out of some misplaced pride?"

"I don't know if she was ever in love with him....But she's definitely not *finished* with him, you know what I mean? Sometimes a man is like, well, like this piece of pie when you're supposed to be on a diet. You stick your fork in it, you break it up, you move it around on your plate, you put all this work into *not* eating it. You're still obsessed with it."

"Really?" Kitty was so taken by this analogy that she stopped in mid-bite. "I've never felt that way about a man. Or a pie, for that matter."

"Well, Aunt Kitty, you've never left so much as a crumb behind."

Brookport, Mass Homicide Detective Lieutenant Starletta Duvall, Star to her friends, has gone shopping with her best friend, Vee, who's going to serve up traditional Black southern fare in a cold northern city. (From Judith Smith-Levin's *The Hoodoo Man*. PB. NY: Ballantine Publishing Group. 1998.)

Shoppers recovering from Christmas dinner crowded the supermarket, getting the goods for the all-important New Year's feast. The first meal of the year set the tone for the rest of it. Good food and food drink insured good luck.

Star pushed the cart while Vee piled groceries inside....

"Tomatoes." Vee pointed toward the produce section. "You get them while I talk to the butcher."...

"Go on." Vee took the cart, and shooed her toward the produce department. She watched Star for a moment, then wheeled the cart toward the meat counter. Behind the glass window, she saw a young man arranging pork chops in a plastic tray. She pushed the service buzzer.

The young man looked up and smiled.

Vee's heart jumped into her mouth. Her blood froze....

                *   *   *

She propelled Star toward the meat counter, stopping a few feet short of the glass window. "Look. Look in there."

Star tilted her head. "What am I looking at?"...

"I can't believe you don't recognize him," Vee whispered through clenched teeth. "That's Carlyle Biggs!"

"Don't you remember? Christmas, about seven years ago in New York City? He killed his whole family!"...

                *   *   *

"It's tradition," Vee said. "You know you got to eat hog's head and black-eyed peas for your first meal right after midnight to bring good luck in the new year."...

"And have you ever seen pig faces pass these lips?"

"That's why your luck is so bad."...

"I'd rather eat a fried baloney sandwich on Wonder Bread," Star said. "Besides, if you buy a pig's head, you're on the bus or walking, 'cause you ain't bringing it in my car."

PI Kinsey Millhone has surrogate parents both of whose identities rest in food preparation. Rosie runs the tavern where Kinsey eats lots of dinners, and Henry, her landlord, mostly meets up with Kinsey in his kitchen where he earns a small living from baking goodies. Rosie's ministrations must be taken with a dose of grating motherly advice, whereas Henry reminds us of an unconditionally loving dad. (From Sue Grafton's *"B" is for Burglar*. HB. NY: Holt Rinehart and Winston. 1985.)

I peered in his back window on my way out, and spotted him in the kitchen rolling out puff pasty dough. He's a former commercial baker who supplements his social security these days doing up breads and sweets....I tapped on the glass and he motioned me in. Henry is what I like to think of as an octogenarian "hunk."...

That afternoon, he was wearing a red rag around his head pirate-style, his tanned forearms bare and powdered with flour, his fingers as long and nimble as a monkey's as he gathered the dough and turned it halfway. He was using a length of chilled pipe as a rolling pin and he paused to flour it while he worked, coaxing the pastry into a rectangle.

...:"You making napoleons?"

He nodded. "I'm catering a tea for someone up the street. What are you up to, besides a run?"

*   *   *

"I mean it. I'm tired of feeling helpless and afraid," I said.

Henry puffed his cheeks up and blew a raspberry....Big talk, his face said, but you don't fool me a bit. He cracked an egg on the counter and opened it up with one hand, letting the white slip through his fingers into a cup. He put the yolk in a bowl and took up another egg, repeating the process with his eyes pinned on me.

*   *   *

"Look...I just don't want to be a victim anymore. I'm sick of it."

Henry cradled the bowl in his arms, whisking the eggs with a practiced ease. When I do that, the eggs always slop out the side.

He said, "When were you ever a victim?..."

You can reach Sue Grafton at *sue@suegrafton.com* or through her web site *http://www.suegrafton.com*. The web site includes Grafton's bio, a write-up about Kinsey's early years, and a test of knowledge about Kinsey, Henry, and Santa Teresa.

Helma Zukas, Bellehaven amateur sleuth, counts as one of her part-ners-in-detecting whacky Ruth Winthrop from the same Michigan high school class. The two picked up Helma's 87-year-old Aunt Em at the air-port in Seattle and weren't back in Bellehaven a few hours when there was a murder practically on the doorstep. Very early the next morning Helma awakens to the odor of heavy fried food. Where'd this come from? And, oh hi, Ruth, why not join us for breakfast? (From Jo Dereske's *Final Notice*. PB. NY: Avon Books. 1998.)

"What are you cooking?" she [Helma] asked, nodding to the pots and pans....

"Potatoes and eggs and ham." She tapped a small kettle with steam escaping between the rim and lid. "And prunes to give you good health. I stewed them with wine. After last night we need strong food."

"But I don't have any of those foods, except the eggs." Helma had planned soft poached eggs, warmed croissants, and fresh orange juice, tea with warm milk.

"I know," Aunt Em said sadly. "You must shop more often; you were out of everything. I went from neighbor to neighbor." She tsk-tsked. "Some of them weren't even up...."

When she returned to the dining room, Aunt Em was dishing food onto three plates: crusty fried potatoes and onions, shiny with grease; thick slices of pink ham with translucent fat curling around the edges; eggs over easy fried in butter; dessert bowls of prunes; tall glasses of orange juice; and cups of coffee. Helma's stomach blanched. It was more food than she ate in two meals, more fat than she ate in a week....

A piece of potato fell from Aunt Em's spatula to the floor. She picked it up, mumbled a few words in Lithuanian, kissed it, and placed it on her plate.

And when all three were seated, their heaping plates in front of them, Ruth raised her glass of orange juice to Aunt Em and said, "Your first morning in Bellehaven. It can only get better...we hope."

Aunt Em raised her own juice and the three clicked glasses.

"Eat up," Aunt Em told them, dabbing her lips with her napkin. "And then we'll solve the murder."

Why is there so little vegetarianism in mainstream detective novels? Is it because mystery writers themselves aren't into it? Must real sleuths eat red meat? Or is vegetarianism, rightly or wrongly, associated with long hair and sandals, vegan spartanism, and *Laurel's Kitchen*, with its 2,000 ways to fix beans and rice?

PI Elizabeth Chase who operates out of Escondido, California, uses the paranormal and astrology to help her investigations. She is looking into a possible murder and here turns for help from best friend Linda who works on a TV psychic hotline. Linda has already warned Elizabeth that she is frightened for her. Now Elizabeth has been shot at and is afraid to stay in her own home. (From Martha C. Lawrence's *Murder in Scorpio*. PB. NY: St Martin's Paperbacks. 1996.)

Linda was holding down a table in the outside dining area of Kung Food, a culinary haven for vegetarians. She sat in the shade of a jasmine-covered trellis, looking regal as always....She is large and handsome and looks like she belongs to another time....Her presence is at once commanding and mysterious....

She stood up as I approached and took me into her arms, filling me up with her generous love.

"Ahh," I purred.

"Hmm," she said, holding me at arm's length and appraising me. She made little tsking noises. "A little fearful energy around you, eh? Sit down; I'll clear you."

We took our seats, and Linda closed her eyes. She took a loud, deep breath and exhaled noisily....As she worked I could feel the energy moving, as if the very molecules that surrounded us were beginning to dance. I closed my eyes and saw colors blending and separating around me. For the first time all day I felt sensations approaching peacefulness, warmth, and comfort....

Our waitress, a petite brunette who wore her hair in two long thick braids, approached our table. This being the type of vegetarian restaurant where metaphysicians hang out, a woman in trance at the table was 'no big.' In deference to Linda's meditation, our waitress leaned over me, braids swaying, and spoke softly. "What can I get for you here?"

"Chamomile tea and a honey-nut muffin," Linda said joyously without opening her eyes.

"Make it a double," I said.

After several minutes Linda opened her eyes. "Right now, Elizabeth, I recommend about ten doses of white light an hour. You are in some deep shit, honey."

Kate Shugak, Alaskan PI, is working for Old Sam, another Shugak, on board the tender *Freya* out of Cordova. There's been a murder and Old Sam was outraged that Kate deliberately was rude to a woman preacher she suspected. Sam wanted her to apologize, and, forgetting she was speaking to an elder, she sassed him. For that, Sam hurled her into the water and let her walk five squishy miles to their next meeting place, where cooled downed, she said, "I'm sorry, uncle. I was rude. Please forgive me." Hours later, it's Sam's turn, an indirect, symbolic turn. Joyce Shugak is Kate's Auntie whom she wants to protect from the suspicions of State Trooper Chopin. (From Dana Stabenow's *Killing Grounds*. PB. NY: Berkley Publishing Group, Berkley Prime Crime. 1999.)

...."What's for breakfast?"

"Try lunch," Old Sam said. "How about pork chops and applesauce?"

Pork chops and applesauce was Kate's favorite meal in the whole world. As a child she'd gotten it only as a special treat because none of the Park rats raised pigs and, after you added on the air freight, pork in the Park was more expensive than filet mignon in New York City. Old Sam knew this perfectly well, and Kate realized that the offering of pork chops and applesauce was his way of showing his affection, alleviating his anxiety and ministering to her needs. Not that he would for a moment outwardly demonstrate anything of the kind...."Sounds great," she said.

"Good," he said gruffly. "I'll serve it up."

When Old Sam cooked, he cooked comprehensively. There were, besides the aforementioned pork chops and applesauce, chicken adobo, sweet and sour spareribs...mashed potatoes, creamed corn, green beans with bacon and onions, and fruit salad. Kate spooned some of the fruit salad on her plate and said, "Hey, great, no marshmallows. You remembered."

Old Sam frowned ferociously. "We're out."

"Oh." Kate prudently said no more....Everything was delicious, and when she finished she sat back and reflected on how nearly impossible it was to despair on a full stomach.

That comfortable...thought was challenged in the next thirty seconds, when Trooper Chopin pushed back his plate...and announced his intention of visiting Joyce Shugak...and she knew he was not going to be...misled or otherwise diverted this time.

In Eugene, Oregon, for the past six months, attorney Barbara Holloway has been running a storefront practice out of Martin's Fine Foods, helping people without resources to buy homes, get divorces, file bankruptcies. Her father, Frank Holloway, is also a lawyer; she used to be part of his law firm and her name is still on the masthead in hope she'll come back.

Barbara is defending a woman accused of killing her child, but she's out of money and asks her dad if his law firm would cover the expenses, a debt she'll pay back in the future. He refuses and for days they don't speak. Finally, it is the memory of food and how it was used in the family to make amends that brings Barbara to her father's door. (From Kate Wilhelm's *The Best Defense*. PB. NY: Ballantine Books, a Fawcett Crest Book. 1995.)

Well, Barbara thought, back in her car, not moving yet, she had set a lot of wheels aspin. She felt as if all around her things were in motion that had not been only a few days ago, and she was tired and hungry.

She drove through town without caring that traffic was heavy now, not caring how long she had to wait at the red lights. On impulse she drove toward Skinner Butte Park and the house her father had bought. She slowed down when she saw his car in the driveway. She could park, go ring the bell, and say, "Hey, I'm hungry." And he would put his arm around her shoulder and say, "Well, let's go eat." That's what her mother would have done, she thought, and they both would have pretended nothing had happened. She drove past the house and went home.

On her porch was a second potted geranium, white with a card that read: *One looked pretty lonesome. I watered them both.*

She returned to her car and drove back to his house. When he opened the door, she said, "Hey, I'm hungry," and he said, "Well, let's go eat." His arm felt good around her shoulder.

They walked to a neighborhood German restaurant, where they had big fat sausages, mashed potatoes, coleslaw, and dark beer. "Save room for strudel," Frank warned when they ordered. "This time of year it will be with fresh cherries."

There's a great scene in Julie Smith's *New Orleans Mourning* (1991) in which Cookie Lamoreux, a childhood friend of Officer Skip Langdon, whips up a sumptuous dinner for her and her lover, and another of Skip's friends from way back in junior high. The paella is so sensational everyone says Cookie oughta open a restaurant. He scoffs. Then the question gets asked, if you could do anything you wanted with your life, what would it be? He could have answered in macho wise-crack style—rocket scientist, brain surgeon, rock star. But to Skip's surprise, he says thoughtfully, he'd be a cook. She reflects on whether they all have actually, finally, grown up and are ready to become friends at a serious level.

Typically a woman has a wide circle of friends. We make friends at work, at church, where we volunteer. We get to know the parents of our kids' friends. We take lots of classes, yoga, aerobic exercise, continuing education, which add more friends to our address book. In contrast, a sleuth is a solitary soul, depending on just a few well-chosen, close-at-hand confidants—her landlord, upstairs neighbor, a favorite aunt, a chum from childhood. All of whom don't have to ask what she'd like most to eat.

Chapter 18
I'm Only Saying This For Your Own Good

"We're going to help you," Aunt Em said. "We three have gone through more men in our lifetimes than…"

"Tsk, tsk," Mrs. Whitney said….She looked at Helma. "We have some ideas you can share with your policeman." (From Jo Dereske's *Miss Zukas in Death's Shadow*.) (Which just goes to show that aunties can sometimes be helpful and sometimes a pain in the butt.)

Why is it so many female sleuths lose their mothers, if not their fathers, at a tender age and have to be raised by a grandmother or an aunt? One, it makes them independent; two, it makes them different from most of us; three, it allows them to relate to more interesting significant others perhaps than mothers.

When mother is in the picture, she wheedles at her daughter to find a husband, change her job, and phone her more often. There is this great scene in Edna Buchanan's *Suitable for Framing* where a reporter screams, "Mother, phone the police right now and tell them your hairdresser's home is being burgled, even as we speak." The latest Miami scam was to "borrow" a car for "an emergency" and then return the car with theater tickets "in appreciation." Then when the folks were at the theater, the burglars cleaned them out. But Mother didn't know her hairdresser's last name or address, so any crime would be the fault of her daughter. Why? Because had daughter returned Mom's call right away, Mom could have phoned the beauty shop and saved the day.

Which is why, instead of mom, we have grandmas and nieces, sisters and brothers-in-law, aunties and uncles, tavern owners and barkeeps with attitude.

Santa Teresa, CA, PI Kinsey Millhone's first choice of comfort food is a chilled glass of chardonnay. Which, since she's lost all her money on one of those bad hair days, she has to pay for by listening to one person's advice as to how to avoid same. (From Sue Grafton's *"D" is for Deadbeat*. HB. NY: Henry Holt and Company. 1987.)

Rosie's is the tavern in my neighborhood, run by herself, a Hungarian woman in her sixties, short and top-heavy, with dyed red hair that recently had looked like a cross between terra cotta floor tile and canned pumpkin pie filling. Rosie is an autocrat—outspoken, overbearing, suspicious of strangers. She cooks like a dream when it suits her, but she usually wants to dictate what you should eat at any given meal. She's protective, sometimes generous, often irritating. Like your best friend's cranky grandmother, she's someone you endure for the sake of peace. I hang out at her establishment because it's unpretentious and it's only half a block away from my place....

That night when I walked in, she took one look at my face and poured me a glass of white wine from her personal supply. I moved to my favorite booth at the rear....Within moments, Rosie materialized at the table and set the glass of wine in front of me.

"Somebody just busted out the window of my car and stole everything I hold dear, including my gun," I said.

"I've got some *sóska leves* for you," she announced. "And after that, you gonna have a salad made with celery root, some chicken paprikas, some of

Henry's good rolls, cabbage strudel, and deep-fried cherries if you're good and clean up your plate. It's on the house, on account of your troubles, only think about this one thing while you eat. If you had a good man in your life, this would never happen to you and that's all I'm gonna say."

I laughed for the first time in days.

Helma Zukas, Bellehaven, WA, librarian, has a widowed mother, Lillian, who lives across town from her. They get together for Sunday dinner and the odd lunch at Saul's Deli. After these sandwiches, Lillian reminds her daughter that Chief of Police Gallant's wife has up and left him and that somebody ought to take a hint. (From Jo Dereske's *Miss Zukas and the Library Murders*. PB. NY: Avon Books. 1994.)

Helma's mother sliced the crusts from her avocado and cream cheese sandwich and then cut each half sandwich in half again.

"This is way too much for me to eat," she said. "They give you such big servings." She folded the crusts inside a napkin and set them at the edge of the table like a gift package. Saul's Deli was crowded…

"Are you going to eat your dill?" Lillian asked.

"No. Would you like it?"

"Rather than let it go to waste."

Helma forked the dill pickle and transferred it to her mother's plate. Lillian held out her bowl of fruit. Only some miniature species of Concord grapes were left.

"Would you like a grape?"

"I don't eat purple food," Helma reminded her.

"Of course, dear. I forgot."

Using her fork and knife, Lillian tidily cut the dill pickle into half-inch disks. Then she leaned across the table and said in a husky voice, "Now, dear. I want you to tell me about the murder—the *real* story, not the silly blather that's in the *Daily News*."

Helma sighed.…

Lillian laughed. "Getting away with murder. That sounds like one of your father's weak jokes. I see they have some yummy-looking chocolate cheesecake at the counter. Let's split a piece."

"No thanks, Mother."

"A third?"

"Not for me, but you go ahead."

"Oh, no, I could never eat a whole piece," Lillian said, looking soft-eyed toward the counter.

An ongoing internal plot within the Kate Shugak series is the friction between Kate and her grandmother, Ekaterina, who smarts that Kate wants to live on her own in the wilderness, apart from her kin. Here, Kate has come to ask Ekaterina's help in finding two Anglos lost in Denali National Park, and to get around their simmering personal battle, Kate asks for one of her comfort foods, cocoa, which the old lady is pleased as punch to prepare. (From Dana Stabenow's *A Cold Day for Murder*. PB. NY: Ballantine Publishing Group, a Berkley Book. 1992.)

…She poured oil into the skillet and let it heat, rolled the remaining dough into loaves and put them in the oven. When the grease began to sputter she tore off chunks of the dough she had retained and fried it a golden brown on both sides. She put the pieces on a chipped plate and set it on the table with a cube of butter and a shaker of powdered sugar. By then the water was boiling. From a cupboard she took two mugs, a can of evaporated milk and a 48-ounce can of Nestle's Quik. She put three heaping teaspoonfuls of the powdered chocolate in each mug, punched holes in the can of milk and half filled the mugs, topping them off the rest of the way with boiling water. Steam rose and the smell of sweet chocolate mingled with the aroma of fried bread and made Kate's mouth water. Ekaterina reached for a spoon.

"Don't, emaa," Kate said, reaching for the mug…."You know I like it lumpy." She took the spoon out of the mug, took a piece of fried bread from the plate, dipped it and took a bite, as absorbed in the right balance of cocoa to fried bread at thirty years of age as she had been at three....

Kate's free hand sifted through the drift of papers on the kitchen table, and came up with a two-page document typed on legal-size paper. She read the first paragraph, read it a second time, and raised her eyes to look again at the old woman. "I thought this was a dead issue."...

Kate sighed. "Oh, emaa."

Food's a super way to control others, the more so if they're ravenous. Sometimes a sleuth uses others' hunger to get them to do her bidding. Sometimes it's the other way around. As in the case of bounty hunter Stephanie Plum who has made two compromises to survive: she works for her cousin Vinnie and spends more time than she'd like at her parents' home where the food is free. They want to fix her up with a balding, fat butcher, but Stephanie isn't about to live the rest of her life with a man who spends his days "stuffing giblets up chicken butts" (*One for the Money*). Here she's debating whether to eat at Burger King or Pizza Hut when mom calls. (From Janet Evanovich's *Two for the Dough*. PB. NY: Simon & Schuster, Pocket Books. 1996.)

"Stephanie...I have a big potful of stuffed cabbages. And spice cake for dessert."

"Sounds good," I said, "but I've made plans for this evening."

"What plans?"

"Dinner plans."

"Do you have a date?"

"No."

"Then you don't have any plans."

"There's more to life than dates."

"Like what?"

"Like work."

"I've got vanilla ice cream, too, for the spice cake," she said.

"Is it low-fat ice cream?"

"No, it's the expensive kind that comes in the little cardboard tub."

"Okay," I said. "I'll be there."

Stephanie Plum lusts after two very sexy guys. There's Joe Morelli, plainclothes cop who feeds her sausage sandwiches and pizza and may have a thing going with another woman, Terry Gilman. Then there's Ranger, Cuban-American, ex-special forces, Stephanie's mentor who fixes her healthful salads and reminds her that the goal of life should be to have a pure mind and body.

"Do you have a pure mind and body?" she asks. "Not right now," he responds, eyes locked on hers. Control is on her mind a lot. When hormones threaten to take over, she turns to Snickers, a solution that works as long as the 7-Eleven is open.

Joe asks her to a wedding. After she determines it isn't her own, she consents. Terry is there, and blows Joe a kiss. Then she meets his Grandma Bella, who offers a strategy that goes beyond chocolate. (From Janet Evanovich's *High Five*. PB. NY: St. Martin's Paperbacks. 1999.)

…She took my hand and dragged me after her. "Come. You should meet the family."

I looked back at Joe and mouthed "Help!"

"You're on your own," Joe said. "I need a drink. A big one."

"This is Joe's cousin, Louis," Grandma Bella said. "Louis fools around on his wife."

Louis looked like a thirty-year-old loaf of fresh raised white bread. Soft and plump. Scarfing down appetizers. He stood next to a small olive-skinned woman, and from the look she gave him, I assumed they were married.

"Grandma Bella," he said, croaky-voiced, his cheeks mottled in red, mouth stuffed with crab balls. "I would never—"

"Silence," she said. "I know these things. You can't lie to me. I'll put the eye on you."

Louis sucked in some crab and clutched his throat. His face got red, then purple. He flailed his arms.

"He's choking!" I said.

Grandma Bella tapped her finger to her eye and smiled like the wicked witch in *The Wizard of Oz*. I gave Louis a good hard thwack between his shoulder blades, and the crab ball flew out of his mouth. Grandma Bella leaned close to Louis. "You cheat again, and next time I'll kill you," she said.

She moved off toward a group of women. "One thing you learn about Morelli men," she said to me. "You don't let them get away with a thing."

Joe nudged me from behind and put a drink in my hand. "How's it going?"

"Pretty good. Grandma Bella put the eye on Louis." I took a sip. "Champagne?"

"All out of cyanide," he said.

Ruby Crane has been estranged from her older sister Phyllis for 13 years. But here Phyllis has manipulated Ruby into leaving the tiny town of Sable, Michigan, where Ruby ekes out a living as a forgery detector, to come to Albuquerque to bail her out of big time trouble. Phyllis's manipulation goes so far as to try to come between Ruby and her brain-damaged teenage daughter, Jesse. Has Ruby traveled all this way to help, only to be abused? (From Jo Dereske's *Short Cut*. PB. NY: Dell Publishing. 1998.)

Everything expansive, expensive, and orderly. The decor might have been taken from an architectural magazine. It was as perfect—and impersonal—as Phyllis's office. No photos or cartoons were magneted to the refrigerator, no shaky stacks of mail or magazines like Ruby kept. The effect was of coolness and polite good behavior.

…"It's a beautiful home," she said. "Did you design it?"

Phyllis nodded....

As they passed through the kitchen, Ruby noticed a ceramic bowl of Reese's peanut butter cups on the counter, Jesse's favorite candy....

..."We're eating in tonight, do you mind? You probably expected Mexican food, but Salina's made a pot roast...."

*   *   *

"It's a clear night," Phyllis told Jesse after they'd finished slices of frozen carrot cake. "I set up a telescope in the back courtyard so you can see Hale-Bopp."

She couldn't have said anything to endear her more to Jesse....They sat in Phyllis's dining room, candles on the table, the overhead chandelier off, and the glass door to the rear courtyard open to the night....

They'd eaten late, after darkness had fallen, and once Phyllis had raised her head. "Hear that?" she asked Jesse. "Coyote."

They paused, forks poised, listening to the eerie lone voice waver and rise, holding its note and then dropping to a series of yips.

"I hope they don't keep you awake."

We are being so polite, Ruby thought, treading on spun glass, biting back words, trying to remain impersonal. Only one more day, she told herself. She could keep it up for one more day.

How does the mother of NYPD Detective April Woo, who lives with her parents, show her disapproval of April's job? Cold shredded jellied eel and black and smelly ten-thousand-year-old eggs. In contrast, the mother of April's would-be lover, Detective Sergeant Mike Sanchez, shows her acceptance of his life's work with food piled heavenward and lovingly lingered over. (From Leslie Glass's *Judging Time*. PB. NY: Penguin Group, Signet. 1999.)

April blew air out of her nose, thinking of some of the delicate habits of her people. Before she'd left Chinatown, she'd assumed that rotting garbage on the street and a dozen people speed-eating from the same plate were normal. Her family and friends dug into the communal serving platters with their chopsticks. They hoisted succulent morsels across great expanses to their faces and shoveled food into their mouths, making great slurp, slurp, slurping noises with an urgency that might lead an outsider to think this was the last meal anyone would ever get.

This, however, was not the case at Mike's mother's table. At Sunday lunch six weeks ago, the one time April had eaten there, Mike's mother, who was as well fleshed and smiling as Sai Yuan Woo [April's mother] was skinny and scowling, had worn a purple dress that looked like taffeta and was cut low enough to show off her ample bosom. Maria Sanchez served fastidiously. She filled all the plates with the different foods from the platters in the center of the table, using a separate serving spoon for each platter. When everybody's plate was piled high with food, the four people at the table ate slowly. They put their forks and knives down frequently to savor the tastes and talk in the manner of people who had eaten not long ago and would soon eat again.

And how does the father of New Orleans homicide detective Skip Langdon show his disapproval of her job? By not speaking to her. Until now. Skip's mother's invited her to dinner. Along with Ted and Nan Gilkerson, Conrad, Skip's brother, and Conrad's wife, Camille. Skip is seeing a therapist for depression after killing a bad guy. (From Julie Smith's *The Kindness of Strangers*. PB. NY: Ballantine Books, an Ivy Book. 1997.)

Her father came in and pecked her. "Skip. How's it going?" As if there weren't years of partial estrangement between them.

Camille gave her a hug, Conrad barely nodded. "How're things at the cop shop?"

"Actually, I'm taking a leave of absence."

She watched as her father's face fell, thinking how ironic it was that he'd stopped speaking to her because she had joined the police department and had seemingly only started again because she'd done so well it reflected on him.

Her mother handed her a glass of white wine and went to answer the door.

"Why is that?" her father asked, trying to keep the disapproval out of his voice....

"Ah. The prodigal daughter." Ted kissed her....

"How are things on America's worst police force? When are they making you chief?"

Conrad said: "I'd be ashamed to say what I do if I were you."...

..."It's not her fault the cops are killing each other. Is it, Skip?"

Skip smiled. "I'm innocent."...

"What's the inside story on that?" Nan asked. She accepted a drink and settled on a sofa.

"You know as much as I do. This young cop's accused of...shooting her former partner...."

Conrad said, "And that was the same week a Tulane student claimed she got raped by a cop."

"Hey, nobody's perfect." They laughed, but Skip was stung.... ...She was suddenly touched by her father's pride in her accomplishments—he probably had to put up with this kind of garbage a lot.

She tried to keep it light, obediently telling war stories until her mother called them to dinner.

Kat Colorado is a Sacramento PI whose cop boyfriend, Hank, is in a huff because she doesn't want to marry him. Kat's best friend is Charity, a nationally syndicated advice columnist. Unfortunately, the common sense present in the column is missing from the columnist's personal life. Charity has just met a cop named Al and turns to the most unlikely person for marriage counseling, independent-minded Kat who likes Chinese takeout. (From Karen Kijewski's *Kat's Cradle*. PB. NY: Bantam Books. 1992.)

…"I brought Chinese food, all right?"

"Wonderful. I'm starving and glad you're here." I hugged her…

She scooped up her Coke and followed me inside. "Okay, Kat, do you think I should get married?"

"Not unless you've learned a lot since I last saw you. Your choice in men is terrible."…

"You guys just met."

"We had lunch and dinner and stayed up all night talking." She blushed. "And stuff. Want some of this, Kat?"

"Sure. You've only been widowed a year or so, Charity. Take your time; enjoy getting to know a lot of people." We ate in silence for a while.

She broke it. "I called Hank today. I needed to ask him about something."

"What?"

"Police procedure on runaways. I told him you looked run-down and unhappy."

"I wish you'd mind your own business."

"Okay."

She helped herself to the rest of the almond chicken. I sat and stared stupidly at a green pepper congealing in sauce.

"What did he say?" I asked finally.

"Hmmm? Oh, Hank." She started in greedily on the rest of the fried rice. "That it has been real hot in Vegas, that he was working a lot of overtime, and—"

"Charity." I said it in a dangerous tone of voice.

"He told me to mind my own business too, only he was nicer about it." She speared a water chestnut and grinned….

"Read your fortune." She handed me a cookie.

I broke it open, eating as I read, "'An out-of-town visitor will arrive soon.'"

"Ha," said Charity. "I rest my case. Mine says: 'Expect a proposal.' Well, well," she said smugly.

In the middle of U. S. marshal Lilly Bennett's investigation into the death of the wealthiest man in town, town being Roundup, Wyoming, Lilly's mother is planning a lavish wedding for one of Lilly's goddaughters. Here Lilly takes a break from business lunches to visit her mother. The tender topic of why Lilly has never found a husband naturally arises. (From Marne Davis Kellogg's *Tramp*. PB. NY: Bantam Books. 1998.)

"*Buenos días,*" he said. "Your mother's out on the front porch."

"Thanks, Manny," I said, and grabbed a handful of powdered sugar-dusted macaroons....

I sat down, poured myself a cup of coffee...and arranged my cookies in a line on the table in front of me. I smiled at Mother....She'd always been thin as a rail....I could be thin, too....If I wanted to eat as little and smoke as much as she did....

Mañuel uncorked a bottle of cold white wine and filled our glasses. Chicken sandwiches with extra mayonnaise and the crusts cut off, sliced tomatoes, and clumps of fresh watercress sat on the plates....

She took a small bite of her sandwich and then signaled for Mañuel to take it away.

"Delicious," she said....

"And now, at this point, I don't think we'd mind if you got married in a gas station in Chihuahua. To the owner, of course."

I laughed and finished my lunch, knowing she'd mind very much....

*   *   *

I have mirrors all around my bathtub, and one time I was lying in the tub watching the movie about the *Sports Illustrated* swimsuit issue and one of the models was Cheryl Tiegs, close to my age [50], and she looked all right, not as great as the other models but all right for a middle-aged woman. And I was thinking I probably looked that good, too.

Then I stood up. And there in all those mirrors was the reality of my body, which looks absolutely *nothing* like Cheryl Tiegs's....I screamed and fell down into the bath, way below the rim...and I haven't taken such a good look at myself since.

After fifteen years away, San Francisco attorney Alma Bashears has returned to Contrary, Kentucky, to defend her brother Vernon against a murder charge. When she gets him released from jail a party awaits them at the family home in the hollows of Appalachia. Merl aka Grammy is Alma and Vernon's mother. (From Tess Collins's *The Law of Revenge*. PB. NY: Ballantine Books, an Ivy Book. 1997.)

...The house smelled of creamed corn, mashed potatoes, biscuits, fried green tomatoes, and deer steak with gravy....

Merl bounced down on the couch and whisked her arm through his and he said, "Momma, I'm hungry as a dog."

"There's food enough for an army and it's all for you, precious."...

"Will y'all be quiet," Vernon said loudly, holding one hand over the receiver. "Yeah, honey," he said into the phone, "a back rub sounds good."

Alma pushed the disconnect button....

Her mother raised a hand as if she were going to slap Alma....

...Larry Joe stood in the doorway and hollered toward the kitchen. "Grammy's gonna whip Aunt Alma!" He bit into an Oreo cookie, chocolate crumbs dusting the side of his face. The kitchen emptied, and the family, all balancing plates of food, wedged themselves into the living room and stared. No one spoke. They just kept gobbling their food and waiting to see if anything was going to happen.

Alma felt as if she were starring in a Fellini movie. Her mother shrank down, embarrassed, and busily brushed crumbs off Larry Joe's mouth. "You can sometimes be the dirtiest little boy," she said, and kissed his cheek.

"Well, guess what, everybody," Vernon said in a jolly voice as though hoping to ease the tension, "I been out of the pokey for less than two hours and I already got four dates."...

...Mamaw called out from the kitchen, "This food is getting cold. I don't know what's so important in there, but if you want any of it, you better come and eat it now!"

Everyone moved at the sound of Mamaw's voice.

Liz James works as a writer for the Houston Mental Health Center. At a Powerful Woman seminar led by Kate Quinlan, one of Liz's colleagues, Liz witnesses the delivery of the body of Kate's husband right in front of all those women. Wow. Here, Liz is having dinner with her fiancé Nick, her sister Margaret and brother-in-law Raoul. (From Karen Hanson Stuyck's *Lethal Lessons*. PB. NY: Berkley Publishing Group, Berkley Prime Crime. 1997.)

"What is that woman's problem?" my sister, Margaret, inquired loudly. "First she encourages the women in her workshop to run over their husbands with their cars and to assault their bosses. Then she goes and shoots her own husband."

Raoul...glanced up from his veal. "At least she practices what she preaches."

I set down my fork, which was holding a mouthful of rather uninspired eggplant parmigiana. "Kate *didn't* kill her husband...."

Margaret finished chewing her salad, daintily blotted her mouth with her napkin, then came out swinging....

Margaret took a sip of wine, holding up one finger in case anyone at the table was planning to usurp the spotlight. "So can't you see how brilliant it was for Kate to send herself the body at her own seminar? Dozens of people are there to watch her open the box and witness how totally shocked she was when she encountered her husband's corpse."

"Except," Nick pointed out, "the police obviously think the same thing you do. So it wasn't that brilliant a scheme after all. Or"—he munched on a breadstick, his head tilted to the side—"maybe the police just always figure the husband or wife is the most likely suspect...."

My sister waited until my mouth was filled with eggplant before she launched her next volley. "We need to get our heads together on planning this wedding," she said, looking at Nick. "Since Liz seems to be so busy with this Powerful Woman seminar, maybe you should be the one who comes with me to the caterers next week."

Nick opened his mouth to reply, took one look at my face, and closed his mouth.

Will Rosie ever serve up chicken paprikas in honor of Kinsey's single-hood? Will Lilly's mother rejoice that her daughter eats all her lunch and asks for more? Will bounty-hunter Stephanie Plum's mom ever serve a potful of stuffed cabbages without trying to fix her up?

Not likely. Think how boring our sleuths' lives would be without the coaxing and cajoling, the whining and complaining, the disapproval and snide remarks.

Another end of chapter quiz. Who's The Author? Her protagonist's name is Nanette. Nan's an amateur sleuth with a Masters degree in French. She lives at the edge of New York City's Gramercy Park and plays a tenor sax on the streets to pay for her groceries. Needless to say, her fridge and cabinets are mostly bare and her Mom's eager that she marry a real provider. But when Nan eats, she eats well, deep frying fresh sardines in Greek olive oil to serve with linguine, garlic, and little green peas for dinner. Or serving poached eggs with wafer-thin toast without the crusts for breakfast. She's crazy about Paris so when Mom sends her over to find out what has happened to Auntie Viv, she says Coq au vin and is on her way.

There we get treated to meals and drinks at Café Cloche, Au Pactole, Café Flore, Bricktops, Au Père Tranquille, Deux Magots, and unnamed little bistros where Nanette is overcome by the smell of onion and rosemary, rabbit and sweetbreads, cheeses and rich red wine. All this is, of course, mingled with murder.

CHAPTER 19
UPPER AND LOWER CRUSTS

"I opened both pats and broke off a band of hot roll, which I buttered and ate, nearly moaning aloud. The dough was soft and moist, the glaze dripping down between the coils. Nothing like fear to generate an appetite for comfort foods...." (From whom else but Sue Grafton in *"K" is for Killer*.)

Food scenes are a convenient way to spell out the social standing of the folks that sleuths deal with. *What* folks eat, *where* they eat, *how* they eat, *when* they eat, says who they are. On the fringes of society, at the top, or somewhere in between. Food scenes also spell out *why* a sleuth finds herself in a particular locale.

The latter is the case in Linda Fairstein's *Final Jeopardy*. NYC assistant D. A. Alexandra Cooper and homicide detective Mike Chapman are looking into a murder up in Martha's Vineyard which is a pretty toney place, but the victim's last meal was basic, simple—big, juicy fried clams, the best on the island. So where's the best place, asks Mike. Alex leads him to The Bite, a tiny wooden shack by the side of the road with two picnic tables, where the owner serves up clams, fries, chowder, and, oh yes, important information.

And just where does Colorado attorney Cinda Hayes find herself in Marianne Wesson's *A Suggestion of Death*? Boulder's espresso parlors and coffee shop-cum-used bookstores are hundreds of miles away. Instead, after a day of galleries and museums, hot twisted pretzels and coffee from street vendors, Cinda finds herself in "Calvin's" facing Classic Chinese. Roast squab with frog legs, braised sea cucumber with duck feet, chicken in a baked clay carapace, plum wine. A meal that lasts from 7:30 until 11 at which time her lover (the *why* she's there) would love to take her to the hot new trio at Zinno. *Where* can only be the Big Apple.

In Barbara D'Amato's *Hard Tack*, amateur sleuth and investigative reporter Cat Marsala has her bodily priorities down cold: "Oh, the sheer joy of being in dry clothes, warm, not seasick, and eating food! You can say what you want for intellectual pleasures. Give me food first every time. *Then* we'll talk."

Cat's assigned to write a story for a Chicago magazine on how to sail a luxury boat on Lake Michigan through the eyes of a novice. A storm hits and then they are becalmed. In the meantime, bodies pile up, engines and radio fail, supplies run low. But the rich, unused to failure, lunch expansively, certain a fair wind will blow their way soon. (From Barbara D'Amato's *Hard Tack*. PB. NY: Worldwide Mystery. 1992.)

Emery had napped, risen, washed the breakfast dishes, then made a meal that will sound inappropriate for lunch in July. But on this particular clammy, foggy day it was exactly right. He had baked all the potatoes left on board. He broiled steaks to order. There was sour cream with or without chives for the potatoes, and butter, though we were beginning to run low on that....

Everybody aboard snarfed it up as if it were their last meal.

All of the living, that is....

I decided to walk the boat like a cop walking a beat. I could cover the whole boat in four minutes without rushing.

Emery was in the galley wringing his hands....

..."I gotta get to a grocery store."

I had not realized this was our major problem. I thought a dead body in a berth and a sabotaged motor and radio was it. I said, "Why?"

"We're practically out of food."

"That can't be. I saw tons of it."

"We ate it. Oh, there are a few odds and ends. We've got lots of champagne...."

And there we sat....Emery brought up a tray of champagne, caviar, Cheez Whiz, and crackers....

I was starving. Finally I spread some Cheez Whiz on a cracker and pushed caviar on top.

PI V.I. Warshawski is gratefully divorced from fellow law student Dick Yarborough, but every once in a while they meet up and she's reminded of the differences in their lives. Dick has married Teri—wealthy, stunningly beautiful—"so much more suited to Dick's combination of ambition and weakness than I was." He's now a partner in a law firm catering to big business. Does it bother her, all that money? She admits that "perhaps it did rankle that I had been the promising graduate, third in our class, with a dozen job offers, and now I couldn't afford a new pair of running shoes."

Still, wealth doesn't guarantee mannered behavior by Dick or any other of his pals. In a chapter titled "Feeding Frenzy," V.I. watches them hit the buffet during a charity concert intermission for Settlement House. (From Sara Paretsky's *Guardian Angel*. PB. NY: Dell Publishing. 1993.)

...Four tables, formed into an enormous rectangle, were covered with staggering amounts of food: shrimp molded into mountains, giant bowls of strawberries, cakes, rolls, salads, platters of raw oysters. The shorter sides of the rectangle held hot dishes. From my perch I couldn't make out the contents very clearly, but thought egg rolls and chicken livers jostled next to fried mushrooms and crab cakes. In the middle of the two long sides, white-capped men poised carving knives over giant haunches of beef and ham.

People were stampeding to get at the spread before it vanished. I noticed Teri's bronze breastplate in the first surge toward the shrimp mountain. She was riding Dick's wake as he snatched shrimps with the frenzy of a man who feared his just share would be lost if he didn't grab it fast. While stuffing shrimp into his mouth he talked earnestly to two other men in evening garb, who were plunging into the oysters. As they slowly moved toward the roast beef in the middle they punctuated their conversation by stabbing at olives, crab cakes, endives, whatever lay in their path....

"I feel like Pharoah watching the locusts descend," a familiar voice said behind me.

I turned to see Freeman Carter....Freeman was the only partner who ever talked to the womenfolk without showing what a big favor he was doing us....

Garner Quinn has sworn off writing true-crime books. But when true-crime colleague TJ Sterling, hot on the trail of an uncaught murderer, tells her he's found the guy, Garner's interest is revived. Then TJ is found shot to death and the police say suicide. Garner suspects otherwise. Here she has come to comfort TJ's widow, who lives in the exclusive community of Cheswick Forest, Charlottesville, Virginia. (From Jane Waterhouse's *Shadow Walk*. PB. NY: Berkley Publishing Group, Berkley Prime Crime. 1999.)

"It must've really bugged TJ," I commented, "living under a microscope like this."...

"Actually, moving here was his idea. As much as he made fun of it, Tom secretly enjoyed Cheswick's snobbery—be a darlin' and grab that salad for me, will you? I thought we'd eat out in the sunroom."

I picked up the bowl and followed her into a bright airy nook off the kitchen. The table had already been set for lunch. "I find myself coming in here a lot," Caroline said, setting down our glasses. "The dining room seems so big now—"....

"It's beautiful," I said honestly....Swags of translucent white fabric floated like clouds over the French doors. A chandelier rained a whimsical cascade of stars overhead, and the chairs were upholstered in a bold animal print....

...."Is it too sunny for you?"

"No, I'm fine." I took four of the dainty sandwiches passed to me, and filled my salad bowl with a small mountain of dressed greens. Caroline chose a single pale wedge of watercress. Now that she'd finally stopped fussing, she looked lost, as though unsure of what to do with her meager portion of food.

"So TJ picked out this house?" I prompted gently.

"Oh, yes." She rallied a little....

Suddenly it made sense to me—the clubbiness, the la-de-da neighbors, all this rampant elitism. How TJ would've relished infiltrating these closely guarded ranks! With Caroline's pedigree as a password, he'd been able to inveigle his way in; after that, it would've been business as usual. I pictured him at dinner parties, *good old Tom*, captivating the Cheswickian upper crust with his easy charm while, in his brain, he sliced and diced them.

Cooks are good at doing more than one thing at a time. Meaning they can be rolling dough or stirring a pot or waiting for the water to boil and observing details that have nothing to do with cooking. But do have to do with crime among the upper crust.

Here Kinsey Millhone has deliberately put herself on tea duty so that she can pump the family cook about the family. It's Christie, the wife of the accused, who needs the comfort of tea, if Kinsey ever gets around to it. (From Sue Grafton's *"M" is for Malice*. HB. NY: Henry Holt and Company. 1996.)

She was standing at the island with a cutting board in front of her, smashing garlic with the blade of a Chinese cleaver. She was wrapped in a white apron with a white cotton scarf around her head, looking as round and as squeezable as a roll of toilet paper....She lifted the blade. Under it, the hapless garlic had been crushed like albino cockroaches, the peel sliding off with the flick of a knife tip.

"I thought I'd fix Christie a cup of tea," I said. "She needs something in her system—do you have a piece of fruit?"

Enid pointed at the refrigerator. "There are grapes in there. Tea bags up in the cabinet. I'd do it myself, but I'm trying to get this sauce under way. If you set up a tray, I'll take it in to her."

"No problem. You go right ahead."

She leaned to her left and slid open a compartment in which the trays were stored, pulling out a teak server with a rim around the edge. She placed it on the marble counter next to six big cans of crushed tomatoes, two cans of tomato paste, a basket of yellow onions, and a can of olive oil....

She dropped her eyes to her work. She was tapping the Chinese cleaver in a rapid little dance that reduced all the garlic to the size of rice grains. "They searched for the shoes all day yesterday. You've never seen anything like it. Going through all the closets and trash cans, digging in the flower beds."

I made a little mouth noise of interest. It was clear Enid had an avid interest in all the trappings of police work.

Jane da Silva doesn't get paid for what she does, but she stands to inherit the interest off her Uncle Harold's sizable trust if she solves two "hopeless cases" a year. Those "nasty old trustees" managing her Uncle Harold's Foundation for Righting Wrongs must decide what qualifies as "hopeless." She faces a Catch 22 at every critical turn: If she involves the police in her investigation, and they put their considerable skills and resources into wrapping it up, what was once hopeless is no more.

In this scene, she's in Victoria, British Columbia, trying to track down a Canadian woman who may have been a witness to a murder. It's breakfast at the Empress Hotel, a much-to-be-envied repast. Time to indulge the senses, all of 'em. (From K. K. Beck's *Amateur Night*. PB. NY: Warner Books, Mysterious Press. 1994.)

In the restaurant, she settled into a corner table with a view of the room, and ordered eggs Benedict. She skimmed over the international news....

There was also a story about some tourists from Quebec who'd been collecting hallucinogenic mushrooms on the Queen Charlotte Islands to the north. Some of the Haida natives had come upon them...held a gun to their heads and forced them to consume their entire sackful of mushrooms. The tourists had been flown by float plane to a medical clinic where they'd had their stomachs pumped....

She put the paper down, turned her attention to her eggs Benedict, and looked around the incredibly civilized room, quiet except for the chink of glasses and cutlery and low murmurs. At the table next to her sat a good-looking man in a dark suit, who appeared as if he were on a business trip. His thick brown hair was still a little wet above his collar from his morning shower, and he had an appealing, freshly shaved look.

...There was something romantic about the idea of strangers in transit, and the delicious sense she got when traveling of never knowing what might happen. Which was probably why she'd traveled so much.

He caught her gaze, smiled at her, and she found herself smiling back....

Leslie Frost is a world-class violinist and a spy run by the mysterious Maxine out of Berlin. The setting here is a fund-raiser in Washington, D.C., full of the usual suspects. U. S. President Bobby Marvel, noted for his sexual wantonness, is expected to attend. Leslie is escorted by social

mover Fausto, also her current accompanist. Justine is the President's secretary. (From Janice Weber's *Hot Ticket*. PB. NY: Warner Books. 2000.)

First a little touchie-feelie with the metal detectors at the front door,
then air kisses from the indebted host....

"When do you expect the guest of honor?"

"He's on his way."

"My God! We'd better find the oysters before he does!" Fausto took me
to the rear salon....The men looked corporate, the women excited:
Marvel the Magnificent was about to touch them. Another calcium-defi-
cient septuagenarian approached. "You're the violinist, aren't you? We saw
you in Paris. You wore a divine St. Laurent."

"Really! What did I play?"

Her eyes bulged, as if I had just asked her age....

...Fausto downed two glasses of champagne as she castigated the government for abandoning the arts. America was becoming a nation of bar-
barians.

"Correct," he agreed, spearing a strip of smoked salmon and dangling it
high above his mouth before swallowing it whole. "There's no self-control
in this country anymore." Four olives went down the hatch. He sidled his
leviathan stomach inches from the woman's plate of hors d'oeuvres.
"Thank God Bobby's in charge."

..."Think of the alternative."

"I do! Every day!" Fausto delicately harvested three chicken livers from
a passing platter. Suddenly he stopped chewing. "Look what the wind
blew in!...Hello, Justine. That dress is absolutely volcanic."...

..."Shouldn't you two be home practicing for your little concert?"

"You know how it is. Every so often you've got to give the digits a rest."
Fausto swallowed his last chicken liver. "I hope Bobby's oiled his tongue
tonight. Judith's packed the place with horny women. Yourself excepted,
of course."

To begin our transition from upper to lower crusts we look to Mesa
Verde park ranger Anna Pigeon, in New York City to help her ailing sister.
She has found lodging in a cottage on Liberty Island with a friend who
also works for the National Park Service. This setting for a gourmet lunch
is among the dark, derelict, overgrown buildings of Ellis Island, a far cry
from Colorado's bright, bold, back country. (From Nevada Barr's *Liberty
Falling*. PB. NY: HarperCollins Publishers, Avon Books. 2000.)

Before descending to Manhattan's end, where the NPS boat docked,
she indulged in a pleasure not available in small towns. She foraged for
food: crisp lettuce at a vegetable stand, fresh bread from a bakery, pasta
and coffee and wine, each item from its own store. Each lovingly selected
and anticipated. The convenience of supermarkets, the tossing of pack-
aged goods into a rolling metal cart, saved time but did little to fill a
woman's primal urge to hunt and gather.

             *   *   *

Having packed a lunch gleaned from the gourmet forage of the previous day—raspberry truffles, blue corn chips, smoked catfish pate, sweet
pickles and some peachy-colored muffinlike item that looked determined
to keep one regular, Anna pushed open the kitchen door.

             *   *   *

A ranger could have made the footprints. A ranger who'd never walked
the wilderness, depended on her boots and muscles to carry her that last
twenty miles out to a cold beer and a hot bath. Anna huffed, a noise very
like the "Harumph!" found in England's comedies. The sound made her
smile at her own snobbery. Still and all, she doubted the tracks were made
by a ranger....

In the hallway Anna lost the trail. Away from the windows, the rubble was
of larger chunks and a harder consistency. Not a good medium for tracking.

A glance at her watch told her it was one-thirty. She had to abandon the hunt or give up her picnic lunch. Since she didn't know why she was so intent on tracking a person she had no pressing need to find, hunger won out.

Continuing our descent from upper to lower crusts, here's a scene between two co-owners of CHAPS, a country-western tavern on the San Francisco peninsula. The senior partner is Zack Hunter who is a rich TV star; the junior partner is Charlie Plato who lives in a loft above CHAPS as a security guard. Zack and Charlie are a team as well in the sleuthing business. Here they meet up at the low-down tavern for a bite of high-class food. (From Margaret Chittenden's *Don't Forget To Die*. PB. NY: Kensington Publishing Corporation. 1999.)

...."What's in the cooler?" I asked to change the subject.

He reached down and hefted the container onto the bar, opened it and took out a glass jar full of dark gray blobs. "Leftover caviar from the weddin'. Seemed a pity to waste it."

Sliding off his stool, he went around the bar and rooted under it until he came up with a pack of crackers. "Should be toast points, but we'll make do,"...

In some ways Zack is culturally challenged. He never heard of Plato, the philosopher my Greek Father had always insisted was our ancestral relative; when Bristow [the bridegroom in the weddin'] quotes Shakespeare he goes blank....But the aunt who took him in when he was seventeen...taught him about the niceties of life, such as wines and caviar....

With a small spoon, he piled caviar on a cracker, gave it a squirt of juice from a lemon wedge he'd brought along and held it to my mouth. "Here you go, darlin'."

A few months back I would have said there is surely nothing more weakening to the knees and brain than a sexy green-eyed man gazing at your mouth and offering it food. A reversal of Eve and the apple. Fortunately, I was immune now. Mind over matter....

...I remembered my father telling me that Picasso loved Beluga caviar and bought it with cash wrapped in one of his drawings. I almost shared that anecdote with Zack, but was afraid he'd say, "Who?"

Like a baby bird, I opened my mouth for more. Two more cracker loads later, I was feeling much more kindly toward Zack than I'd felt in a while.

"K" is for Killer starts with Janice Kepler, shift manager at a coffee shop, entreating Kinsey Millhone to find the killer of her daughter, Lorna Kepler. Now, nearing the end of her investigation, Kinsey, after a frightening interview in the back of a shiny black stretch limousine that shrieked M-A-F-I-A, visits Janice. (From Sue Grafton's *"K" is for Killer*. HB. NY: Henry Holt and Company. 1994.)

...Janice had spotted me when I came in, and she appeared at the table with a coffee pot in hand. There was a setup in front of me: napkin, silverware, thick white ceramic cup turned upside down on a matching saucer. I turned the cup right-side up, and she filled it. I left it on the table so she couldn't see how badly my hands were shaking.

"You look like you could use this," she said. "You're white as a sheet."

"Can you talk?"

..."Soon as the party at table five clears out," she said....She put the pot down and moved back to her station, pausing to pick up an order from the kitchen pass-through.

When she returned, she was toting an oversize cinnamon roll and two pats of butter wrapped in silver paper. "I brought you a snack. You look like you could use a little jolt of sugar with your caffeine."

"Thanks. This looks great."...

...I paused to lick butter from my fingers, and then I wiped them on a paper napkin. "Did you know Lorna was supposed to get married in Las Vegas the weekend she died?"

Janice looked at me as if I had begun to speak a foreign language and she was waiting for subtitles to appear at the bottom of the screen. "Where in the world did you hear such a thing?"

Betty Trenka has been called out of retirement to clear out the files of Sid Edwards, the company president she worked for. Sid is disabled by a stroke and Junior Edwards wants his office. But it's hard for Betty to concentrate on those files after two murders, one being that of Sid's wife. Betty's chief suspects are Tommy and Bennie who have been in loads of trouble with the law before. And who just happen to be the luncheonette counterman's chief suspects as well. (From Joyce Christmas's *Downsized to Death*. PB. NY: Ballantine Books, a Fawcett Gold Medal Book. 1997.)

…Near noon, she'd managed to get to the *G* drawer, and considered that she'd made good progress.

"Is that lunch place across the street still as lousy as ever?"

"You bet," Bennie said.

"Then I think it's time for me to see if they've kept up their standards for grilled cheese sandwiches."…

"Old friends, I see," Betty said as she passed Bennie and Tommy. "Hello, Tommy." The last time she'd seen Tommy was at the greenhouse, the day after Mr. Takahashi's murder….

Betty hurried across the street to the luncheonette, but felt the two men's eyes watching her. She turned slightly as she entered the steamy, noisy luncheonette—and saw the two of them conferring, heads together.

The counterman looked her up and down and beamed. "Back again, are you? I knew retirement wouldn't take."

"I'm still retired," Betty said. "I'm just here to clean up a mess or two."

"Grilled cheese and tomato, I'll bet," the counterman said.

"You never forget, do you?"

"Not me. What kind of messes? I hear the old lady, the wife of the boss, got killed. They ain't askin' you to solve the crime, are they?" He peered through the steamed-up window. "Cause if they are, you start with Bennie Mallis...."

"Bennie's outside right now, talking to a big fellow. Ever seen them here?"...

"Yeah, I seen him around here with Mallis. And if they're best buds, you're right. He's nobody I'd want to see my daughter hanging with. Not Mallis, neither."...

"The grilled cheese was excellent, as always," Betty said. "It's nice to know that some things never change...."

Boston PI Carlotta Carlyle has discovered her very mysterious client Drew Manley in the backseat of her car under her raincoat. He wants to talk. They find a place on the wrong side of the tracks promising Chinese/American. (From Linda Barnes's *Cold Case*. HB. NY: Delacorte Press. 1997.)

The interior was generic suburban Chinese place. I could have described the fish tank, the dark carved wood, the vases filled with plastic carnations, the garish dragon paintings without venturing inside.

A sign said "PLEASE SEAT YOURSELF." Evidently business wasn't good enough to keep a lunchtime hostess busy....

He ordered tea. I ordered hot and sour soup along with hot and spicy green beans, surprised to see both items on the mostly Mandarin menu....

The sulky girl made a few scratches on her order pad, and disappeared, taking tiny steps that hardly ruffled her long traditional garb. Daughter or niece of the owner, I decided. Less than fond of her job....

...The waitress slopped tea on the table. I wiped it up with a napkin and gave her the eye. I took a sip of hot and sour soup. Disappointingly bland....

Dr. Manley took a gulp of tea, eyed the restaurant as though checking for spies....

"Go to your car, get what I left there. We can discuss it."

"If it's a check, I'm ripping it up."

"Fine." He flagged the waitress. "I'll have more tea while I wait," he said.

Underneath my raincoat and a lone gym sneaker, I found another manila envelope....

The waitress told me the old guy had gone to the bathroom. I paid the bill while I waited. After a good twelve minutes, I went to the men's room door and knocked. No response.

I returned to the table. The tiny Chinese girl came to collect her due.

"How much did he give you?" I asked

"What?"

"To tell me he went to the john?"

She smirked. "Twenty," she said.

I stiffed her on the tip....

Britt Montero, Miami police beat reporter, doesn't think a kid named Howie is really bad. He's been informing on a juvenile carjacking gang, *and* he helps an old lady who lives next to the garage of a big shopping mall. Britt sees him accept a box from the old lady and disappear into the garage. Britt follows him to the garage roof. (From Edna Buchanan's *Suitable for Framing*. PB. NY: Hyperion. 1995.)

"You followed me," he said accusingly.

"You got it. Now what are you doing up here?"

..."This my pad, man. This is where I stay."...

"Come on in. I'll show you."

He acted house-proud....

"It ain't too bad. 'Fore that I stayed in a car for a while and in an empty house. Want some coffee?"

"Sure." I sat on the milk crate and watched....

"It ain't bad at all." He measured instant coffee into two plastic mugs....He opened a jar crammed with paper packets of sugar and powdered cream, probably from the food court in the mall....

"You like the pink ones, the blue ones, or the real sugar?" He sifted through the paper packets, the perfect host.

"The real stuff," I said. "I think those others are bad for you."...

...He opened the box with a greedy flourish of anticipation. Half a dozen homemade brownies nestled on napkins inside.

He passed me one, along with a mug of coffee.

"Mmmmm." I savored the first bite....

It felt cozy up here atop Miami in the evening breeze with steaming coffee and rich chocolate treats. Almost like camping out....

"I don't do too much round here, you know," he said solemnly, "'cause I live here. Don't wanna make trouble where you live."

"Yeah, the mob has a phrase for it." He offered another brownie. Tempted, I declined. "You're so skinny," I said.

*   *   *

..."He [a kid called FMJ] ain't shooting 'cause of the car, he's shooting 'cause he likes it; the dude likes hurting people."

A sudden shudder tickled my spine. Must have been the caffeine and the chocolate cavorting through my system.

"You can't go on living like this, Howie...."

The upper crust is pointedly spelled out in caviar, foie gras, oysters, smoked salmon, champagne and tiramisu. While the lower crust is signaled by steak sandwiches, instant coffee, cinnamon rolls, diet cola, beer and bologna, Wonderbread and Cheez Whiz. But no matter what world the sleuth's inhabiting, she's got to be able to digest it all. Even the most unlikely combinations.

CHAPTER 20
LET'S START WITH SOMETHING
TO EAT

How to get a plot underway with food? Legions of women writers get food into that first sentence. How about this? "The colorful gourmet jelly beans were lined up across Amanda Roberts's desk in a precise row—lime, grape, orange, ice-blue mint, peanut butter, strawberry diaquiri, banana, chocolate. She studied the orderly procession listlessly, then dug into the jar on her desk for another handful, absentmindedly popping one into her mouth. Licorice, she realized with a grimace. It figured." This is how Sherryl Woods starts out *Bank On It*.

A salami sandwich is how Dorothy Gilman begins *Mrs. Pollifax Pursued*. After saying to heck with cholesterol, Emily Pollifax fixes herself a sandwich with her husband Cyrus's favorite sausage. Returning to her gardening, she begins to wonder if maybe the men attending tomorrow's Garden Club meeting might not prefer salami as well, rather than the cucumber sandwiches sitting in the fridge under a damp cloth. Back to the refrigerator, but lo and behold, the salami's vanished. How'd that happen? What's it mean? To find out you'll have to pursue Mrs. Pollifax yourself.

Investigative reporter Jessica James of Rochester, NY, is looking into the background of her mother's current lover with the help of *her* lover, Mafia boss Marcus Andrelli. Her mother, Kate James, has just flown in from California to disrupt Jessica's apartment for one. (From Meg O'Brien's *Hare Today, Gone Tomorrow*. PB. NY: Bantam Books. 1991.)

When I woke there was the smell of fresh coffee, the sound of dishes clattering in the kitchen, and Kate James's happy little hum. Mom always did hum around food.

I love living alone. Yet, there's something to be said for lying in bed and listening to the clink of silver or glass in the kitchen. It takes you back to when you were a kid....

*　　　　　　*　　　　　　*

The phone rang....

..."Why don't I pick you up around eight?" Marcus said. "We'll go to dinner."

"I can't. I, uh...I've sort of got company."

"Oh. Someone special?"

"My mom," I mumbled....

"You could invite me over," he said.

"For *dinner*? With my *mom*?" He had to be kidding.

"Why not?"

"Marcus, you aren't exactly the kind of catch a girl brings home to dinner."

"Try me," he said.

"No way. How would I explain about you—"

"Jesse," Mom called from the kitchen, "if that's your mobster friend you're talking to, tell him we're having seafood casserole and there's plenty to go around."...

As we sat over a steaming seafood casserole, Marcus couldn't have been more at home. I forget sometimes that he was once part of a warm Italian family. They must have gathered around the dinner table drinking wine and dunking biscòtti, teasing each other and telling stories of what happened that day....

"Have another piece of garlic bread?" She beamed.

"Thank you," Marcus enthused. "It's excellent bread. Did you buy it here in the neighborhood?"

"From DiAngelo's, down on the corner."

"I grew up with Connie DiAngelo," Marcus reminisced. "A wonderful family."

"Lovely people," Mom agreed.

I felt like I was at the Mad Hatter's tea party.

Dinner as a diviner to death? Here we have the twenty-year reunion of amateur sleuth Helma Zukas's Scoop River (Michigan) High School graduating class. She promised long ago that she would organize it and having smartly invested her HS account in Microsoft, Helma has planned and completely paid for the perfect Pacific Northwest getaway for her classmates. Ruth is Helma's best friend. (From Jo Dereske's *Miss Zukas and the Island Murders*. PB. NY: Avon Books. 1995.)

"Tonight's fun is free form," Ruth told him. "Just a casual dinner... menu gleaned from the terrific Pacific...."

"I'd like to propose a toast," Michael Petronas said, standing and raising his glass of wine. "To Scoop River."

"Scoop River," they repeated, clinking beer bottles, wine glasses, and coffee cups together....

Waiters entered from the kitchen, bearing plates of asparagus salad with citrus vinaigrette.

Ricky took a bite, then called to the waiter, "Do you have any Thousand Island dressing, something with a little more 'chunk' to it?"

Ruth and Helma exchanged quick glances. Helma studiously looked down and cut up an asparagus tip, refusing to give Ricky the satisfaction.

The entree was grilled salmon with a shrimp sauce accompanied by roasted potatoes with rosemary, and sauteed spinach. Baskets of warm sourdough bread sat at each corner of the table.

It was perfect. Helma mentally added a generous tip for the kitchen staff.

"You know," Lolly said brightly, "I like seafood best when it has breading on it, the crispy kind."

"And deep fried?" Ruth asked. "With French fries and catsup?"

"That's *right*," Lolly squealed. She poked at a shrimp. "This is kinda naked."

"Did you ever eat at Armedo's next to the bowling alley back home?" Wilson asked the table in general. "They *really* gave you a lot of food for your money."

"Too bad there isn't any gravy for these potatoes."

"Has this bread gone off? It tastes sour."

Helma hastily stood. "Why don't we go around the table and each relate our experiences since graduation."

"How I spent my life," Michael commented.

"All right, you go first," Helma told Michael.

"Okay. Get ready to be impressed, everybody. I teach high school English."

Sergeant Kathy Mallory is looking into the death of her adoptive father, also a cop, Louis Markowitz. For years Louis had played poker with medical examiner, Dr. Edward Slope, a rabbi, and a lawyer. Two weeks after Louis's death, the three have gathered at Rabbi Kaplan's to receive Louis's good friend, Charles Butler, who will take his place. "Mallory" plays no role in this scene, other than she was the "last woman" to leave Louis's house, and his love saved her life. (From Carol O'Connell's *Mallory's Oracle*. PB. London: Hutchinson, Arrow Books Limited, Random House UK Limited. 1995.)

Slope wandered into the kitchen to stand at the open door of the refrigerator. Louis Markowitz's refrigerator had been much like this one, as he recalled. Not so long ago, Louis's shelves had been filled with real food, built from a woman's blueprint of shopping lists and recipes, the makings of meals past and meals to come, warm colors of fruit and cool green vegetables, condiments and mysterious, unlabeled jars of liquids. When the last woman had gone from Louis's house, the refrigerator had changed its character, becoming shabby in its accumulation of deli bags and frozen dinners....

Now Slope stared at Anna Kaplan's well stocked shelves. Food is love, said this refrigerator.

He was assessing bowls and pots and checking under the lids of Tupperware when the doorbell rang....

He clutched a Tupperware container to his chest and made the contorted face of a man who would rather not cry. He set the plastic container on the tray. What was missing? he wondered as he picked up the tray. When the bell rang again, announcing a fourth person, the tray fell from his hands....

When he was again in full possession of everything he had lost, he carried the tray down the narrow hall and into the rabbi's den....

Slope liked this man immediately. He looked at the faces of his friends, and, like himself, they were unconsciously, accidentally smiling....

"I inherited his chair." Charles eyed the tray of sandwich makings with the discrimination of a connoisseur, and passed over the Cheddar cheese for the Swiss.

Two deaths so far in NYPD Detective Kathy Mallory's latest case which involves a band of aging magicians, the most mysterious of whom is Malakhai. In this early scene Mallory has chosen to interrogate Malakhai in one of the city's trendiest eateries. Background: Louisa was Malakhai's wife many, many years ago. She died in Paris during WWII in a trick gone wrong. (From Carol O'Connell's *Shell Game*. PB. London: Hutchinson, Arrow Books Limited, Random House UK Limited. 2000.)

Lest any illicit smoke escape the enclosure, an air-purification system was hard at work in the main dining room....In this odor-free section, non-smokers observed the diners caged in glass as historical exhibits from the days before the sterilization of New York City....

When she removed her coat, the black cashmere blazer and satin-trimmed jeans also passed inspection. The *maitre d'* mouthed the words, *Oh, yes.* The people in his waiting line wore more formal attire, but Mallory was dressed in money....

"Good evening."..."You're right on time."..."And I mean to the second."

In lieu of hello, she said, "You got a lot of mileage out of that German uniform. You wore it the day you took Louisa out of the transit camp—and again the night you shot her."...

He signaled to the waiter and pointed to the empty bottle...."I remember it well—superb tailoring. It belonged to an SS officer."

"Did you kill that officer?"

"No. Sorry to disappoint you, Mallory." He blew a smoke ring and watched it rise into the blades of the fan....

The waiter appeared with a tray balanced at shoulder level. After unfolding a stand with his free hand, he set his burden down, then rearranged all the items on a tabletop barely large enough to accommodate three plates and silverware, glasses, a bottle, an ashtray and a purse. Mallory and Malakhai watched in silent fascination as the waiter altered the laws of physics to expand space, creating more room for a basket of bread, a candle, another wine bottle and a large plate of hors-d'oeuvres.

"I couldn't have done that," said Malakhai.

Sharon McCone, San Francisco PI, has been hired by a well-known photographer to find his missing roommate, Jane Anthony. Sharon tracks down the owner of the last place where Jane worked, a hospice for the wealthy. Once Dr. Allen Keller realizes that Sharon is not there about his impending divorce, he welcomes her into his home. (From Marcia Muller's *Games to Keep the Dark Away.* PB. NY: Warner Books, Mysterious Press. 1990.)

"I like them gooey," he said over his shoulder, "but I keep breaking the yolks."

"I like them that way too." I followed him. "There are two kinds of people: the ones who break the yolk before frying the egg and the ones who don't. It's like people who use sandwich spread versus people who use real mayonnaise."

"And Scotch drinkers versus bourbon drinkers. Or people who eat small curd cottage cheese, as opposed to the ones who like large curds." Keller led me into a large, tiled kitchen. It was spotlessly clean except for the stove top, which was littered with egg shells. A partly fried egg with a broken yolk sat in congealing grease in a frying pan. There were several more eggs in the sink. Keller motioned at the stove: "See what you can do. Fix one for yourself if you're hungry."

Never shy where food was concerned, I jumped at the invitation; after all, it was almost five o'clock....

..."By the way, since it's not me you're after, what're you investigating?..."

After I'd bitten into my sandwich and gotten yolk all over my chin, I dug into my bag and took out Snelling's photo of Jane Anthony. "Do you remember this woman?"

To reap the generous benefits from Uncle Harold's trust fund, Jane da Silva is obliged to carry on his work solving "hopeless" cases for people who otherwise could not afford help. Posing as a writer for *Seafood Now*, Jane has gone to Norway to solve the murder of a young woman. Her agenda calls for her to dine out with a woman named Ragnhild, who turns out to be very unhappy with Americans. Could there possibly be a connection between the girl's murder and fishy politics? (From K. K. Beck's *Cold Smoked*. PB. NY: Warner Books, Mysterious Press. 1996.)

Jane smiled and tried to look sympathetic. "I suppose people are afraid the world is running out of whales."

"We have eighty-five thousand minke whales off our coast," Ragnhild said heatedly. "And we want to harvest a few for our own use."

Jane nodded and pretended again to read the Norwegian menu. She wondered if whale was on it.

Ragnhild shook her head sadly. "…How many buffaloes are left in America?"

Jane felt on firm ground here. She wasn't supposed to know anything about hoofed animals. "I have no idea," she said.

"Tell them!" said Ragnhild, getting shrill. "Tell them in America that we're fed up. When we had the Olympics we were told the Americans wouldn't like us to eat reindeer, either. They think of this one with the red nose. What is he called?"

"Rudolph," said Jane.

"These fanatics have already ruined our fur business."

"What should we eat?" said Jane, handing over the menu.

"The moose should be good," said Ragnhild.

"I had moose last night," said Jane ….

She ended up with a first course of reindeer…served with a piquant brown sauce; then came cod with melted butter, tasty except for the disconcerting fact that the cod's decapitated head, its eye removed, lay in slack-jawed profile on the side of the plate. Jane assumed this was for visual interest and made no attempt to eat it, but when her companion looked down at her plate with a little frown, she was afraid she was going to be scolded for leaving it untouched.

Instead Ragnhild said, "It is a pity the tongue isn't there, but we sell those to the Japanese."

New Orleans restaurant owner Arthur Hebert (pronounced A-Bear) has been shot by one of his kids. Homicide detective Skip Langdon is trying to find out which one. She goes to interview Nina Phillips, restaurant manager, only to find Arthur's widow, Sugar, sitting beside Nina who is ordering the day's supplies. Reed is Sugar's daughter. (From Julie Smith's *House of Blues*. PB. NY: Ballantine Books, an Ivy Book. 1996.)

…"I need four cases of shrimp, please, sir; a hundred pounds of crawfish; fifteen pounds of alligator; fifteen pounds of frog legs; five gallons of oysters; seventy pounds of pompano fillet …."…"No. No crab today."

Sugar shook her head violently.

"Just a minute, Mr. Daroca."

Sugar said, "What do you mean no crab? We have nine crab dishes on the menu."

"Jumbo lump crabmeat's eighteen-fifty a pound."…

"If I bought crab at that price, we'd have to charge so much for it, no one would order it."

"Well, can't you get imitation crab?"

"Your husband always said, 'This is *Hebert's*, Ms. Phillips. You order crab remoulade, it better be crab.'"

"We'll just do half and half," said Sugar. "Nobody'll know the difference." Her expression said she was absolutely confident no one had ever had such a clever idea.

"Reed tried that about five years ago. You know what happened? The chef walked out."

"Can't we just get a new chef?"…

…"Sugar, you've had a bad shock.…You shouldn't be here, stressing yourself out at a time like this."…

"Nina Phillips, don't you patronize me."

"I'm not patronizing you.…"

"It's not your restaurant."

..."Sugar, honey...you have to remember, your husband was raised in this business....You can't just walk in one morning and take over a multi-million dollar business."

Sugar looked as if she couldn't decide whether to destroy the room or cry. It was a small child's anger and hurt Skip saw on her face.

She must have been some mom. *Skip thought.* A giant-sized four-year-old.

Patricia Delaney is an "investigative consultant." She lives just outside Cincinnati. She went off today to collect from a client, only to find a dead woman in the client's swimming pool. Now a few pages later she decides she's going to try to forget the whole thing with a deluxe pizza, dry red wine, and her faithful pal. (From Sharon Gwyn Short's *Past Pretense*. PB. NY: Ballantine Books, a Fawcett Gold Medal Book. 1996.)

Patricia opened the door a crack, and a dog started whining and pawing to get out. Inside the house, the phone was ringing. Patricia closed her eyes. This was how the nightmare had started this afternoon—an eternity ago. Patricia at a door, a dog eager for attention on the other side. Then she had crossed the threshold from just another day to a day made in hell.

But this is your door, your home, your dog....

Patricia laughed. She was carrying a pizza box, on top of which was a video and the day's mail. "I told you I'd be right back. I got a Mama LaRosa's deluxe, with anchovies. So let me get settled in, and we'll eat."...

...A quiet evening at home, alone with Sammie, a pizza loaded with all the goodies, and the soothing patter of the Nick and Nora Charles characters in *The Thin Man*. Simple, as normal as pumpkin pie on Thanksgiving....

...Sammie whined. Patricia turned and looked at him. "Okay. If you're as hungry as me, you're nearly starving."

One slice of pizza, cut up, in the dog's bowl for Sammie, a few slices for her plus a nice glass of dry red wine....She grinned to herself. Home sweet home....She nibbled on pizza and sipped the wine as she sorted through the day's mail....

Nope, I'm not figuring it out tonight, Patricia thought. She carried her plate and glass back to the kitchen and poured herself another glass of dry red wine. Sammie was snoring contentedly....Time for the oh-so-civilized detecting antics in *The Thin Man.*

April Henry uses morning break time at Oregon Motor Vehicles to allow Claire Montrose, vanity plate verifier and amateur sleuth, to tell a good friend about a mysterious painting left to her by a relative she hardly knew. You *know* these gals work for the state. Their break is super stale coffee in a dim room furnished with glowing vending machines and at the same 15 minutes every day. Ever heard of a "warm wiener welcome"? Does it have to do with food or sex or both? To find out more about wieners and to discover the secrets of this marvelous painting you'll have to check out April Henry's 1999 *Circles of Confusion.*

To introduce a country setting, important secondary characters, and a tense internal plot, J. A. Jance has Cochise County Sheriff Joanna Brady fix dinner for her closest friend and their daughters at Joanna's ranch. But even steaming, foil-wrapped potatoes, butter, sour cream, chopped green onions, and a scrumptious freshly baked meatloaf can't get Joanna's haggard and depressed friend eating again. The scene ends with Joanna and daughter Jenny feeding and watering their menagerie. *Outlaw Mountain* (HarperCollinsPublishers, Avon Books, 2000), like Jance's other books, has tender, life-affirming moments, here in the "feeding frenzy" of eager animals munching oats and hay to offset the rejection of food from Joanna's needful friend.

Food goes down good in the middle of a novel as well. Housewife Louise Eldridge is a binge gardener whose passion for growing things is flowering in her new home in suburban Washington, D.C. Her husband is settled into a cozy job in the State Department and daughter Jane is making new friends. The only flaw in Louise's personal Eden is a damp, dank corner of yard that needs filling with mulch. Purist that she is, she gathers up bags of leaves from neighborhood curbs. But the bags hold more than leaves, and the police must be called. Detective Geraghty is interviewing Louise. (From Ann Ripley's *Mulch*. PB. NY: Bantam Books. 1998.)

...She felt primitive: hungry, headachy, unbathed, wearing yesterday's clothes. Then she took a piece of toast and spread it with a little home-made jam. "Now you go ahead. Ask your questions." She gave him a fleeting smile and took a big bite of toast.

Geraghty looked more sober now. His smile was gone. "Well, ma'am, I told you I thought this situation was no fault of your own. That doesn't mean there won't be some suspicion attached to someone in this house...."

Louise gulped the toast down her unwilling esophagus....

..."I am afraid that although this check will include you and even your daughter, it will focus heavily on your husband." He looked up at her, his face redder than usual.

She felt queasy again. "Tell me just why that is."

"Well, the body is a woman's, relatively young. Young woman killed; points to a man usually. Only rarely another woman. Dismemberment points to a man, except...for some historic exceptions."

Louise's voice was dull. "This was a young woman. Who was she?"

Geraghty hesitated, then said, "We don't know that yet. You know we found only about half of her body: two freckled forearms, two upper arms, part of a leg, and part of a torso. No head. No feet. No hands...hands are gone."...

"...Exactly what do you want from us?"

"Not us, Mrs. Eldridge. I want to know about you. So why don't you just finish your breakfast there, and then we'll take a little ride around the route where you picked up leaf bags. That way we can kill two birds with one stone."

Another midway meal. Attorney Annie MacPherson has merged her own small law firm with one of Seattle's largest. When her boss, Gordon Barclay, invites her to lunch at Ray's Boathouse, she learns he's about to break away and create a firm of his own. Will she join him? Barclay has his dark side, an affair with his secretary that ended with her suicide just nights ago. Still, lunch at Ray's may be the shot in the arm Annie needs. (From Janet L. Smith's *Practice to Deceive*. PB. NY: Ballantine Books, an Ivy Book. 1993.)

When Kristen returned for their orders, Annie opted for the seared ling cod with roasted red-pepper aioli, while Barclay ordered the sauteed scallops, asking the waitress to be sure the chef didn't overcook them....

"...A life without risk is boring. Don't you think I know it's unusual for a man my age, a senior partner...to strike off on his own? That's why I want to do it, to show them I still have the right stuff."...

"I need someone with a general practice background....Someone with good trial experience....A woman to balance the rowdy crew I've already lined up...."

Gordon paused while Kristen trotted over to clear the plates. "Dessert, Annie? They have a wonderful chocolate decadence here."

"No, just coffee. Black."...

Annie paused, sipping her coffee. "When do you need an answer?"

"The sooner the better. By this weekend at the latest."...

Barclay held the door and Annie walked outside into the fresh air. A parking valet...materialized and took Barclay's ticket. "Car, sir?"

"Mercedes sedan."

"Yes sir."...

"Wait, Gordon, my sunglasses. I think I left them on the table...." Annie turned back in the direction of the restaurant.

She had only taken a step or two when it happened. First there was a sharp crack, then two more. A woman somewhere was screaming. She heard Barclay's voice, rising above the others, but couldn't make out the words. What was wrong, why were there so many people? Then she felt the stinging. Sharp, hot, a thousand needles. Terrible pain. Someone pulled Annie to the ground and shielded her body.

Susan Dunlap can always be counted on to glue her novels together with jelly donuts, pizza, and takeout. Here, Detective Jill Smith talks with PI Herman Ott about one Beverly Zagoya, mountaineer, currently pitching an Everest expedition. Ott claims Zagoya killed three people on a previous expedition.

The conversation at Ott's office is followed up with Jill back in her own office with her buddies Howard and Pereira. (From Susan Dunlap's *Diamond in the Buff*. PB. NY: Dell Publishing. 1991.)

…"Ott, climbers die. It's a fact of the sport."

He slammed the window shut and spun to face me. "Do I have to spell it out for you? Okay. *A*: there was a safer route. *B*: that route was longer. *C*: the expedition didn't have enough supplies to take the safer route. Because, *D*: Zagoya didn't plan well enough. Got it?"

"But Ott, there are a lot of variables—"

Ott was actually shaking. "Smith, the woman cut corners buying food. *Food*, for Chrissakes….They don't have Seven-Elevens on the top of the Himalaya. She as good as killed those three people."…

*   *   *

When I got back to the office, Howard was sitting facing into the room, the yard or more of his legs sprawled across it, his feet resting against my desk. On the edge of his desk sat Pereira, *her* feet propped on his lower drawer, her chin covered with powdered sugar.

"Where'd you find that doughnut?..." Still eyeing her sugared chin, I demanded, "You didn't eat the last one, did you?"...

...Howard leaned forward and opened my bottom drawer. "But there is one jelly." He pulled out a napkin-wrapped mound.

I unwrapped. "Ah, Howard. You're a fine man."

"Finer than you think." He extricated a thermos and poured. The smell of Peet's coffee floated up....

...I recounted what Herman Ott had told me about the three deaths on the Zagoya expedition....

"...I figured by now you"—I eyed Pereira—"would have gotten me a lead from the Humboldt County guys."

"And I have."..."And lots, lots more...."

Boston PI Angela Matelli has been hired by her old Marine Corps boss Ev Morrow to find his missing fourteen-year-old daughter Edie. Edie's best friend, Rachel, has been murdered. Was this Edie's fate as well? Midway in the novel, Ev has come to Angela's apartment to catch up on her investigation. (From Wendi Lee's *Missing Eden*. PB. NY: Worldwide Mystery. 1999.)

We sat in companionable silence, munching bakery cookies and sipping coffee.

Ev broke the quiet. "I miss her so much. Do you think there's a chance she's still alive?" He blinked several times....This sort of nurturing wasn't my strength. I was more comfortable with making dinner for a troubled person, nourishing the body rather than the soul....

...God help me, I couldn't stop myself. I leaned over for the kiss that was inevitable....

*   *   *

"Sorry about that, Chief," were my next words....Before he could answer me, I picked up our empty coffee mugs and went into the kitchen....

Ev was the first available man I was attracted to...and I'd probably just screwed up my chances of anything coming of this. A drop of hot coffee splashed, stinging my wrist. I jumped, set the pot down, shook my hand, and cursed.

"Everything all right in there?" Ev called from the living room....

...What an incredibly selfish bitch I was. Here was a guy who was worried about his little girl, and I'm drooling over him like a starving woman over a piece of filet mignon....

*   *   *

"Hey, Angie, remember when that obnoxious corporal was transferred into our unit?"

I chuckled....

"Think he ever found out who put the chicken carcass in his air vent?" I had flirted with the corporal back at the office while Ev sneaked into the guy's room, unscrewed the grillwork to the air vent, and slipped the chicken carcass into it....Finally, the big day came for inspection. The captain came by, screwed up her nose, and demanded to know where the reek was coming from.

"He had tears in his eyes while she yelled at him," I said, gasping for air....

These clever authors are good at using food to end their books as well. There's no better scene than when Benni Harper goes out to her father's and grandmother's ranch to unwind after a difficult case. Throughout Earlene Fowler's *Fool's Puzzle*, Benni has irrationally blamed herself for her husband's accidental death. Ready to toss a jar of strawberry preserves into a ravine as a symbolic gesture that might purge her lingering guilt, she hears her husband's voice saying, get practical. Why toss away a perfectly good jar of strawberry jam when the toast's just waiting in the kitchen? For what happens next in that kitchen, you'll have to read *Fool's Puzzle* to the very end.

Just as you'll have to read Julie Smith's *Dead in the Water* to the end if you want to know how to spoil Thanksgiving turkey and dressing with slimy eyeless hagfish and puffers containing the world's deadliest nerve toxin. Talk of feeding is rife in this Monterey gig of attorney Rebecca Schwartz. From first page to last page it's sushi, pizza, cappuccino, radicchio, tuna sandwiches, huevos rancheros, chile rellenos, moo shu pork, crab cakes, lunch after lunch, dinner after dinner. You can't beat Smith's way with words. A friend dangles Monterey's outlet stores in front of Rebecca like cookies before a kid. The friend's mother describes her daughter as cool as a cucumber. Whom Rebecca quickly upgrades to cool as a whole truckload of cucumbers. Little girls look as smug as cats used to lapping cream, not chowing chow. Jell-O is used to describe (1) a giant sea slug, (2) fat under some guy's T-shirt, and (3) Rebecca's knees when faced with the price of a new BMW.

So, toast and jam is a chance to discuss a leaf bag full of body parts. A fried egg sandwich an occasion for flashing the picture of a missing woman. Midday coffee and donuts the opportunity for cops discussing the evidence. Even the simplest of food scenes can advance a storyline, explore players, define conflicts, and bring about resolution. And from start to finish, there's seldom a snack for its own sake.

CHAPTER 21
STIRRING IN SUSPENSE

Sue Grafton does it so well. Starting with *"A" is for Alibi* where she has PI Kinsey Millhone eat one of the "most sensual" meals she's ever had with a guy whose face is described as "shadowed," "stark," and "fearful." What about him makes Kinsey as tense as a joke snake ready to jump out of a box? Why does she feel he's holding something back? Why aren't her feminist sensibilities offended when he orders for her? Are we witnessing seduction over a buttery pâté, sautéed sand dabs, succulent green grapes, and raspberries dolloped with tart cream? For sure, you have to keep reading to find out.

Plots have got to have suspense, lots of suspense. Here's how it's done—with glasses of chilled white wine, a thermos of coffee, hot milk and honey.

V.I. Warshawski, feisty, independent Chicago PI: "My theory of detection resembles Julia Child's approach to cooking: grab a lot of ingredients from the shelves, put them in a pot and stir, and see what happens....Maybe it was time to let things simmer a bit and see if the smell of cooking gave me any new ideas."

Stirring the pot can lead to death threats, and death threats can lead to deadly action. V.I. is on her way home from a stressful afternoon with the partner of a woman who was murdered. V.I. knew the victim well and blames herself for her death. (From Sara Paretsky's *Killing Orders*. PB. NY: Dell Publishing. 1993.)

...I needed comfort food tonight.

...The thickly falling snow coagulated the traffic even after rush hour. All food starting with *p* is comfort food, I thought: pasta, potato chips, pretzels, peanut butter, pastrami, pizza, pastry...By the time I reached the Belmont exit I had quite a list....

...Ran up the stairs fast, stooping low....I met a body half again as big as mine....Using the flashlight I smashed where I thought his jaw should be. It connected with bone....I sensed his arm coming up toward my face. I ducked and fell over in a rolling ball, felt liquid on the back of my neck. Heard him tearing down the stairs....

...The back of my neck began burning as though I'd been stung by fifty wasps....I...got into the apartment....I ran to the bathroom shedding clothes....leaped into the tub....

Soaking wet and shivering I climbed out....

...Shock, half my mind thought clinically....Hot milk—that would do, hot milk with lots of honey....I had to hold the cup close to my body to keep from spilling it all over me....

When the phone rang I jumped....It was Lotty....

When the phone rang again, I was ready for it...."How are your eyes, Miss Warshawski?..."

Who chopped down the lemon tree? Who's making the anonymous phone calls? Who cracked a pane in the front window of the house on Garber Street in Berkeley, California? PI Jeri Howard has to figure out which of the eight housemates is the target and why. What better bribe than breakfast out for an impecunious student, in this case Rachel, who also happens to volunteer at an abortion clinic. (From Janet Dawson's *A Credible Threat*. PB. NY: Ballantine Books, a Fawcett Crest Book. 1997.)

On weekends there was a long wait to get a table at Rick and Ann's, but now, on a weekday, we'd been able to walk right in. Rachel, with unabashed enjoyment, dug into a stack of buttermilk pancakes. My omelet, with layers of eggplant, tomatoes, and feta cheese, was so large as to be daunting, but I was making a concerted effort to reduce its dimensions....

"So what do you want to talk about, Jeri?" Rachel reached for the syrup and poured another dollop on her pancakes. "Besides men."

I polished off a forkful of my omelet before answering. "About what's happening at the house."...

"Strange," Rachel continued. "This is the first time whoever is doing this has talked. Always before it was—" She stopped, fork in midair. "Menacing presence. But no words."...

"You thought of something," I said as Rachel frowned.

"Yes, I did." She looked thoughtful. "The last time I was at the clinic, I'm sure I heard one of the protesters call my first name. I think it was a man. What if he found out my last name, where I live, my phone number?..."

Our server appeared at the table and I asked her to box up the rest of the omelet, which had defeated me....

"Thanks for breakfast," Rachel told me as we stood....

I stuck the box containing the remains of the omelet into the little refrigerator tucked under a worktable at the back of my long narrow office. Then I wrote myself a note that read, "Take leftovers home." Otherwise the box would sit there, forgotten, contents growing mold, until I began to wonder what was causing the smell.

In *Edwin of the Iron Shoes*, PI Sharon McCone is working for All Souls Legal Cooperative in San Francisco investigating the murder of an antique dealer. This makes a lot of people uncomfortable. She finds herself being chased, but manages to break away and run to the famous Cliff House. (From Marcia Muller's *Edwin of the Iron Shoes*. PB. NY: Warner Books, Mysterious Press. 1990.)

Ahead I saw the stairs to the dining room and the upper bar. I wanted to find shelter in the ladies' room, but its downstairs location would be a trap. I climbed slowly, my knees weak. The bar was crowded and brightly lit, a cheerful haven from the dismal, foggy sea beyond huge windows....

A group of people in Levi's and windbreakers occupied a table in the far window bay. As I stood there, one of them, a woman with a round, freckled face and dark hair spied me....

"Hey, Sharon! Hello! Come on over!"

It was my friend Paula Mercer, a fine arts graduate from Berkeley who worked for the de Young Museum.

Almost collapsing with relief, I started across the bar. The group rearranged themselves as Paula greeted me, introducing everyone by first names and adding asides that led me to believe they were part of the local arts and crafts crowd. As I sat down and one of the guys called for another glass of wine, I glanced at the entryway.

Frankie stood there, his shiny suit rumpled and sweat-stained, his tie askew. His eyes scanned the room and came to rest on me. Our glances locked, and an icy dread frosted my limbs.

"Sharon?" Paul's voice was concerned. "What's the matter?"

I dragged my eyes away from Frankie. "What?"...

The waitress placed a glass of Chablis in front of me, and I grabbed it, gulping deeply. "I'll be all right," I said. "I'm just in a little trouble...Will you help me?"

"Of course."

"Don't leave me, that's all. Not for a second...."

If you asked Kate Austen to define herself, she'd call herself a single mom first, then lover of homicide detective Michael Stone, then fledgling art consultant. She's investigating the death of friend Mona. The police say suicide but the facts don't fit: Mona was found with a bottle of Glenfiddich, and she drank gin. Kate searches Mona's home and finds evidence of an affair conducted at The Timbercreek Lodge. While she's there, UPS delivers a box that contains expensive cuff links engraved with the letter "S." An affair gone sour? When Kate starts to think murder, everyone looks like a villain. Here, attending a school fund-raiser, she chats up Laurelle Simms's husband, Paul. (From Jonnie Jacobs's *Murder Among Friends*. PB. NY: Kensington Publishing Corporation. 1996.)

I made a sweep of the buffet, fixed myself a mini ham sandwich, then loaded my plate with an assortment of fancy delicacies....

...The bartender appeared and Paul pulled out his billfold. "Let me get this. What'll you have?"

"White wine."

He turned to the bartender. "A glass of the Hidden Cellars chenin blanc and a double Glenfiddich, straight, no ice...."

The auctioneer's voice boomed from the other side of the room. "Going once, going twice, sold to the beautiful lady in blue."

There was a swell of clapping. Laurelle shrieked and waved to Paul.

"Looks like you just bought yourself a weekend at Sea Ranch," I said....

"...To my mind, Mendocino is a much nicer place....There's a place I like to stay, sort of off the beaten track...."

"Sounds nice."

"It is. The place is called The Timbercreek Lodge...."

My gaze drifted from the glass of scotch to his raised arm, where it froze on the black ebony cufflinks.

Simms. The initial "S...."

"I...I need to get home early," I stammered. "Sitters, you know...."

...My original plan had been to find the car and call Michael, but with the attendant waiting to slip the BMW into my spot, I couldn't simply sit there.

When I got to the bottom of the hill, I turned onto the main road, then pulled off to the shoulder to make the call. I was punching in the number when I felt a hand reach over from the back seat and take the phone from me.

"I'd rather you didn't do that," Paul said.

You can write Jonnie Jacobs at *jonnie@netcom.com* or visit her web site at *http://www.nmomysteries.com/main.htm.*

Ex-cop Hannah Barlow of Laguna Beach is beginning a second career as a lawyer. She's looking into the disappearance of Father Kostka, a priest who was researching the history of a woman being considered for sainthood. It's all mixed up with Sanctus, an arch-conservative Catholic group.

In this scene Barlow finally meets Father Occhipinti, Sanctus's leader, at the home of a wealthy Sanctus supporter. Intellectually she makes the usual assumptions about someone who is a priest, but on another level she senses something else. Food gives it away. (From Carroll Lachnit's *A Blessed Death*. PB. NY: Berkley Publishing Group, Berkley Prime Crime. 1996.)

On the terrace, a dozen men in perfect khaki pants and starchy camouflage jackets sipped cocktails and cleaned rifles....At the end of the terrace, three young Latino men reached into baskets, pulled out the limp bodies of doves, and calmly stripped them of their feathers.

...Occhipinti was sitting at an oak table that was covered with platters of fruit and cheese. Behind him, a spit of tiny dove breasts turned and sizzled in the flames of a stone fireplace. A waiter was standing next to the Occhipinti, his neck outstretched, as though waiting for the ax.

Occhipinti was praying under his breath. Latin or Spanish, Hannah thought....Behind a granite counter, a cook slapped masa into circles and stole glances at the men....

Occhipinti turned and said something to the cook in Spanish, and she laughed, a little nervously. She held up the masa and, from what Hannah could understand, told him her secret for perfect *pupusas*. Hannah knew the food well. The cornmeal pockets stuffed with cheese were a culinary treasure from El Salvador. An immigrant family's *pupuseria* near Hannah's apartment had sustained her while she studied for the bar exam....

"...Father Kostka is a member of Sanctus, isn't he?"

Occhipinti said nothing for a moment....But, finally, he nodded. "We pray for our brother to be brought back safely from the hands of his enemies."

"What enemies?"...

"There are alliances, networks, satrapies that honeycomb the Church. A gay church here. A liberation theology camp there. Pro-choice Catholics. Women priests....These things are very wrong, to us...."

When senior Eugenia Potter finds pottery shards on her Arizona ranch, she signs herself up for the Women's Hike into History at an archeological camp near Mesa Verde to learn more about an ancient mystery: Why did the Anasazi build the cliff dwellings when they did, and why after only 100 years did they leave? Before they can begin to guess, one of the women is found dead (accident or murder?) and sixteen teenagers with guides disappear into the wilderness. Police, parents, and the press over-take the camp, but the women had paid to hike and hike they would. But their leader Susan deceives them, forcing them to hike to a point of no return, at least for that evening. Thankfully, Bingo the cook shows up to serve them some tasty campfire grub. (From Nancy Pickard's [based on the character created by Virginia Rich] *The Blue Corn Murders*. PB. NY: Dell Publishing. 1999.)

Dinner was simple: steaks dredged in fresh chopped garlic and grilled over an open flame; corn on the cob cooked in foil over the fire; green salad that Bingo had prepared back on campus; and pecan brownies iced with chocolate....

While they ate, Bingo told them what happened…after they left. "It's a zoo back there. Dinnertime for the reporter animals. They're feasting on this. Sixteen kids missing. Parallels to ancient history. It's so dramatic, they're slobbering all over themselves. We've got cable news. Foreign press."…

When Madeline and Lillian complained about the trick that Susan had pulled on them to get them here, the little chef's reaction was only to laugh at them. "Hah. Maybe you accidentally uncovered the secret of the Anasazi," she said, grinning. Susan and Genia exchanged startled glances. "Maybe their leader told all the poor suckers they were only going to take a little hike over to the next mesa. Only when they got there and turned around to go back, he said, 'Not so fast! I say we're heading south, and guess who's holding the water?'"…

She looked up, saw the effect she'd had on the others…."…What I mean is, so maybe something like that happened to the Anasazi, too, you know?"…

"Bingo?" Susan's tone was straightforward. "There's not much evidence of that, of what you just suggested. No sign, really of a forced march, or bodies strewn along the way."

But the chef had the last word. "After another eight hundred years, there may not be much sign of any of us, Susan."

It's Sunday brunch at Tortilla Flats, a Santa Fe family restaurant. Forensic psychiatrist Dr. Sylvia Strange is meeting friend Rosie Sanchez, prison administrator, to discuss a deeply disturbed inmate at Rosie's prison who's up for parole. (From Sarah Lovett's *Dangerous Attachments*. PB. NY: Ballantine Books, an Ivy Book. 1996.)

"I'm in a tight spot," Sylvia said as she slid into the booth. She waited while the waitress set a huge platter of stuffed tortilla, beans, rice, and a side of grease-puffed sopaipillas in front of Rosie….

"Share these with me," Rosie said pushing the basket of sopaipillas and a plastic squeeze-bottle of honey toward Sylvia. "I'm listening."

Sylvia set the envelope containing the pouch on the table....

Rosie pointed to her full mouth and wrinkled her nose quizzically. After she swallowed, she said, "What is that?"...

She watched while Rosie slit open the plastic runner with a polished nail....

"Is that what I think it is?" Rosie asked....

"An ear?" Sylvia kept her voice low....

"Where the hell did it come from? Whose is it?"

Sylvia took a swallow of coffee....

She held up her thumb and said, "First, I'd like to avoid getting my source fired. Second," her index finger joined her thumb, "I'm not at liberty to speculate on the ownership of the pouch. It should've gone directly to you in the first place."

"Why didn't it?"

Sylvia dropped her hands to the table, tore off a piece of sopaipilla, and leaned forward. "Because he was scared." The crispy golden dough disappeared between her lips....

..."If this is a human ear, then I have to seriously consider the likelihood that it came from my body snatcher."

"It's human," Sylvia said.

"What's the rest of this stuff? A ring, hair, teeth...a gallstone? *Jesus*. It's a medicine pouch, isn't it?..."

Rosie pushed her plate away and reached for her purse where she carefully stowed the baggie and its contents....

"Brunch is on me."

While sailing in her 40-foot sloop off the Seattle coast, sailing instructor Kellie Montgomery spots a luxury sailboat drifting toward rocks. Owners Donald and Miranda Moyer are dead, slain. But Kellie owes Donald a big one—after all he was the lawyer who helped her adopt a baby 20 years ago. The investigation takes her to Bremerton, Washington, where she meets the Chapmans and learns that not every Moyer client is a happy client. (From Valerie Wilcox's *Sins of Silence*. PB. NY: Berkley Publishing Group, Berkley Prime Crime. 1998.)

...She [Betty Chapman] stood at the sound of footsteps on the wooden porch and ran to greet the short, wiry man who strode through the front door....

"She's here about Donald Moyer."...

"You want to eat lunch out here?" she asked.

He nodded distractedly....

She turned to me. "Could I bring you something, too? I've got plenty."

I was hungry, but just the thought of liver and onions—not to mention the smell, trailing after Betty Chapman like cheap perfume—was enough to quell my appetite. I shook my head....

Betty bustled into the room again, this time carrying a plastic tray with a single mug of coffee on it. I wondered where his lunch was, but Chapman didn't seem to notice....

He picked up his coffee mug as if to take another sip, but waved it at his wife instead. "Good God, Betts, when do I get some lunch?"

She jumped up from the couch....

"You were saying about Moyer," I prompted.

"He suckered us in but good. Even invited us out on that fancy boat of his...."

Lucy's wild barking stopped further conversation. We both turned toward the kitchen. "Jesus H.," said Chapman, sniffing at the air. "Something's burning." He bounded out of the recliner and raced for the kitchen like the devil was after him....

Clouds of thick black smoke billowed out at us....

"Is Betty all right?"

..."She wasn't in the kitchen."

"Where is she?"...

"Hell if I know." He shrugged...."She was gone three days the last time....Only it was chili that got burned then."...

Common prescription medicines are the weapons of choice in Nancy Pickard's *Generous Death*. In high enough doses, even pain killers and hypertension medicine can do the job, especially if mixed with alcohol or coffee. Amateur sleuth Jenny Cain already has three poisonings on her plate when the fourth potential victim, elderly Minnie Mimbs, ventures out into the night at the request of church custodian James Turner, to look at a roof cracking under the weight of snow. (From Nancy Pickard's *Generous Death*. PB. NY: Simon & Schuster, Pocket Books. 1987.)

It was so still inside the chapel that she could hear the snow shift on the door. She peered up into the darkness at the suspect ceiling, listening for creaks and looking for cracks. Well, she didn't hear or see any signs of impending disaster, but James would show her....

"Mrs. Mimbs."

Her old heart jumped violently as the figure walked out of the shadows at the front of the chapel. She laughed a little in surprise and relief when she saw who it was.

"Glory! You startled me," she said and sank into the hard seat of a walnut pew. "I didn't expect anyone but James Turner."

"I'm waiting for him, too."

"Oh, for heaven's sake. I can't imagine why James would bother you about our roof...."

"No bother. But it's freezing in here, don't you think? I've brought a thermos of coffee—here, I'll pour some for you."

"I never drink coffee after six P.M.," she said regretfully. "Oh, be careful, you've spilled some! You didn't burn yourself?"

"No. Just got a little on the floor, I'm afraid. Actually it's decaffeinated, if that's what you're worried about."

"Oh, well in that case, I don't mind if I do." She reached out grateful hands for the steaming plastic cup. "If it's decaffeinated, I don't think I'll have any trouble sleeping tonight, do you?"

"No, you'll sleep just fine."

Minnie sipped. Goodness, the coffee tasted awfully sweet, but the warmth was wonderful. Where *was* that James Turner?

NYC John Jay College of Criminal Justice psychology professor Mackenzie "Mac" Griffin has come home to Rogiston, Connecticut, where her academic parents live and where her brother Chad has just purchased the local art gallery—whose previous owner has since washed up on the beach. At 11:30 on this Sunday morning Chad has gone off briefly to the gallery, while Mac helps Stella, the very Scottish housekeeper, prepare dinner. (From Jeanne McCafferty's *Artist Unknown*. PB. London: Headline. 1995.)

Stella's Sunday dinners were always big, always delicious, and always served at 2:30 on the dot. Knowing how sacrosanct Stella's schedule was, and knowing that Chad had said he was only going to be an hour or so, Mac began to notice the time around 1:15. At 1:30, the phone rang. Stella answered, and after a hearty "Wherrre are ya, lad?" and an answer that evidently didn't satisfy her, she said "She's right here," and handed the phone to Mackenzie. "It's your brrrother," she said. "Remind him the roast comes out of the oven in thirty minutes."

Chad's voice sounded funny from the first syllable. "Mac, I know this sounds like the old game, but don't say anything, okay?"

"Okay," she responded hesitantly.

"I need you to get over here right now."

"What...?"

"Don't say anything." He sounded worse to her ears. "Just get over here."...

Mac heard the phone clunk down in her ear.

"Okay," Mac said, still cheery, pretending she was still talking to her brother....

"I'm just going over to the gallery to help Chad with something for a minute," she said, avoiding eye contact.

"Did you tell the boy the roast will be out of the oven in thirty minutes?" Stella asked, knowing full well that Mackenzie hadn't.

"I'll tell him. I'm going to pick him up."...

...What in the world was the matter with Chad? He sounded awful on the phone.

She pulled up in front of the gallery and quickly walked to the front door.

In this prosperous town of expensive cars, there was no reason for her to notice the expensive dark sedan parked beyond the gallery, on the other side of the street.

We'll end with examples of Patricia Cornwell's use of coincidence, real or imagined, in building suspense. In *From Potter's Field* (G. P. Putnam's Sons, 1996), Kay Scarpetta, Chief Medical Examiner for the State of Virginia, sees villainy personified in the person of Temple Brooks Gault. While in New York investigating Gault's most recent killing, Kay and Benton Wesley, her lover and FBI head of criminal profiling, stop at an Italian restaurant near the crime scene. The restaurant name is Scaletta, close enough to Kay's name to draw them through the doors. They ask Eugenio, maitre d', about the origin of the name and learn that someone called Scarpetta has been there before them. Someone unusual, with red hair, long black leather coat, Italian trousers, but not Italian. The man paid with an American Express credit card in the name of "Scarpetta, K." K, for Kirk, the man claimed. Kay looks through her wallet. Her card is missing. She had lent it to her niece Lucy. How could it have been stolen?

In *Cause of Death* (G. P. Putnam's Sons, 1997), it's New Year's Eve. Kay, Richmond Police Captain Pete Marino, and niece Lucy, are camped out at a weathered beach cottage. The three play to character with Pete as protective male, Lucy as youthful cynic, and Kay as appeaser, trying to set everything right with a scrumptious dinner. Pete goes out for firewood. Lucy watches from the window and becomes concerned when she thinks he turned his flashlight off. But he doesn't have a flashlight, Kay says. She grabs her gun and runs into Marino loaded down with wood. They search the grounds, but only boot prints remain. Kay escapes into a glass of wine and tells herself it's all coincidence. She grates Parmesan, arranges figs, melon, and proscuitto, and won't consider getting the hell out of there until after a champagne dinner.

CHAPTER 22
FOOD FORESHADOWING EVENTS

"It's in honor of *El Dia de los Muertos*," Maralyn Wilson said, joining them. "The Day of the Dead...." (From Corinne Holt Sawyer's *Murder Ole!*)

Foreshadowing: a subtle preparation for what lies ahead. It builds suspense, it feels like a premonition. It teases and hints of the future direction of the story. Chapter One of Carolyn Wheat's *Troubled Waters* (good foreshadowing title) finds NYC lawyer Cassandra Jameson on a flight to Toledo, Ohio, she really, really, really does not want to take. So she downs two Bloody Marys, but as the plane lands, fear like a lump of cold oatmeal hits her stomach. Ignoring the seat belt sign she dives for the toilet and upchucks—a portent of scenes ahead. Such as Chapter 3's recollected county fair of 1969 when young Cassie, on a protest march, is nauseated by the smells of bratwurst and saltwater taffy. Which will she lose first she wonders, her nerve or her breakfast? There's even a picnic scene (Chapter 11) involving politicians who refuse to eat anything because they must follow it up with a campaign lunch, the cardinal rule of politics being only eat what constituents provide and do it in their faces. To show voters they are real men, the two slurp greasy Hungarian sausages with extra onions, while hoping that the inevitable heartburn doesn't send them to the emergency room. No one does food and drink better than Carolyn Wheat.

Another Carolyn most adept at foreshadowing is Hart. Two examples. Senior sleuth Henrietta O'Dwyer Collins, "Henrie O," has been invited by media magnate Chase Prescott to meet all the friends and family he suspects of trying to poison him. He lives on an island off the coast of South Carolina. The party spends a lot of time at the pool, and in this first scene Hart sets us up for a later death. You can inquire about the Henrie O series at *HenrieO@carolynhart.com.* Her web site is *http://www.CarolynHart.com.* (From Carolyn Hart's *Dead Man's Island.* PB. NY: Bantam Books. 1994.)

...Chase was working out, swimming with a slow, steady freestyle.

The breakfast patio was twenty yards from the pool. In good weather the setting would be idyllic. There was...elegantly prepared food: fresh fruit including papaya and kiwi, Danish pastries hot and buttery, cereals, meats, cheese, eggs, and exquisite coffee....

Chase finished his workout....Then, with a casual wave toward his audience, and, yes, I'm sure he knew we were all watching, he loped across to the hot tub, took the steps two at a time, and jumped into the steamy water.

*   *   *

Another breakfast scene on the patio. A hurricane is moving into the area and the only boat they can use for escape mysteriously explodes. Time is running out. There's a possibility that one of the group was able to make brief telephone contact with the Savannah Coast Guard station. Henrie O seeks out Chase to tell him the good news. He's in the pool.

"Good," he said simply. He locked both hands and slammed the water. A plume of water geysered up and splashed over me....

He was revitalized, his dark eyes flashing, a triumphant smile lighting his handsome face....

"Well," I said lightly, "if they're going to be here in half an hour, you'd better get dressed, Chase. I think I'll have some breakfast."

"Yeah...great idea." He shivered, hesitated, then said briskly, "But I'm going to get warm first."

Lightning splintered the sky. Thunder boomed.

It was closer now.

Not here yet.

But close.

Chase started up the path to the hot tub.

I almost called out to him. A hot tub wouldn't be my choice with an electrical storm coming....

Second example. Mystery bookstore owner Annie Laurance Darling has meticulously planned a centennial celebration of Agatha Christie's birth at the Palmetto House on Broward's Rock Island, South Carolina. Early in the festivities the guests—writers, editors, publishers, and one reviled critic, Neil Bledsoe—sit down to an all-English dinner. Lady Gwendolyn is the guest of honor, Max is Annie's husband, Laurel is Max's mother, and Henny, Annie's employee. (From Carolyn Hart's *The Christie Caper*. PB. NY: Bantam Books, a Bantam Crime Line Book. 1992.)

...The food was perfect...oyster soup, roast beef of Old England, Yorkshire pudding, roast potatoes, curried chicken with rice, syllabub or tea, and, of course, a hearty serving at meal's end of clotted cream and fresh strawberries or sherry trifle. Lady Gwendolyn enjoyed it so much, in fact, that spatters of the golden cream adorned the front of her pink-flowered lavender dress.

But as she scraped the last microdot of cream from her dish, the old author swept the table with a troubled glance. "The brew is bubbling."

Annie stiffened. Max frowned. Laurel bent forward in rapt attention, but Henny only half hid a yawn behind her napkin.

Lady Gwendolyn absently swiped her spoon again in her empty bowl.

Laurel...offered her dessert.

The old lady happily plunged her spoon into the full bowl. "I do abhor waste." Not quite indistinctly, despite the deployment of her spoon heaped with golden cream, Lady Gwendolyn continued thoughtfully, "I took the opportunity prior to the opening session to visit with those who have been linked to Bledsoe...."

...Those bright, questing blue eyes swept the dining room. "Much is happening around us—all the result of the intermixture of characters assembled here." The old author's tone was somber. "Bledsoe, of course, is the focal point...."

Lady Gwendolyn absently smoothed her upswept hair...."I sense a purpose, a plan....Whatever it is, I fear he will achieve it at all costs."

Angela Benbow and Caledonia Wingate are residents of Camden-sur-Mer, retirement home for the well-heeled. Whenever a resident meets an unnatural death, Angela and Caledonia are there to probe. But murder doesn't happen every day, so they and other residents—tired of gluing sticks together to make picture frames and tissue holders—convince the activities director they need adult challenges. After several Spanish lessons they travel to Tijuana, Mexico. Might their little party return to the hotel reduced in number on this auspicious day? (From Corinne Holt Sawyer's *Murder Ole!* PB. NY: Ballantine Books, a Fawcett Crest Book. 1998.)

...To the amazement of the visitors from Camden-sur-Mer, the air was redolent with the scent of meat roasting over open fires, meat that would be put into tacos on order. Big pots of rice simmered on small stoves. And there were at least four carts where the proprietors peeled mangos or cucumbers and placed them on sticks for the customers to carry away and nibble as they strolled along. Apples, half-melons, and pineapple were also available for skewered snacks. There were several small stands labeled *Refrescos* that sold drinks—a few of the well-known bottled variety, but since these were very expensive, most of the sales were of a brightly colored, fruity-smelling concoction dispensed in big plastic cups, filled with ice from battered zinc tubs.

"Don't drink any of that stuff," Angela hissed to Caledonia. "It's the ice. You don't know what water it's been made from."

"Don't worry," Caledonia hissed back. "I never did like Kool-Aid, and if I'm not mistaken, this is the genuine article. Hey, look at the little skulls!" At another booth there was an assortment that looked incredibly morbid, but was proving highly popular with the Mexican patrons; candy had been used to shape tiny skulls, little coffins, miniature skeletons, and children were buying the little objects with apparent delight. "What's going on?" Caledonia asked in wonder.

The setting is the northern California mountains where San Francisco PI Maggie Elliott has gone to recover from Chronic Fatigue Syndrome. The day before she arrives two hikers are attacked, one dead, one left for dead. At the invitation of Jim Pepper, Maggie attends a Native American dance ceremony. To ensure a good year, a medicine man has been praying for days up on the mountain. But to catch a glimpse of him at his prayers spells doom for the observer. (From Elizabeth Atwood Taylor's *The Northwest Murders*. PB. NY: Ballantine Books, an Ivy Book. 1994.)

…"We're making acorn soup. You want to help?"

"Sure—what can I do?"

"Follow that path there down to the river, you'll see a place with a lot of rocks. Gather up some big ones.…They're to put in the soup to heat it up.…"

"Eeech!" I screamed before I could stop myself, jerking back and looking up at a tall Indian....

By the time I'd made several more trips, the soup was boiling and I helped ladle it out...into white polystyrene cups. People then went on to another table where grilled salmon, various casseroles, and pies and cakes were laid out in great abundance.

As I helped myself to the food I spotted Jim Pepper across the field, listening to the dour Indian who'd surprised me....

"...How do you like the acorn soup?"

"Don't know yet." I took a small sip and said noncommittally, "ummm." Rather like thin oatmeal, it was basically kind of tasteless considering all the trouble it is to make...."Who was that tall, sort of mean-looking man you were talking to just before I came over?"

..."You know him?"

"No. I saw him down by the river, is all...."

Jim hesitated, then said soberly, "...he happened to see the *fut-a-way-non*—the medicine man—going up the mountain the last day."

"He's not supposed to survive the year, you mean, because he saw the medicine man?"

"That's the old belief....he doesn't believe in all that old stuff, but he seemed a little nervous about it."

*   *   *

...I wondered about the new year ahead, what it held up its sleeve. Would I get well?

PI Sharon McCone works for the All Souls Legal Cooperative, San Francisco. But the times, they are a'changin'. All Souls was created in the 1960's to provide low-cost legal service, but new partners want to abolish the sliding fee scale and move far away from the people they now serve. Hank Zahn, Sharon's boss, is struggling with how to deal with the new

partners' demands. Sharon is unaware of this struggle until she explores
the refrigerator in the old Victorian house that they use as an office. (From
Marcia Muller's *There's Nothing to be Afraid Of.* PB. NY: Warner Books,
Mysterious Press. 1990.)

...I continued along the narrow corridor to my boss, Hank Zahn's
office. But the door was shut and a Do Not Disturb sign...hung on the
knob. I looked at it, debated knocking anyway, then went all the way to
the rear of the house to the big country kitchen. No one was there, and
none of the usual unwashed coffee cups and dishes cluttered the counters.
The flat feeling was fast becoming a depression.

I went over to the refrigerator and looked in. A couple of bottles of
Calistoga Water, some limp celery, condiments, and a withered lime. No
wine, no big pots of Hank's famous beef stew, not even the alfalfa sprouts
the co-op's health food addicts favored. I shut the fridge door and leaned
against it, sighing.

For several months now there had been a change in the atmosphere at
All Souls. Once warm, friendly, and easygoing, it was now cold and tense.
People no longer took their meals here or organized impromptu parties;
several of the attorneys had moved out of the living quarters on the second
floor. There were conferences behind closed doors, and I was always running across people in furtive discussions in odd places like the service
porch.

When left-leaning lawyer Willa Jansson is offered $90,000 a year to
work for a right-leaning law firm, she tells her father who's waving *Das
Kapital* in her face: "I'm going to represent banks! I'm going to open a
charge account! I'm going to buy a decent couch! And the world is not
going to go to hell because of it...." Shortly thereafter she begins to suspect she was hired for more than her lawyering skills. Her new boss is poisoned with hemlock which is exactly what happened to her previous boss.
Here, Willa's just partaken of Bloody Marys with the remaining office

staff. Minutes later, San Francisco homicide inspector Krisbaum drops by. Good idea. (From Lia Matera's *Hidden Agenda*. PB. NY: Ballantine Books. 1992.)

I swallowed more of the tabascoey drink...

I could feel myself flush. My shirt was sticking to my back....

...My mouth felt blistered and my throat burned....My eyes were beginning to tear. It would be just my luck to get sick on top of everything else....

I leaned against the wall, massaging my throat. I felt like I'd just bitten into a jalapeno. My mouth and eyes were watering. I didn't feel able to talk....

I wiped a film of moisture off my checks. Why was the office so warm?...

...Then I struggled to my office. I sat heavily in my leather chair, turning it so I could look out the window....

I swiveled in my chair. "Inspector Kris—!" I swallowed several times. What was wrong with my throat?...

Krisbaum was about to say something snide, I could tell by the clucking sound he made. But I was feeling too awful to maintain eye contact. I pressed the heels of my hands to my sinuses. They felt swollen, like a sudden head cold: worse, though—almost scalded.

"Hey!" Krisbaum's voice was sharp. "What the hell's wrong?"

He knelt beside my chair, pulling my hands off my face. My eyes were streaming. "What's the matter?" He sounded angry.

I shook my head. "I feel—I don't know. Fluish. Like I've been eating hot peppers."

"Oh, Christ! Come on!"

Lia Matera can be e-mailed through her web site, *http://www.scruz.net/~lmatera/LiaMatera.html.*

Time and time again, for over forty years, Judith Poole has been look-ing for her boyfriend's body in the Washington mountains. Helma Zukas and her sidekick, Ruth Winthrop, come across her on a hike which high-lights the differences in the women through the food they bring along. Helma has already determined that Ruth did *not* bring, as per Helma's instructions, the Ten Essentials and a whole lot more. (From Jo Dereske's *Out of Circulation*. PB. NY: Avon Books. 1997.)

"I heard the helicopter," Judith Poole said as they sat around her fire. Soft darkness surrounded them, carrying a chill that was easily repelled by the fire and an extra layer of clothing. They'd eaten: Helma a pleasant bowl of reconstituted chicken soup from her store of labeled plastic bags of meals, a roll, and dried banana chips; Ruth a crushed bag of potato chips, cheese sticks, two Reese's peanut butter cups, and, Helma sus-pected, a generous splash of whiskey in her coffee....

"If I don't find poor Roger first, who will? Years from now, he'd only be a curiosity. He *expects* me to find him."

Helma and Ruth stared at this healthy, perfectly reasonable-appearing woman explaining how bodies were preserved by snow and cold, her alert eyes touched by light, her voice as matter-of-fact as if she were discussing preserving peaches. "Sometimes they can even detect the last meal, hun-dreds of years later," she finished.

Helma's tea was cold, Ruth's cup was empty. Judith Poole jerked once as if she'd thumped to earth, and said, with a cheery little chortle, "Oh my, I sound daft, don't I? Except for going down the mountain to buy provisions, I've been up here six weeks. I couldn't let such good weather go to waste."

PI Trade Ellis, forty-something, owns the Vaca Grande ranch north of Tucson. She's investigating decades-old murders with little to go on except the recovering memories of a client. Trade's chief suspect is the client's father, Phelan Brewster, known for his vicious guard dogs. For her first visit to the Phelan ranch, Trade loaded up with Big Macs which she threw from her truck to the attacking trio. They gobbled them up and she learned an important fact: his dogs were not professionally trained or they wouldn't have taken the food. Now she's back in the saddle with more Big Macs, which Macs just might appear a third time. (From Sinclair Browning's *The Sporting Club*. PB. NY: A Bantam Crime Line Book. 2000.)

Phelan Brewster's dogs, all three of them, came charging up the hill, barking furiously and snapping their big white teeth. They circled Gray....

Gray knew about bad dogs....The dust was killing my contacts and tears ran down my face as I concentrated on staying with the twisting, spinning horse as he kicked and struck.

The German shepherd whimpered and flew ass over teakettle into a prickly pear cactus. Her misfortune was enough to deter the other two and they backed away....

...I groped in my shirt for a Big Mac, tore the paper from it and threw it to the ground, away from the horse's feet....

...It was blissfully quiet as the dogs gulped the burgers and Gray stood, knowing he was now in no danger from the furious canines.

"Good girls," I said. "Sweet puppies."...

The dogs were back, but this time they were not snarling and ready to have my horse for lunch. The tide had turned as they realized that Gray was Meals on Wheels.

"Good girls." I repeated. I reached around to the cantle bag and brought out more Big Macs, unwrapping them and tearing them into pieces...."Here you go, pretty baby," I crooned....

Finally out of hamburgers, I sat there among the dogs for a while, talking quietly to them....

As I turned back to the west, Brewster's dogs continued to follow me. I stopped when I neared the fence opening and told them to "go home." They didn't. So I had to sit on the horse for another fifteen minutes until a jackrabbit finally came darting across their path and all three of them took after it, leaving me alone in the desert with my gray Arabian horse.

Forty years ago on Good Friday a crime was observed by two idiot savants. The police believed they did it and institutionalized them, apart. Neither would ever talk about what happened.

Enter Christine Bennett, 30, out of a convent only a month, who's taken up residence in Oakwood, NY. There she meets James, one of the twins.

The twins can recall their own experiences on any date given them. In this scene, Chris brings the two together in the belief that each really inhabits half a personality. Maybe together they can recall what happened 40 years ago. You can contact Lee Harris at *mysmurder@aol.com* or through her web site: *http://www.nmomysteries.com/main.htm*. (From Lee Harris's *The Good Friday Murder*. PB. NY: Ballantine Publishing Group, a Fawcett Gold Medal Book. 1992.)

The twins sat opposite each other, and I sat on the side between. "I'm Chris," I said.

"I'm Robert."

"I'm James."

"I brought you here on an airplane today," I said to Robert. "Do you remember that?"

He smiled at me and shook his head....

"Do you remember my name?"

"Chris," they chorused.

"That's right. Chris Bennett....I'd like to be friends with you."

The dinner was hamburgers and french fries, a can of Coke, and vanilla ice cream, an all-American meal to celebrate our country's birthday.

"Do you like hamburgers?" I asked.

"I like mine with ketchup," James said.

"Here's some ketchup." I picked up the sealed packet that was on his tray and tore it open. "You can squeeze it on," I explained, showing him.

"Where's the bottle?"

"The bottle's in the kitchen. It's easier to use these on a tray."

"I like that," Robert said. He had managed to open his ketchup packet himself only with slight damage. He wiped up the spilled red sauce with his napkin.

"This is a good Fourth of July dinner," I said. "You know that today is the Fourth of July, don't you?" I addressed the question to both of them.

"No, it's not," Robert answered. He didn't seem upset at my error. He was smiling.

"Sure it is. It's Wednesday, July fourth."

"Today is April ninth," James said. "It's Easter Sunday."

Patricia Cornwell plays a game with us in *Body of Evidence* (Avon Books, 1992) with two scenes that we realize after the fact parallel each other. One is very early in the book, one, very late. Early on, Virginia State Medical Examiner Kay Scarpetta and her sidekick Richmond Police Captain Pete Marino are investigating the violent death of writer Beryl Madison in her own home. They poke around her kitchen, trying to guess how she spent her last minutes. The refrigerator holds only a shriveled lemon, butter, moldy Havarti, condiments, and tonic water. The liquor cabinet is over-flowing with expensive booze, including a bottle of rare Haitian Barbancourt Rhum she brought back from Key West, where she'd been hiding for months. They know she flew home that night from Florida, even though her life was in danger. What's most troubling is that she left her gun on the kitchen counter to answer the door. She apparently deactivated the alarm, let someone in, and set the alarm again. For whom would she do that? In one of the last scenes of the book, Kay returns to Richmond, VA, well aware she's a target of the killer. Marino meets her at the airport, takes her home, but is called away on an emergency. Kay comforts herself in the kitchen with Scotch and bemoans the fact that her suitcase is lost and her

.38 inside it. The doorbell rings. She looks out and deactivates the alarm…*Body of Evidence* points up one more source of tension tied to fore-shadowing. Because we readers, naturally, have picked up on clues that the sleuth is stubbornly ignoring. Haven't we?

Chapter 23
The Last Bite: Food as Motive and Weapon

"At that instant, shouts rang out...mingling with a single masculine scream. 'Dear Lord,' Brother Danny said. He dropped the box of sugar cubes which broke open, scattering snowy cubes across the dark tile floor." (From Jo Dereske's *Miss Zukas in Death's Shadow*.)

How might an author express contempt and loathing through food, short of using it as a weapon? For the cook, there's serving hot food stone cold, and cold food at 75 smelly degrees. Taking *al dente* to a whole new level of undercooking. Burning expensive T-bones and lobster to shriveled cinders. Dishing up Franco American night after night—until the outraged eater demands stew and you can tip some Alpo into a pan.

For the eater there's showing up so late the meal is ruined. Or announcing too late that she is a vegetarian or allergic. Or comparing the fare unfavorably with his mother's recipes.

Food as motive? The Great Sourdough Starter Auction was to take place in the office of attorney Rebecca Schwartz, except that Peter Martinelli, owner of the frozen doughball, got bumped off before the bidding could begin. Here Rebecca and her law partner Chris pay a visit to a suspect baker. (From Julie Smith's *The Sourdough Wars*. PB. NY: Ballantine Books, an Ivy Book. 1992.)

Within seconds, Sally had laid a small feast on her long smooth pine table—pâté, butter, cornichons, a little white wine, and her own sourdough. I tried the bread with a little butter first, not polluting it with pâté. It was like candy.

...it wasn't sweet or anything, but so melt-in-your-mouth perfect that that's what came to mind. I said, "Chris. Try this bread. You won't believe it."

As Chris did, Sally leaned forward, hands twitching. She watched Chris taste and hardly gave her time to swallow before she spoke: "Do you think it's okay?"

"It's the greatest," said Chris. "Nobody else is making anything like it."

I helped myself to more, this time with pâté. "Is it because the other bakeries are so big? You have better quality control?"

Sally shook her head. "I could bake just as good a bread if I had to do it in million-loaf batches. If only I had the opportunity."

"Why on earth," asked Chris, "do you want the Martinelli starter? You honestly think you could improve on this?"

"You really think it's that good?"

"You know it is."

..."The way things work in this country, a thing is good if people think so. You've got to have a gimmick. A scam, to get their attention."

"You feel you haven't had the recognition you deserve," I said....

"And you think if you had the starter other people would think your bread was special?"

She nodded.

"What we came for," I said, "is to tell you there was a second batch of starter. Whoever stole it didn't get it all."

She looked like a woman who'd just been told her child wasn't on that wrecked schoolbus after all.

The house is Victorian, perched high above the Ohio River in Pittsburgh. Leigh Koslow, jobless advertising copywriter, has just moved in with its owner, her cousin Cara, who needs looking after. Cara is seven months pregnant with a husband working overseas. On Leigh's first morning, she finds a body in the terrace hammock. It is Paul Fischer, the previous owner, and eleven years embalmed, bearing a note saying "Get out of my house." Shortly thereafter Leigh and Cara find another deposit on the patio. This time food is used to deliver the message. (From Edie Claire's *Never Buried*. PB. NY: Penguin Group, Signet. 1999.)

"Cara," Leigh asked with a yawn as her cousin joined her outside, "when did you throw out fish?"

Cara stepped over to investigate the assortment of fish and fish portions scattered over her patio. " I didn't," she said matter-of-factly....

Cara stooped and poked a nearly whole fish with her toe. Her eyes narrowed. "Leigh," she said intently, "look at this."

Leigh...squatted down for a closer look....She squinted at the red streaks. "It looks like a U," she announced.

Cara grabbed a stick...and picked the edge of another fish to flip it over. "And here," she said, "this one is marked too. It looks like somebody tried to make a six, or a G." Leigh and Cara exchanged a brief glance, then began gathering the fish and turning them paint side up.

There were five fish in all, but thanks to the crows, several were no longer in one piece. Leigh undertook the anatomic reconstructions while Cara puzzled over the red markings. When fish number five had most of its body reoriented, the women stood back.

"We have two T's, a G, a U, and an E," Cara announced. "Lovely. Any ideas?"...

"TUTEG?" Leigh hypothesized. "UGTET?"

"Maybe it's two words," Cara said thoughtfully. "Like EAT GUT without the A."

...her eyes met Leigh's as a new possibility struck them. Wordlessly, they began searching again. After a few moments Leigh found the majority of a sixth fish under a shrub.

"Well," she announced, pushing it next to the others with a stick. "It's not an A, it's an O."

Suddenly her blood ran cold.

GET OUT....

...How exactly should one respond to a threat spelled out in fish?

Parties and receptions are a popular venue for poisonings. Here amateur sleuth Mandy Pepper takes her mother Bea to the lavish 50th birthday party of TV producer Lyle Zacharias. Lyle has invited anyone who had anything to do with his illustrative history, including unhappy ex-wives and bitter ex-partners. Bea knows only the kinder side of Lyle and bakes him his favorite tarts. In the first scene, Bea and Lyle meet up in the hotel's kitchen. In the second scene, Lyle is giving a post-dinner speech. (From Gillian Roberts's *With Friends Like These*... PB. NY: Ballantine Books. 1994.)

...."I baked you tarts, Lyle," she said. "Fifty of them. All different flavors, all special, the way you used to like them."

"Now, Bea," he said, "that's not fair! I'm an old man now! I have to count calories and fat grams. I have to practice Olympic level self-control, and now—my favorite food in the world, Bea's tarts—how could you do this to me?"...."Tell me you aren't tempting me with the one with the macadamias and peaches...."

"I certainly am....But I never thought you'd remember."

"Unfortunately for my waistline, I remember it all too well...."

...My mother catalogued the varieties in the tin. Lyle chuckled and said he would have a vicarious eating thrill. She described the strawberry-kirsch tart. He made low, sexy sounds of appreciation. I felt unutterably depressed. Another unsolicited, hazard-free, sensation-free sensual experience. After safe sex, safe eating....

..."Like that song in *Annie*," Lyle said. "Tomorrow. The tarts will come out—tomorrow, but I can't touch them until then....I'll ration myself. One a day, like an incredibly delicious vitamin pill. I'll cut back on the cottage cheese, to save calories."...

*   *   *

"For all—of—you here, thanks for—this—that—moment I—wanted." The rhythm was...punctuated by gasps, and he was skipping words. The hairs on the back of my neck prickled. This couldn't be an attack of stage fright....

Wheezing like a fireplace bellows, Lyle forced more words out. "Who...poison me?"

I ran like hell for the phone.

Was using food as a weapon the start of a career in crime? This is what PI Kinsey Millhone has to say. What a way to get back. What a way to start a novel. (From Sue Grafton's *"N" is for Noose*. HB. NY: Henry Holt and Company. 1998.)

Personally, I hated grade school, having been cursed with a curious combination of timidity and rebellion. School was a minefield of unwritten rules that everyone but me seemed to sense and accept. My parents had died in a car crash when I was five, so school felt like a continuum of the same villainy and betrayal. I was inclined to upchuck without provocation which didn't endear me to the janitor or classmates sitting in my vicinity. I can still remember the sensation of recently erupted hot juices collecting in my lap while students on either side of me flocked away in distaste. Far from experiencing shame, I felt a sly satisfaction, the power of the victim wreaking digestive revenge. I'd be sent down to the school nurse where I could lie on a cot until my aunt Gin came to fetch me. Often at lunchtime (before I learned to barf at will) I'd beg to go home swearing to look both ways when I was crossing the street, promising not to talk to strangers even if they offered sweets. My teachers rebuffed every plaintive request, so I was doomed to remain; fearful and anxious, undersized, fighting back tears. By the time I was eight, I learned to quit asking. I simply left when it suited me and suffered the consequences later. What were they going to do, shoot me down in cold blood?

In Susan Dunlap's fifth crime book in her Jill Smith series the plot revolves around the competition among three Paris-trained gourmet chefs. What irony, sending in to investigate the murder of chef Mitch Biekma a detective whose idea of dinner is a hamburger. Here Jill interrogates the chef's widow in the front garden and then the kitchen of the fabulous Paradise Restaurant where a bowl of soup made with leeks, baby carrots, greens, eggplant, onions, and dill was Mitch's last supper. (From Susan Dunlap's *A Dinner to Die For*. PB. NY: Dell Publishing. 1990.)

…"I'm Detective Smith. Are you Laura Biekma?"

"Mitch was so proud of this garden." She shook her head. "He saw a beauty—no, that's not it. No, a stylishness—that's it—a stylishness that most people couldn't. At first I wondered if he was just saying that because he'd committed himself and didn't want to look a fool. But no, he really loved it. It's almost fitting that he should die…"

*   *   *

She set a small bottle on the table, the type of milk bottle I had seen only in nostalgia ads. "It's so unfair. Why did he have to die now, just when he'd finally found his place?"

"What do you mean, Mrs. Biekma?"

..."Maybe Mitch was too talented. Nothing ever challenged him....There were always five or six half-done projects lying around our apartment. Before he'd finish, he'd find something else and be all enthusiastic about it. I thought that's the way our life would be, just scraping by, my working at the gas company all day....Then he decided to open a restaurant. And it was as if overnight he grew up. I'll tell you, when he went to Paris to cooking school, I thought it was just another hobby, and when he came back, wouldn't have bet on it lasting a month. But he stuck with it. He even took courses in accounting and business management, and if you knew Mitch you'd know how much he hated stuff like that. And then, just when people recognized that Paradise was the best..." She sniffed back tears, swallowed hard, and then, concentrating all her attention, lifted her coffee cup and drank.

It's March, mud slide and silly season on the Russian River. Time for the annual spoof of "country-ness" by the denizens of Henderson. The party begins with The Biggest Slug contest, followed by The Slug Race. But it's the third event that concerns us here, Slug Tasting. This year among the five judges is Edwina Henderson, event organizer and biggest booster of the town named for her family. Vejay Haskell, yuppie dropout from San Francisco turned rural meter reader, sips a brandy and soda as she watches the proceedings. (From Susan Dunlap's *The Last Annual Slugfest*. PB. NY: Dell Publishing. 1994.)

"Take a good look, judges," Bert said. "Breathe in the aroma of garlic, and tomato sauce, and sautéed mollusk. Look for the best, the most slug-filled portions." He clapped his hands slowly, starting the audience off on the rhythmic accompaniment to the halting pace of the judges as he led them around the front of the table, stopping them in front of each dish....

Bert picked up the first tray, of what appeared to be shrimp cocktails in long-stemmed crystal, and held it out for the audience to see. "Looks pretty tasty, doesn't it?"...

"One bite," Bert Lucci directed. "Just enough to pass judgment. All together now. Get those tasty little fellows on your spoons, judges. Wait. No cutting! You can handle a whole one, right, folks?"...

"Okay, judges, all together now."

They raised their pizzas and stuffed them in. The audience held its breath, but it didn't take long to realize that what we had here was an anti-climax. Rosa's cooking had overcome the event. Even Curry Cunningham couldn't disguise his enjoyment.

"So, judges, what's your verdict? You've had Slug Cocktail, not a universal favorite. Then there was Frittata with Slime Sauce, Slug Stroganoff, and now Slug Pizza. Give us your verdicts, judges." Bert poked the microphone at Curry Cunningham.

"Pizza."

"Pizza," Angelina seconded.

Father Calloway agreed, and though it was clear that Edwina Henderson begrudged the decision, she gave it her nod....

The main room was virtually empty when a scream came from the kitchen.

I ran in.

Angelina Rudd was propped against the stove. Her mouth hung open. She was staring down at the floor, where Edwina Henderson lay.

District Judge Deborah Knott is in High Point, North Carolina, during the week of the International Home Furnishings Market, which sounds like the sorriest excuse in the world to party. In a food court Deborah meets a very strange lady, Mrs. Jernigan, from whom she accepts a stolen entrance badge. Into the market parties they go, accepting complimentary tote bags. Deborah meets up with an old beau, Chan, she hasn't seen in years, and is introduced to his current romantic interest, the lovely Drew Patterson of furniture makers Fitch and Patterson. (From Margaret Maron's *Killer Market*. PB. NY: Warner Books. 1999.)

...Taste and dignity did not seem to be considerations of the American Leathergoods Wholesale Association's party....

We [Deborah and Chan] snaked our way through laughing, perspiring dancers to the far end of the room where two long serving tables stood draped in blue calico. On one of them, several shiny galvanized washtubs held ice and five or six different brands of beer. The other table featured huge platters of Texas-style ribs, fried chicken, jalapeño cornbread, corn on the cob, and some sinfully rich-looking chocolate brownies....

As I came up to Mrs. Jernigan, I saw her slip a zip-lock plastic bag filled with fried chicken into the new Fitch and Patterson bag between her feet....She reminded me of my Aunt Sister, who keeps similar plastic bags stashed in her carryall bag because, and I quote, "I just can't stand to see good food go to waste."...

"Mrs. Jernigan—"

She completed her raid on the table with a couple of brownies, then looked up at me with a cold eye....

*   *   *

More dancers surged forward to stoke up. I still wasn't hungry but Drew fixed a plate for Chan with a proprietary air. "Cornbread, hon?"

"Yes, ma'am. And what about a couple of those brownies?" he said hungrily....

*   *   *

The cowboy boots looked familiar.

"Chan?"

He didn't move and his breathing seemed shallow and irregular.

I touched a pulse point on his neck and the heartbeat was almost unde-tectable. An odor of alcohol, chocolate and sour vomit emanated from the cushion beneath his head....

"Call an ambulance," I gasped. "It's Chan. Up at the Swingtyme place. I think he's dying."

Margaret Maron's web site is *http://www.margaretmaron.com*.

A case of cannibalism? That's the proposition National Park Ranger Anna Pigeon is asked to consider when the wife of a staffer goes missing. Anna's been transferred from Texas to Lake Superior environs. Her cohorts are a dysfunctional group who are brought together more than they like by managers who feel the need for potlucks, Chrismooses, and chocolate pigouts. This particular party is to celebrate a marriage. Anna notices that Scotty Butkus, also a law enforcement ranger, is drinking way too much, again. Tinker and Damien are volunteers who conduct nature walks for the tourists, and who are very, very observant. (From Nevada Barr's *A Superior Death*. PB. NY: Avon Books. 1995.)

...Scotty knocked over his beer. Cigarette butts were floating out of the ashtray and down the white tablecloth on a foaming tide. Anna guessed he was drunk....
...She cast her eye around for some likely reason to excuse herself....
Damien and Tinker provided it....
They led her out of the restaurant and down to the water....
"What's the problem?" Anna asked.
"We think Scotty has eaten his wife," Tinker confided.

*   *   *

Anna...sat on the floor of Tinker and Damien's room in the old house half a mile back from the harbor....
"So. Scotty's wife—Donna—hasn't been around for a few days?"
"Seven," Damien said....

Tinker said: "Donna had promised to cut my hair. In return I was going to teach her how to use some of the herbs here...."

"You watched the house," Anna said....

"Nothing....We never saw Donna."...

"Then this," Tinker said gravely. She turned to a brick-and-board bookcase....She took a small glass container so clean it looked polished....

..."We would not have come to you had we not found proof Scotty devoured his wife. It is a serious charge."

Anna lifted the jar carefully from Tinker's hand....

"A jar," Anna said blankly.

"A pickle relish jar..." Damien encouraged her.

..."Heinz," Tinker added.

"That"—Damien pointed to the little bottle..."is not an isolated incident. The last food order Scotty Butkus sent to Bob's Foods included an order for an entire case of pickle relish."...

..."'Twenty-seven Bottles of Relish'!" Anna exclaimed. It was a short story about a man who had consumed evidence of his wife's murder, with relish as the condiment.

"That's what we think," Tinker said.

When Summerfield, Montana, pathologist Dr. Grace Severance finds a note on her kitchen table telling her to "stay out of it," she knows her investigation into the murder of Roscoe Moss has gotten up somebody's nose. Then the spare key to the house goes missing. Returning alone to her lakeside home one night, she finds muddy footprints at the back door. From what direction will the attack come? Tampered pills? A bomb? (From Margaret Scherf's *The Beaded Banana*. HB. NY: Doubleday. 1978.)

Stop it, she told herself....

Suddenly she was aware of a sort of scratching noise. She stiffened, listening. The sound stopped. Then there it was again, a scratching or scraping. She was not anxious to get out of bed and look, but she pulled on her dressing gown, turned on the light, and something shot down the hall.

"It's a chipmunk," she said aloud. "He must have fallen down the fireplace chimney." She opened the back door and the glass door to the patio, but the thing would not go out....

Maybe if she left the room and was quiet, he would find his way out. She made instant coffee, got out the carton of cream and pinched it open, then changed her mind and went back to bed. She would take care of the chipmunk in the morning. She remembered leaving the cream out, but she did not get up to put it in the refrigerator.

The sun woke her. The sky was clear and bright, nothing had gone wrong in the house, it was a normal summer morning. You were an idiot last night, she told herself....

She went to the kitchen, wondering where the chipmunk had tucked himself in for the night. The answer to that question was on the kitchen counter. He lay there, in his beautiful striped coat, quite dead. Beside him the overturned carton had spilled cream into the sink and down on the floor.

From the look of him, she guessed he had died almost instantly, without pain. Before she picked up the carton and sniffed it, she knew what it would smell like. Almonds. Cyanide....

A prominent businessman named Russell Fortier has disappeared into thin air. New Orleans homicide detective Skip Langdon has been assigned to the case. Of all things, Skip's psychologist friend Cindy Lou is involved. Scene One: Cindy Lou. Scene Two: Featured is a PI whom Skip finds with a big hole in his chest and his mouth open, in a big round O. (From Julie Smith's *82 Desire*. PB. NY: Ballantine Books, an Ivy Book. 1999.)

Davis Deluxe had caused Skip to gain five pounds since getting transferred. It was a great neighborhood restaurant—red plaid on the tables, Dr. King on the wall, butter beans on your plate....

"I'm in a heap of shit, girlfriend."

"What's going on?" Skip put down the menu, deciding once again on the fried chicken.

"Well, I was seeing a married man."...

...She was shaking her head. "I don't like it. From the little I knew of him, he was your basic solid family man."

Skip almost dropped her fork. "Oh, right. And you're part of the family? What do you mean, you barely know him, by the way?"...

"Then we saw each other a second time and he couldn't get it up. He was feeling so damn guilty about cheating on his wife; you know that one? I swear, married men aren't worth messing with."

"I'm going to type that out and tape it to your refrigerator. You don't get to eat till you repeat it ten times."

"I never eat at home anyway."...

*   *   *

The coroner's van came, and then the crime lab...."Phew-ee, how come no one smelled him before?"

"You couldn't with the door closed. I know—I was first on the scene. The question is, how come nobody heard the shot?..."

"Potato, probably. Look—see that spot over there—betcha anything that's potato."

Some months ago, there had been an extremely well-publicized murder in which the perps had stuck a potato on a gun barrel as a silencer. Now everyone was doing it. Maybe that accounted for the surprised look on the man's face—if you saw a potato, you had to fear the worst.

Helma Zukas and Ruth Winthrop are working off a traffic ticket at Bellehaven, WA's Promise Mission by serving up meals to the hungry. Brother Danny is in charge. Chairman of the grant committee, Quentin Vernon Boyd, has been murdered on the hill behind the mission. Forrest is an old classmate of the sleuths who has arrived from Michigan—out of the blue to, of all things, ask Helma to marry him. Helma has said she'd think it over. (From Jo Dereske's *Miss Zukas in Death's Shadow*. PB. NY: Avon Books. 1999.)

"…The subject is murder, ma'am." Ruth pulled a box from the grocery bag like a magician. "Ta-ta. Sugar cubes. Remember the night QVB bought the farm and Brother Danny came running in all hot and bothered?…What does Brother Danny do?"

"He…" Helma began.

"Exactly right," Ruth said. She held the box of sugar cubes at waist height. "He drops them." Ruth released the box and it fell to the kitchen's tile floor, crunching one corner. "So what do you think of that?" Ruth asked, bowing as if she expected applause.…

They spent the next fifteen minutes dropping the box of sugar cubes from knee high to Ruth standing on one of Helma's dining room chairs and holding the box as high as the ceiling. The cubes crumbled; the box grew lumpy; granules of sugar seeped out of the cardboard corners onto the floor, but the box did not break.…

"He may have opened the box on the way into the building to save time," Helma suggested.

"Could be," Ruth said, tapping her chin. "Or, he never went out to buy sugar cubes at all.…"

                    *   *   *

"You and Forrest have your heart-to-heart yet?"

Helma shook her head.

"Hey, murder's a piece of cake compared to that," Ruth said.

When you think about all the different meanings food has, we ordinary folk share most of them with female sleuths. Like them, we happily use food as fuel, to communicate and celebrate, and for comfort. Like them, we less happily use food as escape and to control others. But we part company when it comes to using food to reward informers, or looking for clues in food, or considering food as a possible motive, or, the ultimate, deducing food was the actual means whereby a crime has been committed. And we certainly don't have to worry about it being used as a way to get us to quit our sleuthing, permanently.

AFTERWORD

Have no doubts about America's love affair with food. While putting this book together, one Sunday's comics contained no fewer than 14 strips featuring food. Toast with grape jelly was the favorite fare, appearing in *Peanuts*, *For Better or Worse*, and *Bobo's Progress*. *Luann* had made a meatloaf, while hot dogs were served in *Mutts*. The *Lockhorns* were having salad. Strawberry Frosted Pop-Tarts were debated in *The Boondocks*, while salt was savored in the kitchens of Camelot. Kitchens were also the settings for *The Duplex*, *Crankshaft*, and *Shoe*, while *Doonesbury* and *Frank and Ernest* found themselves at the supermarket. *Sally Forth* was at yet another office party, *Adam* was doing backyard barbecue, and the fishes in *Sherman's Lagoon* were, naturally, sampling other fishes. *Garfield* scarfed up his dinner in seconds and asked for, naturally, seconds.

So, what better way to spend our time than reading our favorite genre, mainstream detective fiction—not culinary or cats or dogs or gardening—and going for gastronomic scenes done with words rather than pictures. What did we come up with?

First of all, some books were so replete with food scenes, every chapter could have been given a food title. Food was very often used to start a novel, and it was a rare first page that did not mention something to stuff in your mouth. We have confronted mainstream authors with our copies of their books, with myriad post-its sprouting from the pages, only to be told, "Omigod, I couldn't possibly have used food that often!" Then we would tell them that the post-its were just the BEST scenes.

Okay, back to the basic hypothesis. As we suspected, the protagonist's personality was spelled out by what she ate. No set meal times, junk food on the run, empty cupboards and fridge, restaurant fare? They stood for serious sleuthing, going it alone, a woman set apart from the ordinary rules of ladylike behavior, most likely a PI or a cop. Amateurs were more like us, cooking for themselves and others and enjoying the process.

No surprise either that food scenes introduced secondary characters and their various roles in the main character's life. When working partners got together to discuss a case, it was over hot and spicy Chinese, burgers and fries, pastrami on rye. Friends and relatives proved helpful or unhelpful over food, either serving up pot roast or goulash admonishing, "I'm only saying this for your own good, but…" Or treating the sleuth to a gourmet meal out with comforting words that encouraged the sleuth to confide worries and doubts. Lovers typically mixed romps in the sack with foraging for breakfast and dinner.

Now for the unanticipated. "When are you going to find yourself a good man?" We fully expected the stereotypic PI and cop to steer away from a long-term, stable relationship, but we were floored by the pressure she was under from relatives and friends to get married. When the phone rang and she said, "Oh, hi, Mom," you just knew what topic mom would get around to. After telling her daughter that she didn't eat right.

Of course, the dubious character of many lovers was a good way to keep the women single, but gives rise to the question, are there any "good men" out there?

"Not a suitable job for a woman!" We were also taken aback by these same well-meaning secondary characters' opinions that the sleuth get a less dangerous, more traditionally female occupation. Sleuths' sisters and total strangers felt they had a right to demand greater conformity. "Private detective? I didn't think there was such a thing, except on television shows."

"My idea of good nutrition now is Taco Bell Lite." Was the amount of junk food consumed over the top? We think so. Cops and PIs in real life turn to junk food when they're especially stressed, but they couldn't eat the amounts depicted in these novels and stay in shape. And, for the record, authors have confessed that plunking chocolate addiction onto their protagonists is pure projection.

"Weighty Issues," "Aging's Not for Sissies," "Truth About Sleuths and Pets," and "Kids R Not Some of Us" were unpredicted topics of concern. Weight and aging are "women's topics"—just look at any Scene Section of your local newspaper. So while the typical youthful sleuth was lean and fit, there was also room in these books for ruminations about being overweight and getting older. Both covered nicely by Kiki Goldstein's need for Moon Pies and Ding Dongs. A goodly number of sleuths worried about their alcohol intake, while others drank a lot and let other people worry. While chilled white wine has achieved the status of an acceptable comfort food, we have to ask ourselves, why do the hard liquor scenes usually have a man in them? To put the onus on him?

The number of kids and pets was not anticipated. Both complicate a sleuth's life with their dependence and the need for the sleuth to be seriously responsible. But kids are definitely another "women's topic," and who takes care of the family pets in our households?

Mucho humor was a very pleasant surprise. Who can forget Catherine Sayler's lunch table joke about the man who took a year's leave to have a sex change? The sandwich-making scenes in "C" and "L"? The Chardonnay scene in Rebecca Rothenberg's *Shy Tulip Murders*? Or Sonora Blair pouring the disgusting dregs of her coffee in a squeaky clean cop's cup? Humor with food was *the* method of handling the "issue" of social class whether rich, poor, or in-between.

The variety of food scenes amazed us. Because the amateur female has been around since the days when that's the only kind of sleuth a woman could be—in and out of fiction—women authors have become practiced at moving a plot along with meals.

Which brings us back to the fact that our original premise was borne out. Women authors skillfully use food preparation not only to advance action, but to flesh out the sleuth and her fellow characters. Every component of these novels also was served by powerful scenes at the supermarket, seafood shack, station house, ship's galley, and annual slugfest.

ABOUT THE AUTHORS

This is Patricia Wells Lunneborg's seventh nonfiction book since her retirement as a professor of psychology. She's authored two other books about women police officers. Roberta Wells Ryan, 61-year-old retired writer-editor, is living out her fantasy of being a cop as a uniformed volunteer in her hometown police department in Sequim, Washington. Pat can be reached at *Lunneborg@home.com*. Bobbie can be reached at *BobbieRyan@aol.com*.

References

Andrews, Sarah. *Tensleep*. PB. NY: Penguin Group, Signet. 1995, pp. 14, 16-17.

Ayres, Noreen. *A World the Color of Salt*. PB. NY: Avon Books. 1993, pp. 103-105.

Barnes, Linda. *A Trouble of Fools*. PB. NY: Ballantine Books, a Fawcett Crest Book. 1990, desc.

Barnes, Linda. *The Snake Tattoo*. PB. NY: Ballantine Books, a Fawcett Crest Book. 1990, desc.

Barnes, Linda. *Coyote*. PB. NY: Dell Publishing. 1991, pp. 153-156.

Barnes, Linda. *Steel Guitar*. PB. NY: Dell Publishing. 1993, pp. 32-34, 37-38, 40.

Barnes, Linda. *Steel Guitar*. PB. NY: Dell Publishing. 1993, pp. 32-34, 37-38, 40.

Barnes, Linda. *Snapshot*. PB. NY: Dell Publishing. 1994, pp. 70-71.

Barnes, Linda. *Hardware*. PB. NY: Dell Publishing. 1996, pp. 175-177.

Barnes, Linda. *Cold Case*. HB. NY: Delacorte Press. 1997, pp. 129-131, 133-134.

Barr, Nevada. *Track of the Cat*. PB. NY: Avon Books. 1994, p. 169.

Barr, Nevada. *A Superior Death*. PB. NY: Avon Books. 1995, pp. 36-44.

Barr, Nevada. *Ill Wind*. PB. NY: Avon Books. 1995, pp. 240-241.

Barr, Nevada. *Endangered Species*. PB. NY: Avon Books. 1997, pp. 98-100.

Barr, Nevada. *Liberty Falling*. PB. NY: HarperCollins Publishing, Avon Books. 2000, pp. 114, 116, 125-126.

Beck, K. K. *A Hopeless Case*. PB. NY: Warner Books, Mysterious Press. 1993, pp. 4-7.

Beck, K. K. *Amateur Night*. PB. NY: Warner Books, Mysterious Press. 1994, pp. 210, 177, 94-96.

Beck, K. K. *Electric City*. PB. NY: Warner Books, Mysterious Press. 1995, pp. 192-193.

Beck, K. K. *Cold Smoked*. PB. NY: Warner Books, Mysterious Press. 1996, pp. 83-84.

Benke, Patricia. *Above the Law*. PB. NY: Avon Books. 1997, pp. 169-171.

Benke, Patricia. *Cruel Justice*. PB. NY: Avon Books. 1999, pp. 5-8.

Berry, Carole. *Death of a Downsizer*. PB. NY: Berkley Publishing Group, Berkley Prime Crime. 1999, pp. 172-173.

Bland, Eleanor Taylor. *Gone Quiet*. PB. NY: Penguin Group, Signet. 1995, pp. 77-78.

Block, Barbara. *Vanishing Act*. PB. NY: Kensington Publishing Corporation. 1999, pp. 118-120.

Browning, Sinclair. *The Last Song Dogs*. PB. NY: A Bantam Crime Line Book. 1999, pp. 116-117, 119, 182.

Browning, Sinclair. *The Sporting Club*. PB. NY: A Bantam Crime Line Book. 2000, pp. 121-123.

Buchanan, Edna. *Contents Under Pressure*. PB. NY: Avon Books. 1994, pp. 57-61, 63-64.

Buchanan, Edna. *Miami, It's Murder.* PB. NY: Avon Books. 1995, pp. 37-39.

Buchanan, Edna. *Suitable for Framing.* PB. NY: Hyperion. 1995, pp. 101-104, 106-107.

Carter, Charlotte. *Rhode Island Red.* PB. London: Serpent's Tail. 1997, desc.

Carter, Charlotte. *Coq Au Vin.* PB. London: Serpent's Tail. 1999, desc.

Chittenden, Margaret. *Dead Men Don't Dance.* PB. NY: Kensington Publishing Corporation. 1998, pp. 207-209, 213-214.

Chittenden, Margaret. *Dead Beat and Deadly.* PB. NY: Kensington Publishing Corporation. 1998, pp. 124-125.

Chittenden, Margaret. *Don't Forget To Die.* PB. NY: Kensington Publishing Corporation. 1999, pp. 29-30.

Christmas, Joyce. *Downsized to Death.* PB. NY: Ballantine Books, a Fawcett Gold Medal Book. 1997, pp. 168-171.

Christmas, Joyce. *Mood to Murder.* PB. NY: Ballantine Books, a Fawcett Gold Medal Book. 1999, pp. 172-173.

Claire, Edie. *Never Buried.* PB. NY: Penguin Group, Signet. 1999, pp. 65-66.

Coburn, Laura. *A Missing Suspect.* PB. NY: Penguin Group, Onyx. 1998, pp. 173-174, 176-177.

Coel, Margaret. *The Story Teller.* PB. NY: Berkley Publishing Group, Berkley Prime Crime. 1999, pp. 130-133.

Coel, Margaret. *The Lost Bird.* PB. NY: Penguin Putnam, Berkley Prime Crime. 1999, desc.

Collins, Tess. *The Law of Revenge.* PB. NY: Ballantine Books, an Ivy Book. 1997, pp. 95-99.

Cooper, Susan Rogers. *A Crooked Little House.* PB. NY: Avon Books. 1999, desc.

Cooper, Susan Rogers. *One, Two, What Did Daddy Do?* PB. NY: Avon Books. 1996, pp. 30-32, 75.

Cornwell, Patricia. *Body of Evidence.* PB. NY: Avon Books. 1992, desc.

Cornwell, Patricia. *All That Remains.* PB. NY: Avon Books.1993, desc.

Cornwell, Patricia. *Cruel & Unusual.* PB. NY: Avon Books. 1994, desc.

Cornwell, Patricia. *From Potter's Field.* PB. NY: G. P. Putnam's Sons, Berkley Books. 1996, desc.

Cornwell, Patricia. *Cause of Death.* PB. NY: G.P. Putnam's Sons, Berkley Books. 1997, desc.

Cornwell, Patricia. *Point of Origin.* HB. NY: G. P. Putnam's Sons. 1998, desc.

Cornwell, Patricia. *Unnatural Exposure.* PB. NY: G. P. Putnam's Sons, Berkley Books. 1998, desc.

Cornwell, Patricia. *Black Notice.* HB. NY: G. P. Putnam's Sons. 1999, desc.

Dain, Catherine. *Walk a Crooked Mile.* PB. NY: Berkley Publishing Group, a Jove Book. 1994, pp. 75, 48-49, 8-9.

Dain, Catherine. *Dead Man's Hand.* PB. NY: Berkley Prime Crime Book. 1997, desc.

D'Amato, Barbara. *Hard Tack.* PB. NY: Worldwide Mystery. 1992, pp. 148, 163-165, 222.

D'Amato, Barbara. *Hardball.* PB. NY: Worldwide Mystery. 1993, desc.

Dawson, Janet. *A Credible Threat.* PB. NY: Ballantine Books, a Fawcett Crest Book. 1997, pp. 67-68, 72, 74.

Dentinger, Jane. *Death Mask.* PB. NY: Penguin Books. 1994, desc.

Dentinger, Jane. *Who Dropped Peter Pan?* PB. NY: Penguin Books. 1996, pp. 65-66.

Dereske, Jo. *Miss Zukas and the Library Murders.* PB. NY: Avon Books. 1994, pp. 48-49, 52.

Dereske, Jo. *Miss Zukas and the Island Murders*. PB. NY: Avon Books. 1995, pp. 67, 70-71.

Dereske, Jo. *Miss Zukas and the Stroke of Death*. PB. NY: Avon Books. 1995, pp. 71-75.

Dereske, Jo. *Miss Zukas and the Raven's Dance*. PB. NY: Avon Books. 1996, pp. 188-189, 193.

Dereske, Jo. *Savage Cut*. PB. NY: Dell Publishing. 1996, pp. 104, 107, 110, 119-120, 122-123.

Dereske, Jo. *Cut and Dry*. PB. NY: Dell Publishing. 1997, pp. 17, 36-37, 42-43.

Dereske, Jo. *Out of Circulation*. PB. NY: Avon Books. 1997, pp. 62-63, 65.

Dereske, Jo. *Short Cut*. PB. NY: Dell Publishing. 1998, pp. 70, 74.

Dereske, Jo. *Final Notice*. PB. NY: Avon Books. 1998, pp. 69-71.

Dereske, Jo. *Miss Zukas in Death's Shadow*. PB. NY: Avon Books. 1999, pp. 21, 141, 177, 178, 180.

Dreyer, Eileen. *Bad Medicine*. PB. NY: HarperCollins Publishing, HarperPaperbacks. 1995, pp. 43, 169-172, 179.

Dunbar, Sophie. *Shiveree*. PB. Philadelphia: Intrigue Press. 1999, pp. 107-110.

Dunlap, Susan. *Too Close to the Edge*. PB. NY: Dell Publishing. 1989, pp. 58-59.

Dunlap, Susan. *A Dinner to Die For*. PB. NY: Dell Publishing. 1990, pp. 94-96.

Dunlap, Susan. *Pious Deception*. PB. NY: Dell Publishing. 1990, pp. 141-142.

Dunlap, Susan. *As A Favor*. PB. NY: Dell Publishing. 1991, pp. 12-15.

Dunlap, Susan. *Diamond in the Buff*. PB. NY: Dell Publishing. 1991, pp. 117-120.

Dunlap, Susan. *Karma*. PB. NY: Dell Publishing. 1991, pp. 195-198.

Dunlap, Susan. *Rogue Wave*. PB. NY: Dell Publishing. 1992, pp. 85-87.

Dunlap, Susan. *Death and Taxes*. PB. NY: Dell Publishing. 1993, pp. 248-249, 252.

Dunlap, Susan. *The Bohemian Connection*. PB. NY: Dell Publishing. 1994, pp. 123, 125-128.

Dunlap, Susan. *An Equal Opportunity Death*. PB. NY: Dell Publishing. 1994, pp. 199-201.

Dunlap, Susan. *The Last Annual Slugfest*. PB. NY: Dell Publishing. 1994, pp. 28-29, 36-37, 39.

Dunlap, Susan. *Time Expired*. PB. NY: Dell Publishing. 1994, pp. 137-138.

Dunlap, Susan. *High Fall*. PB. NY: Dell Publishing. 1995, pp. 288-289.

Dunlap, Susan. *Sudden Exposure*. PB. NY: Dell Publishing. 1997, pp. 61, 186-187.

Dunlap, Susan. *Cop Out*. PB. NY: Dell Publishing. 1998, pp. 172-173, 175-176.

Edwards, Grace. *A Toast Before Dying*. PB. NY: Bantam Books. 1999, pp. 184-188.

Eichler, Selma. *Murder Can Singe Your Old Flame*. PB. NY: Penguin Group, Signet. 1999, pp. 54-55, 59-60.

English, Brenda. *Corruption of Power*. PB. NY: Berkley Publishing Group, Berkley Prime Crime. 1998, pp. 25-28.

English, Brenda. *Corruption of Justice*. PB. NY: Berkley Publishing Group, Berkley Prime Crime. 1999, pp. 230-232, 234.

Evanovich, Janet. *One for the Money*. PB. NY: HarperCollins Publishing, HarperPaperbacks. 1995, pp. 7-9, 65-66.

Evanovich, Janet. *Two for the Dough*. PB. NY: Simon & Schuster, Pocket Books. 1996, p. 83.

Evanovich, Janet. *Three to Get Deadly*. HB. NY: Scribner. 1997, pp. 150, 198-199.

Evanovich, Janet. *Four to Score*. PB. NY: St. Martin's Paperbacks. 1998, pp. 75-76.

Evanovich, Janet. *High Five*. PB. NY: St. Martin's Paperbacks. 1999, pp. 27, 158-159.

Evanovich, Janet. *Hot Six*. HB. NY: St. Martin's Press. 2000, pp. 14-18.

Fairstein, Linda. *Final Jeopardy*. PB. London: Warner Books. 1998, desc.

Fairstein, Linda. *Likely To Die*. PB. London: Warner Books. 1998, desc.

Fairstein, Linda. *Cold Hit*. PB. London: Little, Brown and Company. 1999, desc.

Forrest, Katherine. *Murder by Tradition*. PB. Tallahassee: Naiad Press. 1998, pp. 122-124.

Fowler, Earlene. *Fool's Puzzle*. PB. NY: Berkley Publishing Group, Berkley Prime Crime. 1995, desc.

Fowler, Earlene. *Kansas Troubles*. PB. NY: Berkley Publishing Group, Berkley Prime Crime. 1997, desc.

French, Linda. *Steeped in Murder*. PB. NY: Avon Books. 1999, pp. 128-129, 181-182.

Frommer, Sara H. *Murder & Sullivan*. PB. Toronto: Worldwide Mystery. 1998, pp. 92-96.

Garcia-Aguilera, Carolina. *Bloody Waters*. HB. NY: G. P. Putnam's Sons. 1996, pp. 46-47, 49-50.

Garcia-Aguilera, Carolina. *Bloody Shame*. HB. NY: G. P. Putnam's Sons. 1997, pp. 74, 191-192.

George, Anne. *Murder On A Girls' Night Out*. PB. NY: Avon Books. 1996, pp. 146-148.

Gilman, Dorothy. *Mrs. Pollifax Pursued*. PB. NY: Ballantine Books, a Fawcett Crest Book. 1995, desc.

Gilpatrick, Noreen. *Shadow of Death*. PB. NY: Warner Books, Mysterious Press. 1996, pp. 60, 62-63.

Glass, Leslie. *Loving Time*. PB. NY: Bantam Books. 1997, pp. 301, 350-353.

Glass, Leslie. *Judging Time*. PB. NY: Penguin Group, Signet. 1999, pp. 64-65.

Glass, Leslie. *Stealing Time*. PB. NY: Penguin Putnam, Inc., Signet. 1999, pp. 220-224, 227.

Grafton, Sue. *"A" is for Alibi*. HB. NY: Holt Rinehart and Winston. 1982, desc.

Grafton, Sue. *"B" is for Burglar*. HB. NY: Holt Rinehart and Winston. 1985, pp. 66-68.

Grafton, Sue. *"C" is for Corpse*. HB. NY: Henry Holt and Company. 1986, pp. 67-68.

Grafton, Sue. *"D" is for Deadbeat*. HB. NY: Henry Holt and Company. 1987, pp. 103-104.

Grafton, Sue. *"E" is for Evidence*. HB. NY: Henry Holt and Company. 1988, pp. 66, 68.

Grafton, Sue. *"F" is for Fugitive*. HB. NY: Henry Holt and Company. 1989, desc.

Grafton, Sue. *"G" is for Gumshoe*. HB. NY: Henry Holt and Company. 1990, pp. 58-59.

Grafton, Sue. *"H" is for Homicide*. HB. NY: Henry Holt and Company. 1991, pp.175-176.

Grafton, Sue. *"I" is for Innocent*. HB. NY: Henry Holt and Company. 1992, pp. 148-149.

Grafton, Sue. *"J" is for Judgment*. HB. NY: Henry Holt and Company. 1993, pp. 111-112.

Grafton, Sue. *"K" is for Killer*. HB. NY: Henry Holt and Company. 1994, pp. 181-182.

Grafton, Sue. *"L" is for Lawless*. PB. NY: Henry Holt and Company. 1995, pp. 36-37.

Grafton, Sue. *"M" is for Malice*. PB. NY: Henry Holt and Company. 1996, pp. 214-216.

Grafton, Sue. *"N" is for Noose*. HB. NY: Henry Holt and Company. 1998, p. 49.

Grafton, Sue. *"O" is for Outlaw*. HB. NY: Henry Holt and Company. 1999, pp. 149-151.

Grant, Anne Underwood. *Smoke Screen*. PB. NY: Dell Publishing. 1998, pp. 223-225.

Grant, Linda. *Random Access Murder*. PB. NY: Avon Books. 1988, pp. 110-111.

Grant, Linda. *Blind Trust*. PB. NY: Ballantine Books, an Ivy Book. 1991, pp. 146-148.

Grant, Linda. *A Woman's Place*. PB. NY: Ballantine Books, an Ivy Book. 1995, pp. 19-20.

Grant, Linda. *Vampire Bytes*. PB. NY: Ballantine Books, an Ivy Book. 1999, pp. 250-251, 256-258.

Griffin, Annie. *A Very Eligible Corpse*. PB. NY: Berkley Publishing Group, Berkley Prime Crime. 1998, pp. 50-51.

Hager, Jean. *Seven Black Stones*. PB. NY: Warner Books, Mysterious Press. 1996, pp. 173-175, 177-178.

Harris, Charlaine. *Shakespeare's Champion*. PB. NY: Dell Publishing. 1998, pp. 74-77, 79-80.

Harris, Lee. *The Good Friday Murder*. PB. NY: Ballantine Publishing Group, a Fawcett Gold Medal Book. 1992, pp. 138-139.

Hart, Carolyn. *Death on Demand*. PB. NY: Bantam Books. 1989, p. 109.

Hart, Carolyn. *The Christie Caper*. PB. NY: Bantam Books, a Bantam Crime Line Book. 1992, pp. 143-144.

Hart, Carolyn. *Dead Man's Island*. PB. NY: Bantam Books. 1994, pp. 74-75, 215-217.

Hartzmark, Gini. *Final Option*. PB. NY: Ballantine Books, an Ivy Book. 1994, pp. 111-112.

Henry, April. *Circles of Confusion*. PB. NY: HarperCollins Publishers, HarperPaperbacks. 1999, desc.

Herndon, Nancy. *Casanova Crimes*. PB. NY: Berkley Publishing Group, Berkley Prime Crime. 1999, pp. 84-86.

Hess, Joan. *A Diet to Die For*. PB. NY: Ballantine Books. 1993, pp. 5, 11, 14, 16, 26, 39, 52-53.

Hightower, Lynn. *Eyeshot*. HB. NY: HarperCollins Publishing. 1996, pp. 133-136.

Hightower, Lynn. *Flashpoint*. PB. NY: HarperCollins Publishing, Harper Paperbacks. 1996, pp. 157-158, 160-162, 166.

Hightower, Lynn. *No Good Deed*. PB. NY: Dell Publishing. 1998, pp. 169-170.

Hightower, Lynn. *The Debt Collector*. PB. NY: Delacorte Press. 2000, pp. 105-108.

Holtzer, Susan. *Black Diamond.* PB. NY: St. Martin's Paperbacks. 1998, pp. 136-137, 140-141.

Hornsby, Wendy. *Midnight Baby.* PB. NY: Penguin Group, Signet. 1994, pp. 9, 22, 54-56.

Jackson, Hialeah. *The Alligator's Farewell.* PB. NY: Dell Publishing. 1999, pp. 219-223.

Jacobs, Jonnie. *Murder Among Friends.* PB. NY: Kensington Publishing Corporation. 1996, pp. 208-213.

Jaffe, Jody. *Horse of a Different Killer.* PB. NY: Ballantine Books, an Ivy Book. 1996, pp. 34-35.

Jance, J. A. *Skeleton Canyon.* PB. NY: Avon Books. 1997, pp. 220-222.

Jance, J. A. *Rattlesnake Crossing.* PB. NY: Avon Books. 1998, pp. 132-133, 11.

Jance, J. A. *Outlaw Mountain.* PB. NY: HarperCollins Publishers, Avon Books. 2000, desc.

Jordan, B. B. *Principal Investigation.* PB. NY: Berkley Publishing Group, Berkley Prime Crime. 1997, pp. 97-99.

Kellogg, Marne Davis. *Tramp.* PB. NY: Bantam Books. 1998, pp. 144-145, 148-150, 156.

Kellogg, Marne Davis. *Nothing But Gossip.* PB. NY: Bantam Books. 1999, pp. 175, 177-179.

Kennett, Shirley. *Chameleon.* PB. NY: Kensington Publishing Corporation, Pinnacle. 1999, pp. 123, 127-128.

Kijewski, Karen. *Kat's Cradle.* PB. NY: Bantam Books. 1992, pp. 148-149.

King, Laurie R. *A Grave Talent.* PB. NY: Bantam Books. 1995, pp. 14-15, 51-52.

King, Laurie R. *With Child*. PB. NY: Bantam Books. 1997, pp. 9-10.

Knight, Kathryn Lasky. *Trace Elements*. PB. NY: Simon & Schuster, Pocket Books. 1987, pp. 72-74.

Krich, Rochelle. *Blood Money*. HB. NY: Avon Books. 1999, pp. 8-11.

Lachnit, Carroll. *A Blessed Death*. PB. NY: Berkley Publishing Group, Berkley Prime Crime. 1996, pp. 102-103, 105-106.

Lanier, Virginia. *A Brace of Bloodhounds*. PB. NY: HarperCollins Publishing, HarperPaperbacks. 1998, pp. 7-8.

Law, Janice. *A Safe Place to Die*. PB. NY: Worldwide Mystery. 1995, pp. 17, 124-125.

Lawrence, Martha C. *Murder in Scorpio*. PB. NY: St Martin's Paperbacks. 1996, pp. 178-179.

Lee, Wendi. *Missing Eden*. PB. NY: Worldwide Mystery. 1999, pp. 160-163.

Lippman, Laura. *Baltimore Blues*. PB. NY: Avon Books. 1997, pp. 150-151.

Lippman, Laura. *Charm City*. PB. NY: Avon Books. 1997, pp. 11-14.

Lippman, Laura. *Butchers Hill*. PB. NY: Avon Books. 1998, pp. 38-39.

Lippman, Laura. *In Big Trouble*. PB. NY: Avon Books. 1999, pp. 15, 21, 23-24.

Lordon, Randye. *Mother May I*. PB. NY: Avon Books. 1998, pp. 18-19, 21, 24-25.

Lovett, Sarah. *Dangerous Attachments*. PB. NY: Ballantine Books, an Ivy Book. 1996, pp. 58-61.

Lovett, Sarah. *Acquired Motives*. PB. NY: Ballantine Books, an Ivy Book. 1997, pp. 13, 15-17.

Malmont, Valerie. *Death Pays the Rose Rent*. PB. NY: Dell Publishing. 1998, desc.

Maracotta, Lindsay. *The Dead Hollywood Moms Society.* PB. NY: Avon Books. 1997, pp. 141-145, 147.

Maron, Margaret. *Killer Market.* PB. NY: Warner Books. 1999, pp. 26, 28, 30, 33, 39, 72-73.

Matera, Lia. *Hidden Agenda.* PB. NY: Ballantine Books. 1992, pp. 23, 130-133.

Mathews, Francine. *Death in a Mood Indigo.* PB. NY: Bantam Books. 1998, pp. 232-234, 236.

Matthews, Alex. *Secret's Shadow.* PB. Angel Fire, New Mexico: Intrigue Press. 1998, pp. 305-307.

Matthews, Alex. *Satan's Silence.* PB. Angel Fire, New Mexico: Intrigue Press. 1998, pp. 240-243.

McCafferty, Jeanne. *Artist Unknown.* PB. London: Headline. 1995, pp. 36-38.

McCrumb, Sharyn. *If I'd Killed Him When I Met Him...*PB. NY: Ballantine Books, a Fawcett Gold Medal Book. 1996, pp. 136-138.

McKevett, G. A. *Just Desserts.* PB. NY: Kensington Publishing Corporation, a Fawcett Gold Medal Book. 1996, pp. 128-131, 133-134.

Meier, Leslie. *Back to School Murder.* PB. NY: Kensington Publishing Corporation. 1998, pp. 232, 234-236.

Moore, Miriam Ann. *Stayin' Alive.* PB. NY: Avon Books. 1998, pp. 99-100.

Moseley, Margaret. *The Fourth Steven.* PB. NY: Berkley Publishing Group, Berkley Prime Crime. 1998, pp. 50-53.

Muller, Marcia. *The Cheshire Cat's Eye.* PB. NY: Warner Books, Mysterious Press. 1990, pp. 11, 13-15.

Muller, Marcia. *Edwin of the Iron Shoes.* PB. NY: Warner Books, Mysterious Press. 1990, pp. 117-119.

Muller, Marcia. *Games to Keep the Dark Away.* PB. NY: Warner Books, Mysterious Press. 1990, pp. 53-55.

Muller, Marcia. *Leave a Message for Willie.* PB. NY: Warner Books, Mysterious Press. 1990, pp. 22-26, 209, 213-214.

Muller, Marcia. *There's Nothing to be Afraid Of.* PB. NY: Warner Books, Mysterious Press. 1990, pp. 47-48.

Muller, Marcia. *Eye of the Storm.* PB. NY: Warner Books, Mysterious Press. 1993, pp. 8-10.

Muller, Marcia. *Wolf in the Shadows.* PB. NY: Warner Books, Mysterious Press. 1994, pp. 212, 244, 258.

Muller, Marcia. *Till the Butchers Cut Him Down.* PB. NY: Warner Books. 1995, pp. 150-151.

Muller, Marcia. *A Wild and Lonely Place.* PB. NY: Warner Books. 1995, desc.

Muller, Marcia. *A Walk Through the Fire.* PB. NY: Warner Books. 1999, desc.

Muller, Marcia. *Listen to the Silence.* HB. NY: Warner Books, Mysterious Press. 2000, pp. 191-193.

Muller, Marcia. *Ask the Cards a Question.* PB. London: Women's Press Limited. 2000. First published by St. Martin's Press, 1982, desc.

Munger, Katy. *Money to Burn.* PB. NY: Avon Books. 1999, pp. 25-27.

O'Brien, Meg. *Hare Today, Gone Tomorrow.* PB. NY: Bantam Books. 1991, pp. 11, 23-25.

O'Connell, Carol. *Mallory's Oracle.* PB. London: Hutchinson, Arrow Books Limited, Random House UK Limited. 1995, pp. 54-56.

O'Connell, Carol. *The Man Who Lied to Women.* PB. London: Hutchinson, Arrow Books Limited, Random House UK Limited. 1996, pp. 242-243.

O'Connell, Carol. *Killing Critics*. PB. NY: Berkley Publishing Group, a Jove Book. 1997, pp. 129-131.

O'Connell, Carol. *Stone Angel*. PB. NY: Berkley Publishing Group, a Jove Book. 1998, pp. 59-60.

O'Connell, Carol. *Shell Game*. PB. London: Hutchinson, Arrow Books Limited, Random House UK Limited. 2000, pp. 185-188.

O'Kane, Leslie. *The Cold Hard Fax*. PB. NY: Ballantine Publishing Group, a Fawcett Gold Medal Book. 1998, pp. 257-259.

Pade, Victoria. *Divorce Can Be Murder*. PB. NY: Dell Publishing. 1999, pp. 84-86.

Padgett, Abigail. *The Dollmaker's Daughters*. PB. NY: Warner Books. 1998, pp. 132-134.

Paretsky, Sara. *Deadlock*. PB. NY: Ballantine Books. 1986, pp. 35, 37, 39, 84, 114.

Paretsky, Sara. *Bitter Medicine*. PB. NY: Ballantine Books. 1988, pp. 174-177.

Paretsky, Sara. *Blood Shot*. HB. NY: Dell Publishing. 1989, pp. 163-164.

Paretsky, Sara. *Indemnity Only*. HB. NY: Delacorte Press. 1991, pp. 161-162, 72, 74, 76.

Paretsky, Sara. *Guardian Angel*. PB. NY: Dell Publishing. 1993, pp. 218, 20-21.

Paretsky, Sara. *Killing Orders*. PB. NY: Dell Publishing. 1993, pp. 58, 121-125.

Paretsky, Sara. *Tunnel Vision*. PB. NY: Dell Publishing. 1995, pp. 42, 28, 136, 143.

Paretsky, Sara. *Hard Time*. PB. London: Penguin Books. 1999, desc.

Paul, Barbara. *Full Frontal Murder*. HB. NY: Scribner. 1997, pp. 131-132.

Pickard, Nancy. *Generous Death*. PB. NY: Simon & Schuster, Pocket Books. 1987, pp. 157-158.

Pickard, Nancy. *Dead Crazy*. PB. NY: Simon & Schuster, Pocket Books. 1989, pp. 169-170, 173-174.

Pickard, Nancy. *I.O.U.* PB. NY: Simon & Schuster, Pocket Books. 1992, pp. 50-51.

Pickard, Nancy. *Confession*. HB. NY: Simon & Schuster, Pocket Books. 1994, pp. 50, 47-48.

Pickard, Nancy. *But I Wouldn't Want to Die There*. PB. NY: Simon & Schuster, Pocket Books, a Pocket Star Book. 1994, pp. 200-202.

Pickard, Nancy. *Twilight*. PB. NY: Simon & Schuster, Pocket Books. 1995, desc.

Pickard, Nancy, based on the character created by Virginia Rich, *The Blue Corn Murders*. PB. NY: Dell Publishing. 1999, pp. 233-236.

Piesman, Marissa. *Personal Effects*. PB. NY: Simon & Schuster, Pocket Books. 1991, pp. 110-111.

Prowell, Sandra West. *The Killing of Monday Brown*. PB. NY: Bantam Books. 1996, pp. 63-66.

Prowell, Sandra West. *By Evil Means*. PB. NY: Bantam Books. 1997, pp. 198-199.

Ripley, Ann. *Mulch*. PB. NY: Bantam Books. 1998, pp. 113-114.

Roberts, Gillian. *With Friends Like These...*PB. NY: Ballantine Books. 1994, pp. 25, 29-30, 58, 60.

Rothenberg, Rebecca. *The Shy Tulip Murders*. PB. NY: Warner Books, Mysterious Press. 1997, pp. 6, 14-15.

Rozan, S. J. *A Bitter Feast*. PB. NY: St. Martin's Paperbacks. 1999, pp. 79, 74-76.

Salter, Anna. *Shiny Water*. PB. NY: Simon & Schuster, Pocket Books, a Pocket Star Book. 1998, desc.

Saulnier, Beth. *Reliable Sources*. PB. NY: Mysterious Press Paperback, a Time Warner Company. 1999, pp. 153-155.

Saulnier, Beth. *Distemper*. PB. NY: Mysterious Press Paperback, a Time Warner Company. 2000, pp. 93, 95, 97.

Sawyer, Corinne Holt. *The J. Alfred Prufrock Murders*. PB. NY: Ballantine Books, a Fawcett Crest Book. 1989, pp. 104-107.

Sawyer, Corinne Holt. *Murder in Gray and White*. PB. NY: Ballantine Books, a Fawcett Crest Book. 1991, pp. 192-194.

Sawyer, Corinne Holt. *Murder Has No Calories*. PB. NY: Ballantine Books. 1995, pp. 128-132.

Sawyer, Corinne Holt. *Murder Ole!* PB. NY: Ballantine Books, a Fawcett Crest Book. 1998, p. 49.

Scherf, Margaret. *The Beaded Banana*. HB. NY: Doubleday. 1978, pp. 140-141.

Scoppettone, Sandra. *My Sweet Untraceable You*. PB. London: Little, Brown and Company (UK), Virago Press. 1996, pp. 3-4, 144, 232-233.

Short, Sharon Gwyn. *Past Pretense*. PB. NY: Ballantine Books, a Fawcett Gold Medal Book. 1996, pp. 60-61, 63.

Sibley, Celestine. *Spider in the Sink*. PB. NY: HarperCollins Publishing, HarperPaperbacks. 1998, pp. 62-63.

Smith, Barbara Burnett. *Celebration in Purple Sage*. PB. Toronto: Worldwide Mystery. 1998, pp. 222-223.

Smith, Cynthia. *Silver and Guilt*. PB. NY: Berkley Publishing Group, Berkley Prime Crime. 1998, pp. 106-107.

Smith, Cynthia. *Royals and Rogues.* PB. NY: Berkley Publishing Group, Berkley Prime Crime. 1998, pp. 44-46.

Smith, Janet L. *Practice to Deceive.* PB. NY: Ballantine Books, an Ivy Book. 1993, pp. 105, 108-111.

Smith, Janet L. *A Vintage Murder.* PB. NY: Ballantine Books, an Ivy Book. 1995, pp.19, 157-158.

Smith, Julie. *Death Turns a Trick.* PB. NY: Ivy Books. 1982, desc.

Smith, Julie. *New Orleans Mourning.* PB. NY: Ballantine Books, an Ivy Book. 1991, desc.

Smith, Julie. *Dead in the Water.* PB. NY: Ivy Books. 1991, desc.

Smith, Julie. *The Axeman's Jazz.* PB. NY: Ballantine Books, an Ivy Book. 1992, desc.

Smith, Julie. *The Sourdough Wars.* PB. NY: Ballantine Books, an Ivy Book. 1992, pp. 61-62.

Smith, Julie. *Other People's Skeletons.* PB. NY: Ivy Books. 1993, desc.

Smith, Julie. *Jazz Funeral.* PB. NY: Ballantine Books, an Ivy Book. 1994, pp. 127, 129, 131.

Smith, Julie. *New Orleans Beat.* PB. NY: Ballantine Books, an Ivy Book. 1995, pp. 150-151.

Smith, Julie. *House of Blues.* PB. NY: Ballantine Books, an Ivy Book. 1996, pp. 44-45.

Smith, Julie. *The Kindness of Strangers.* PB. NY: Ballantine Books, an Ivy Book. 1997, pp. 77-79.

Smith, Julie. *82 Desire.* PB. NY: Ballantine Books, an Ivy Book. 1999, pp. 17, 19-20, 40-41.

Smith-Levin, Judith. *The Hoodoo Man.* PB. NY: Ballantine Publishing Group. 1998, pp. 51-53, 55-56.

Speart, Jessica. *Tortoise Soup*. PB. NY: Avon Books. 1998, pp. 9, 13, 20, 24, 28.

Stabenow, Dana. *A Cold Day for Murder*. PB. NY: Ballantine Publishing Group, a Berkley Book. 1992, pp. 45-47.

Stabenow, Dana. *Dead in the Water*. PB. NY: Berkley Publishing Group, Berkley Prime Crime. 1993, pp. 117-119.

Stabenow, Dana. *Play with Fire*. PB. NY: Berkley Publishing Group, Berkley Prime Crime. 1996, pp. 199-201, 204-205.

Stabenow, Dana. *Killing Grounds*. PB. NY: Berkley Publishing Group, Berkley Prime Crime. 1999, pp. 179-181.

Stabenow, Dana. *Midnight Come Again*. HB. NY: St. Martin's Minotaur. 2000, pp. 157, 159-160.

Stuyck, Karen Hanson. *Lethal Lessons*. PB. NY: Berkley Publishing Group, Berkley Prime Crime. 1997, pp. 47-48, 50.

Sultan, Faye and Kennedy, Teresa. *Help Line*. HB. NY: Doubleday. 1999, pp. 162-163, 166, 169.

Taylor, Elizabeth Atwood. *The Northwest Murders*. PB. NY: Ballantine Books, an Ivy Book. 1994, pp. 48-50, 53.

Tishy, Cecelia. *Jealous Heart*. PB. NY: Penguin Group, Signet. 1999, pp. 162, 164-166.

Trocheck, Kathy Hogan. *Every Crooked Nanny*. PB. NY: HarperCollins Publishing, HarperPaperbacks. 1993, pp. 3, 45-47.

Trocheck, Kathy Hogan. *To Live & Die in Dixie*. PB. NY: HarperCollins Publishing, HarperPaperbacks. 1994, pp. 152-154.

Trocheck, Kathy Hogan. *Happy Never After*. PB. NY: HarperCollins Publishing, HarperPaperbacks. 1996, pp. 102-105.

Viets, Elaine. *Rubout*. PB. NY: Dell Publishing. 1998, pp. 56-59, 62.

Viets, Elaine. *Doc in the Box*. PB. NY: Dell Publishing. 2000, pp. 26-27.

Walker, Mary Willis. *The Red Scream*. PB. NY: Bantam Books. 1995, pp. 39, 42, 48-49, 51.

Walker, Mary Willis. *Under the Beetle's Cellar*. PB. NY: Bantam Books. 1996, pp. 145-146.

Walker, Mary Willis. *All the Dead Lie Down*. PB. London: HarperCollins Publishers, Collins Crime. 1999, pp. 191-193, 197-198.

Warner, Penny. *Dead Body Language*. PB. NY: Bantam Books, a Bantam Crime Line Book. 1997, pp. 39-41.

Waterhouse, Jane. *Shadow Walk*. PB. NY: Berkley Publishing Group, Berkley Prime Crime. 1999, pp. 129-130.

Weber, Janice. *Hot Ticket*. PB. NY: Warner Books. 2000, pp. 140-141.

Wesley, Valerie Wilson. *Devil's Gonna Get Him*. PB. NY: Avon Books. 1996, desc.

Wesson, Marianne. *Render Up the Body*. HB. NY: HarperCollins Publishing. 1998, pp. 96, 98.

Wesson, Marianne. *A Suggestion of Death*. PB. London: Headline Book Publishing. 1999, desc.

West, Chassie. *Killing Kin*. PB. NY: HarperCollins Publishing, Avon Books. 2000, pp. 102-105.

Wheat, Carolyn. *Mean Streak*. PB. NY: Berkley Publishing Group, Berkley Prime Crime. 1997, pp. 12-15.

Wheat, Carolyn. *Troubled Waters*. PB. Harpenden, Herts, UK: No Exit Press. 1999, desc.

Wilcox, Valerie. *Sins of Silence*. PB. NY: Berkley Publishing Group, Berkley Prime Crime. 1998, pp. 141-144, 146-147, 149.

Wilhelm, Kate. *The Best Defense.* PB. NY: Ballantine Books, a Fawcett Crest Book. 1995, pp. 140-141.

Wilson, Barbara. *Sisters of the Road.* PB. Seattle: Seal Press. 1986, pp. 144-147.

Wilson, Barbara Jaye. *Death Brims Over.* PB. NY: Avon Books. 1997, pp. 150-152.

Wings, Mary. *She Came Too Late.* PB. London: Women's Press. 1995, pp. 131-134.

Wolzien, Valerie. *Deck the Halls with Murder.* PB. NY: Ballantine Publishing Group, a Fawcett Gold Medal Book. 1998, pp. 159-161.

Woods, Sherryl. *Bank On It.* PB. NY: Warner Books. 1993, pp. 179-181.

Zukowski, Sharon. *Leap of Faith.* PB. NY: Penguin Group, Signet. 1995, pp. 49-51.

ACKNOWLEDGEMENTS

Gathering permissions to reproduce the many excerpts that make up *Food, Drink, and the Female Sleuth* was a process beyond imagining. Because we were publishing with iUniverse.com, we needed world rights for both print and electronic formats. Fortunately many of the authors own all of their rights and were able to grant permission without fuss. For the others, permissions from publishers were a must. It was never simple. One person handled print rights, another, electronic, or research might uncover that it was the author's agent after all who was in control, or, surprise, surprise, it was the author, but she didn't know it.

You'll note in the References that some titles are followed by "desc" rather than page numbers. These brief descriptions were used when a book was read so late, it was impractical to try to get permission to excerpt. Or, in other cases, when permission to excerpt was denied.

Along the way we made friends with the permissions editors. They must be among the least appreciated people in the publishing world, receiving as they do up to a hundred requests a day, each requiring a dig through the contract files to make some legal determination of who owns what where. Our sincere thanks to them for the work they did and for waiving the usual use fees. Without these waivers the book would not have been published.

It's time to name names: At the top of the list is Carol Christianson, permissions editor for Random House, Inc. She handles all of the Dell books, all of Delacorte Press, and all of Bantam Books. We deluged her with requests, far more than any other editor, and through it all she remained courteous and supportive, often responding within twenty-four hours. Another stalwart supporter was Peter London, permissions manager at HarperCollins Publishers, Inc., who expedited our requests by bringing in an extra staff person. Voilá, it was done. Agnes Fisher, permissions manager at Simon & Schuster, broke new ground, bringing about a change to Simon & Schuster's policy to deny approval for requests from authors whose books would be published online. She was able to waive the use fee, something never done even internally between Simon & Schuster divisions, by proposing we reduce the length of the excerpts in question. Gladly. A special word of thanks to Florence Eichin, permissions manager, Penguin Putnam Inc., whose department has been struggling over the past year with an enormous backlog of permission requests, the result of recent mergers. She granted a blanket provisional approval for those titles by authors who had given their okay, allowing us to move ahead until she was ready to give them her personal attention.

The catalyst for *Food, Drink,...* was Sue Grafton's alphabet series. Permission to use excerpts from her books without charge was essential. Our great appreciation to her agents, Paul Cirone and Molly Friedrich, of the Aaron Priest Agency, and to Mimi Ross, permissions manager at Henry Holt and Company. They wanted it to happen.

Others who paved the way: Laura Russo of St. Martin's Press, whose enthusiasm for the project kept us both going; Michael Graves, also of Random House, Inc., who handled all of our many Ballantine Book requests; Denise Bontoft and Paul Rodger of Random House UK in London; Kimberly Ingersoll, Jennifer Minerva, and Michael Healey, Trade Permissions Department, Warner Books, Inc.; George Phocas of Intrigue Press; Jean McGinley of Hyperion; Tery Hamlin of Worldwide Mystery, Walker and Company; Adam Levison of Kensington Books. Three agents were especially helpful: Robert Gottlieb, head of the Trident Group and agent for Janet Evanovich; Nicole Pitesa of the Sandra Dijkstra Agency, who was relentless in her quest to gain approval from a number of foreign publishers who had some say about books by Rochelle Krich and Abigail Padgett; and Richard Curtis, agent for G. A. McKevett, who is championing the cause of authors to retain their electronic rights.

Special thanks to Nicole Hollander, creator of Sylvia, for permission to use her cartoon which couldn't have made a more timely appearance. And, last but not least, thanks to Sgt. Sheri Crain of the Sequim, WA Police Department for permission to use her work station on the cover photo.